Praise for *Blood Roses*

'The writing is scalpel-sharp, the unrelenting savagery of the Nazi occupation vividly painted. I spent the entire novel feeling glad that I never had to live through such a time. Placing a serial killer in a Nazi-occupied city during the Second World War was a masterstroke. With this book, Jackson will rightfully be regarded as one of the UK's finest crime writers'

Ben Kane, *Sunday Times* bestselling author of *Napoleon's Spy*

'A compelling, evocative story of evil stalking amidst the chaos of war'

Giles Kristian, *Sunday Times* bestselling author of *Where Blood Runs Cold*

'Jackson has written an utterly compelling novel ... which contrives to be both a public and private story, admirably plotted and beautifully put together. It is a remarkable piece of work, a fine piece of craftsmanship'

Scotsman

'A taut, tense thriller that immerses you in war-torn Warsaw as police detective Jan Kalisz faces an impossible choice: save his family, his country or his soul. Gutsy and gripping, this is perfect for fans of Chris Lloyd and Robert Harris'

D. V. Bishop, author of *Ritual of Fire*

'*Blood Roses* is a dark, twisting thriller that powerfully recreates the brutal Nazi occupation of Warsaw and dramatises the desperate plight of those forced to collaborate while secretly working for the Resistance. Jan Kalisz, Douglas Jackson's police officer hero, is the natural-born heir to the late Philip Kerr's Bernie Gunther'

Andrew Taylor, *Sunday Times* bestselling author of the Marwood and Lovett series

'Jackson has created a brilliant mash-up of WW2 thriller and a serial killer chiller, and in so doing brings a fresh perspective to both. Sharp, intelligent writing that makes for a compelling read'

Alison Belsham, author of *The Girls on Chalk Hill*

'This suspenseful serial killer novel by an experienced historical novelist transcends some of the sub-genre's limitations and makes for a remarkable crime debut... What raises it to another level is the atmospheric evocation of a city in the process of being systematically obliterated by the Germans and brought to life again by Jackson's pen... Gripping stuff and a series that could develop into something impressive and a goldmine for Philip Kerr Bernie Gunther fans'

Maxim Jakubowski, *Crime Time*

'Douglas is a master of historical fiction... *Blood Roses* is exciting, claustrophobic and disturbing at times, but ultimately it's a hugely satisfying and thrilling read'

Steven A McKay, author of *Sword of the Saxons*

'A dark story set against dark times, you practically need a torch to read it'

Alec Marsh, author of *Rule Britannia*

'Two men with double lives, a police officer and a serial killer, collide in Nazi-occupied Poland in this richly researched novel. Jackson brings the tension, brutality and paranoia of Warsaw into murderous life. A fine portrait of a people suffering oppression as well as a knife-edge thriller'

Douglas Skelton, author of *A Thief's Justice*

'This is a clever, compelling crime story full of historical detail. Jan Kalisz is a dazzling addition to the canon of compromised heroes, a man desperately trying to keep his family alive without losing his soul. Part police-procedural, part serial killer novel but also so much more, *Blood Roses* brings home the sheer brutalism and horror of life in Nazi-occupied Poland while still delivering a thrilling wartime adventure story. I can't wait to read the next one'

Russ Thomas, author of *Firewatching*

Blood Roses

Douglas Jackson is the author of seventeen historical novels and mystery thrillers, including the critically acclaimed nine-book Hero of Rome series. He was born in Jedburgh in the Scottish Borders and now lives in Stirling. Originally a journalist by profession he rose to become Assistant Editor of the *Scotsman* before leaving to be a full-time writer in 2009.

Also by Douglas Jackson

The Warsaw Quartet

Blood Roses
Blood Sacrifice

DOUGLAS JACKSON

Blood Roses

10 CANELO

First published in the United Kingdom in 2024 by Canelo

This edition published in the United Kingdom in 2024 by

Canelo
Unit 9, 5th Floor
Cargo Works, 1-2 Hatfields
London SE1 9PG
United Kingdom

A CIP catalogue record for this book is available from the British Library.

Ebook ISBN 978 1 80436 592 2
Hardback ISBN 978 1 80436 748 3
Paperback ISBN 978 1 80436 590 8

Cover design by Black Sheep

Cover images © Alamy and Shutterstock

Look for more great books at www.canelo.co

Printed and bound in Great Britain by Clays Ltd, Elcograf S.p.A.

1

GLOSSARY

German ranks

Hauptsturmführer	SS rank, equivalent to a captain
Obergruppenführer	SS rank, equivalent to a general
Oberleutnant	Wehrmacht rank, equivalent to a captain
Obersturmführer	SS rank, equivalent to a lieutenant
Unterscharführer	SS rank, equivalent to a corporal
Wachtmeister	Wehrmacht rank, equivalent to a company sergeant major

Arbeitskarte	Work permit
Gestapo Geheim Staatspolizei	the Secret State Police
Judenrat (pl **Judenräte**)	Jewish council
Kriminalpolizei	German plain clothes police force, also **Kripo**
Landser	A German rank and file soldier
Ordnungspolizei	German uniformed police, also **Orpo**
Raucherkarte	Permit to buy tobacco
SD Sicherheitsdienst	Reich Security Service
Seifenkarte	Permit to buy soap
Selbstschutz	Paramilitary groups of Polish-domiciled ethnic Germans
Sicherheitspolizei	Nazi security police, also **Sipo**
SS Schutzstaffel	originally Hitler's personal bodyguard, later expanded to become a powerful military force

Volksdeutsche	Ethnic Germans without German citizenship

Polish words

Aleja	Avenue, as in Aleja Szucha
dziękuję	Thank you
łapanka	Round-up
lodówka	Fridge
Ogrod	Garden, as in Ogrod Saxi, the Saxon Gardens
Policja Państwowa	Polish State Police. Also known as 'the Blues'
Pomścimy Wawer	We will avenge Wawer
Szkopy	Insulting Polish slang for Germans
to nic	It's nothing
Ulica	Street
Wigilia	Vigil, also the traditional Polish Christmas Eve celebration

PART ONE: INSPIRATION

PROLOGUE

The Artist

Munich

Beads of sweat formed like minute diamonds among the silken hairs on her upper lip.

How to capture them?

The Artist chewed on the flesh inside his cheek, his ultra-fine brush hovering over the palette. A combination of Venetian red, white and yellow ochre had perfectly matched the soft glow of her skin, complementing the hair that fell to her shoulders in waves of pale gold. His cerulean blue captured the translucence of her gown, and, with the deftest of touches, her eyes, too, as they glistened in the slanted, dust-flecked rays of the afternoon sun.

But those beads of sweat… A dab of white, perhaps blended with ultramarine to provide depth? Yes, that was the key to what you *saw*, but how did one represent their translucence, the fragile bond between liquid and flesh that could be broken an instant after brush touched canvas?

He looked up from the picture to find her watching him. *Of course*. He forced a smile. 'We'll rest now, I think, Ilse. Perhaps you would like something to eat?'

She moved purposefully to the table of food that had been the focus of her attention all morning.

He backed away from the canvas, frowning as he studied the part-completed portrait from a new angle. Not too bad, really. He was definitely improving. Yet the subtleties that divided the great from the merely good continued to elude him.

The squeak of a chair leg on the wooden floor drew his attention back to the girl. Despite her obvious hunger, Ilse ate delicately, nibbling at the food with perfect white teeth that shone like newly harvested pearls. She had lived with hunger so long, he decided, that it was ingrained in her nature to fight it. Yet hunger had made her more beautiful, accentuating the fine cheekbones which, allied to her piercing blue eyes and a long, elegant nose, gave her the face of an Aryan goddess.

It was this pale beauty that first drew him to her as she sat in a secluded spot in the Luitpoldpark; a slim, angular figure in her mid-teens, with a shopgirl's overall hitched up to catch the sun on her long legs. Her beauty had drawn him in, but also her obvious poverty and a third, equally important, trait: she was a solitary person.

He had always been able to find the solitary ones, those who avoided social contact and sought out the shadows and the fringes.

Her beauty was neither exciting nor stimulating: it was a challenge. Any journeyman could illustrate the mundane, but to discover and portray the indefinable, almost spiritual, essence that made an object extraordinary was the mark of the true artist.

She put the bread and ham aside and opened her mouth to speak, but before she could say anything he switched on the little black 'People's Radio' that sat by the fireplace and turned up the volume. He wasn't interested in anything she had to say.

Not the usual Bruckner symphony today, or even the new man, Karajan, but the instantly familiar stentorian tones of the

Führer in full flow filled the room. He heard a thump behind him and looked round to discover that Ilse had leapt to her feet with her right arm extended.

'You're in the BDM?' He should have realised: almost every girl of her age would be a member of the *Bund Deutscher Mädel*, the female equivalent of the *Hitlerjugend*, the Hitler Youth.

'Of course.'

A frown tugged at the corners of her lips. She thought he was making fun of her.

He smiled and the wary expression faded. 'If I'd known, I would have painted you in uniform.'

'Perhaps next time...' She let him know she liked the idea. 'The Führer is speaking in Berlin.' Her eyes shone with the light of pure worship.

The Artist nodded distractedly, and they listened as Adolf Hitler assured cheering Berliners that his patience with the Czechs was at an end, and there was still a reckoning to come for Poland.

'...*The most difficult problem which faced me was the relation between Germany and Poland. There was a danger that the conception of a "hereditary enmity" might take possession of our people and of the Polish people... I know quite well that I should not have succeeded if Poland at that time had had a democratic constitution. For these democracies which are overflowing with phrases about peace are the most bloodthirsty instigators of war...*'

It went on for ten minutes before a raucous, repeated chorus of *Sieg Heil* signalled the end of the speech.

'What does it mean?' Ilse asked. 'Will there be a war?'

'I don't know.' He'd been wondering the same thing. 'If the Poles have any sense they will give in to the Führer's demands.' Maybe it was for the best, but then... War brought opportunities. 'Now, Ilse, we shall resume.' He removed the half-finished canvas from the easel and replaced it with a large pad of white paper. 'Something a little different – a life study.' He allowed a sternness into his voice that hadn't been there earlier. 'Disrobe and sit by the window.'

'But, sir...' The irritating Bavarian sing-song whine was more pronounced when she became agitated. 'I have never... It would not be proper. My family...'

Her family, according to Ilse, was scraping a living on a ramshackle smallholding up some valley outside Bad Tölz and couldn't care less about her. Her false reluctance could only be a negotiating ploy.

'You need not concern yourself with your virtue,' his voice softened, 'nor even your modesty. I am an artist and you are my model. An artist looks beyond the reality. He sees only shape and form. However,' he conceded gracefully, 'I note your concern and will be willing to pay a little extra.'

With a show of reluctance, the girl agreed to accept an additional one mark fifty and disappeared into the bedroom. A few minutes later she shuffled back into the room naked, with her hands covering her breasts.

'Yes,' he said, encouraging her to the cushioned seat, 'just there. Now, angle your body towards me so the sun catches your breasts. Hold your chin up and direct your eyes towards the window.' She shuffled until she was in the position she thought he wanted. He studied the composition carefully and picked up a piece of charcoal. No, it wouldn't do, and he didn't hide his irritation. 'Cross your feet. No, no... Keep your knees slightly apart. Good. Left hand on your upper thigh, and let the right hang by your side.'

Satisfied, he began to draw.

She had an almost boyish figure, yet with the unmistakable curves of the female form. Small, upturned breasts with pink nipples, protruding ribs testifying to her recent privations, a narrow waist and the long tapering legs of a dancer; a surprisingly dark tuft of pubic hair at the convergence of the thighs.

'What are those flowers?'

The instinct to snarl at her was strong, but it was immediately overwhelmed by another even more powerful sensation. The flowers. 'They're a type of rose. *Rosa centifolia pomponia.*' His voice seemed to come from far away. He paused in his work, his breath catching in his throat and something melting inside.

Her mention of the flowers had opened his mind to the true nature of his genius. The *inner* person was what he sought, not this pale, uninteresting outer shell. When he resumed, the charcoal strokes quickened and his hand seemed to take on a life of its own. The drawing altered, shapes appearing on the outline of the taut abdomen where there had previously been none: at first spirals and coils, but swiftly they evolved into petals, stems, leaves and buds, a close approximation of the roses on the windowsill. The beauty within, that he would bring out for all to see. A whole constellation the naked eye could not witness while it was constrained by the flesh.

'You must come again, Ilse.' He struggled to keep the excitement from his voice. 'One night after work. If you like, you could wear your BDM uniform.' He sensed her smiling; he knew the suggestion would appeal to her. 'Now, hold very still.'

He was so moved by the prospect of what was to come, the hand with the charcoal shook. When next they met, she would not only be his subject; her body would supply the canvas and palette for a true masterpiece.

CHAPTER 1

Warsaw, 16 September 1939

'Pain is good.' The reassuring voice seemed to come from very far away. 'It means you're alive.'

Jan Kalisz attempted to open his eyes, but someone seemed to have glued them shut. His entire body throbbed, and his skull felt as if it had been split in two. The soft touch of a damp cloth dabbed gently at his eyelids and, after a few moments, he tried again with more success.

Light seemed to explode in his brain so fiercely he almost cried out with the agony of it. He tried to rise, but firm hands on his shoulders pushed him back. It was hard to breathe.

'Stay still.' A woman's voice, quiet, but confident in her authority over him. His nostrils twitched at the familiar smell of disinfectant. Doubtfully, he tried his eyes again, screwing them up so the light wasn't quite as severe. He was rewarded by a blur of white uniform and a head of dark curls.

'Maria?' The word emerged as a mumbled groan.

'My name is Sister Emilia,' the blur corrected him, 'and you are in the Social Security Hospital on Red Cross Street in central Warsaw.'

A moment of almost unbearable relief – he was home – accompanied by the inevitable mystery. 'How did I…?'

'I'm sorry, Lieutenant.' She shook her head. 'I can't tell you anything, because I don't know anything. You must be patient.'

'But… the war?' The images came back in a rush. Death and explosions and fear in the green hell of an anonymous forest. His brave boys had fought the Nazis all the way from the Warta river to Warsaw, losing casualties every day until, inevitably, it had been his turn. 'My men? I have to get back to my unit.'

'Not till you're well, young man.' The stern tone was offset by the water glass she put to his lips. 'Lie back and I'll fetch Doctor Novak. He'll explain everything.'

When she'd left, Kalisz considered his surroundings. A room of his own, which was surprising for a lowly lieutenant in the intelligence section of the army reserve. He'd been at this hospital once before, he remembered, to identify a corpse, in his peacetime guise as an investigator in the *Policja Państwowa* – the State Police. He ran his hands gingerly over his scalp, then over his chest and down his body. His ribs were wrapped in a broad bandage strapped as tight as a steel band, which explained his difficulty breathing. Surprisingly, he could feel no sign of a wound. He'd been certain he'd been hit by a large piece of shrapnel, but it seemed not. His left thigh was different – bandaged from hip to knee. The cloth hid some kind of thick pad that no doubt covered a specific injury. Everything else was in its proper place, and seemingly in working order.

He turned his attention back to the room. Clean, white painted walls. A small window that must look out on to Czerwonego Krzyża. Beside the bed, a chair, and some kind of small cupboard with a tray on top that held a flask of water, the glass, an empty ceramic ashtray and a night light with a plain cloth shade. Spartan, one might call it, but for the little print of the Virgin Mary beaming benevolently from the far wall. He stared at it for a long time, then remembered to thank her with a prayer.

As he completed his devotions, a diminutive figure in a white coat bustled in without knocking. Short, round and somewhere beyond middle-aged, the doctor had thick dark hair that stood up like a hedgehog's spines and a moustache you could strain soup through. Kalisz waited patiently as he was studied by small, over-bright eyes.

'Quite right, my boy.' The man looked knowingly from Kalisz to the picture. 'I'm not religious myself, but in times of trial we must avail ourselves of all the help we can get.' He accompanied the words with a nod, as if an unspoken diagnosis had been confirmed. 'I'm Novak. You'll be hurting, yes? Hardly a surprise after all your body's been through. Three cracked ribs that'll nip like the devil for a while. We took a large splinter of wood out of your leg – six inches higher and you'd have been singing soprano – but it didn't touch anything important. It was the skull that worried me most. They said the force of the blast threw you head first into a tree—'

'They?'

But Novak had already moved on. 'We expected multiple skull fractures, perhaps even a depression, but your cranium must be made of concrete because I believe you've escaped with just a severe concussion. How does it feel?'

'As if someone hit me with a hammer.' He ran his fingers through his hair and grimaced. 'My scalp feels as if it's covered in tiny shards of glass, but I can't find anything.'

Novak nodded. 'A classic symptom. A little rest and we'll soon have you back on your feet.'

'How long?' Kalisz wasn't going to be soft-soaped into an indefinite convalescence. 'I must get back to my unit. My men need me.'

'Slow down,' the little doctor insisted. 'You have to be patient. Look at you. You can't walk and you can't lift anything.

That means you can't march and you can't fire a gun. Until I'm satisfied with that head of yours you won't be going anywhere.'

'How long?' Kalisz persisted.

Novak whipped a small torch from the breast pocket of his white coat and shone it into his patient's eyes, one after the other. He stood back with a long sigh. 'A week, at best. Perhaps two, depending on the circumstances.'

Kalisz groaned. 'In two weeks the war could be over. Warsaw could be surrounded in one.' Something struck him. 'I don't even know what day it is.'

Novak had gone very still, and when Kalisz looked up he noticed the light had faded from the doctor's eyes.

'What is it?'

'Today is Saturday. Saturday, the sixteenth of September. The Germans completed their encirclement of the city yesterday. Warsaw is already surrounded.'

Kalisz felt the world fall away beneath him. Everything he and his comrades had suffered, fought and died for since the Nazi divisions crossed the Polish border two weeks earlier had been for nothing. As he closed his eyes he heard the door handle turn.

'Don't give up hope, Lieutenant,' Novak said gently. 'That's an order from your doctor. By the way…' A slight hesitation, and Kalisz's well-trained ears detected a subtle change in tone. Did he hear conspiracy? 'You'll have a visitor tonight.'

CHAPTER 2

A signal flare arced into the night sky to burst in a kaleidoscope of colour that illuminated the street below in patches of red, purple and green, blue, yellow and pink.

'Oh, shit,' someone whispered.

Jan Kalisz felt oddly cheated. War wasn't supposed to be so exotic. The war he fought was a war of dull greens, mud brown and field grey, occasionally enlivened by a splash of arterial crimson. This was all wrong.

'Lieutenant?' A hand shook his shoulder and, with a thrill of fear, he realised the German assault troops had used the cover of darkness to manhandle a small field artillery piece into the roadway. In the stark glare of the flare, Kalisz felt the barrel was aimed directly at him. It was like staring down a railway tunnel. The gun captain stood with his hand raised, ready to shoot. Worse, hundreds of curiously faceless stormtroopers had managed to creep forward to line the streets within fifty metres of the barricade of wrecked trams and cars. Kalisz knew there was something he should do, but for the life of him, he couldn't remember what it was.

The arm came down and his world was transformed into an explosion of light and heat that seared his eyeballs and threw him backwards. The wrecked tram that sheltered him rose up and balanced on its nose for a moment, trying to decide which way to fall, before toppling to one side to crush the unfortunate soldier beside him.

'This way.' At last he found his voice. He pointed to a burnt-out house not far from the barricade. Corporal Bukowski was twenty paces ahead when he entered the building at the same time as an artillery round from the German cannon. An enormous blast rocked Kalisz, while what was left of the corporal was hurled into the street, a smouldering bundle of rags. He'd liked Bukowski.

'Lieutenant?' The hand was back, the voice more urgent. Kalisz wanted to tell whoever owned it they should be shooting at Germans, but when he tried to speak all that emerged was a mew of terror. When he opened his eyes it was pitch dark, but he sensed another presence looming over him. 'You were having a nightmare.'

A cultured voice, someone used to wielding command. An army officer, perhaps an aristocrat of the type Kalisz's father so despised.

'Who in God's name are you and what do you want?' The surreal dream, with its elements of fantasy and chilling reality, had left Kalisz bathed in sweat and in no mood for polite conversation.

'As to who I am, that doesn't matter,' the invisible man said. 'I'll get to why I'm here in my own good time.'

'What time is it?'

'About four, probably.'

'You keep strange hours.'

'These are strange times. I would have been here earlier, but… Well, you'll hear about it in a few hours anyway. Thirty Soviet divisions crossed the Polish frontier at three this morning, near Kresy.'

'Christ, no.' Kalisz felt as if someone had hit his heart with a hammer.

'I'm sorry, but there's no doubt. We expect them to be in Lwów by morning, though the messages we're getting are confusing. The only certainty is that the Germans are giving up ground – it all seems to have been arranged in advance – and our fellows don't know whether to fight the Reds or not.'

'I have a brother with the Frontier Protection Force—'

'It's to be hoped he'll be safe.' Kalisz sensed a mental shrug that might have been sympathy or might not. 'The main thing for you and me is that it makes our meeting all the more important.'

Now Kalisz was intrigued, but he wasn't buying what the invisible man was selling just yet. 'How will I know until I hear what it is?'

'We are agreed that the intervention of the Soviet army means it's only a matter of time before Poland is defeated? That if there was the least hope before, it's now gone?'

'We were never strong enough to conduct a war on two fronts,' Kalisz agreed reluctantly. For the Polish military it had always been an unfortunate, but indisputable truth.

'Therefore we must think of the future.'

'My only wish is to get out of here and rejoin my unit.'

'Very worthy, I'm sure.' A sardonic edge now to the voice from the darkness. 'For the moment you aren't fit to go anywhere. If I can't persuade you my offer is the better option, you can cheerfully go and throw yourself under a tank, though what good you think that will do your country or your family is unclear to me— Christ!'

The building seemed to jump beneath them as a massive explosion erupted not far away, followed by a second, and then a third. They waited in the dark, counting the seconds till the one with the hospital's name on it arrived. But tonight, it seemed, it wasn't their turn. Kalisz had a feeling his mystery visitor would have quite liked to dive under the bed, but was much too well-mannered to do the sensible thing. If he'd been fit, he'd have beaten him to it.

'Two hundred and fifty kilo heavies.' He was surprised how steady his voice was. 'From Heinkel 111s, probably. A trick they learned in Spain. They use the large bombs to blow the roof tiles off, and the incendiaries that make up the rest of the load finish the job. They're going for the city power plant across by the river.'

'Efficient, the Germans, yes?'

'Very.'

The visitor hesitated for a moment. 'We have an idea how it will work from what's happened in Prague and Vienna. It will be bad.' He meant after the surrender, but it seemed he couldn't bring himself to say it. Maybe not made of iron after all, Kalisz's guest. 'We just don't know quite how bad. It'll be worse for the Jews, of course, but then it always is.'

Kalisz had a vision of the Feinbaums, his neighbours across the hall: a watchmaker, his wife and twin sons, always unfailingly polite and in no way suited for what was to come. 'I'm a cop, Mr Whoever You Are. Your sob stories are wasted on me.' But his voice said something different and the other man knew it.

'Then I'll get to the point. When the Nazis take over Warsaw they will have to work with the people who run the city, or at least what's left of it. That means power workers to restore the generating facilities and the lines, the water and sewage officials, telephone engineers, the railwaymen and the roadsweepers. And the police.'

'No.' Kalisz could see what was coming; it felt as if he was standing in front of a freight train with his legs encased in concrete.

'We want you to go back to work, Lieutenant Kalisz. We want you to work with the Germans.'

'You've got the wrong man.'

'Have I?' The invisible man paused, as if he were flicking through a notebook, but of course he couldn't be. Not in the dark. 'Investigator Jan Kalisz, Department V, State Police. Born July 1907. Unexceptional academic record, but thrived in the police. A degree in criminal psychology from Warsaw University. Two awards for bravery in the field. Mother of German origin.' Another pause, so Kalisz could reflect on that. 'You speak German, but more importantly, you understand the Germans. You'll be working for us, of course. We believe the police will be central to much of what their administration wants to achieve in Warsaw. The Nazis are perfectly capable of making people disappear – *Nacht und Nebel*, into the night and fog. But for some reason, they also want the world to admire their sense of justice. You won't only tell us what the enemy is going to do, you'll be able to tell us what they're thinking. It will feel like a defeat, and it will be. It will feel like the end, but it must not be the end, it must only be a beginning. Poland will fight on, Lieutenant, and you can do more for Poland behind a desk than crushed beneath a tank.'

Kalisz wasn't fooled by his visitor's clarion call to patriotism. He'd served for a while in the political police and he knew how counter-intelligence operations worked. Amateurs didn't last five minutes. This might as well be an invitation to commit suicide. All right, not so different from what he had planned for himself, but a man had the right to choose his own end. It made him angry that they thought he could be controlled like this. 'Who is this *us*? This *we* –' he forced himself up off the bed – 'who think they know me better than I know myself?'

'*We* are a group of people who serve the Polish state,' the invisible man's voice hardened in its turn, 'which will continue to exist whatever befalls this nation. We've been preparing for this eventuality for quite some time. Our organisation is small, but it will be the seed from which Polish pride is restored. What the Nazis destroy, we will rebuild. Those they attack, we will protect. Those they kill, we will avenge. They will learn to fear us, Lieutenant, and the most important lesson from Berlin these last years is that they will strike out at those they fear.' A shadowy figure loomed out of the dark to face Kalisz. He stood beside the bed, his features a contrast of dark planes and pale flesh, part-hidden beneath the broad brim of a homburg hat. Only the eyes were distinct, glittering like chips of polished onyx. 'Do not misunderstand me, Lieutenant. They will try to annihilate us with every weapon at their disposal. If we are to survive and take the fight to them, we will need all the help we can get. You have been selected with great care. By returning to work you can save lives, possibly many hundreds of lives.'

Kalisz felt his anger fade. He'd long ago learned not to allow emotions to overcome logic. Perhaps the man had a point. If Warsaw was indeed surrounded, in all likelihood the city would fall before he left his hospital bed. At least this way he could continue the fight. But he wouldn't be led to the sacrifice like a sheep. He needed assurances.

'Do you truly believe they're going to allow someone who was an intelligence officer to even be in the same room as their innermost secrets?'

'When you leave here you won't be a former reserve intelligence officer,' his visitor explained patiently. 'You will be a former reserve corporal clerk. We'll alter your personnel file, so you were injured in the first days of the war and took no part in the fighting against them. You'll have a certificate that says you're unfit for active military service. You will report to me, and only to me.' He paused to allow Kalisz time to appreciate this evidence of his value. 'Any information you supply will be filtered through a dozen other sources to disguise its origin. You will be forced to lie. You will be forced to steal. You will be working alongside people you will have to deceive. All things that may seem unacceptable to a man who has spent his life maintaining law and order. I understand that. Much easier for someone like you to pick up a gun and go out to Mokotów or Praga to die. But other men – and women, too – are willing to die to keep the flame of freedom alive in Poland. At this very moment they are stockpiling weapons and preparing places of sanctuary. Theirs will not be an honourable war. They will fight from the shadows and they will meet their end in the shadows. Some of them will die screaming under the most terrible torture. All of them understand that, but still they will fight, because it is their duty.'

Kalisz felt his heart swell to fill his chest and his throat. Was it pride, or apprehension at what was to come? Either way, it made no difference. He'd made his decision. 'Then I will be honoured to fight alongside them.'

'We'll arrange a system of signals.' The invisible man was all business now. 'A choice of two or three meeting places each month. You will make the final decision. Think about locations. It must always be wherever is most convenient for you and somewhere you feel safe, but we'll never meet in the same place twice. There will be an emergency protocol, some way you can let us know you want an immediate meeting, and likewise for us.'

Kalisz was doubtful. 'It seems complicated.'

'We want you to feel secure. We learned a lot from the Reds in the Twenties and Thirties. The MVD taught them well.'

'Not so many Polish communists left,' Kalisz reflected. 'Marshal Piłsudski and the colonels saw to that. The political police hounded them until they found they had urgent business in Moscow.'

'As I said, we've learned from them. We'll do better.'

'I hope so.'

Eventually, the visitor sensed Kalisz was close to exhaustion. They arranged an initial meeting at the Krasiński Library, near Kalisz's home. It would take place the first day after he was released from hospital, with a fallback two days later, just in case.

'Will my wife be permitted to know what I am doing?'

'I'm afraid that won't be possible. It would be dangerous for both of you.'

CHAPTER 3

24 September 1939

Jan Kalisz had experienced war at first hand, along with the destruction and death that went hand in hand with it, but what the Nazis had done to Warsaw was beyond all comprehension. Entire apartment buildings had been thrown into the street in great avalanches of rubble, leaving gaps like pulled teeth in the façade of the once elegant avenue of Nowy Świat. Whole blocks virtually turned to dust, with perhaps a chimney standing like a Roman column in the midst of the wreckage, or a surviving wall, the pictures still hanging and a fireplace waiting to be set. Among the piles of wreckage, shattered families foraged for what little survived of their lives, or perhaps to uncover the remains of relatives who had occupied these homes. Rich or poor, the German bombs didn't differentiate. The Ford passed two men in evening dress struggling with a large wardrobe, followed by a woman in a ball gown and pearls, her back hunched to take the weight of the sack of bedding across her shoulder. Firefighters hosed down the smouldering rubble to stop the wreckage reigniting, and hospital crews hung about in hopeless little groups with empty stretchers at their feet.

The driver steered the car round a pair of dead horses blocking the middle of the street, people already surrounding them like vultures to harvest the meat. Kalisz must have made some sort of internal groan, because the man half-turned and said, 'This isn't the worst of it. Out in Wola there are whole streets where every house is destroyed.'

At the top of the street, where it transformed into Krakowskie Przedmieście, they turned right past the familiar statue of the astronomer Nicolaus Copernicus, which gave Kalisz's street its name. Another right into Kopernika. No damage here that Kalisz could see, thank God. Despite the black mood brought on by all the destruction he'd witnessed, his heart beat a little faster at the thought of seeing his family again. 'Number 35, it's on the right.'

There'd been times when he'd been certain he'd never see his home again.

The driver drew up in front of the apartment block. He got out of the car and opened the door for Kalisz, helping him out with surprising care for a man who looked capable of tearing a Warsaw telephone directory in half. '*Dziękuję*,' Kalisz thanked him.

'*To nic.*' The driver shrugged, but whether he meant the fare was nothing, or that the favour needed no repayment, Kalisz couldn't tell.

When the car drove off, he stood in the street, staring at the familiar surroundings. There weren't many people about, and those who were kept their eyes down as if they were ashamed. That's what war did. Forced you to choose between lives. The easiest way to survive was not to care what happened to anybody else.

Kalisz had half-expected Maria to meet him in the street, and he felt a curious mixture of disappointment and relief that she might have been called in to work. He looked up at the narrow windows of his apartment on the top floor, but could see no sign of life. Number 35 was as he'd left it, every balcony festooned with flower baskets that created a sunburst of colour against the dark stone, the residents clinging to normality as the world collapsed around them. Red-and-white Polish flags hung from every second window. *Kopernika says fuck the war.*

Kalisz climbed the narrow stone stairway one careful step at a time, trying by trial and error to find the angle that caused his leg the least pain. By the time he reached the top floor he was breathing like an old man.

A moment's hesitation, then, and a little stab of something that felt surprisingly like fear. Finally, he fumbled for his keys until he found the one to the apartment door. It opened with a squeak that reminded him he'd promised to oil the hinges a month before. He stepped into the dark hallway and closed the door behind him.

'Surprise!' A light flicked on and Maria was standing in front of him, her face wreathed in a smile, and somehow looking more beautiful than he'd ever seen her. She was wearing her favourite dress, the blue one with tiny white flowers. Stefan stood a step behind, slim, with a shock of dark hair, a sombre, bright-eyed miniature of his father, embarrassed to be part of the ceremony. For ceremony it was. Maria held a round loaf on a white cloth. An egg cup filled with salt had been sunk into the centre of the bread. Bread and salt, the traditional Polish welcome for a returning loved one. Good bread, freely given, with salt and goodwill.

Kalisz struggled to keep his hands from shaking as he accepted the gift. He went through the ancient ritual, breaking off a small piece of bread and dipping it in the salt. When he put it in his mouth, his throat was so dry he had difficulty swallowing.

'Under the circumstances we thought a party would be inappropriate.' Maria hugged the boy to her side. 'But Stefan was determined that we should celebrate the return of his father, the hero.'

Kalisz put the bread aside on the hall table and wrapped his arms around his wife and the child they'd created together, enjoying their warmth and a sense of belonging that could be replicated nowhere else on earth. He closed his eyes. To be loved…

He kissed Maria and she led him into the main room, where a bottle of pale Żywiec beer sat beside a cake decorated in patriotic red and white. She saw his look and shrugged. 'Maybe the last of either for a while. Commissar Starzyński has been asking people not to hoard food, but every day things become harder to find.'

It wasn't the largest apartment in the block, but a decent size for a small family, with a proper kitchen *and* a bathroom, not just a WC. They'd shared the labour of decorating the place with a job lot of floral wallpaper, and furnished it with a little grudging help from Maria's father. August Klimecki was a former army officer who believed his daughter could do much better than a lowly cop. Fortunately, he was also sensible enough to know that if he refused permission to marry Kalisz, she'd have gone ahead and done it anyway.

'Dada?' Stefan stood with a cake knife in his hand and a plate in the other. It seemed to Kalisz that his son had grown another inch in the month he'd been away. A new confidence, too, as if his father's absence had forced him to accept greater responsibilities, which Kalisz sensed, not without a certain pride, he had enjoyed. A sharp hiss announced that Maria had opened the beer.

'We should share it,' Kalisz suggested, cutting a slice of the cake and putting it on Stefan's plate.

'Listen to your nurse, Jani.' Maria shook her head and handed him the glass. 'You're the one who needs to build his strength up. How is your leg?'

'It will take a while to heal properly, but it looks worse than it is.' He smiled. 'At least I have a nurse to change my bandages. The ribs are painful, but I can move relatively freely. They were more worried about my head. Fortunately, it turns out we Kaliszes are blessed with armoured skulls. To us.' He raised the glass of golden lager and smiled at his son.

'I'm afraid I have to work later,' Maria said.

'Yes?' Meaning, *you don't have to go.*

'They need me, Jan.'

'Not out at the institute, surely? It must be on the front line by now.'

'You must have forgotten.' She pushed a rebellious tendril of dark hair out of her eyes. 'They moved the patients into hospitals in the city centre. I'm looking after ten beds in the children's hospital, so just round the corner.'

'I thought, maybe…' He glanced significantly at Stefan, who was devouring his cake as if he'd never eaten one before.

'You must be feeling better.' She smiled. 'Maybe later, huh?'

They tried to keep the war outside the front door for their short time together, but didn't quite manage it. Stefan wanted to hear about fighting the Germans and Kalisz gave him the Boy Scout version of crawling through the bushes, distant explosions and heroic Polish attacks pushing the enemy back. He sensed Stefan didn't believe a word, but the boy didn't push him, for which Kalisz was grateful. When they discussed news of friends and relatives, the talk ended up being about how much damage had been done to someone's house, a cousin who'd lost a son, or a family forced to move in with more fortunate siblings.

'The last we heard, Tadeusz was still with his squadron.' Maria spoke lightly, but Kalisz knew the words hid a deeper concern. Tadeusz was her twenty-year-old brother, a fighter pilot. The Luftwaffe had all but wiped out the Polish Air Force. 'They've suffered losses, but Father still has contacts in the general staff. He says we would have been informed if anything had happened to him, so we must keep our spirits up. Henryk?'

'No news yet,' Kalisz said. Henryk was Kalisz's younger brother and a sergeant in the Polish Frontier Protection Force. 'But he was down on the Romanian border, and I hear many of our boys escaped that way rather than be captured by the Germans or the Russians.'

Too soon, Maria stood up. 'I have to go,' she announced with what Kalisz sensed was forced enthusiasm for Stefan's benefit. 'My shift finishes at midnight.' Stefan flinched away as she bent to kiss him on the forehead, but Kalisz's lips were more welcoming. 'Don't wait up. You need your rest.'

Kalisz followed her to the door. Then their heads were together, their tears mingling, and he could taste salt on her lips.

'Oh, Jani.' She gave an unladylike sniff. 'I thought you were gone.'

'For a while I thought so, too,' he admitted. 'The Germans never stopped coming.'

'I hate them.' The force behind her words surprised him. Hatred was so alien to her nature. 'A week ago, Ochota was in the front line, but our soldiers drove them back. We had to evacuate our patients. They say forty Nazi tanks were destroyed, but there were so many of our dead they buried them in parks and gardens – there was no space in the cemeteries.'

'We can't let them win, Marysia.'

'I don't want to lose you, Jan,' she whispered, 'but…'

But.

Kalisz understood with an intuition a thousand years in the making. Poland's men had been sent off to war with that 'but' since Baidar the Savage appeared on the eastern horizon with his Mongol *tumen* – the terrible Hordes of Ten Thousand – in the time of Henry the Pious. That 'but' meant: Honour demands your presence in battle. Honour demands your courage. Honour demands your blood. And if Honour demands your death, so be it. We women will stay at home and till the fields and go hungry and if, some day, the barbarian comes and you are not there to protect us, we will endure what must be endured. But…

He kissed her again. After a moment she pulled away and put on her coat, arranging her hair in front of the hall mirror.

'You look beautiful, as always.'

'Flatterer.' She punched him lightly on the arm. She reached for the door and hesitated.

'It's good to have you home, Jani. But for how long?'

The question took Kalisz by surprise, his mind lulled by the unfamiliar cosiness of the afternoon together. 'I'm not sure,' he mumbled. 'They say I'm definitely not fit for any kind of active service yet. I have a certificate.'

'A certificate?'

'To prove I'm not a deserter or a malingerer.'

'Pfaw.' An explosion of breath escaped from her pursed lips. 'Who would ever think such a thing of you?'

'I'm to have a medical in two weeks, but I suppose it's up to me to decide if I feel fit enough before that.'

Maria nodded. 'We'll talk later.' She kissed his cheek. 'Make sure Stefan goes to bed at a reasonable time. He'll try to keep you up all night.'

When she was gone, Kalisz leaned against the wall in the darkness.

'Is something wrong, Dada?' Stefan's concerned face appeared in the doorway.

'It's been a long day.' Kalisz straightened and forced a smile. 'I forgot to thank you for looking after Mama while I was away. You've made me a very proud father.'

The boy looked at his feet for a moment, torn between embarrassment and pride.

–

Later, Kalisz turned out the lamp and went to the bedroom. With some difficulty, he struggled out of the civilian suit Maria had sent to the hospital and changed into his pyjamas. Sleep eluded him despite a weariness close to exhaustion, and worry gnawed at him like a starving dog. *What will tomorrow bring, if this was what a good day felt like?* He listened to the sound of the guns – closer than last night, he thought – until he heard the sound of the front door opening and closing. He drew the covers over him, turned on his side and pretended to sleep.

The gentle click of the bedroom door and snick of a suspender belt being unhooked was followed by the rustle of silk as Maria undressed. The thought of her naked body, the soft curves and dark shadows, created an almost unbearable longing, but Kalisz didn't move. Couldn't. The sound of the nightdress being pulled over her head. She lifted the cover and slipped in beside him, snuggling up close for warmth.

'You're late,' he whispered.

'The wounded,' she sighed. 'There were so many of them. Those poor boys, some of them not much older than Stefan. They were in so much pain. I couldn't help them, Jan. It was terrible.'

He took her in his arms. 'Of course, you helped them. Believe me, I know what it's like to wake up wounded in a hospital among strangers. A smile. The touch of a woman's hand. The sound of her voice. Even if you had nothing else to offer, it would still give them comfort.'

'You truly think so?' She hesitated. 'Jani, I'd thought we might… I wanted to, but I'm so tired. I just couldn't.'

'There'll be other nights, my love.'

Maria squeezed her thanks and turned over. Kalisz stared into the darkness, concentrating on the sound of her breathing and wondering about tomorrow.

CHAPTER 4

The Artist

Berlin

The Artist sat back on a wooden park bench in the Tiergarten, watching a twenty-strong group of teenage BDM girls in white T-shirts and black shorts going through an energetic gymnastic exercise. They'd just completed a set of enthusiastic star jumps and were now doing vaults over each other's backs. Two or three of the girls interested him as potential subjects, but there was no question of approaching them as a group.

After the sheer visceral self-indulgence in Munich, he'd experienced a moment of terror that had restrained him from repeating the exercise. Several people must have seen him and Ilse together, perhaps even on the way to the studio. It would only take one word in the wrong place...

Fear of detection had also meant he'd been unable to complete what he'd begun and, in retrospect, it felt like a squalid wasted opportunity. He wanted so much more. Had so much more to offer. What was the point of creating something astonishing and then concealing it from the world? Recently, he'd experienced the urge growing inside him like a living thing, twisting his guts and searing his brain. Waves of what felt like electric pulses built up inside his head to the point where sometimes he thought it would explode. An intelligent man, he knew how he would be perceived by other intelligent men. A monster, they'd call him. A psychopath.

But, to The Artist, what he felt and what he'd done was entirely logical. He saw his life as a wheel, with every experience a line that converged on a central point. Each humiliation he'd suffered contributed to the cumulative total like chemicals being poured into a solution. Sooner or later there had to be a violent reaction.

He'd hoped the capital would provide new opportunities, but instead all he'd found was frustration. Suitable material was there at every turn. Hitler and the Nazis had created a German youth filled with confidence and a sense of adventure, disciplined, but independent of mind and strong of body. His train of thought was disturbed by a shouted order, and his heart beat a little faster as the BDM troop leader stripped off her T-shirt and shorts to reveal a bathing costume. Her charges followed suit and marched after her to the sparkling waters of the lake. All but one.

He'd noticed her earlier because, in the company of her athletic sisterhood, she'd looked as out of place as a carthorse among thoroughbreds. Chubby, bespectacled and flat-footed, her attempts to emulate the graceful movements of the others had appeared almost comical, culminating in a moment of humiliation when instead of vaulting her companion, she'd merely collapsed on top of her. As the others laughed she'd been berated by the troop leader, a sharp-featured woman in her late twenties with a shrill voice that carried to where he sat. From the one-sided conversation, he gathered the girl wanted to be excused something, and this was confirmed as she sat glumly on the bank, shaded from the sun by a tall willow, while the others took to the water.

The Artist rose to his feet and, taking care to stay out of sight of the swimmers, strolled along the bank towards her until something caught his attention. Taking out his sketchbook and with pencil in hand, he sat down about a dozen paces from her and began drawing an innocuous-looking plant among the reeds. She would probably have ignored him, but for the tune he habitually whistled as he sketched. As it was, he could sense her eyes on him, and he turned towards her with a look he liked to believe combined curiosity and mild confusion, as if he'd just been struck by unexpected inspiration. Now he began to sketch in earnest, with the focus on the girl.

'Are you drawing me?' To his surprise, she had a voice at odds with her appearance – soft and melodious.

'Yes.' He smiled. 'I hope you don't mind. Would you like to see the sketch? I'm quite pleased with it.'

She stared at the grass between her feet. 'I doubt it would be very nice. Everyone says I'm fat and ugly.'

Yet there was an element of self-mockery to the words. He could tell she was interested despite her natural wariness, and he sensed a deep desire to avoid any situation which would bring her more hurt. He stood up and crossed the space between them, again keeping the tree between him and the gimlet-eyed troop leader and her charges. 'Then I can assure you everyone is wrong. Look.' He handed her the sketchbook.

The moment she saw his likeness of her, her expression altered. 'Why, you've made me quite pretty.'

Her tone still contained a hint of suspicion, but he was ready for that. There was no sign of the other girls leaving the lake yet. He had time. He must use it well. 'Because you *are* pretty,' he said. 'An artist sees beauty in everything. In fact, I would like to paint you.' A bark of bitter laughter escaped her. Now she was certain he was mocking her. 'No,' he said. 'It is true. Have you heard of an artist named Gerard van Honthorst?'

'I know little of art,' she said.

'He was a great painter, a master, during the Dutch Golden Age. Why, his paintings would fill an entire gallery with images of girls just like you. Girls whose beauty transcends the normal.' Van Honthorst's subjects had mainly been prostitutes, but she didn't need to know that. 'An artist is nothing without his subject. His inspiration. We call it his Muse. You will be my Muse…?'

Still she wouldn't reveal her name. 'My parents would never allow it.' She said it with a hint of regret.

'Which is why you must not ask them,' The Artist said. 'Look.' He handed her a scribbled note torn from the sketch-book. A time and a place. 'Don't make a final decision now. Meet me here and we can discuss it further. Now, I must go, or I'll be late for church.'

The troop leader was chivvying her girls from the water. He'd done what he could. Either she would come or she wouldn't. He gave her a last smile and turned to walk away.

'Renata,' she called to him softly. 'My name is Renata.'

–

Renata lay on her back on the rough wooden workbench, pinned by leather straps that bit deep into her snowy flesh at the shoulder and hips, and her wrists shackled to ringbolts on either flank. Her dark eyes bulged with terror and muted whimpers emerged from behind the gag.

Good, she is quite conscious now.

He picked up the scalpel and held it where she could see it, enjoying the feeling of power as she bucked against her fetters in a vain attempt to avoid her fate. Her heaving chest and stomach drew his attention, and for a moment he had the most delicious liquid feeling inside as he contemplated eviscerating her while she still lived.

But no, it wouldn't do.

He drew the scalpel across the taut skin of Renata's throat in one precise movement before stepping well clear of the twin fountains of blood from her severed carotid arteries. As he waited for her to bleed out, he reflected on how much he'd learned from Renata and her predecessors. For one thing, chloroform in its current state of development did not bring about the kind of instant oblivion that would save him so much trouble. It was something he must think on. There would be books in the university library that might provide a solution. And it was surprising how quickly the vibrant colours of the organs faded when they were liberated from the sanctuary of the body cavity. An artist could not work without vivid colours, so today he would experiment with a shallow bath of olive oil, in the hope they would keep their condition.

She was quite dead now; he could resume his work in peace. He began his cut at the pubis, making an incision that ran up across the abdomen to the breastbone, exposing the first colours of the palette he would work from.

He worked quickly, taking only what he needed. His creation must be in position and completed by daylight. He had lied to Renata. She was never going to be his Muse. That distinction lay with the vase of flowers by the window – *Rosa centifolia pomponia*. Now he sought to replicate them, but it was far from simple. The different textures – rigidity or elasticity of the individual organs and parts – provided different challenges for his scalpel. He knew almost immediately that tonight would not be perfect, but he was enough of an artist to understand that perfection came only with constant practice.

When he'd created the individual elements and stored them in the oil container, he hosed down the body – he'd been attracted to this place by the workshop's drainage pit – and wrapped it in a sheet. Renata had no interest for him now, but he knew his work would not be understood without the context of the crucible that had provided the original components. When he carried her through to the garage area and placed her in the trunk of his car, he was surprised by how light she was.

He'd identified the perfect spot earlier, and it didn't take long to drive from the workshop back to the Tiergarten, and a dirt track that led through an area of forest. What made it perfect was that it was far enough from any main thoroughfare to make it unlikely he'd be disturbed, but well enough used by walkers and riders in daytime to ensure his creation would be found. He parked and switched off the headlights, lifted the body from the trunk, and placed it beside the track in a cross configuration, a refinement calculated to suggest Renata's killing had some sort of religious motivation. When he was satisfied with her positioning, he returned to the car and retrieved a torch from the glove compartment and the box containing the oiled body parts from the rear seat. He quickly found the flat area of hard-packed earth he'd picked out as his canvas earlier. Yet he discovered the torchlight made it impossible to identify the components by their colour beneath their viscous coating. Worse, they kept slipping through his fingers to become contaminated by dirt. Plainly the oil had been a mistake. Still, he willed himself to be calm and continued to place the elements as well as he could.

The voices from the trees to his right froze him for a moment, and the beams of a pair of torches reached out towards him. No time to think or they'd be on him. He switched off his own torch and ran for the car, opening the door and throwing himself into the driver's seat in the same movement. A moment of sheer horror as he fumbled for the key, only to remember he'd left it in the ignition.

He rejoiced as the engine fired on the first turn, and he engaged gear and accelerated into the darkness, depending on memory to keep him safely on the track for fifty nerve-shredding metres before he switched on the headlights.

He could have wept; so many things had gone wrong. Yet a single consolation eased his disappointment.

How many more Renatas were still out there waiting for him?

CHAPTER 5

Warsaw

Next morning, Kalisz put together a breakfast of bread, pickles and a couple of hard-boiled eggs, eaten in his pyjamas. When he was done, he selected a clean shirt, dark tie and his grey work suit, the trousers a little looser around the waist than he remembered.

He unlocked a drawer in the oak chest beside the bed and placed the contents on the bedcover. The police-issue Nagant revolver slipped easily from the polished leather shoulder holster. He checked the action, automatically making sure the cylinder was empty, and peered down the length of the barrel. Compact and reliable, Kalisz preferred the Nagant to the Browning automatics some of his colleagues carried; it was lighter, with a shorter barrel and less prone to jam. Of course, every gun had a downside. This one's was the double-action trigger, which had a heavy pull, and the time it took to reload. If you fired the seven rounds without bringing down your man, you might as well use it as a club. Kalisz had spent countless hours at the range practising with the gun until he was rated expert. Not that he particularly wanted to shoot anyone, but if he had to, he wasn't going to miss. He loaded the cylinder with 7.62mm ammunition from a box in the drawer and slid his arms through the straps of the shoulder holster, snapping the flap into place over the gun. The familiar action made him grin. Fast draws were for Tom Mix movies, and he didn't want it falling out on the tram when he bent over.

It was only when he reached Krakowskie that he remembered there *were* no trams.

–

Department V: a kind of second homecoming.

The department headquarters at Nowy Sjazd 1 stood across the road from the west bank of the river Vistula, near the Kierbedź Bridge, with an entrance from the viaduct at the level of the fourth floor.

Through the swing doors and into the reception area. A nod of recognition from the sergeant behind the desk. He wore the dark navy uniform that gave him and his comrades their nickname – 'The Blues' – but the short-barrelled Mannlicher rifle leaning against the wall beside his seat and the military-style helmet sitting on the pack next to it provided ample evidence of the changed times. As he walked by, Kalisz was reminded of the exhortation by the Inspector General of the *Policja Państwowa*, Josef Kordian, to his officers a year earlier, as Hitler began to increase the pressure on Poland to relinquish the Danzig Corridor. 'Remember you are a soldier. Always practise a soldier's skills.'

To his right, a passage to the interview rooms and the holding cells. To his left, a bank of desks armed with type-writers that would normally be filled with secretaries clattering out reports, but now inhabited by two bored-looking women drinking what smelled like coffee. The two storeys below were occupied by other departments and, taking up the entire ground floor, the rather dull Warsaw railway museum.

Kalisz made his way up the stairs. The white paintwork had long ago mutated into a pale nicotine yellow, and bare threads and patches of polished wood showed through the scuffed surface of the linoleum. He emerged directly into the detectives' room, inhaling the scent of dried sweat, stale cigarettes and cheap pomade with as much pleasure as if it had been an exotic perfume.

'Shit, it's Kalisz, we must have won the war.'

Ten or twelve heads turned towards him – about half the number who'd normally inhabit the battered desks. 'Go screw yourself, Witold,' someone – Mosicki – snarled at the joker. 'At least he picked up a rifle. What did you do?'

'I've got a heart condition.' Witold spread his hands. 'What could I do?'

He was offered several options, most of them physically impossible, and hurriedly went back to the paper on his desk. Kalisz took time to look round the room. Just what he'd expected. Too old, too fat, and one or two who were fit enough, but would always find an excuse not to fight. Some of them wouldn't meet his eyes, but a couple nodded grimly, pleased, in their gruff way, to see him.

'Looks like you gents are expecting a storm.' Kalisz pointed to the sandbag-covered windows on the river side of the building, blocked up entirely apart from a narrow rifle slit at the centre.

'Welcome to the impregnable Vistula Line.' Edelman, as bald as an egg and with a boozer's beetroot nose, picked up a rifle that had been sitting at his feet, went to the nearest window and stuck it through the slit to menace the far bank of the river. 'If *Szkopy* comes, we're supposed to fight to the death. We're taking bets Witold will die of fright before they fire the first shot. What do you think, Jan?'

'Enough of this. Get back to your work.' The order came from an enormously fat man who emerged from one of the offices at the rear of the room. Kalisz felt an instant surge of pleasure. Bruno Litauer had been the best detective in the state police until advancing years, overindulgence and downright disillusionment had driven him close to the grave. That's why the commander of Warsaw's police had given him Kalisz as second in command. Bruno sat in his office and ensured the paperwork had no holes in it, and Kalisz did the legwork leading the twenty investigators in Nowy Sjazd 1. Litauer's face lit up when he recognised the cause of the commotion. 'Jani! We thought we'd lost you. Mary, mother of Christ, am I glad to see you. Wait there.' He vanished into his office and reappeared a few moments later, squeezing himself into his suit jacket and cramming the battered fedora that was his trademark on his head. 'Mosicki, you're in charge until we get back.'

The appointment was greeted by a chorus of groans, but Litauer was already on the way out, moving surprisingly nimbly for such a large man. They took the stairs to Mariensztat on the level of the river. 'Come on, we'll see if there's anything to eat,' Litauer announced. 'Rylski will be getting the place ready for lunch, if there is anything for lunch, but we might find something at the market.' They passed the restaurant where Litauer liked to entertain visiting dignitaries. An ancient waiter in a white jacket was laying tables outside, and Bruno called to him.

'Hey, Poldek. They say the Huns will requisition all the best restaurants in Warsaw for themselves, so you shouldn't have anything to worry about.'

'At least they'll be better tippers than you cheapskate cops,' the man grunted without looking up from his task.

It was business as usual at the market in the shadow of the viaduct. Everyone had something to sell or trade, so long as it wasn't food. But the shabby traders behind the makeshift counters knew what was coming, and that they'd need all the help they could get to survive it. So today nothing was too much for the chief investigator of Warsaw Central. Somehow a hunk of bread and hard Koryciński cheese was discovered – a miracle, surely? – and wrapped in an old copy of the *Kurier*.

'We'll find a seat by the river, eh?'

'Sure.' Kalisz followed his boss. They settled in on a wooden bench by the water gauge tower overlooking one of the numerous marinas where the pleasure steamers berthed. Today the marina was empty, and Kalisz guessed the riverboat men had taken their families out of the city to escape the bombing. On the far side of the choppy grey waters, he could see more marinas and bathing stations. Despite the constant sound of artillery and the twenty-four-hour bombing raids, fragile, narrow-winged terns and graceful black-headed gulls still quartered the river, seeking out a meal.

Litauer broke the bread in half and tore off a piece of newspaper to use as a plate. 'They're coming, Jan.' He waved the crust towards the far side of the river, where dark pillars of smoke scored the horizon. 'Maybe not today, or tomorrow, but we won't be able to stop them. Did you know that if the wind's in the right direction you can hear the sound of small arms fire from the tower of the Church of Our Lady? They're that close.'

'You climbed a church tower, Bruno?' Kalisz feigned astonishment.

A guffaw of laughter shook Litauer's prodigious frame. 'These days I have trouble climbing on to a chair. But,' his voice turned serious, 'you know what I mean. There's no stopping these Nazi bastards now. This talk of the French and English is just that – talk. We're on our own and we have to deal with it. The one thing we have in our favour as cops is that they're going to need us.'

Kalisz suppressed a shiver at the echo of the Invisible Man's words. 'You truly believe that?'

'Of course. The Germans love order, you know that. Hell, you're practically German yourself. Without cops there is only chaos. We're already seeing it. There's been so much looting out in Powązki we're just letting them get on with it. People see a burnt-out shop and think, "Why should I leave this for the Nazis?" So they take what they want. Then they get a taste for it. That kind of thing will offend the Germans. It certainly offends me. So you're going to be important. My German is limited to "*Zwei Bier bitte*". I'm going to need you to help me deal with them.'

Kalisz accepted this horse manure in the spirit with which it was offered. To his certain knowledge, Bruno's German was just about as good as his own, but if the boss wanted to play the dumb Polack, who was he to argue?

Litauer reached inside his jacket and brought out a folded piece of paper. 'This is who we have in the holding cells. I'm in two minds what to do with them. What do you think?'

Kalisz took the list. A couple of petty thieves and two of more interest. Petrov, whom they called 'The Bulgarian'. A smuggler of cigarettes and fine wines, as far as they knew. Maybe a few other things besides. Kalisz recalled he operated out of an office in Marszałkowska and had contacts in City Hall. The other, Hershel Rozenblum, was a Jewish forger who could turn out ten-zloty notes of superior quality to the government's. This addiction to excellence had been his downfall, because they stood out like diamonds in a dungheap, and if Hershel was short, he tended to rely on his own products. Kalisz rather liked him. If you wanted to impress your friends with a Picasso line drawing, Rozenblum would run it up in an afternoon. A minor Old Master would take a week. He didn't touch anything really good because, with beguiling modesty, he would admit, 'I don't have their talent and who wants to do sub-standard work, sir?'

'No mass murderers in this bunch.' Kalisz gave his verdict. 'But it would go badly with a couple of them if the Nazis laid hands on them. I'd turn them loose.'

'All right, Jan. I trust your judgement.'

'I'll talk to them before they go. Let them know they owe us.'

'Good idea. And… Jan?'

'Yes?'

'Unless you're thinking of shooting yourself with it, best hand in your personal weapon now. All it will do is get you killed.' Bruno patted him on the shoulder. 'Maybe it won't be so bad after all. Maybe after they swallow us they'll cough us right back up again, like a dog with a warty old toad.'

–

Back in the office, Kalisz pulled the files on the four men in the cells, paying particular attention to the two he'd identified. As the day wore on a glimmer of a possibility – perhaps an opportunity? – began to form. *We will need all the help we can get.* Why not?

'If it was up to me, I'd lock you up and throw away the key.' Kalisz repeated the speech to Rozenblum he'd already given Petrov. The sharp-featured Jewish forger sat with his back to the cell wall, listening with a disconcerted frown on his face. 'But for some reason,' Kalisz continued, 'the boss has come over all soft-hearted. He reckons at a time like this a man should be with his family. So we're letting you go.' Rozenblum let out a long breath and his body seemed to deflate like a balloon. Clearly he'd been considering his future with as much interest as Kalisz, and it hadn't looked too bright. 'This doesn't mean the charges are going away. We have plenty of evidence and the government doesn't like people printing money without its say-so. You're still operating out of that little warehouse out on Miła?'

'Yes, sir, and thank you, sir.'

'Don't thank me. Just remember that if someone comes knocking in a week or a month, make sure you do the right thing.'

'The right thing, sir?'

'Trust me, Mr Rozenblum, you'll know it when it happens.'

–

It had been Investigator Kalisz's habit, before *all this*, to be last out of the office, apart from the night cover, and with so little manpower there'd be no night cover. So no one thought it odd that he was still there as they all drifted off to their homes.

Once he was alone, Kalisz rummaged through the department store cupboard until he found a nearly new leather attaché case he hadn't used since he was first promoted. Maria had bought it for him, but the Department V old guard found it so hilarious that he'd abandoned it after a week. He opened the straps and placed the Rozenblum and Petrov files inside. But why only two? The Warsaw Central records were held in dozens of filing cabinets in a dusty room that ran the length of the top floor. Before he went up to retrieve them, he wrote down a list of possibles: a backstreet gunsmith out in Mokotów, who hid behind a perfectly legitimate clock repair business; a bent civil servant suspected, but never convicted, of stealing blank passports, driving licences and travel permits; another two men, and one woman, all of them living on the margins, beyond officialdom, but people who could get things *done*. Seven files.

Could he take more? Not without arousing suspicion from the guard on the front desk.

He found he was sweating and his hands shook. If this was what it was like before the Germans came, what would it be like later?

CHAPTER 6

In daylight, the Invisible Man had none of the powerful presence he held in Kalisz's memory. They were of a similar height, which an optimist would have called medium. The suit he wore smelled of a lifetime spent in cheap boarding houses, his shirt collar was frayed, short wisps of white cotton fluttering in the strong wind, and his homburg hat looked as if someone had recently sat on it. A salesman, perhaps? A door-to-door purveyor of household insurance or cheap jewellery, but not a very successful one.

He'd sounded young, but the face, though the skin remained smooth and unblemished, had been forged for a man much older. Sunken cheeks, a chin barely worth the name, and the eyes, which Kalisz had imagined glowing with passion, seemed almost bored, framed by black-rimmed spectacles and barely fathomable behind their thick lenses. At least they were until he heard what was in the attaché case.

Not such a clever idea after all, as it turned out. Had horrified outrage ever been so eloquently expressed? Hands pushed deep into the pockets of his thin raincoat, he turned to Kalisz. 'Are you quite mad?'

'There was no risk.' Kalisz tried without success to radiate equal composure. 'When the time comes, each of these people can be of important service to you – to us.'

'No risk? How do you know one of your colleagues hasn't tagged these files for the Gestapo? "They were in their places

45

at 6.12 p.m. on the afternoon of 26 September, at 8 a.m. on the 27th they were discovered missing. Four people were in a position to remove them, the suspect with the closest proximity is a certain—"'

'I've worked with these men for five years.'

'As they've worked with you.'

'What is that supposed to mean?'

'You know exactly what I mean, Investigator, but what is done cannot be undone. They know you and they trust you. That's one of the reasons you were selected. It's not just that you have access. You have influence. You possess a combination of attributes which we believe one day may place you in a position to make a genuine difference. We put our trust in you, and you jeopardise *everything* for a few names we probably already have. Understand this, Investigator…' He brought his mouth close to Kalisz's ear as if he were imparting a commercial secret. 'You cannot impress me. I don't care how clever you are, or how cunning, or how brave. The only thing I care about is how effective you can be, and for how long.'

His rebuke delivered, he looked up at the ruins of the Krasiński Library, which three days earlier had been a master-piece of neoclassical architecture. 'I never thought it would come to this.'

'No?'

'They seem to have deliberately targeted the most beautiful and most loved buildings in the city. That is not the mark of soldiers, it is the mark of the Beast. There is a reason they are known as Huns.'

'If this is how they treat our buildings, how will they treat our people?'

The other man nodded. Now Kalisz was beginning to understand. 'It is already happening in the occupied areas.

Anyone who gives the slightest affront is shot. Mass round-ups in cases of suspected sabotage. The deliberate and systematic destruction of Jewish communities and massacre of their populations.'

They walked on in silence, past the blackened remains of Staniewski Brothers Circus, avoiding piles of rubble and a charred carcass left lying in the centre of the road. It was big and four-legged. A horse? Possibly one of the beautiful, exotic zebras Kalisz remembered pulling a chariot-load of clowns at the performance he'd attended with Stefan. A lamp post leaned at an impossible angle in front of the music conservatory at the end of the street, the top six feet hanging down like an old-fashioned gallows. Kalisz pursed his lips at the imagery.

'Your job,' the Invisible Man continued, 'distasteful as it will undoubtedly be, is to bow to the conquerors, impress them with your diligence, accept their rebukes, ignore their provocations and win their trust.'

'In other words, do nothing.'

'Precisely.'

'For how long?'

'For as long as it takes.'

Kalisz voiced the thought that had been troubling him. 'What if they ask me to do something that is unacceptable to me?'

A heartbeat's pause, but the tone said that this, like everything else, had been considered. 'We accept that must be your decision. Every man has a line he will not cross. But you'll have to bear in mind that any refusal will have its consequences and we may not be able to help.'

'Very well.' Kalisz nodded. 'When will I know to contact you?'

'That, too, will be your decision. Have you decided on an emergency protocol?'

'Can you have someone make a regular pass by the apartment building?'

The Invisible Man considered the question for a moment. 'That should be possible.'

'There's a small window on the top floor. A storeroom. The curtain is always kept closed. If it's open, I want a meeting.'

The other man liked the idea. No risks on the agent's side and minimal on the watcher's. 'The location?'

'The back entrance to the university gardens off Browarna. On the way to work next morning I'll step inside the gate.'

'I'll be there. For our regular meetings we'll use the procedure you suggested. The fountain and the chalk?' He reached inside his pocket and handed over a packet of coloured chalks of the kind teachers used. 'We can talk about the details later.' He hesitated for a moment. 'Should there be a difficulty, you'll know my replacement by his tie. It will be the same colour as this.' He ignored Kalisz's look of disquiet and pointed to the powder-blue strip of nylon at his neck. 'It's just a precaution. He won't know your identity and it will be up to you to initiate contact. My superiors have also ordered me to offer you this.'

He handed over a small ring box. Kalisz opened it to reveal a single white capsule. 'Is this what I think it is?' A sharp nod, like a blackbird pecking at a snail shell. 'Then no.' He handed the box back.

'They are not gentle with spies.'

'I'll take my chances.'

'Very well.' Kalisz had a feeling the meeting was terminated, but his companion paused in the act of turning away. 'May I make an observation, Investigator?'

'Of course.'

'You are a proud man,' he said. 'In other circumstances that would be a worthy attribute, but if these people sense pride in you, they will undoubtedly kill you.'

Kalisz gave him a look the Invisible Man didn't care for. 'I'll bear it in mind. Wait,' he called as the other man began to walk off.

'Yes?'

'Do you have a name?'

For a moment the pale face looked bemused, as if the thought had never occurred to him. Eventually, he came up with a pseudonym that pleased him.

'You may call me Kazimierz.'

CHAPTER 7

The Artist

Berlin

The Artist studied himself in the mirror. Yes, he rather liked this new look. He'd always had what people called a fine figure: tall and slim, with a narrow waist and shoulders that, if not quite broad, were at least solid. The uniform set it off to perfection. A tailored grey jacket with black collar tabs, the right embroidered with the silver lightning flashes of the SS and on the left, the vertical line of three diamonds that denoted his rank of *Obersturmführer*. The patch on his right arm rather spoiled the overall effect, but they'd insisted he had to have something that showed he wasn't *quite* the real thing, even if they hadn't been certain exactly what it should be. He completed the effect with the peaked officer's cap, setting it at what he deemed a sufficiently rakish angle. The handsome face with its cold eyes stared back at him, the silver Death's Head above the peak lending a sinister effect that he found stirred something inside. *Oh yes, so many possibilities*.

The appointment had happened rather suddenly and had come as a complete surprise. His profession had always been regarded as rather boring, but an SS general had suddenly taken an interest in his particular talents. They needed someone to perform a special task, and The Artist was the man with the qualities required to make a success of it. Germany required him in Poland, which suited him perfectly well in the circumstances, and the rank and uniform were an added bonus. As a former reservist, the basic military training he'd undergone had proved only a minor hardship.

What mattered was that the SS uniform gave him authority, and with authority came opportunity. He had a feeling his new posting would provide him with many such opportunities. But there was no hurry. The anticipation and the knowledge of what he was capable of was almost as thrilling as the act itself. After the debacle in the Tiergarten – how could he have been so foolish as to forget the forest wardens and their relentless pursuit of poachers? – he'd decided to rein in his appetites for a time. For some reason, the anticipated outcry and accompanying headlines had never manifested themselves. In a way he was disappointed; he would have liked to see the appreciation of his work in the newspapers. To walk the streets knowing people feared his presence, but were unaware of it. Perhaps they would even have given him a name?

With a last admiring glance at the mirror, he shrugged on his greatcoat and picked up his suitcase. A car was waiting outside to take him to the station. When he reached the terminal, a porter accompanied him to his compartment. On the opposite track another engine had just pulled in, and weary-looking Wehrmacht soldiers stumbled from their berths onto the platform, some of them wearing bandages over recently acquired wounds. Some front-line unit sent back for a rest. Warsaw may have surrendered, but the stubborn Poles continued to fight elsewhere. Clearly there was still work to do.

Chalked on the side of the nearest car was a pledge he was quite certain was already being fulfilled.

Wir fahren nach Polen um Juden zu versohlen.

'We're off to Poland to beat up the Jews.'

Personally, he had nothing against the Jews. His first chemistry teacher, old Bronstein, had been a Jew who proudly wore the Iron Cross he'd won at Verdun. Every war had its victims, and it was just that the Führer had singled out the Jews for this one. There was nothing to be done about it.

A ticket collector appeared at the doorway, almost bowing at the sight of the SS runes and the Death's Head emblem on his cap. Normally the fawning servility would have made The Artist smile, but his face remained a mask of icy dismissal. The railway worker hesitated, uncertain whether to ask for his ticket. He made the man wait while he reached slowly inside his greatcoat and produced his travel warrant. He looked away during the cursory inspection.

'Enjoy your trip, *Herr Obersturmführer.*'

The Artist raised a languid hand for the return of the warrant. 'I intend to.'

CHAPTER 8

Warsaw

The difference between victory and defeat was written plain on the faces of the two columns of men passing each other on opposite sides of the street. On the far side, a straggling procession of tattered scarecrows in ill-fitting military over-coats and crumpled mud-brown field caps shuffled towards the railway station, carrying their worldly belongings in bulging packs slung diagonally across their shoulders. They had pinched, grey features, downturned mouths, and their dull, disinterested eyes never left the cobbles or the neck of the man in front. The contrast between the despondent Polish prisoners of war on their way to an uncertain captivity and the soldiers marching in the opposite direction couldn't have been greater.

Led by a bespectacled Wehrmacht major on a chestnut horse, their iron-shod jackboots slammed into the conquered Polish cobbles with enough force to strike sparks, and they sang a song about a girl they'd left behind in Bavaria. It was a love song, but somehow these tall, handsome young German boys managed to make it threatening and aggressive. They marched with their rifles slung, their heads high and their chins out. Beneath the curved rims of their steel helmets their eyes were restless and bright, searching the surroundings for the fruits of victory. For this was no ceremonial procession. These were the front-line troops who had hounded the Polish army to destruction.

Kalisz watched them march past from a shop doorway, rank after dusty grey rank, and wondered how he had ever believed they could be defeated. They looked invincible, and their smug, imperious expressions told him they believed it. Yet they could be killed. He'd killed enough of them himself to disprove that theory. The problem was that there were so many of them. They just kept coming.

He felt a terrible hollow sadness for Warsaw. His city. This was the way an enemy stripped a conquered capital of its identity. Perhaps even its soul, who could tell? First they sent in the scouts on their motorcycle–sidecar combinations to make sure some deceitful Pole hadn't planted a landmine or set up an ambush. Then came the billeting officers – if a few thousand families had to be thrown out of their homes, well, that was what happened when you were at the wrong end of a war – followed by the marching bands and the endless lines of *Landsers*: farm boys and factory workers who'd been told they had a God-given right to rule. Even their belt buckles told them so. *Gott Mit Uns*, they said: God is with us. And after the soldiers would come the exploiters, the bureaucrats, and the men in leather coats with dead eyes and a limitless capacity for inflicting pain.

Bile rose in Kalisz's throat and he was filled with a self-destructive loathing. He had to get away before the anger growing inside him made him do something foolish. The large woman standing next to him felt it, too, because she put a warning hand on his arm. He turned to look at her. A Slavic face with coarse, reddened features and hooded eyes filled with motherly compassion. Tears ran unchecked down her cheeks. She shook her head slowly, unable to find the words. Kalisz nodded to tell her he understood, unhooked his arm and walked away.

Deathly quiet in Department V. The twelve who'd originally greeted him on his return had shrunk to nine. Mosicki and two other investigators had decided not to turn up that day. Through the open door of his office, Bruno, glum and grey-faced, looked up and raised a hand with a smoking cigarette in salute before returning to the papers on his desk. Kalisz took his seat and opened a file the boss had left for him, a report on the looting out in Powązki. But he couldn't concentrate. His eyes drifted to the windows on the river side of the office, now stripped of their protective and potentially provocative sandbags. He could just make out smoke from the smouldering ruins of Praga drifting along the far bank.

'Did you see the bastards?' Edelman demanded. 'A fucking brass band. Parading up and down as if they own the place.' Witold hissed at him to be quiet, but the other man only glared at him. 'If you let them know you're scared of them, they'll stomp all over you,' he growled. 'They want our co-operation? Well, there are different kinds of co-operation, and you don't get if you don't give. Maybe I'll co-operate and maybe I won't. We'll see.'

'No point in antagonising them on the first day.' Kalisz kept his voice low. 'Better to wait and see how things go.'

'I thought you'd be the last one to turn the other cheek, Jan.' Edelman regarded him with something close to scorn. 'The war's changed you.'

Kalisz picked up the file, pretending to read it, and Edelman lapsed back into silence. As the minutes passed the tension in the room increased. Kalisz felt his stomach begin to knot, the way a piece of string does when you twist it in different directions at either end. Something clattered to the floor in Bruno's office, and the men started and looked nervously at each other.

The room went still at the sound of a car engine. Nobody breathed until it became apparent this one wasn't for them.

Or was it? Another car drew up, this time accompanied by the sound of slamming doors. Kalisz glanced towards Bruno's office. The big man was staring at the top of the stairs, his mouth a thin line and his jaw set like concrete. He held his hands clutched together on the desk, and Kalisz could see he was trying to stop them shaking. The main door crashed back and boots thundered on the wooden stairs. A Nazi officer appeared, SS flashes on his collar and the silver Death's Head on his peaked cap, and marched directly to Litauer's office. He was followed by six jackbooted soldiers wearing steel helmets and with submachine pistols unslung and ready to fire. Four of the men accompanied the officer while the others turned their weapons threateningly on Kalisz and his companions.

Kalisz froze beneath the dark eye of a machine pistol's muzzle. 'Don't move.' Did his voice really sound that calm? The soldier holding the gun was little more than a boy, but he seemed angry at the situation in which he found himself and he had his finger on the trigger. All it would take was the slightest increase in pressure. Kalisz recognised the weapon as an MP38, a gleaming combination of blue-black metal and plastic. It had a folding stock and a long box magazine that held thirty-two rounds of 9mm ammunition. A single burst from an MP38 could cut a man in half. Kalisz had seen the results and they weren't pretty.

'*Holen Sie sich zurück gegen die Wand.*' The words were accompanied by a jerk of the barrel.

'He wants us to stand back against the wall,' Kalisz translated. 'I suggest we do it slowly and without any sudden movements.'

He took his hands off the desk and held them at shoulder height as he carefully rose and stepped clear. His eyes never left the man with the gun, but he heard the sound of chairs scraping back as the others complied. He shuffled backwards in the direction of the nearest wall, praying he didn't fall over a chair and give the SS man an excuse to shoot. Meanwhile, a sharp, guttural conversation was taking place in Bruno Litauer's office. The officer, a hawk-faced man in his early thirties, had evidently lost patience with whatever he was being told, because they heard a crack like a pistol shot and Bruno reeled back, stunned by an open-handed slap to the head. Kalisz noted that the German had worn a pair of black leather gloves to ensure his skin wasn't contaminated by Polish sweat – or blood.

A moment later, Bruno was hustled out by four escorts, their hands on his shoulders or grabbing handfuls of his shiny suit jacket. Fear and consternation distorted the big man's chalk-white face. He looked wildly at Kalisz as they hauled him bodily down the stairs, with the toes of his shoes rattling against the individual treads. A second later the officer marched after them with a sour look on his face, not looking left or right.

They heard the slam of car doors, accompanied, Kalisz had a feeling, by a yelp of pain, before the sound of engines revved up and then faded. For a moment the only noise was the harsh breathing of frightened men whose minds reeled with the devastating speed and ruthlessness of the arrest. Kalisz caught the eye of the young guard. The anger had been replaced by an expression of amused contempt. Clearly, he was enjoying their fear.

'I think I've pissed my pants.' Edelman's belligerence hadn't lasted long.

'*Sprechen Sie nicht*,' the guard snapped.

The two SS men herded them into a small windowless room normally used for conferences and closed the door, leaving them in darkness. An investigator called Stolarski, a man in his late forties but one of the newer members of the team, produced a cigarette lighter to illuminate a ring of faces in its eerie, flickering light.

'What the fuck was that all about?' whispered Witold. 'I thought poor old Bruno was going to have a heart attack.'

'They're trying to put the frighteners on us,' Stolarski said.

'They fucking succeeded. When they lined us up against the wall… Edelman wasn't the only one pissing his pants, I can tell you.'

'That was just a figure of speech,' a voice insisted from the back of the huddle.

'Sure. That puddle you were standing in, that was just a figure of speech, too. Not so tough now, eh, Edelman?'

'They were armed. If I'd had my pistol…'

'You can have mine,' Stolarski offered.

A hissed chorus of 'Whaaaaat?' None of them had any doubt what would happen if anyone was found with a gun.

'A joke.'

'Well, keep them to yourself. You're not saying much, Jan.' Witold sought Kalisz out by the door. 'I suppose you're in charge of the department now. What do you think they're up to? Why did they arrest the boss?'

Kalisz had been asking himself the same question. 'Bruno thought they'd need us to help them keep order.' He kept his voice low. 'But it looks as if they have a different idea. Maybe he was on a list. The Gestapo like their lists, and that's all it would take.'

'What about us?'

A groan went up as Stolarski's lighter sputtered and went out, plunging them back into darkness.

'We'll just have to wait and see.' No point in voicing his own fear that the Nazis would send Poland's police to camps in Germany in the wake of her soldiers. If that happened, he'd have to somehow get a note to Maria. How would she and Stefan survive if he was taken away, perhaps for a year or more? And so much for Kazimierz's grand plan. Kalisz wouldn't be much good to him staring at a barbed wire fence somewhere in Silesia.

It was an hour by the luminous dial of Kalisz's watch, but it seemed much, much longer, what with the stink of Witold's farts – at least, everybody blamed Witold – that made the stifling, airless atmosphere toxic, and Edelman's constant grumbling. Outside the room they could hear the sound of movement and furniture being shifted. By the time the door opened to flood them with a blinding light, they'd almost have been grateful to be carted off to a prison camp.

Kalisz squinted at the helmeted figure silhouetted in the doorway. The man stood there just long enough for them to start wondering if the room was about to be filled with flying lead before he spoke.

'*Spricht irgendwer Deutsch?*'

Kalisz felt every eye on him as he took a step forward.

'*Ich spreche Deutsch.*'

CHAPTER 9

One of the soldiers covered Kalisz with a machine pistol while the other searched him with quick, practised hands. When they were satisfied, the taller German prodded him towards Bruno's office with a playful nudge of the gun barrel in his ribs. By now, more soldiers – he guessed they were from the Sipo, the Nazi Security Police – were busy rummaging through the investigators' desks. Kalisz had a moment of panic as he tried to remember if there was anything in his desk that would cause offence. A difficult question, that. He had a feeling that just about anything would offend them.

'Name?' the guard demanded as he consulted a sheet of paper by the office door.

'Kalisz, Jan. Investigator. Department V.' The SS man gave him a look that said *we'll see about that*. But it seemed he was on the list. The only question was whether that was good or bad.

'*Hauptsturmführer* Hoth will see you now.'

The soldier tapped on the door and a gruff voice told him to enter. Kalisz heard his name being spoken and the guard ushered him into the familiar room. Familiar, apart from the man behind the big wooden desk. A solid, almost square individual, with what Kalisz thought of as a very Germanic face, a mouth that might have been scored by a knife point and a jutting, determined chin. The owner wore his crow-black hair swept back from a broad brow and kept his eyes on whatever he'd been reading.

Kalisz took in an immaculately tailored uniform of field grey, with the silver runes on one collar tab and a combination of diamonds and stripes on the other. A Walther pistol lay on the desktop within reach of his right hand. If Kalisz remembered correctly, the Walther had the advantage of being a double-action weapon, which meant it could be carried with a round in the chamber. The SS officer lifted his head with a sharp movement, and Kalisz straightened to his full height under the gaze of pale, washed-out eyes.

'Kalisz?' A soft voice, but the tone of a busy man irritated by this diversion from the normal course of his routine. Apparently, he had more important things to do than make decisions about puzzling little Polish policemen.

'Yes, sir.'

The eyes went back to the document and Kalisz felt an unfamiliar thrill of fear. How much did they know about him? He'd sat on the other side of a desk in similar situations to understand that this was a piece of theatre designed to make him feel uneasy, but that didn't make it any less disturbing. 'Born Silesia, 25 July 1907?'

'Yes, sir.'

'Yes, Herr *Hauptsturmführer*, if you please.'

'My apologies, Herr *Hauptsturmführer*.'

'Your German is very good.'

'Thank you, Herr *Hauptsturmführer*. My grandmother was from Köslin on the—'

'I know where Köslin is. She was German?'

'Yes, Herr… She died in the influenza epidemic after the war.'

'A German, yet you fought her countrymen?'

Kalisz froze as he saw the trap. Kazimierz had said his records would be doctored, but the Gestapo could have access to an earlier version. Was he listed on the page as a lieutenant of intelligence or a corporal clerk? 'I was a reservist, Herr *Hauptsturmführer.*' He couldn't hide the nervousness in his voice and he knew that to this man, fear would be like blood to a shark. 'I was called up,' he hurried on, 'but I never reached my unit. I was wounded before I fired a shot and given a full discharge.'

The German produced an audible sigh of frustration. *Why did it always have to be like this with these people?* The right hand crept towards the Walther and Kalisz had to bunch his fists to stop his own hands shaking. Before the fingers reached the gun, they slipped beneath the desk and some sort of buzzer sounded in the investigators' room. Kalisz would have applauded this swift, new and very Teutonic addition to office efficiency, but he was too busy trying to stay upright on his rubber legs.

A uniformed aide appeared at the door. '*Hauptsturmführer* Hoth?'

'Fetch Steinhuber.' The aide gave the Hitler salute and disappeared again. 'I think you are lying to me, Kalisz.'

'No, sir... Herr *Hauptsturmführer.*' Kalisz could feel sweat trickling down his back. He measured the distance to the Walther. Could he get to it before the Nazi bastard moved? At least he would take one of them with him. But what if the pistol wasn't armed?

'A clever fellow like you with such a fine command of German – I think you hunted our friends in the *Selbstschutz* who were so helpful during the campaign.' Kalisz took his eye off the gun and relaxed a little. The *Selbstschutz* were paramilitary groups of Polish-based ethnic Germans who had provided the Nazis with intelligence, and sabotaged bridges and supply routes. No doubt someone had been investigating them, but it certainly hadn't been him, and Hoth could have no evidence that he had. 'There have been many instances of atrocities against the *Volksdeutsche* of Poland. Perhaps you were involved?'

'I assure the Herr *Hauptsturmführer* I was wounded and spent the first weeks of the campaign in hospital. The records...'

Hoth looked up sharply, his pale eyes glistening with menace. 'Destroyed, we are told. Convenient, don't you think? Come in.'

A young officer in an SS field cap joined them in the office. 'You wanted to see me, sir?'

'This man claims to have been so badly injured he couldn't have fought against us. What do you think?' Hoth turned to face Kalisz again. 'Steinhuber is from the SS Medical Corps,' he said. 'He will soon find out the truth of it.'

'You were wounded?' From Steinhuber, it sounded like an accusation.

'In the leg, ribs and head, sir,' Kalisz confirmed. 'I recovered quickly enough from the concussion, but my thigh—'

'Let me see it.'

'Sir?'

'Your leg, man. Let me see the wound.'

'But, sir...' Kalisz fumbled ineffectually at his belt.

'He's seen a leg before,' Hoth growled. 'Get on with it.'

'Of course, Herr *Hauptsturmführer*.' Kalisz felt his face redden as he hurriedly unbuttoned his trousers and allowed them to drop to his ankles, turning so that the scar on his left thigh was visible to the young doctor.

Steinhuber tapped a long, elegant finger against his upper lip. 'You were fortunate.' He pulled a wooden spatula from his tunic pocket and bent to study the ugly, puckered lightning flash that ran diagonally across Kalisz's upper thigh towards his groin. 'Shrapnel?'

'A piece of tree branch, sir.' Kalisz winced as the spatula tested the inflamed flesh.

'It's healing well,' Steinhuber murmured to himself. 'An inch one way and the femoral artery would be gone, a couple of inches the other and it would have gelded him.'

'Well?' Hoth demanded.

Steinhuber straightened. 'If he was wounded when he says he was, this injury would have kept him out of the fighting for three weeks to a month.'

'And was he?'

Steinhuber bent for a second examination and Kalisz held his breath. 'I see no reason to think otherwise, sir.'

'Very well, Steinhuber. That is all for now.' Steinhuber left the office with a perfectly executed Hitler salute. Hoth raised his right hand perfunctorily in reply. He turned to glare at Kalisz. 'Are you going to stand with your trousers around your ankles all day?'

'No, Herr *Hauptsturmführer*.' As he bent to pull up his trousers, Kalisz felt a surge of relief. He had a suspicion he owed his freedom – perhaps his life – to something cooked up in the hospital to make the wound look worse than it actually had been.

'You must understand –' *Hauptsturmführer* Hoth's face twisted into a frown, as if he couldn't quite believe his theory had been disproved – 'we can't be too careful with you tricky Poles. Why, your own chief, Commissar Litauer, no doubt in peacetime a perfectly honourable policeman, was involved with some clique of army officers who are pledged to make life difficult for us. Perhaps they even approached you?'

Kalisz went cold again. 'No, Herr *Hauptsturmführer*.'

'Of course not.' Hoth shook his bull's head. 'Because they don't trust you, Kalisz. Blood will out, and you will always be an outsider among the Poles. You still consider yourself a Pole?'

'I… Yes, sir.'

'Natural, I suppose.' An equal measure of regret and understanding in the gruff tone. A different Hoth, this – the disappointed headmaster prepared to be conciliatory. 'But understand this, Kalisz. We're already discovering that there are two kinds of Poles. The Poles who accept their current situation and are happy to work with us – then the others, like your man Litauer, who still have to be taught the realities of life. Am I making sense to you?'

Kalisz bowed his head, hating himself in a way he knew he was going to have to become accustomed to. 'Thank you for explaining the situation to me so clearly, Herr *Hauptsturmführer*.'

'Good.' Hoth was all business again. 'Now, you'll not be surprised to hear that there are going to be some changes around here.'

–

Kalisz's head reeled as the two guards escorted him back to the conference room. For one thing, Kazimierz had been wrong. He would never understand Germans. Someone had restored the electricity in the room, and every eye turned to him as he was ushered through the door. 'They won't be questioning anyone else for the moment,' he announced, to the relief of the other detectives. 'That doesn't mean we aren't under suspicion. We have to prove they can trust us.'

'So what happens now?' Edelman seemed to have recovered some of his bounce.

'We're no longer investigators.' A shocked silence greeted Kalisz's words. 'The new head of Department V, a man called

Hoth, who, by the way, is a former Commissar in the Berlin Kripo, says we're no longer required. We'll be replaced by a few *Volksdeutsche* cops from Danzig and Silesia.'

'Christ, Jan, we can't let them do this to us. We have families, bills to pay.' Witold wasn't the only one complaining. There were groans and angry muttering at the thought of their jobs being taken over by some German yokels. Kalisz sympathised with them, but...

'*Hauptsturmführer* Hoth wasn't in a negotiating mood, Witold, and unless you want to take the Bruno way out, I wouldn't mention it. Another reason he doesn't need Polish investigators is that his bosses expect a rapid and permanent decline in Warsaw's crime rate.'

'He's got a fucking big shock coming if he thinks that,' Edelman butted in, to a chorus of agreement.

'They'll pick up the professional crims and anyone they think might oppose them, regardless of whether they've done anything,' Kalisz continued. 'And then it's off to a camp where they're beyond the reach of the law. You may not think it's justice as we understand it, and you'd be right, but we're no longer in charge. The good news – if you can call it that – is that we still have a part to play, and we'll continue to be paid.'

He explained what Hoth had told him. The investigators of Department V and the other district investigation offices would become glorified filing clerks. Today they'd start moving the files of convicted and suspected criminals down to the lower floor, which was being evacuated for the purpose, set up desks, and begin to sift the files into assigned groups. At the end of each day the files would be gathered and taken away to be actioned by another department. For the sake of efficiency, all the files from Warsaw's various police departments would be processed at Nowy Sjazd 1.

'Another department?' Edelman said. 'You mean the Gestapo or the SS, and "actioned" means these poor bastards will be dragged off to those camps you mentioned, whether they're guilty or not.'

'I didn't ask Hoth what happens to the files after we process them,' Kalisz said wearily. 'I doubt you would have either, Edelman.'

But Kalisz could see on their faces that not a man in the room doubted Edelman was right.

Edelman glared at him. 'They have a name for people like us.'

'Yes, they do.' Kalisz matched his look. 'Survivors.'

PART TWO: COMPOSITION

CHAPTER 10

The Artist

The Artist decided he liked Warsaw. True, much of the city had been reduced to rubble, but it gave what survived a certain nobility: a dignified grandeur, similar to the shattered remains of an ancient civilisation that had endured war, famine and flood to exist as a testament of past endeavour, even greatness. A pity it would soon all be gone.

As part of his preparations for his new position, he'd attended a conference in Würzburg on the post-war future of Poland. Warsaw, as it now was, had no role in it. The Führer had ordered that the city be almost completely razed and all evidence of its place in European history wiped away. What little remained would form the foundation of a moderately proportioned German town, inhabited entirely by ethnic Germans and their Polish servants. As he turned from Marszałkowska into Aleja Jerozolimskie, with submissive Poles stepping aside on the pavement and doffing their caps to him, he felt an electric surge of power. These people knew nothing of their future or his part in it.

He passed a pretty little park with a makeshift wooden gallows in the centre. Four men and a woman hung suspended by their necks like so much ripening fruit, while a group of soldiers stood around them, smoking and chatting together. A burst of laughter made him smile. Death, destruction and chaos:

the perfect combination to allow him to take the step he'd anticipated for so long. The expectation gave him an almost sexual thrill. Who would notice one more disappearance when hundreds vanished every day? What was one more dead body in a city populated by the dead and the soon to be dead?

He'd spent the morning touring the city. It had disappointed him that so little remained of the Royal Castle, but he'd been impressed with the artwork in the churches he'd visited. The expedition allowed him to familiarise himself with the city centre, and he'd identified several potential opportunities. It also had a dual purpose, which was yet to be fulfilled. Still, he had plenty of time.

Not too far away, on the edge of the Vistula escarpment, stood the National Museum of Poland: four great modernistic sandstone monoliths that would have made the Führer proud. Not to his taste, particularly, and out of character with the rest of the city, but impressive in their own way. A security detail had set up a checkpoint across the road, but they let him through readily enough. He strolled past a line of grey-painted trucks until he was opposite the front entrance, where a pair of guards stopped him at the bottom of the concrete steps. He could hear the sound of hammering, and every few moments soldiers would appear, carrying narrow timber packing cases or boxes of varying sizes.

'I'm sorry, sir,' the guard said after inspecting his papers. 'I can't allow you inside. There's a special operation in progress.'

The Artist pursed his lips. 'What kind of special operation?'

'I'm not at liberty to say, sir.'

'What's going on here?' a voice demanded from the top of the stairs. 'Who are you?'

The Artist looked up to find an SS captain staring down at him, with his hands on his hips.

72

'A German and an art lover.' He shrugged. 'Also a fellow SS officer, as I'm sure you've noticed. I've just arrived in the city and I'd heard the museum has a fine collection of Old Masters. It looks as if I'm just in time.'

The captain marched down the stairs and put out his hand. The Artist handed over his paybook and the man flicked through, checking the photograph against the features in front of him. 'Most recent posting SS *Junkerschule* Bad Tölz?'

'They wanted me for a special assignment. I was fast-tracked through the training.'

'Tough, eh? I'm Berger. Likewise on special assignment.' He handed back the paybook and gave The Artist a speculative look. 'All right, art lover, you can come in as long as you stay out of the way.' He turned and ran up the steps and The Artist followed. 'Old Masters? We have plenty of Old Masters.'

'I prefer the Dutch school.' He answered the unspoken question. 'Vermeer, Rubens, Van Honthorst, but especially Rembrandt. I find the Italians too fussy, and if I'm honest, overly religious.'

'A pity.' Berger took off his peaked cap and ran a hand over his close-cropped dark hair. 'I could have shown you a very nice Raphael we picked up in Kraków last week. You'll find the Dutch school in the gallery along to your right. If anyone questions your right to be here, just mention my name.'

The Artist thanked him. 'If you don't mind my asking, what's the hurry? From what I hear, we won't be going anywhere soon.'

Berger grinned over his shoulder. 'We're collecting for Reichsminister Göring. If we don't get in and out quickly, we'll end up sharing with Heini and Joey's boys, and *Der Dicke* won't like that.'

73

The Artist joined in with the other man's laughter. Heini and Joey were *Reichsführer* Heinrich Himmler and Josef Goebbels, the equally powerful Minister of Propaganda. *Der Dicke* was Göring's semi-affectionate nickname and referred to his portly stature.

He spent a pleasant hour wandering from gallery to gallery. Meanwhile, men hurried about their business around him, and paintings disappeared one by one to leave gaps on the walls. Should he feel pity as Poland's greatest art collection was dismantled around him? He rather thought not. If the Poles truly wanted it, they should have fought harder to keep it. Better that Rembrandt's rather fine *Painting of a Young Man* – a reluctant sitter if The Artist had ever seen one – should be exhibited where it could be enjoyed by people better equipped, socially and culturally, to appreciate the Dutchman's genius.

When he left the museum, his route purposely took him towards the river and an industrial district of derelict factories and a bombed-out, partially abandoned gas works. It was still early afternoon and only a few people were on the narrow, hemmed-in streets, mostly women of the lower class. The looks he received made him glad it wasn't later in the day, when their menfolk were returning from work. Next time he came this way, it would be in a motor car. Fortunately, when he went a little further he found a cleared area where the men of a Wehrmacht engineering company were building a supply base and fortifying nearby houses as part of its defences. There'd be a permanent presence here that would ensure he and his... interests... were protected.

The Artist asked to see the commander of the engineers, and was presented to a burly young man with an *Oberleutnant*'s insignia on his shoulder tab and a two-day growth of beard on his cheeks. He saw the man's eyes harden and his lips curl as he

74

recognised the SS uniform. For reasons, he supposed, of rivalry, there was no love lost between the branches of the German military.

He gave his name and rank and a perfectly executed Hitler salute that the other man returned with an unhidden lack of enthusiasm. A few soldiers stood watching them with expectant grins on their faces, but The Artist was not here for confrontation. He returned the glare with a smile. 'There's no need to stand on ceremony, *Oberleutnant*…?'

'Halder.' The other man's tone contained no welcome, but The Artist's smile didn't falter.

'*Oberleutnant* Halder, this isn't a formal visit.' He looked around at the grinning men. 'Perhaps we could go somewhere more private?'

Halder stared at him for a moment, then shrugged. 'Sure.' He led the way to a nearby house, where a room had been set up as an office with engineering drawings on the walls. A man was sitting at a desk in the corner, using a set square to draw a plan. 'Leave us,' Halder ordered, and the man got up and left with a puzzled glance. 'All right?'

'You're a man of few words, Herr *Oberleutnant*.' The Artist pulled out a cigarette case and offered it. Halder sniffed, but he accepted. 'Your soldiers seemed to take exception to my presence.'

'That's because they don't much like you people, whatever your rank.'

'And why would that be?'

'Because we've had to clean up after you. My men would rather build a bridge under fire than dig a mass grave, especially one that's going to be filled with women and kids.' Halder's grey eyes took on a distant look and he nodded slowly to himself. 'Once you've done it a few times, maybe you'd just as much like to see that skull you're wearing on your cap in your sights as a Polish eagle. They're out there hoping I'll hear what you say and then rip your throat out. We use a lot of concrete, and, as we engineers say, you can hide a lot of problems under six feet of concrete.'

The Artist laughed. 'As it happens, Herr *Oberleutnant*, I didn't volunteer for the SS, and I didn't come here for an argument. I have certain skills that someone more important than I decided would be of use to the SS, and, like you when I'm given an order, I obey it.' Halder grunted, and his shoulders bunched, but The Artist ignored the threat. 'I'm here to ask a favour. I'm in Warsaw on special assignment, and for reasons that needn't concern you I need somewhere in this area I can store equipment. All I ask is the loan of one of your men who speaks Polish. An hour should suffice.' He allowed the smile to broaden. 'Engineers, after all, are the elite of the army – you're bound to have one.' Despite himself, Halder returned a wry smile. 'I'm prepared to pay, of course. A packet of cigarettes for the pioneer, and a case of brandy for the commander to disburse at his leisure. I would also count it a favour.'

Halder went to the door. 'Kontowski?' he shouted. 'I'm going to regret this. Take another man as an escort. We don't have too many friends around here.'

It took them less than half an hour to find the ideal place: a warehouse hidden away at the end of a narrow dead-end street within two hundred metres of the German supply base. It was currently being used as a workshop, but the bewildered Pole who owned it could only watch as The Artist marched through the double doors and inspected the interior, a trifling space stinking of oil and sweat, but capable of taking two cars at a time.

'Perfect. Tell him I can get a requisition order, or we can do it the easy way – six months' rent up front in Occupation marks.'

The soldier's eyes widened at his largesse, but Kontowski relayed his words.

The negotiations were short and conclusive. The Artist handed over the money, the man produced the keys to the warehouse, and agreed to put the spare set through the letterbox when he'd moved his tools out. The Artist and the soldier walked back towards the supply base. 'No need for anyone to know what went on here,' he told Kontowski. 'A carton of cigarettes each for your trouble, and there'll be a little something inside to say thank you.' The engineers grinned their thanks and he felt a shiver of anticipation as he considered the future. The warehouse, with its familiar raised workbench and nearby drainage pit, was perfect for what he had planned. And soon no one would even be aware of its existence. If he'd calculated correctly, the engineering company would be on their way to France once they'd completed their assignment.

With a little luck, Halder and his companions would be at the front of the attack, and dead before six months were out.

CHAPTER 11

Kalisz arrived home hours later than normal to find the house in darkness. As he fumbled for matches to light the oil lamp, Maria emerged from the bedroom in her dressing gown. She studied his face in the soft, buttery glow that rose to bathe the room. 'Jan, you look exhausted. What happened?'

Kalisz slumped in the armchair. 'It was just a hard day.'

He was avoiding her eyes and she sensed it. 'What happened, Jani?'

'They took Bruno.'

'What?' Maria turned deathly pale.

'They marched him out of his office and dragged him away. The SS. Or the Gestapo.' Kalisz got up, poured himself a thimble-sized glass of Krupnik and threw back the sweet, fiery liquid in a single gulp. 'He was terrified, Maria. Scared half to death. There was nothing we could do. They had guns trained on us.'

Maria's hand went to her mouth. 'You were in danger? But the war is over.'

'No, not in danger. At least so long as we didn't do anything stupid.' He remembered the mocking eyes, daring them to try. 'The war might be over for us, but I don't think it is for them.'

'But what will happen to Bruno? Will they...?'

'I don't know. In Germany they have camps. Maybe they'll take him to one of those. Maybe they'll just question him and release him.' But the way he said it told her he didn't believe that.

She put her arms around him and they stood like that for a while, taking comfort from each other's physical presence, the togetherness of a dozen years of marriage insulating them for a moment from the realities of a day that was not like yesterday, or the day before, or the day before that. A day that was the first of who knew how many that must be endured and survived.

'Jani,' she said softly. 'Perhaps you don't have to do this? You don't have to work for them.'

Kalisz felt an icy fist close on his heart. He'd known this moment would come, but knowing didn't provide an answer. 'I don't think I have a choice, Maria. Our new Nazi boss made it clear that anyone who doesn't work for them won't work at all. He has the power to do that. Worse, he hinted that we might end up like Bruno. I'm not even an investigator any more, I'm just a clerk. And what would we do if I was out of work? We have to eat. We have to pay for the apartment.'

'My father—'

'Your father will be looking out for himself, just like everybody else in Warsaw. He won't be able to help us.'

'Jan, please…'

'It's no use, Maria.' He struggled to keep his tone even. 'Words like compromise and compassion mean nothing to these people. They'll take what they want as a right of conquest. They'll control us. Totally. As they do their own people. They are the masters. We are the servants. If we complain, they will throw us into camps. If we fight back, they will kill us. I saw it today. I looked into the eyes of a young German boy and he dared me to give him an excuse to pull the trigger.'

'But if it's going to be like that, what choice do we have but to resist?' she asked, as if it were the most logical question in the world.

Kalisz closed his eyes and an image of Kazimierz swam into his brain. If he was ever going to tell Maria, now was the time. For a moment he wavered – was on the point of speaking – but then the face was matched by a quiet insistent voice. *It would be dangerous for both of you.*

'With what?' He saw her flinch at the anger and frustration in his voice and hated himself for it. 'We had planes and tanks and artillery and they defeated us. Are we supposed to march into their machine guns waving flags, so the rest of the world can read their newspapers at breakfast and spend a moment mourning the "gallant little Poles" before they turn to the sports pages?'

She took a step back and stared at him. 'I can't believe this is you talking, Jan. The man I kissed before he went off to war would have died before he bent the knee to any Nazi.'

'For God's sake, Maria, that *was* war. This is peace. This is about learning to live with what little we have left.'

'What about dignity and honour and duty?' She almost spat the words. 'Those values we taught Stefan to live his life by. Was that all they were to you, Jan, just words?'

'Dignity won't put food on the table,' he hit back with equal force. 'My honour is my affair, and, as for duty, my duty is to the Polish state. In Warsaw, the Polish state is represented by President Stefan Starzyński, and he has ordered all civil servants to return to their desks. Until he withdraws that order, my duty is to obey it.'

'But he—'

'Is something wrong, Mama?'

'No, Stefan,' Maria said gently, as she turned to find her son rubbing his eyes in his bedroom doorway. 'Dada and I were just discussing his day.'

'Did you see the Germans?'

'Yes, they visited the office.'

'What are they like?'

'Just men. Like us, more or less.'

'I hate them.'

'We'll talk in the morning, Stefan,' his mother said. 'Get some sleep. Remember you're going to Mrs Lewicka for lessons because the school is still closed.'

'I thought I heard shouting.'

'No, just talking.'

'Oh. Well… goodnight.' A moment of hesitation. 'I love you.'

When he was gone, Maria stood with her head bowed. Kalisz took her hand. 'Come,' he said. 'We should get some sleep, too.'

'Promise me, Jani.'

'Promise you what?'

'Promise me you will never do anything to shame us.'

–

Kalisz, Stolarski and two others manoeuvred the last metal filing cabinet down the stairs into the basement room. When they reached the bottom, they lowered it to the ground and stretched their backs, shirts sweat-soaked from the effort.

'Put it beside the rest,' ordered their guard, an SS corporal called Blum. 'And be quick about it.'

'On three,' Kalisz said. 'One, two, three… up.'

With a collective groan, they staggered across the concrete floor with the massive box and deposited it with a dull crunch at the end of a row, the last of seventy-five that had been carried down six flights. The filing cabinets were arranged along one side of the basement, facing a formation of twenty scarred wooden desks and chairs that, from the childish graffiti carved into them, had been commandeered from a nearby school.

Blum sat, his compact black MP38 ready to hand, at a larger desk, the only other furniture in the ill-lit room, beyond two ranks of large packing cases that gave him the impression of being protected by a tank trap.

The disgruntled former investigators of Nowy Sjazd I had been joined by eleven others from various Warsaw districts. Kalisz and his fellow labourers took their seats at the last four unoccupied desks. He expected Blum to give him their instructions so he could translate. To his surprise, the corporal snapped to attention as the sound of footsteps echoed down the stairs, heralding the entrance of *Hauptsturmführer* Hoth and a young officer, who surveyed the scene with quizzical interest.

Hoth cleared his throat, like an opera singer preparing for his aria. 'Good, you have settled into your new accommodation after your manual labours.' Kalisz was surprised at the Nazi's excellent, if idiomatic, Polish. Hoth stood with his hands clasped behind his back and his chest puffed out, surveying the layout and nodding approval.

'I wished to address you directly because you have an important task to complete. It is one which will have a serious impact on the level of criminality in this city, which I am sure, as policemen, we all desire.' He paused, waiting for some sign of approval that never came, before continuing with his speech. 'All files in this building relating to convicted and suspected criminals are now in this room. Your job is to categorise them into four groups, which coincide with the large containers to your front. From left to right they are labelled major criminals, political criminals, habitual criminals of the lesser sort, and Jews. It is of vital importance that you carry out your task with the utmost diligence. If you have any doubts about the category of a file, or if it fits into more than one category, it must be placed in the highest category container that relates to it. For instance, if a man – or a woman, for that matter – is both a Jew and a major criminal, let us say a gangster of note, his or her file should be placed in the major criminal container. However...' Hoth raised his right hand and flourished what looked like a conductor's baton, but turned out to be a red marker pencil. 'It must be marked with a large *J*, thus.' He picked up a file Blum had laid out for him and, with an artistic flourish, scrawled the letter *J* on the front so it was clearly visible to all.

'You will work quickly, but with precision. Any mistakes will be... Well, let us not talk of such things. One last word. You will approach the filing cabinets one person at a time, retrieving such files as you can comfortably transport back to your desk. Likewise, one at a time to the boxes, yes?' He raised a hand and a sharp click punctuated the question as Blum cocked his machine pistol and laid it back on the desk with an executioner's smile. '*Unterscharführer* Blum has my orders to fire the moment he feels under threat. Like me, he is of a nervous disposition. It would not be wise to test just how nervous.'

He half-raised his right arm towards his shoulder before remembering who he was talking to, and turned it into a dismissive wave. With a rueful shake of his head, he left the room with the young SS officer at his heels.

When Hoth was gone, the Poles stared at Blum. The SS man motioned in the direction of the files with the barrel of his machine gun. At first no one moved, and his expression changed from one of benign menace to irritation. 'Get on with it,' he snarled.

'Witold, you go first.' The investigator looked at Kalisz in alarm, but complied. 'The rest of you, follow one at a time.'

Every time he looked up, Kalisz found Blum's eyes on him as the SS man passed the time cleaning and oiling a big pistol. It was a Nagant, and looked disturbingly familiar.

The first time Kalisz marked a *J* on one of the folders, he felt as if he was signing a death warrant.

CHAPTER 12

Had Jan Kalisz been a diarist, he would have written: *Poland is no more. In the space of just three weeks, a once proud nation has been reduced to a historical footnote. Warsaw is now part of a bureaucratic entity called the General Government. Our western provinces have been incorporated into the Third Reich. Refugees from the annexed territories pour into Warsaw by the tens of thousands each day, with dreadful tales of murder squads and mass shootings. Priests, writers, doctors and dentists. Lawyers, journalists, businessmen and landowners. All those the people look to for leadership have been singled out for execution. Dear God, what has our poor nation done to deserve this?*

But diaries, like most forms of communication, were dangerous, so he only thought it. At least your thoughts couldn't be taken away or destroyed or held hostage by the Nazis. He pushed his hands deeper into his overcoat pockets against the cold and made his way towards the river, where he was less likely to be stopped by a patrol.

They'd even taken away Piłsudski Square and the Saxon Gardens. One day, Kalisz had followed his usual route to work only to be stopped by a sign reading '*Nur für Deutsche*' – Only for Germans – backed up by a hulking brute with a rifle. Another large reserved area had been created around the old Ministry for Religious Beliefs building on Aleja Szucha that had been requisitioned by the Gestapo as their headquarters.

Like everyone in Warsaw, Kalisz needed an *Arbeitskarte* if he wanted to work, a *Raucherkarte* if he wanted to buy cigarettes, and a *Seifenkarte* if he wished to wash with what the Germans laughingly called soap, a rock-like substance that refused to raise a lather. He even needed a licence to own a bicycle. Poles had to leave the pavement free for Germans, raise their hats to German officers, and any Polish woman who 'annoyed' a German soldier risked being sent to a military brothel. In short, life in Warsaw was like walking a long, shaky plank with a noose around your neck and your hands tied behind your back.

Hunger was a constant companion. The Nazi-issued ration cards entitled Kalisz to a fifth of the ration allocated to Germans, but a hundred calories a day more than that allowed to the Jews. It was enough – just – to keep a body from starving. Bread was only available through official channels. If people baked their own, they risked being shot, but Poles, being Poles, showed their respect for this law by ignoring it – if they could lay their hands on flour. Still, Kalisz could see the pinched signs of early starvation in the faces of the people around him.

By unspoken agreement, neither he nor Maria had mentioned their... *discussion*... after that night, but the tension remained. She didn't like him working with the Germans and she didn't care if he knew it. On the other hand, she still loved him enough that, for now, she was prepared to tolerate it. She still took him to her bed and let him know she enjoyed what they did together. But now it was a little different. As if she had removed part of her consciousness from the act.

Ice coated the windows of the basement room, and the former investigators worked in their hats and overcoats. It was so cold, they'd named their workplace '*lodówka*' – the Fridge. They'd long since sorted all the files from Department V and new batches arrived overnight from other areas of the city. One by one, they went up to collect an armful of folders to examine.

'Hey, Blum,' Stolarski called. 'This new lot aren't crooks, they're just ordinary employment files.'

Blum looked up from the newspaper he was reading.

'You address me as Herr *Unterscharführer*, Stolarski. Bring them over and let me have a look.' Stolarski did as he was ordered and Blum grunted in annoyance. 'All right. Anyone else who has these, put them back until I find out what's to be done. Take some from one of the other cabinets.' He picked up the internal telephone and called upstairs for instructions. After a few moments, he shook his head. 'They should have gone direct. Move them beside the files to be picked up tonight.'

Before he replaced his batch, Kalisz flicked through the papers on his desk. They were all personnel files from Warsaw University: professors, lecturers and researchers. Puzzled, he returned them to the cabinet and replaced them with a batch of suspected criminals from the tough Ursus factory district on the western outskirts of the city.

–

'Kalisz?' He froze at the sound of his name and his heart pounded fit to break his ribs. They'd been working in the Fridge for long enough to be wary of Blum's hair-trigger temper. 'Report to *Hauptsturmführer* Hoth.'

'At once, sir.'

'At the double, Kalisz.'

'Yes, sir.' Feeling something like nervous anticipation, Kalisz walked through the scantily populated investigators' room and knocked on the door of Hoth's office.

'Enter.'

Kalisz closed the door behind him and took up a position a pace away from Hoth's desk. Directly facing him, on the wall beside the window, hung a large print of Adolf Hitler wearing a brown uniform with a red-and-black swastika armband on the sleeve. The Führer had his right fist on his hip and stared into the middle distance. His hair was perfectly parted, and the familiar toothbrush moustache was firmly clamped between a nose like an axe head and a thin, almost feminine, mouth. His expression reminded Kalisz of a man suffering from severe constipation.

'You sent for me, Herr *Hauptsturmführer?*'

Hoth didn't look up from the document he was studying, but to Kalisz's surprise, he waved towards a chair set slightly to one side of the desk. Kalisz obeyed, but there was something not right about sitting in the presence of an SS officer. He settled for perching on the lip with a straight back, so he could leap to attention when Hoth realised his mistake. His position gave him a view of the papers on the desk, but he studiously ignored them, concentrating instead on the black-and-white photograph of a surprisingly young, and very pretty, blonde woman with two children.

'Idiots,' Hoth muttered. 'They send me idiots. Look here.' He glanced up and waved the paper, his face pink with frustration. 'They arrested the wrong man because they couldn't tell the difference between two street names. By the time one of his friends who spoke German turned up to protest, the SD had already shot him. Any competent German detective who speaks Polish goes straight to the Gestapo, while Kripo has to make do with potato-headed yokels who can barely string two words together and have never investigated anything more important than a broken window.' He sighed. 'If they do happen to speak Polish, the chances are they can't speak German.'

Kalisz kept his expression blank as he listened to Hoth's litany of complaint. If the *Hauptsturmführer* wanted an opinion, he'd no doubt ask. For the moment, it was safer to play dumb.

'Every case takes three or four times longer than it should, and half of them are botched. We're understaffed, but we're still expected to make our quota of arrests. Something has to be done.' Hoth frowned and looked directly at Kalisz. 'Blum assures me you work diligently and give no cause for complaint. You're an intelligent fellow, Kalisz, and obviously competent.' He nodded slowly to himself as some inner thought bore fruit. 'Let's call it the German blood in your veins. I've decided to bring you upstairs as a translator. What do you think of that?'

For a moment, Kalisz couldn't find the words. A jolt of exhilaration shot through him like an electric shock, but it was immediately tempered by his instinct for self-preservation. He was being invited into the tiger's cage and, for all Hoth's flowery compliments, the tiger was never slow to show its teeth. 'I'm very...' *Honoured* was the word that was expected, but he couldn't bring himself to say it. '...flattered, Herr *Hauptsturmführer*,' was the best he could manage.

'Of course,' Hoth mused, 'we'd find a way to increase your rations. We can't put you on the *Volksliste*, you don't meet the requirements for citizenship, but we'll manage something. And you'll be paid in marks.'

'That's very generous, sir.' Maria wouldn't have Nazi currency in the house, so best she didn't hear about this part of the deal. The General Government had pegged the exchange rate of the mark artificially high against the zloty, which would almost double Kalisz's spending power. But all that was secondary to the fact that he'd be operating on the fifth floor. He'd be in a position to hear and see things that could be of genuine value to Kazimierz. Of course, he'd have to be doubly careful, but it would be worth the risk.

'You'll move up to Desk Five immediately,' Hoth continued. 'In the long term I suspect we'll need a pool of interpreters, but for now you'll be working with *Obersturmführer* Ziegler.'

'I'm afraid I don't know the officer, sir.' Kalisz dared to venture.

The SS man took a cigarette from a packet on the desk and lit it with a long match, blowing a cloud of smoke from the left side of his mouth, away from the picture of his family. For a moment he held the cigarette raised elegantly between two fingers in a pose Kalisz thought more suited to a literary salon than a police office. He could tell Hoth was considering how much he needed to know. Enough, at least, for the purposes of departmental efficiency.

'*Obersturmführer* Ziegler is, by career, a lawyer – quite an eminent one. He lectured at the University of Berlin.' A tight smile acknowledged Kalisz for a moment as a fellow cop. They knew what they thought of lawyers, didn't they? 'He was involved in some sort of special operations group, keeping order behind the lines during the takeover. The poor fellow must have had a busy time of it because they've sent him to us for a rest. He has little or no Polish, so God knows what they thought I could use him for, but he's bright, I'm short-staffed, and he's an extra pair of hands. Be here at eight sharp tomorrow. We'll start the pair of you with something simple.'

CHAPTER 13

The Hotel de Saxe

Obersturmführer Willi Ziegler studied the darkened maw of the arched entrance on Kozia with visible distaste. 'So, this is it?'

Kalisz refrained from pointing out the letters thirty centimetres high that spelled out the name of the establishment. 'This is it, Herr *Obersturmführer*,' he confirmed.

'Not the most attractive assignment.'

'No, Herr *Obersturmführer*.'

'I've told you, Kalisz. If we're to work together, you must call me Willi, at least when we're alone.'

'Yes, Herr *Obersturmführer*.'

Ziegler blew through his lips in exasperation. 'All right, have it your own way.'

For anyone who'd experienced the stunning brutality of the Nazi takeover of Warsaw, SS Lieutenant Willi Ziegler was a peculiar sort of German. Tall and slim, with pale, aristocratic features, the young SS officer had an easy charm and seemed determined to be pleasant. Of course, it helped that he viewed Kalisz, working on the fifth floor among Germans and speaking German, as almost one of his own. As Kalisz had guided him through the streets between headquarters and the hotel, he'd shaken his head at the destruction of so many fine buildings and praised the qualities of those that had survived. He'd been especially interested in the churches along the route, and showed his knowledge of religious architecture, of which Warsaw had an abundance. The contrast between the man and the uniform he wore was disconcerting. It made Kalisz all the more resolved to hate him, but he had a feeling it was going to be difficult.

A *Wachtmeister* and a pair of square-jawed thugs from the *Ordnungspolizei* accompanied them, to provide security in case of trouble. Not that anyone expected trouble. This was a routine assignment more suited to a clerk than a detective.

'I suppose our soldiers need to be able to have their recreation somewhere safe, without a threat to their health or their character.' Ziegler tapped the brown file he was carrying against his left palm. 'Let's get on with it.'

They walked through the entrance into a carpeted reception area. The room exuded a faded grandeur entirely in keeping with a hotel that had once been the largest in Warsaw, but had long since been eclipsed by the likes of the Europejski and the Bristol. Worn carpets and chipped wooden furniture added to the air of decline, along with gilt-framed landscapes that hadn't seen a duster in years. To one side of the reception, beyond glass doors, lay the gloomy cavern of an empty bar. The reception desk was staffed by a single elderly male in a shiny black waistcoat and tie, who looked up in alarm when he saw Ziegler's uniform and the slung rifles of the men accompanying him.

Ziegler handed Kalisz the file and stood back.

'We're here to talk to the manager,' Kalisz told the receptionist. 'State business,' he added, just in case there was any doubt.

'Of… Of course, sir,' the old man stammered. 'If you will just wait a second.'

He turned towards a door at the rear of the reception, but Kalisz stopped him with a word. 'No.' He pushed the internal telephone towards him. 'Just give him a call.' He accompanied the order with a grim smile. 'We don't want either of you suddenly discovering you have a very important appointment elsewhere, do we?'

The receptionist licked his lips. 'No, sir.' He picked up the handset and dialled a number. 'Mr Giulietti?' He swallowed. 'The police are here, asking to see you.'

Kalisz heard a muttered curse at the other end of the line. Ziegler studied his surroundings with feigned interest. The escort watched the receptionist with emotionless hunters' eyes as he replaced the phone and placed both hands clearly in sight.

At the sound of footsteps, the *Wachtmeister* automatically half-turned to cover the stairs with his sub-machine gun. A middle-aged man appeared, wearing a tan suit that, like the hotel, had seen better days. He had dark hair worn slicked back, a thin moustache, and the florid features that marked a heavy drinker. Kalisz knew Carlo Giulietti by reputation, but they'd never met. In the past, the hotelier had been suspected of allowing his premises to be used for various nefarious purposes, none of which anyone ever quite managed to prove.

'How may I help you, sirs?' His steps faltered as he recognised Ziegler's SS uniform, but before he could say anything else, Kalisz stepped into his path. He had a feeling Giulietti probably spoke at least some German, and he wanted this conversation to be conducted entirely in Polish.

Kalisz nodded for the receptionist to disappear, and the old man took the hint and slipped away gratefully through the rear door. Kalisz took Giulietti by the shoulder and guided him to the reception desk. He removed a single sheet of paper from the file Ziegler had handed him and placed it face up, so the hotelier could see the official eagle and swastika stamp on the document. 'Sir, this is an order signed by the military commander of Warsaw requisitioning the Hotel de Saxe for use as a military brothel for German officers.'

It took a moment, but when the reality sank in, Giulietti clutched at his chest and went deathly pale. He had to lean against the reception desk to stop himself from collapsing. 'My hotel,' he gasped. 'My livelihood. Mother of Mary, what will become of my family?'

Ziegler didn't understand the words, but he shook his head at the hotelier's theatrical reaction. 'Tell him he will be compensated. We are not thieves.'

Kalisz sensed an opportunity to test whether the SS officer's affability was more than skin deep. 'Sir, this man is an Italian citizen and a neutral. I can attest to his good character. Perhaps he could be allowed to continue in some management role?'

Ziegler considered the suggestion. 'Italian or German, I don't suppose it matters to the general as long as he's competent and he's not a Pole. Of course, the… workers will be supplied by an outside agency under the Reich's control. I'll see if it is possible to arrange it.'

'I'm sure he'll be grateful, sir.' Kalisz turned back to Giulietti and reverted to Polish. 'The officer is happy for you to continue to manage the hotel functions for the moment—'

'So, I'm to be a pimp?'

'You are to supply entertainment and essential services to the heroic officers of the Third Reich,' Kalisz said evenly. 'The essential services will be under German control, naturally, but there will be times when you will be required to take on staff – barmen, cleaners and the like.'

'Yes?'

'Should anyone come to you seeking a position and mention the number twenty-five, you would be wise to accommodate them in the interests of the state. Do I make myself clear?'

Giulietti didn't need to be told twice. 'Number 25' meant the Gestapo headquarters at 25 Szucha Avenue and was already a byword for terror. Of course, the Gestapo would want to know what the Wehrmacht talked about in their moments of relaxation.

'Naturally,' Kalisz allowed his voice to take on a hint of steel, 'any mention of this arrangement would be regarded as an act of sabotage against the state.' If possible, the hotelier turned even paler, but Kalisz had learned long ago that it was sometimes wise to offer a carrot after you'd applied the stick. 'There will also be certain refurbishments and improvements required. You will be able to requisition the materials and labour for these through the city authority.'

'Have you explained everything to him?' Ziegler demanded.

'Yes, sir. He is very grateful for the opportunity.'

'Good. Then get him to sign, so we can put this tawdry business behind us.'

As they turned away, Kalisz heard footsteps on the stairs that stopped abruptly.

'Willi Ziegler?'

Ziegler looked up in astonishment at the tall blond man in the stylishly cut civilian suit, who swept imperiously down the remaining stairs. 'Hans? What in the name of God are you doing in Warsaw?'

The newcomer laughed. 'I'm attached to the Purchasing Commission investigating factories to be taken into German control. It's all very dull, I'm afraid.'

'And they put you here?'

'It's not so bad. I've been here for a few weeks, but hopefully I'll be moving somewhere a little more luxurious soon. An old university friend of ours told me you were here and I thought we might meet up, but not like this. I even brought along a carton of those revolting Turkish cigarettes you smoke.' His eyes drifted to Kalisz, taking in the worn suit and tired shoes.

'My apologies,' Ziegler said. 'Hans Wolff, this is Herr Kalisz of the Warsaw Kripo.' Kalisz saw Wolff dismiss him in a single glance. Just another worthless little Pole. 'So you're in the police now, Willi? How interesting. You must sit down and tell me all about it. You there,' he called to the old man, who'd resumed his place behind the desk. 'Bring us a bottle of your best champagne.'

Ziegler said something about having to return to the office, but Wolff's ebullience wouldn't be denied.

'How long has it been? Eight years? You can tell the office you were questioning me.'

Ziegler looked helplessly at Kalisz.

'I'll inform the Herr *Hauptsturmführer* that you're inspecting the premises, sir.'

'Good – it's settled then.' Wolff grinned. 'Now…'

Kalisz nodded at the *Wachtmeister* and they walked towards the door.

'Champagne, is it?' he heard one of the troopers mutter. 'Fucking officers have it easy.'

–

Kazimierz's eyes lit up behind the thick glasses when Kalisz reported his elevation to the fifth floor, but when he heard about the Hotel de Saxe: 'You did what?'

'I opened the door for you,' Kalisz pointed out. 'It's entirely up to you whether you walk through.'

They were standing in a sheltered corner of a junior school playground not far from Kalisz's street. Like all the other schools in Warsaw, it had been closed since the start of the war and didn't look like reopening any time soon. Someone had written an untidy POLAND SHALL BE FREE in red paint on the brick wall.

Kazimierz nodded thoughtfully. Plainly the de Saxe was a potential intelligence goldmine. Kalisz could tell that the image of all those drunken Wehrmacht officers gossiping to their mistresses – and one another – almost made his mouth water. Yet he knew that inserting someone from the Underground into the hotel staff had to be balanced against the threat to Kalisz's usefulness, which may have just grown a hundredfold.

'I know what you're thinking, Kazimierz,' he said. 'But it's time I was back in the war. I'm in a position to make a difference now.'

'All right.' The Resistance man capitulated. 'But don't take unnecessary risks. Your primary task is to identify those among the enemy who have a weakness. People we can coerce and corrupt. In other words – control.' Kazimierz looked at his watch. 'I need to get back before curfew.'

'You heard about Edelman?'

Edelman had failed to appear at the Fridge one morning, and Blum had told Kalisz cheerfully that he'd been arrested and shot.

'Yes,' Kazimierz nodded morosely. 'He belonged to one of those organisations with an outlandish name – the White Wolves, or some such. Enthusiastic amateurs, but with little idea of security or how the game is played. They were clumsy, but perhaps it's worth the sacrifice if it makes the Germans think so little of us.'

'Is there a possibility they could lead the Gestapo to you. To us?'

'No. We know of them, but they have no perception of who *we* are. And certainly not to you, because you are known personally only to me, and by a *nom de guerre* to others. If there'd been the slightest suspicion you were part of what Edelman was doing, Hoth would never have moved you upstairs. There'll be many more Edelmans before this is finished. Himmler and the Nazi security services have been fighting this kind of war for years against the Communists and the political opposition in Germany. The beginners only have to make a single mistake and the real wolves are among the sheep. The ugly truth of it is that Edelman and his like do us a service by acting as a sort of outpost line between the Germans and the Resistance proper. While they scream in a Gestapo basement, we have the time to save what needs to be saved.'

Kalisz shook his head – *the world we live in* – and turned to go, but Kazimierz drew him back.

'There's one last thing, Jan. Our organisation now has a name – the Union of Armed Struggle. It has the support of every political party apart from the Communists. I've been told to inform you that you are now a lieutenant, with full army pay and pension rights. Congratulations.'

'Thanks.' Kalisz managed a dry smile. 'That should come in useful when they put me up against a wall.'

CHAPTER 14

Three sets of footsteps left individual impressions across the frosted grass as the slanting golden rays of the low November sun cut through the skeletal branches of the park's enormous lime trees. Air as clean and fresh as ice water. A day even the Nazis couldn't spoil.

It had been Maria's idea to get Stefan out of a house that was in danger of turning into a prison for him. With all official schools still closed by German decree, he only had two days of clandestine teaching to keep his mind occupied, and one night of activity during the week with his friends in the Boy Scouts that Kalisz was not supposed to know about. They'd stayed in bed late that Saturday morning, making the most of the stored warmth, but as soon as they'd eaten they broke the news to their son.

Stefan didn't hide his delight, and immediately rushed to bring out the balsa wood model of a Polish P.11 fighter plane he'd almost finished painting. Kalisz had to use his most persuasive diplomacy to convince his son that carrying a plane that was said to have downed over a hundred Luftwaffe bombers might not be the brightest idea when there could be German soldiers about. In the end they settled for a football, and found a flat patch of ground at the base of the park's western slope to have a family kickabout. For ten minutes, Kalisz was able to forget about the insane pressures of his surreal double life and enjoy a semblance of normality, before he noticed an unlikely figure approaching.

'Is this your doing?' he called to Maria.

'Tadeusz,' she cried, ignoring him, and ran to her brother, who hugged her for a moment before they were almost knocked off their feet by the hurtling Stefan.

'Uncle Tad!'

Kalisz's brother-in-law eventually managed to free himself from Stefan's grip and approached him with his hand extended and a broad grin on his face. 'Hello, Jan.'

Kalisz took the hand and shook it, conscious of the horny palm hardened by scores of hours straining at the joystick of a fighter plane. The boyish face was more lined than he remembered, but the self-mocking twinkle in the blue eyes had survived. Tadeusz Klimecki had always displayed the awkward angularity of an overgrown schoolboy, and once more Kalisz marvelled at how Tadeusz managed to force his elongated frame into the cramped cockpit of a warplane. He noticed that though the other man was wearing a long overcoat, beneath it he was dressed in clothes at least one size too small for him.

The question in his eyes must have been apparent, because Tadeusz answered it before he could ask. 'The rear gunner of a Heinkel took a dislike to me,' the younger man confirmed with a broad smile. 'I managed to parachute out, but with true Klimecki luck I ended up splashing down in a lake and almost drowned. Fortunately, a local fisherman had more respect for my skinny carcass than the Luftwaffe, so here I am.' He raised an arm to show inches of flesh at the wrist. 'All my civilian clothes were mislaid during the retreat and I had a feeling our new rulers might take offence at my uniform. I had to raid my old wardrobe at home, and this was the best I could come up with.'

'I'd offer you some of my clothes, Tad, but we're a little mismatched.'

'That's not why I'm here, Jan.'

'I didn't think you were here for the football.' Kalisz noticed the significant look between his brother-in-law and Maria. 'Stefan –' he tossed the boy the ball – 'maybe you'd like to show Mama that new trick you were telling me about?'

Stefan gave him a blank look and Kalisz forced an angry frown. 'Don't come the old soldier with me, young man. We're going to talk about things that don't concern you.'

'I'm not a child.' Stefan hunched his shoulders in a belligerent boxing pose that Kalisz recognised in himself. He knew he shouldn't be surprised at these first signs of youthful rebellion, but it saddened him, because there would inevitably be many more to come and these were dangerous times for the rebellious. All he wanted was for Stefan to be safe – to be untouched by the war – even though it was an unrealistic expectation.

'Do as your dada says, Stefan.' His mother put her arm across his shoulders. 'We'll talk later.'

'He takes after his father,' Tadeusz laughed when they were out of hearing. 'Quick reactions and a quick temper. He'll make a fine fighter pilot some day.'

'Not if I have anything to do with it,' Kalisz assured him. 'So why are you here?' He looked towards his wife. 'I take it this isn't a happy accident?'

'Don't blame Maria, Jan.' Tadeusz's boyish face turned serious. 'I'm leaving for France in a week to return to the fight, and I wanted you to know. They're desperate for pilots to fill the Polish squadrons being formed by the French Air Force. They say we'll be equipped with Caudrons.' He made a face. 'They're not the P.11, not even close, but they fly and they fight, and for the moment that's all that matters.' He hesitated for a moment. 'The fact is, I'd like to invite you along for the trip.'

For a moment Kalisz thought he'd misheard, but Tadeusz's grin confirmed his worst fears.

'You're just the type the army is looking for in France, Jan. Clever and brave – a proven leader. I know you were wounded, but Maria tells me your leg has healed well. My father has been in touch with your former commanding officer. He has a place waiting for you on the intelligence staff of the Fourth Infantry Division. They're putting the unit together at Parthenay, down in Poitou-Charentes, from men who escaped to Romania. Father has arranged everything. Rail warrants to Kraków. A guide who'll take us across the mountains to Slovakia. They'll provide us with false papers to get us through Austria and into Switzerland.'

Kalisz's heart sank as the younger man's eyes shone in anticipation of the great adventure they would have together. Of course it made sense to him. He was a trained soldier, and if Poland was to be recovered from the Nazis, she would need every trained soldier she could lay her hands on. The military effort to free the nation would be conducted beyond the country's borders. So yes, Jan Kalisz should take the opportunity to join it. But he had given his word to Kazimierz. A desperate need to tell Tadeusz that he was *already* fighting rose deep in his belly and expanded into his chest. If it had reached his throat he would have broken, but somehow he suppressed it.

'I'm sorry, Tad.' He almost choked on the words. 'I appreciate the offer, but I can't go. I have to stay here. Maria and Stefan? How would they live without me to provide for them?'

'I'm sorry, Jan,' Tadeusz said after a long silence. 'I'm sure you're right.' Kalisz tensed as he noticed a man in a long overcoat with his hands thrust deep in his pockets among the trees behind his brother-in-law. Tadeusz noticed his look. 'Don't worry,' the younger man assured him. 'He's one of ours. You can't be too careful. There's nothing to stop me going off to war,' he continued. 'I'm young and have no dependants. It's different for a married man, I'm sure. A pity.' Kalisz found himself the focus of penetrating blue eyes, and understood for the first time what made his brother-in-law a successful fighter pilot. 'I would have preferred travelling with a companion, but maybe it's for the best.'

Mother of Christ, why does serving Poland feel like being torn apart by four wild horses. 'Maybe some day...' Kalisz stumbled. He gripped Tadeusz's hand. 'Good luck and good hunting.'

Tadeusz nodded gravely.

'And please tell your father to be very careful. A former high-ranking army officer would be of great interest to them. If he's caught—'

'He knows the dangers, Jan.' Tadeusz brought his head close and his voice dropped to a whisper. 'The old man may think the Charge of the Light Brigade would have been a pleasant way to spend an afternoon, but he's not a fool. These people are professionals. They've been running evaders across the border for a month and they haven't lost anyone yet. Marshal Rydz-Śmigły is back in Warsaw and he's going to make things happen, Jan.'

'Maybe you shouldn't be telling people things like that, Tad.' Kalisz knew Rydz-Śmigły, the commander-in-chief of the Polish armies, had fled to Romania to escape the Nazis and the Russians who had hunted him in the final days of the war. There had been rumours for weeks about his impending return to Poland.

'You're not "people", Jan.' A wry smile flickered on Tadeusz's lips. 'I may be your brother-in-law, but I've always looked up to you as though you were my older brother. When I said you had your reasons, that's exactly what I meant.'

'But I—'

'Do you think I would have come here if I even had the slightest doubts about you?' He glanced towards Maria. 'How you deal with it is up to you. If it were me, I... No.' He sighed. 'You know what's best for your family. But if you're ever in trouble, remember my father will help if he can.'

Kalisz nodded his thanks and Tadeusz went to say goodbye to his sister and Stefan. Kalisz saw him whisper something in Maria's ear that made her bite her lip and her eyes shine.

It had been apparent to Kalisz from the moment he agreed to work with Kazimierz that at some point he would have to deceive his wife. It had never occurred to him that some day she might be driven to deceive him. In Kazimierz's terms, she had devised and implemented an intelligence operation: its sole purpose, to return Jan Kalisz to the fight, willing or otherwise. As they walked back along Oboźna towards the apartment, he was surprised at how much it hurt.

When they reached home, Stefan must have sensed something between his parents, because he immediately announced he was going to his bedroom to finish painting the P.11.

Kalisz stared out of the window across grubby little Kopernika, struggling with the emotions building inside him. He could feel Maria watching him, waiting for him to say something, but he'd made his decision. What more *was* there to say? Better just to let it be.

Clearly, Maria thought otherwise. 'You may go with my blessing, Jan.' A tremble shook her voice. 'And Stefan's. My father has offered us a place in his house until Poland is liberated. Other wives and sons have to endure being parted from their loved ones. Why not us?'

Kalisz shook his head. 'We've discussed this, Maria.' He tried to keep the irritation from his tone. 'Your father is a good man, but it's unfair to place this responsibility on him. This will be a hard winter, probably the worst winter Warsaw will ever endure. August is nearly seventy. He'll find it tough to look after himself, never mind you and a ten-year-old boy.'

'Then surely that's all the more reason for us to go and stay with him.' Maria kept her voice low, but she couldn't hide her frustration. 'I can help care for him and Stefan will do the fetching and carrying. It's time he took some responsibility.'

'Tadeusz told me your father had arranged everything?'

'I asked him to. He was happy to help.'

Kalisz fought to control his frustration. *Doesn't she understand?* 'But don't you see what that means? He's *involved*. He's part of some organisation working against the Nazis.'

'We should be glad *someone* is,' Maria snapped. 'Many officers in my father's old regiment took off their uniforms and hid their weapons rather than surrender. You should be proud of him, Jan. I know I am.'

'Bruno Litauer thought he could do the same, and look what happened to him. They have lists. I've seen them. August will get himself killed or sent to a camp, and if you and Stefan are living with him, they'll take you, too. I can't allow it.'

'Is that what you do?' Maria's voice dripped scorn, and Kalisz felt his face growing red. 'Help them make their lists?'

'Maria—'

'No, Jan. I'll say what I have to say. My father is a patriot. My brother is a patriot. I thought the man I married was a patriot.'

'I have a responsibility to you and Stefan,' Kalisz protested, hating himself for it.

'You have a greater responsibility... to Poland. When you left hospital you were keen to get back into the fight.'

'That was before we surrendered.'

'Tadeusz hasn't surrendered.' Maria spat the words like machine-gun bullets. 'My father hasn't surrendered. All those soldiers and pilots who escaped to France didn't surrender, or the naval officers who sailed their ships to English ports.'

'I've made my decision, Maria.'

It was too much for her. Her face contorted in fury, and she stormed from the table and disappeared into the kitchen. Kalisz considered going after his wife, but he knew nothing he said would improve the situation. Maria thought he was a coward – or worse, a traitor – and there was nothing he could do about it. Snared in a trap of his own making.

Later, as Maria prepared for bed, he reflected on the bitter irony that his situation appeared to be transparent to everyone in her family except his wife. They didn't know exactly what he did, but instinct told them he was doing something. The problem was that, if it was so obvious to Tad and his father, sooner or later it would become obvious to the Germans. And that was the moment it would undoubtedly kill him.

Later, as they lay on opposite sides of the bed, he asked Maria what Tadeusz had said to her.

'He told me to trust you.'

CHAPTER 15

Christmas Eve, 1939

Christmas 1939 might have been a subdued affair for the Kalisz family, but between them they managed to salvage something of the atmosphere of previous years. On the eve of the festival, Kalisz's father Stanisław wandered off with a fishing rod to a pond he'd kept secret for years, and managed to catch a small but plump carp to form the centrepiece of the traditional *Wigilia* celebration. Kalisz himself spent the exorbitant sum of fourteen zloty on a meagre Christmas tree, thanks to the German marks Maria suspected he was bringing home, but never found. Maria's contribution was the beetroot soup they consumed while the carp cooled, courtesy of the grateful parents of one of her patients at the children's hospital. Stefan had decorated the tree with painted silver stars made from old cardboard boxes. Maria's father, August, arrived late, but had never been more welcome than when he produced a bottle of Scotch whisky he'd kept for the occasion, and which brought gasps of appreciation from the adults present.

'To Tadeusz –' Kalisz toasted his brother-in-law – 'and all our brothers who are so far from home tonight.'

'To Tadeusz and all our brothers.' They echoed the salute in voices made gruff by pride, and Maria wasn't the only one who wiped away a tear.

'Do you have any news of him, August?' Kalisz asked as the tall, silver-haired aristocrat poured four more generous measures of tawny liquid, while Maria served the flaky white flesh of the carp with Stefan's help.

'The last we heard –' Kalisz sensed a significant inflection on the *we* – 'he was still in Slovakia, waiting for the correct papers to cross Austria to Switzerland. Since the *Anschluss* the Austrian Nazis have gone out of their way to be more officious and obnoxious than their German cousins. You can't be too careful.'

'Better there than freezing his…' Stanisław caught his son's look and remembered his manners. They were of a similar height, but where Kalisz's slim torso hinted at muscular power, his father was thin to the point of malnourishment, with deep-set eyes and sunken cheeks that flanked a bitter, thin-lipped mouth. The impression of fragility was an illusion. That scrawny body, all gristle and bone, harboured a surprising strength, and his fists could be as quick as his tongue. 'Sitting in some draughty tent in a French field while your toes turn blue and the snow piles up outside. I remember when—'

'More fish?' Kalisz cut off the lengthy and oft-repeated story of his father's service during the war against the Soviets.

'I don't mind if I do. Never seen a carp better cooked.' Stanisław gave a little bow towards Maria, who returned it with a blush that had more to do with the unfamiliar burn of the whisky in her throat than embarrassment at the fulsome praise.

'You're probably right, Stan.' August and Kalisz's father hadn't always been friends, but their relationship had mellowed over the years, so they could talk politics and not come to blows. 'In any case, nothing will happen until the spring when the French and the British attack.'

'You think they'll come?' Maria sounded sceptical.

'With our Polish boys to add some backbone, there's no doubt of it,' August declared.

'They should have come in September when we were keeping the Germans busy,' Kalisz said quietly, remembering friends who had sacrificed themselves in just that hope.

'Their generals didn't think they had the strength,' the old man growled. 'Now look at them. Up against another fifty or sixty battle-tested divisions, all trained to conduct this *Blitzkrieg*, this Lightning War the newspapers crowed about.' There was an air of dismissal about the way he spoke of the new German tactic. Kalisz had been on the wrong end of it, and he had to bite his tongue to stop himself providing his father-in-law with a little touch of reality. He grinned ruefully and decided he was becoming more like his father every day. He saw Maria looking at him and knew the whisky was showing on his face. He returned his attention to August's assessment of the military situation in the west. 'When the *Blitzkrieg* meets the Maginot Line, there will only be one winner,' the old man predicted.

'But surely the Maginot Line can't attack, Papa?' Stefan, a keen student of military tactics, was confused. 'It is a concrete defensive position.'

'It doesn't need to, Stefan.' August Klimecki's grey eyes had taken on a slightly glazed look. 'You may be assured the arrogance of Hitler and his generals will provoke them into attempting to smash the line.' He placed a knife in a strategic position on the tablecloth to replicate the French defences. 'While the Nazis spend their strength in futile attacks here –' he pointed his fork at the centre of the knife – 'the French, English and our gallant Poles will sweep round –' his finger swept past the knife blade in a broad curve – 'to take them in the flank and drive them back into Germany.'

When you put it like that, it all sounded very simple, but Kalisz had his doubts. Hitler and his generals might be arrogant, but they weren't stupid. By his calculation, August's Allied right hook had swept through neutral Belgium and Holland. If the British and French high commands had thought of that, wouldn't the Nazis?

Two conversations were competing with each other. '…it's a disgrace what they're doing to the Jews…' Kalisz listened to his father with half an ear while August whispered in the other. 'You've heard about Rydz-Śmigły?'

'Is it true?'

'…making men older than me shift great mountains of rubble in all weathers…'

'A heart attack at fifty-five, poor man. Our finest commander gone. Poor Poland.'

'…it's enough to make you weep…'

'Jan, I…' Kalisz sobered as he sensed a change in August's tone that suggested they were entering dangerous territory, but the older man was silenced by a knock at the door that froze the entire room in place. They stared at one another for a moment, wondering who among them had brought this catastrophe upon the house. The seconds passed and they sat back in their chairs, hiding their embarrassment as it became clear this had been a tentative, nervous knock and not at all the frenetic, violent battering that would herald the Gestapo.

Kalisz let out a long breath. 'If you'll excuse me for a moment.' He wiped his lips with his napkin and went out into the hall to answer the door. When he opened it the first person he saw was his neighbour across the hall, Julius Feinbaum, solemn-faced and nervous, twisting his hat in his hands. Feinbaum – tall, skinny and stoop-shouldered – had a watchmaker's business and repair shop on Lipova. It took a few moments before Kalisz noticed the shopkeeper was accompanied by a thin, elderly woman in a worn overcoat and floral headscarf. Like Feinbaum, she wore a blue six-pointed Star of David on a white armband on her right arm. In November the Nazis had issued a decree that all Jews over the age of six years must bear the mark or face the threat of the 'severest punishment'. It was surprising to discover how many of your nodding acquaintances were Jewish when they were branded in this fashion. Surprising to discover how many Varsovians were Jews.

'Investigator Kalisz, pardon me for disturbing your festival.' Feinbaum uttered the words with gruff formality, as if he was attending a police interview and they hadn't been neighbours for years. 'However, I believe this matter is of sufficient urgency that it requires your immediate attention. Mrs Goldberg seeks your help. Her daughter has gone missing.'

Kalisz glanced back into the hallway. He could hear his father and August laughing together. Women walked out of their homes all the time. What did they expect him to do? And at Christmas.

'Perhaps...' Feinbaum cleared his throat to regain Kalisz's attention. 'We could talk in my house?'

'Of course.' Kalisz forced a reassuring smile and followed Feinbaum and the woman across the corridor and through the door of the apartment. To his knowledge he'd only been inside the house twice, both times to help with domestic emergencies. Over the years they'd invited each other socially, but there had never seemed a right time, and he had an unsettling feeling that might not have been the only reason. The first thing he noticed were the spaces on the wall where Feinbaum's paintings had been, their former positions marked by rectangles of unfaded wallpaper. No fine furniture, either, that he'd been so proud of. Feinbaum's wife, Marta, a tiny woman with a permanently sour face that matched her outlook on life, disappeared into the kitchen as the door closed behind him.

Mrs Goldberg stood rigid at the centre of the room, with Feinbaum hovering protectively at her side like a prospective groom. Kalisz saw now that she wasn't elderly, as he'd thought, but probably only in her mid-thirties. She might once have been quite pretty, in a plump-cheeked Slovakian way, but hunger had melted the flesh from her face and her skin was lined and coarsened by work, worry, and now fear.

'I'm not sure what you think I can do for you, Mrs Goldberg, but perhaps you can tell me what happened?'

The woman looked inquiringly at Feinbaum. 'Mrs Goldberg speaks only Yiddish,' he explained. 'I will translate the questions and her answers, if you are willing?'

'Of course.'

'Mrs Goldberg lives on Elektoralna with her husband and four children, near the Holy Spirit Hospital.' Kalisz knew the street. It wasn't too far from his father's apartment. 'On Friday morning her daughter Hannah went out with friends to look for food, but she never returned.'

'Does Mrs Goldberg know where she went?'

Feinbaum translated and nodded as the woman replied, her eyes never leaving Kalisz's face.

'Her friends say they often went to the bombed-out Wielopole shopping hall in Iron-Gate Square. Sometimes, if you are fortunate, you find something under the rubble that had been missed by the shop owners. Tinned food. That sort of thing. There are also cellars, if you're brave enough.'

'And Hannah was brave enough?'

This time Feinbaum didn't need to translate. Mrs Goldberg gravely bowed her head. *Children. What can one do?*

'Hannah is thirteen years old and adventurous. When they were making their way through the ruins to a certain favoured shop, the girls heard a noise. Her friends wanted to go back. There have been fights between rival foragers. Threats have been made, you understand?'

'I understand.' The hungrier people became, the worse it would get. Survival of the fittest and the law of the jungle would rule. It would suit the Nazis to have Poles fighting one another rather than the Wehrmacht.

'In any case, the girls ran off. Hannah laughed at them for their timidity and carried on. Later, after perhaps an hour, when she didn't follow them, they recovered their courage and went back to look for her, but she was nowhere to be found.'

Kalisz thought for a moment. 'When they returned, did they see anyone else? Other foragers? Maybe the ones who made the threats?'

Feinbaum put the question to the woman. 'They didn't stay long because the Germans were there in a big black car, but they remember seeing an old man with a long grey beard and a dark coat, and hearing a strange rattling noise.'

'A rattling noise? Like pots and pans? Something mechanical?'

'She does not know.'

Kalisz paused, rummaging through what he'd been told as if it was a drawer full of long-forgotten keepsakes. On the face of it, the only clues to Hannah's disappearance were the man in the long coat and the threats from the other foragers. But apart from the 'rattling sound', the man could be anyone in Warsaw above the age of fifty. At thirteen, it was unlikely she'd gone off with some boy, but these were different times, and who knew what could happen when the young had to grow up so quickly.

'I take it they've searched the ruins and their surroundings thoroughly?'

'Her husband has done what he can.' Feinbaum shrugged. 'But there are loose girders and holes in the floor. Cellars ready to collapse the moment you enter them. He found nothing.'

'Thank Mrs Goldberg…' Something occurred to Kalisz. 'Oh, there is one thing I wondered. Why is Mrs Goldberg here and not her husband?' Mrs Goldberg's frightened glance at Feinbaum told him she knew enough Polish to understand the question. She was also scared of her husband.

'Mrs Goldberg's husband is a proud man who believes such matters should be kept within his own community.' Feinbaum sounded as if he was apologising for the man. 'It was her friends who persuaded her you would be able to help.'

Kalisz closed his eyes and two pieces of the jigsaw fell into place. *Of course.* 'Isaac Goldberg?'

'Yes, sir. Isaac is the husband of Mrs Goldberg.'

Isaac Goldberg was a feared name in the Yiddish community, and one of the reasons Kalisz and his colleagues in the state police had so little success in solving crimes in Warsaw's Jewish district. Goldberg wasn't the only person who believed Jewish differences should be sorted out within their own community. His gang bosses felt the same, and it was allegedly Isaac who dispensed justice, in the form of forced restitution, beatings and, on possibly two or three occasions, murder.

'What is it that Mrs Goldberg – and you – expect of me, Mr Feinbaum?' The question had to be asked, but Kalisz had a feeling he already knew the answer.

Feinbaum didn't hesitate. 'She hopes you will return to the house with her and speak to the two girls who were with Hannah. She hopes you will agree to help find her daughter.'

Kalisz took a deep breath. Perhaps it was the unaccustomed whisky, but the short discussion had wearied him as much as a two-hour interrogation. He'd already made his decision, but he hesitated long enough to make them believe he was considering it.

'I'm afraid that won't be possible. The curfew... My family... Naturally, I'll do what I can when I return to work on Tuesday. Make inquiries, that sort of thing.' The feeble excuses rang hollow in his head, and he saw the hope fading from Mrs Goldberg's red-rimmed eyes. But what choice did he have? He'd made his decision when he agreed to work for Kazimierz. Poland came before family or reputation. In this case, it must come before friends, and what felt very much like honour. Turning his back on Hannah Goldberg made him feel soiled, but any contact with Isaac Goldberg would inevitably taint him and endanger his position at Nowy Sjazd 1. Even having Mrs Goldberg in the building might cause trouble. His eyes flicked to the window. Was it possible she'd been followed here? One thing was certain. If anyone was on a Gestapo list, it was Isaac Goldberg. 'I'm sorry,' he told them.

He watched a tear run slowly down Mrs Goldberg's cheek as she whispered something to Feinbaum.

The watchmaker looked up, and Kalisz couldn't decide whether it was disappointment or something much worse in his eyes. 'She thanks you for your consideration, sir.'

When he crossed the corridor into his own apartment, Kalisz stood in the darkened hallway for a long time, his heart thundering as if it was trying to escape his chest. He felt like a fly trapped in a spider's web. He could still see and hear and think and reason, but he was helpless against the forces holding him in place. Somehow he fixed his face in a mask of festive geniality and opened the door to the main room.

August Klimecki looked up as he helped Kalisz's father to his feet. The old man's face glowed red, and his features wore a slightly perplexed smile that was testament to the impressive inroads made into the whisky bottle.

'We need to go if we're to be home ahead of curfew,' August said. 'The Nazis are cracking down hard on anyone who breaks it.'

'Take care, August.' Kalisz shook his hand. He offered a hand to his father, but the old man brushed it aside and surprised him by giving him a warm hug and a whisky-scented kiss on the cheek. 'You take care of Maria and the boy, son,' the old man grinned, 'or you'll have me to answer to.'

'Was there a problem?' Maria asked as she emerged from the kitchen.

'Feinbaum needed help with a jammed window sash,' Kalisz lied. 'The damp must have swollen it.'

Kalisz escorted the two older men down to the street with the aid of Stefan's torch, and when he came back he helped Maria wash the glasses. They were kept in a low sideboard in the main room.

As Kalisz put them away, he noticed a cloth bag on the shelf he'd never seen before.

'What's this?' he asked Maria.

'Marta Feinbaum asked me to keep it for her,' she said.

He emptied the bag onto the tablecloth: six gold rings, two set with what looked like quite large diamonds, and two with sapphires; a pearl necklace; two gold pendants, one with a locket holding a picture of a woman's face; four wristwatches; and two pocket watches. He recognised the names Patek Philippe and Breguet.

'These must be worth a lot of money?'

'The Nazis have taken control of Jewish bank accounts.' A touch of defiance now, as if she was prepared to fight for the right to keep the jewellery. 'Marta says there's a rumour they'll come for their valuables.' Kalisz nodded thoughtfully. He'd heard it, too. 'She says if things get bad, we can sell the wristwatch with the crocodile-skin strap. There's a jeweller on Zielna Street – a Pole – who should pay three thousand zloty for it, but under no circumstances should we take less than two. The rest she asks us to keep until…'

'I understand.' He picked up one of the watches and weighed it in his hand. 'We should divide these up and put them with our own jewellery.' He saw her look of surprise. 'We'll make a list, of course, so we don't forget what belongs to the Feinbaums, but if the Germans find them like this—'

'You really think they would search our home?'

Kalisz touched his wife's hand. 'Don't be fooled into thinking my position gives us any kind of protection, Maria. If they suspect me, they'll come for me like all the rest.'

Maria picked up the rings, pendants and necklace. 'I'll put these with my mother's. You can hide the watches among your clothes. Would that work?'

'Yes, I think so.' She went off to the room, leaving Kalisz marvelling at how this small conspiracy had brought them closer together at the same time as his larger one was tearing them apart.

'Maria,' he called softly. 'Did you notice the paint on Stefan's hand earlier?'

'He was painting his stars this morning.'

'No, this was red paint.'

CHAPTER 16

The sound of thunder woke Jan Kalisz two days after Christmas, which was unusual because you didn't normally get thunder in winter. His first reaction was to turn over and go back to sleep, but he froze rigid when the sound was repeated.

'Jan,' Maria hissed. 'The door.'

Kalisz opened his eyes to find his wife staring at him, her eyes wide with fear.

Another volley: *bang bang bang.*

'Don't worry,' he said, with a reassurance he didn't feel.

His mind raced as he threw on his dressing gown and walked swiftly through the house to the front door. *Bang. Bang.* He pulled open the door and froze as he recognised the grey uniform, the SS runes and the Death's Head badge.

'I'm sorry to wake you so early, Kalisz, but this is an emergency. I'll wait in the car.'

Ziegler. Kalisz almost collapsed with relief. He noted that Ziegler, too, must have had an unwanted and unexpected summons. Normally immaculately dressed, tonight his uniform was crumpled and stained and his boots filthy with mud. Above his collar, what might have been a scratch had been camouflaged by some sort of powder.

'Yes, sir.' Kalisz addressed the retreating back as the German bounded down the stairs without pausing.

'And don't worry about breakfast,' Ziegler threw over his shoulder. 'We'll have coffee and bread on the way.'

Coffee, bread *and* ham, as it turned out; proper coffee that didn't taste like oak dust mixed with disinfectant, and bread that melted in your mouth. They travelled east through the half-asleep city in the rear of a black Mercedes 180 driven by a uniformed Orpo. It had snowed overnight and the tyres struggled for grip on the slippery streets. Ziegler explained the rush as they ate.

'We've had word that two German soldiers, members of a construction battalion, have been murdered in a bar out in a place called Wawer. An Orpo company is on its way to meet us there.'

'Do we know how they were killed?' Kalisz asked. Wawer was on the east side of the river, south of Praga.

'I understand they were shot.'

Kalisz looked sceptical. 'If they were killed by a Pole, isn't this something for the Gestapo to investigate?'

'Possibly,' Ziegler acknowledged. 'But *Hauptsturmführer* Hoth wants us there while the initial investigation is carried out. Whatever is done, it must be done according to the legal frame-work of the General Government.' His lips pursed with distaste. 'Hopefully we'll get there in time to question the witnesses before they are subjected to a more rigorous interrogation.'

–

The face of the man who hung by the neck from the bar sign had been battered beyond recognition, and fresh blood sheeted the front of his white shirt. He might not have existed, as far as the two cheerful *Ordnungspolizei* officers who stood chatting together a metre or so below were concerned. The bar was in the centre of the village, at the junction of two streets – a rough place with shuttered windows and cracks in the walls. When they left the warmth of the car, Ziegler marched up to the men and saluted. Kalisz followed a little behind with his hat in his hand, and tried not to look upwards.

The elder of the officers, a major, returned Ziegler's *Heil Hitler* with a dismissive grunt before his eye fell on Kalisz. 'Is this another one?' He gestured to a nearby Orpo private. 'Take him round the corner and put him with the rest.' A volley of shots rang out from close by and Kalisz flinched at the noise. The firing was followed by the massed wailing of what sounded like a substantial number of women.

'Please, sir.' Kalisz appealed to Ziegler as the soldier prodded him, not gently, with his rifle barrel.

The SS officer found his voice. 'I am *Obersturmführer* Ziegler. This is my interpreter. We're with Warsaw Kripo. I have orders to investigate the murder of our two soldiers.'

'Brenner, Orpo.' The major introduced himself with a dry smile. 'And I think you'll find the case has been solved. This man –' he glanced up at the dangling corpse – 'is Bartoszek, the former owner of this fine establishment. When we talked to him, he confessed that he'd allowed his bar to be used by two men on the run, a couple of career criminals – Prasuła and Dąbek. Scrap dealers, they called themselves, the type you look for when the lead on the church roof goes missing.' Another volley of shots and more wailing. Kalisz noticed that Ziegler seemed to barely notice the gunfire. Had the man been drinking? 'Two of our men were also in the bar and an off-duty policeman alerted them. The fools didn't know Dąbek was armed, and he shot them before they could get hold of the Poles.'

'Do you have the killers?' Ziegler asked.

'You'll have to ask *Wachtmeister* Meier.' Brenner smirked as if someone had made a poor joke. 'He's in charge of the paperwork. Esser?' He called over a young soldier. 'Take these gentlemen to *Wachtmeister* Meier and tell him he's to co-operate with them. They're from the Kripo.'

'Sir,' the *Landser* responded. 'If you'll follow me, sir.'

They followed the man along the street and around a corner, feet slipping on the hard-packed snow. The soldier led them across open ground towards a railway line, where a tunnel carried a road beneath the embankment. Walking beside Ziegler, Kalisz could see several dozen women and children gathered about forty or fifty paces short of the tunnel. As they came closer, he discovered the families were being kept away from the entrance by armed soldiers in greatcoats and steel helmets.

Another volley split the cold air, so close it made Kalisz's ears ring. The crowd erupted into new shrieks of anguish, and wisps of thin smoke rose from the far side of the embankment.

'Noisy bitches,' complained the Orpo trooper. 'If you ask me, we should be sorting them out as well. These Poles are fucking savages.'

They made a detour away from the women. Kalisz felt the condemnation of a hundred eyes as he walked through the tense line of guards and into the shadow of the tunnel. Now they heard the sound of shouted orders and men crying out and pleading. A dog barked angrily somewhere and Kalisz could smell powder smoke. And something else: an odd mixture of sweet and metallic that he recognised. He braced himself for what they would see when they emerged into the light.

'Get those bastards forward or we're never going to finish this up,' an irritated voice shouted.

The first thing Kalisz saw as they emerged was a group of about forty men, sitting under the guns of perhaps two thirds as many German guards among the trees about fifty paces away. They ranged in age from beardless boys to elders in their sixties and seventies. Another ten or so were already being herded towards the railway line by SD men, who hurried them along with blows of their rifle butts under the supervision of a red-faced corporal. A cloud of steam hung over the prisoners as their breath turned to mist in the freezing air. Some were still dressed in their pyjamas, but the majority wore trousers and shirts and a few had caps on their heads. There was something odd about the way they moved across the flattened snow, and he noticed they were all barefoot. Most were bruised or bleeding, and at least one of them cradled a broken jaw with his hands.

As Kalisz and Ziegler moved clear of the tunnel, the Pole almost stumbled at the sight that greeted him, even though he'd been expecting it. Along the line of the embankment, little groups of huddled corpses lay in heaped piles. A couple of metres away, a squad of twelve Nazi soldiers waited with their rifles at the ready. Ziegler looked neither at the prisoners, nor the piles of dead, and for all the impression the earlier volleys had made on him, they might have been birdsong.

'*Wachtmeister* Meier?' their escort reported. 'Major Brenner's compliments, and this gent's from the Kripo in Warsaw. He says you're to co-operate with him.'

'As if I haven't got enough to fucking do,' the *Wachtmeister* muttered without looking up from the clipboard he was holding. 'Sorry, sir.' He snapped to attention when he saw the collar tab on Ziegler's uniform jacket.

'We won't keep you long, *Wachtmeister*.' Perhaps it was the apparently prolonged festivities that had him looking so dishevelled, but Ziegler's voice had taken on a flat, entirely disinterested note. Kalisz, with all his experience of war, had seen many reactions to violence and death, but never quite this level of detachment. 'We need to know if the two killers are among the men who have been singled out for punishment.' He turned to Kalisz.

'Prasuła and Dąbek, sir.'

As the *Wachtmeister* consulted his list, Kalisz could hear the firing squad commander ordering the prisoners into position in fractured Polish. 'You will stand facing the embankment. You will not move, or I promise it will be the worse for you and your families. Take off your caps.' The last seemed an incongruous request of men about to die. 'Ready.' Kalisz held his breath. 'Aim.' He closed his eyes and tried to still his shaking hands. He braced himself for what was to come, as if he was one of the doomed Poles standing facing the dirt wall of the embankment. 'Fire.'

The sound of the shots reverberated from the embankment and Kalisz's heart seemed to stop. As the echoes died away, a muffled wail rose from the far side of the tracks. Closer, he could hear a man crying out and another moaning. A pistol shot, the sound almost harmless after the power of the Mauser rifles, followed at intervals by a second and a third. He looked to see the effect of the execution on the waiting men. They sat huddled together, their gaze anywhere but the railway embankment, explosions of breath misting the air. A few muttered encouragement or solace to their companions. One of them stared directly at him, but with the dull, sightless eyes of a man already dead.

'Nobody by that name on the list, I'm afraid, sir,' the *Wachtmeister* apologised.

Ziegler frowned, apparently uncertain what to do next.

'A witness, sir,' Kalisz hissed. 'We're going to need a witness so you can compile your report to *Hauptsturmführer* Hoth.'

'Yes.' Ziegler blinked. 'A witness. *Wachtmeister?*' His voice recovered some of its normal intonation. 'We need one of these men to give us an account of last night's murder.'

'I don't know about…' He shook his head. 'Still, we have a few spares, and in the spirit of co-operation… help yourself. Will you be bringing him back?'

'That depends on what he tells us.'

'Well…' The *Wachtmeister* chuckled. 'It's your funeral.'

Kalisz walked behind Ziegler and approached the little group of condemned men.

'Let him have one,' the sergeant called to the guards.

Kalisz passed through the ring of soldiers. For a moment he was confounded by the unimaginable choice now forced upon him. Who among these doomed human beings deserved life over the others? Old men and young. Bald heads and broad, hunched farmers' shoulders, they sat shivering, their flesh tinged blue by the freezing cold. The scent of fresh excrement hung in the air. Would he have been any different? He searched their faces, but none would meet his eyes apart from the one he'd noticed earlier: a young man in a dirty vest, with a shadow of dark stubble on his jaw. Kalisz reached down and took him by the shoulder strap of his vest. He looked up, startled and wide-eyed with terror.

'No,' Kalisz assured him. 'Not that. Come. You'll be safe with us.'

Fear was instantly replaced by bewilderment and consternation. The man looked around for some lead from his companions, but none even raised his head. After what seemed an age, he responded and struggled to his feet. Kalisz led him, unresisting, beyond the guards, just as the escort arrived to choose the next victims.

'Sir? This is our witness.' Kalisz pulled the man away from the killing ground. 'We can interview him in one of those houses over there.' He indicated some rough hovels about a hundred metres away. Ziegler muttered something to the sergeant and gave a half-hearted Hitler salute before he followed like an obedient child. It was only when they were halfway to the houses and another volley rang out that Kalisz realised he had no idea whether his 'witness' had any knowledge of the events they were supposed to be investigating.

The door of the first house was closed, but Kalisz kicked at the rotten wood until it gave in and pushed his captive inside, forcing him back until he was stopped by the far wall.

'Kalisz, I—'

'Leave this to me, sir.' Kalisz ignored Ziegler's protest. He loomed over the cowering figure slumped against the crumbling plaster. 'You have one chance,' he reverted to Polish, 'and one chance only. You can live or you can die. I need everything you know about last night. Who did it, how it happened and what happened afterwards. Do you understand me?' He nudged the near-comatose figure with his knee. 'I said, do you understand me? What's your name?'

'Baruch, sir. Please don't hurt me.'

'All right, Baruch, what happened?'

'They came for us—'

'No – what happened earlier? What happened in the bar?'

'I wasn't there…'

'No, but you must have talked about it. The whole village would have talked.'

'Yes, sir.' Baruch looked like a drowning man who'd just been thrown a lifebelt. 'There was a girl, Janina. A German dragged her away. She struggled and screamed, but he was too strong for her. An old man who'd been out cutting firewood saw them and alerted the village. About twenty of us went into the woods after the Nazi, but he must have heard us because he abandoned her. We found her on a forest track, with her eyes blackened, but he was long gone.'

'Wait,' Kalisz said. 'So this wasn't just about the two crooks, Prasuła and Dąbek?'

Baruch shook his head. 'No, sir. Stan – that is, Dąbek... The girl was his cousin. He said he'd teach the Germans to mess with his family. He waited until he could borrow a gun from Marian Prasuła and they went to Bart's Bar – he knew these two Germans went there every night – walked in and shot them. My father saw it all. Blood everywhere. The place cleared like smoke. My father came home and said he'd been with us all night, right? And that was it, we thought. No witnesses. Maybe they'd rough up Tony a bit.' He shook his head at his own naivety, glancing fearfully at Ziegler, who listened to the incomprehensible Polish with a frown of concentration. 'But they're not like that. About midnight, somebody kicks the door in and says, "*Raus*, everybody out." Father, he objected, and they gave him a mouthful of rifle butt and kicked four ribs in just for the fun of it.'

'What does he say?' Ziegler demanded.

Kalisz relayed what Baruch had told him.

'Then we have what we came for.'

'I'd like to try to get some more detail out of him.'

Ziegler shrugged as if he didn't care one way or the other.

'What happened next?'

Baruch wiped the back of his hand across his mouth. 'They herded all the men to Poprzeczna Street, and a little later another twenty or thirty were brought from Anin, the village just down the road. We were freezing, but anyone who protested would be beaten. Really beaten. After about three hours an officer appeared, and a Blue told us we were all charged with involvement in the murder of the Nazis. That was it. No lawyer. No defence. We were sentenced to death.'

Kalisz turned to Ziegler. 'He's pleading for his life,' he lied. 'He says he had nothing to do with the killings.'

Ziegler lowered his head and stared at the wooden floor. 'Tell him to go home.'

'Sir?'

'Tell him to go home and stay there, Kalisz.'

'Yes, sir.'

He lifted Baruch to his feet. 'Listen to me, Baruch. You're going to walk out of here and you're going to go home, or somewhere else safe.'

'But my father… my brothers.' His wide eyes whirled in the direction of the railway.

'Look.' Kalisz took him by the front of the vest. 'You have been given a chance to live. Take it. And make sure you remember every detail of what happened last night. Remember every name and every face. Some day there will be a reckoning for this, and whatever you know will be important. Do you understand, Baruch?'

'I think so, sir.'

'By the way, what happened to the old man who saw the German attacking the girl?'

Baruch's eyes drifted in the direction of the embankment and he shook his head.

When Kalisz and Ziegler walked back to the tunnel beneath the railway, the ten remaining survivors of the shooting were hacking at the frozen ground with shovels to provide a grave for the hundred bodies lying a few feet away.

As they dug, their future executioners stood by, smoking and talking among themselves.

CHAPTER 17

Ziegler chain-smoked for most of the journey back to the office, leaving Kalisz to wrestle with the enormity of what he'd witnessed. The murderous ruthlessness of the Nazis came as no surprise, but the scale of the killings stunned him.

A hundred innocent men butchered. Two villages stripped of their breadwinners with the people already close to starvation. And he had a feeling this wasn't an isolated incident in Poland's suffering. There'd been something clinical and workmanlike about the way the soldiers carried out the executions that told him this wasn't the first time they'd done this kind of job.

'Don't think too badly of us Germans for what happened, Kalisz.' Jan blinked as Ziegler's soft voice cut across his thoughts. 'Those fellows were only doing their duty. It is dirty work, but when a military court passes sentence, any soldier who refuses to carry it out is a traitor to his comrades and his people.'

Kalisz could hardly believe what he was hearing. 'You don't think the scale of the retribution was excessive, sir?'

'Excessive?' Ziegler lit another of the scented Turkish cigarettes he'd received from his friend Wolff, and rolled down the window to throw the butt of its predecessor onto the road. Kalisz shivered in the chill blast of the zephyr that entered through the opening. 'Not the punishment, which was carried out in an exemplary manner with no unnecessary cruelty. If you had seen…' He shook his head and the words faded. 'Perhaps the numbers were somewhat surprising, but two German soldiers had been murdered and not one villager attempted to apprehend the killers. Does that not smack of collusion?'

'If you say so, sir.'

Ziegler frowned and lapsed into silence for the space of another mile.

'You are a Catholic, Kalisz? I understand most Poles are?'

'Yes, sir,' Kalisz said tentatively, wary of this new and awkward line of questioning.

'A regular churchgoer?'

'We – that is, my family – attend Mass every Sunday.'

'I, too –' Ziegler's rapt expression seemed to hint that a shared faith gave them a common bond – 'although I haven't had the opportunity so much recently. Army chaplains do not have the same feeling for nuance and subtlety that one's parish priest can bring to the Mass. That is not a criticism,' he said hurriedly. 'Our *Landsers* can be rough types. They wouldn't appreciate a sermon telling them to love their enemies or turn the other cheek, as Luke suggests to us in his Gospel. Matthew is more to their way of thinking. An eye for an eye. But how I long to sit in the quiet calm of a church, kneel in prayer and become closer to God.'

The final sentence contained an element of suggestion that Kalisz chose to ignore. 'Do you truly think God approves of this war, sir?'

Ziegler turned to stare out of the window. 'I do not deny that my faith has been tested, Kalisz, as no doubt has your own. As a German, I must believe God's guiding hand is behind the Führer's efforts to transform my country and restore its pride. How else could he have won the swift and decisive victory he achieved in Poland? Why else would the French and English have stayed their hand when Germany was at its most vulnerable, and Comrade Stalin, so ideologically at odds with Nazism, persuaded to give his approval? You Poles –' now he swivelled to face Kalisz, and his dark eyes took on an almost manic quality – 'have suffered and I fear you will continue to suffer, but your sacrifices will be rewarded by your inclusion in the new Europe which Adolf Hitler will create with God's support. For the moment, he requires Poland's labour, territory and resources to prepare for the next stage of his campaign, but you will see, Kalisz,' Ziegler nodded solemnly, 'in the end he will prove to have been justified.'

'All we Poles have ever asked is to be left in peace, sir.' The words were out before Kalisz knew he'd spoken.

Ziegler stiffened. 'You know better than that, Kalisz.' The SS officer frowned. 'You have German blood and you speak the German language like a German. Perhaps in Warsaw it was different, but in the western districts, people like you were treated worse than animals. Believe me, I have seen the results. The Führer was forced to act before the ethnic Germans in Poland were wiped out altogether. Far from seeking peace, the Poles provoked this war.'

They arrived back at Nowy Sjazd 1 a few minutes later. Kalisz held the car door for Ziegler. 'I apologise if I offended you, sir.' The words stuck in his throat, but they had to be said.

Ziegler replied with a non-committal grunt, but as the car drove off Kalisz made a snap decision to try to retrieve something of value from this terrible day. 'If you please, sir, I have a request to ask of you.'

Ziegler frowned. 'Request?'

'Yes, sir. A Polish girl has gone missing.' The words came out in a rush. 'It happened three days before Christmas, somewhere close to Iron-Gate Square. Her parents are very worried, sir. She had been scavenging for food, and it's a possibility she may have been picked up by the Blues, or perhaps a security patrol. You have access to the records and I thought—'

'Girl?' The German released a grunt of exasperation. 'I sometimes think God only created the female of the species on earth to test us. First this Polish woman in Wawer leading a young German soldier on and then changing her mind – and we have seen the results of that. Now another gets into trouble. Name?' Ziegler plucked a notebook from the breast pocket of his tunic and produced a pencil stub to scrawl the name.

'Hannah Goldberg, sir, and I am very grateful.'

'A Jew?' Ziegler almost smiled at Kalisz's naivety.

'A girl, sir,' the Pole persisted. 'Thirteen years old and lost to her parents.'

The German shook his head, but he wrote the name in the book. 'I, too, have a request.' He raised his eyes from the notebook to meet Kalisz's gaze. 'I would like very much to attend Mass with you at some point.'

Jan Kalisz's heart dropped like a lump of lead into the pit of his stomach. His head was filled with an image of Ziegler marching into church at his side, wearing SS uniform, and every eye turning to see the Nazi and the Polish traitor. But if he wanted the information about Hannah Goldberg, there could only be one answer.

'Of course, sir.' He accompanied the words with an unconvincing smile. 'It would be my pleasure.'

Ziegler walked ahead to report to Hoth, leaving Kalisz standing in the snow under the contemptuous eyes of two freezing sentries. For the first time in ten years, he regretted giving up smoking. Anything to rid himself of the bitter taste of vomit that clogged his throat and the scenes of horror spinning in his head. He tried to think. He had to get the information about the Wawer massacre to Kazimierz and the Underground.

They'd hear about it from other sources, but Kalisz had the names of the officer and units involved. A thought occurred to him. Would it change their plans for the coming insurgency Kazimierz had hinted at? If the price of a pair of German engineers was to be a hundred Polish lives, surely it must? At that rate of exchange, the cost of ambushing a Nazi patrol or bombing an SS barracks could run into thousands of innocents.

Yet – and the thought sent a knife point raking down his spine – there was something about the way Kazimierz referred to his superiors that told Kalisz they might not hesitate to pay it. And what of Jan Kalisz, if these ruthless men decided a sacrifice must be made? There was only one answer to *that*. Still, he would set up the meeting. What else could he do? The only way was forward, though each day might be his last. Now he thought of it, did that make him different from any other Pole? Bizarrely, the macabre thought cheered him. No matter what his family thought of him, if Kazimierz used him, or if the Nazis sneered at their Polish helper, as long as he stayed true to himself *inside*, he would still be the same man. Right up until the moment they strapped him into a chair in Szucha Avenue.

'You can either go inside, or you fuck off,' the taller of the two guards grunted. 'You're making the place look untidy.'

'I'm sorry, sir.' Kalisz bowed his head as he slipped past them into the building.

He kept his eyes down as he climbed the stairs to the fifth floor. He'd almost reached the top when a burly figure barged into him and pushed him against the banister. 'Watch where you're going, you little Polish shit.'

'My apologies, sir.' Kalisz looked up into the twisted features of Günther Gruhl, a *Volksdeutsche* cop drafted into the department from some little one-horse town outside Danzig. The story went that Gruhl, all pent-up anger and heavyweight wrestler's physique under the grey suit, had made a name for himself in the *Selbstschutz* during the invasion, ambushing Polish supply columns and torturing any survivors. He was a committed Nazi with a pathological hatred for Poles, particularly big city Poles. Narrow gimlet eyes and a rat-trap mouth that seemed too small for his broad peasant face gave him an almost simian appearance. Kalisz made to bypass him, but Gruhl took him by the shirt front and lifted him backwards so the banister cut into his spine. His feet were off the ground, and one good heave would send him plummeting five storeys into the stairwell.

'You stinking little cockroach. Just because the boss sees fit to let you work up here, it doesn't make you one of us. He thinks you're a German, Kalisz, because you speak the language and you know how to put on airs and graces. But I know better. I can smell a stinking Pole from fifty paces, and you –' he pushed Kalisz a little further into the void – 'are a stinking Pole. I'll be watching you, and if I think you're up to any of your Polish tricks I'll drop you head first.' He grinned at the thought. 'They won't be able to tell the difference between you and a splatter of strawberry jam. So you'd better stay out of my way and keep your Polack nose clean. Understand?'

Kalisz's hands were still free. When he'd been out on the streets he'd learned a few handy tricks, and with one jab of his fingers he could have blinded the Danziger for life. But injuring Gruhl would mark him out as someone capable of defending himself. Someone strong. With difficulty, he buried the pride Kazimierz had so accurately predicted would get him killed. 'I understand, sir.' He raised his hands submissively. 'If the Herr Investigator would please release me, I have a report to write for the Herr *Hauptsturmführer*.'

Gruhl flicked a glance to his right. Something wasn't right here. He'd expected fear, or resistance, not this calm acceptance.

'That's enough, Gruhl.'

Hauptsturmführer Hoth stood in the doorway of his office with Ziegler, who had the irritated look of a teacher whose star pupil had got into trouble in front of the headmaster.

'Thank you, sir.' Kalisz straightened his tie and ran his fingers through his hair.

Gruhl allowed himself one last flash of contempt before stomping off, flat-footed, down the stairs.

As he walked to his desk, Jan Kalisz made himself a promise.

PART THREE: FRUSTRATION

CHAPTER 18

The Artist

It had been so close. In his imagination he could still smell the stink of her peasant sweat in his nostrils, and the rank essence of female fear that had stimulated him beyond anything he'd ever experienced. He lay naked in his warm bath, contemplating the scratches and bruises she'd inflicted on his body. Yes, it had been a failure, but he didn't regret it for a moment.

He'd been in Wawer by mistake. Christmas festivities had no interest for him, so he'd decided to explore the east side of the river, seeking out places that might interest him, and got hopelessly lost. He parked the car and got out to study his map.

That was when he saw her, collecting twigs and small branches for kindling in the wood beside the road. Just another Polish farm girl wrapped in an old blanket and with rags tied round her legs against the cold. It occurred to him that he might be able to lure her to the car. Was it worth it? He whistled to draw her attention, a jaunty tune designed to place her at ease, but keeping his head down so he could get a covert look at her face without her being able to see his. She looked up, and he was quite shocked to see features that shone with a kind of luminous beauty so rare in these rustic Slavs. He waited; sometimes the poorest of the conquered would approach their conquerors and beg for money and food. Instead, she moved further into the woods.

137

What made it so special was that she had been the prey and he the hunter.

The process of stalking her through the trees had heightened his senses until it felt as if each nerve ending was charged with electricity, and he was astonished she couldn't hear the thunderous pounding of his heart. It had been utterly exhilarating. Closer, and ever closer, using the trees to shield him from sight. Every footstep placed precisely to avoid the twigs that littered the forest floor. He'd even made sure he was downwind in case she caught the scent of the Turkish cigarettes he knew clung to his uniform. Power and menace seemed to grow inside him with each passing second. She was nothing. At least nothing to him. But she would have a family somewhere, and the thought that he was about to take her away from them only increased his excitement.

Once he'd noticed she was following a barely visible path, the outcome had been certain. He'd simply hidden behind the trunk of an ancient oak nearby and waited. The pad with the enhanced chloroform was in the leather satchel by his side. It had taken him several attempts to discover the correct compound and the precise dosage to create the effect he desired. He'd only tested it on dogs so far, strays he'd paid Warsaw street urchins to bring him in the belief he wanted a pet. They had to be of the largest breeds to emulate his intended victims, and three of them had died under the anaesthetic before he'd reached the correct combination. Careful not to make a sound, he opened the straps of the satchel and withdrew the pad.

It should have been simple. She was just a girl and he a grown man with surprise and strength on his side. When she walked past the tree her back was to him, and all he had to do was step out and cover her mouth and nose with the pad.

Instead, it was as if she'd been waiting for him all along, and she had the reactions of a cat. As he reached forward with the pad, an arm came up to block the movement. She twisted so her face was in his chest and her right hand clawed at his eyes, while her left clamped on his wrist. He'd had the impression that she was stocky, but the body beneath the blanket was lithe and muscular, with an impressive farm girl's strength. Now she was pounding at his chest and stomach with her free hand. She screeched something in Polish and, to his alarm, he heard an answering shout from nearby.

For a moment, he didn't know what to do. Somehow he managed to free his hand and push her away. He abandoned any hope of using the chloroform and dropped the pad and lashed out with his fist. A satisfying crunch as his knuckles connected with her nose. She went down, but her hands were still clawing at his legs, so he bent and hit her again.

By now more voices were calling, and he realised there must be a settlement nearby. He picked up the pad and ran to his car.

It had been a failure, even a fiasco, but curiously he had no regrets.

He would remember the feel of that body beneath his hands for a long time.

And the thrill of the hunt compensated for all the rest.

CHAPTER 19

It suited Kalisz to work beyond his assigned hours, and it was growing dark when he took the stairs to the lower level, his mind still in a turmoil after the events earlier in the day. When he reached the ground floor he walked out on to the Vistula Boulevard, and turned south in the direction of the Poniatowski Bridge.

Earlier, Ziegler had stopped by his desk and informed him that no record existed of Hannah Goldberg's arrest or detention, or any information relating to her disappearance. 'But our agreement still stands?'

'Of course, sir.' Kalisz forced a smile. 'The Church of St Joseph of the Visitationists? Perhaps we could meet for evening Mass a week on Sunday.'

Ziegler nodded, but his features took on a knowing look. 'Don't worry, Kalisz,' he said. 'I won't embarrass you.'

Kalisz had his own views about that, but he bid the SS officer a cordial goodnight. He was relieved when Gruhl followed Ziegler from the office, with a last glare in Kalisz's direction. There was one who'd bear watching. Another was Gruhl's companion Müller, an older man who looked benign and harmless, with his round spectacles, dog otter moustache and malodorous meerschaum pipe, but who shared his colleague's virulent hatred of Poles. They seemed to take turns observing him, and he had no doubt they reported their findings to Hoth.

He took the inner road where the boulevard split to accommodate the paths and gardens of the riverside park, and walked past the offices of the water department, which had somehow survived the Luftwaffe's attentions. In that curious lottery of war, the next block had been less fortunate, and the vodka distillery it housed had burned with a curious blue flame that illuminated the surrounding area for the next forty-eight hours. Someone had cleared a path through the distillery ruins to make a short cut to Leszczyńska and he followed it, his shoes kicking up puffs of fine, new-fallen snow.

Around him, fragments of walls stood out like rotting teeth amid the piles of snow-dusted rubble and timber. It was an eerie place in the growing gloom, and he suppressed a shiver. He must have been halfway across the derelict site when he heard the noise from behind and whirled to face the possible threat. Not far away, a brick tumbled from a pile and rolled laboriously onto the path. He searched the shadows at the top of the pile, but if anyone was there, they stayed hidden. He wasn't frightened. Yet. His first thought was that Gruhl and Müller had followed him and the Danziger wanted to continue their 'discussion' of earlier in the day. He could handle that.

It crossed his mind that Kazimierz might have supplied him with a guardian angel, but he dismissed the thought even as it formed. If there was any trouble, he'd have to look out for himself. In the old days he'd carried a flick knife as well as the pistol, but these weren't the old days. If the Nazis found so much as a fruit knife on you in one of their never-ending stop-and-search operations, they'd line you up in front of twelve rifles or throw a noose over the nearest branch.

He quickened his step, bunching his fists, his ears straining for the sound of footsteps behind.

But the immediate danger didn't come from behind. Two young men – just kids, really – in leather jackets and flat caps appeared from the far end of the path and advanced towards him, their breath clouding the cold air. Kalisz could tell from the purposeful way they walked that they meant trouble. He looked over his shoulder, seeking an escape route, only to find two more blocking his exit. As they came closer, he noticed not everyone was nervous about carrying knives. He backed away until a rubble pile at the edge of the path blocked him, and the four young men silently joined forces a few paces to his front.

They stared at him for a long time, eyes killing-bright, filled with a mixture of resolution, righteous anger – and fear. Not their usual night out this, he decided, despite the glittering blades they clutched in their fists. Just kids sent to do a job. Or maybe they'd decided for themselves. Heard a whisper about what had happened out in Wawer. *Something has to be done. Let's go out and send* them *a message.* Two of them were sweating despite the cold, and held their knives awkwardly, as if they were warding off evil. The third's hand shook violently, and not because of the frost. But the tallest – a young man with curly blond hair and a slight squint – held his blade rock steady at the height of Kalisz's abdomen.

Kalisz met his stare. *Believe me, if I'm going down, boy, I'm taking you with me.* Mother of Christ, they were so young. He could see the tall boy building himself up to make the first move.

Kalisz decided not to allow him the initiative.

'Whatever it is you want, lads, I don't have it.' He kept his tone light and held his hands away from his sides, submissive, but ready.

Three of them glanced nervously at one another, as if this wasn't part of the script, but the leader's eyes never left him. 'Tell him, Poldek.' The teenager's voice was gruff with stress.

A boy with spectacles and a freckled face reached into the inside pocket of his jacket and drew out a piece of paper. When he spoke, his voice was so high Kalisz almost laughed. But that was before he understood what the kid was saying.

'You are a traitor to your country and your people.' The boy paused to clear his throat, spitting into the dust, though whether it was an insult or through nervousness was difficult to tell. 'You have been found guilty of collaborating with the enemy by the Warsaw Defenders of Freedom and the sentence is—'

'Hold on,' Kalisz interrupted. 'Found guilty when? Where was the trial? What's the evidence against me? You can't try a man without giving him a chance to defend himself, or that makes you the same as them. What happened to Polish justice?'

'A traitor doesn't deserve a trial,' the tall kid snapped. 'And your guilt is declared for all to see every time you walk into an office filled with SS and Gestapo. The sentence is death.'

Jesus and all his saints, how has it come to this?

'And you're here to carry it out?' The disbelief in his voice made the tall boy's nostrils flare, and he took a step forward. Kalisz brought his fists up and his would-be executioner froze in mid-stride.

'Don't think I'm going to make it easy for you, son.' Kalisz allowed himself a shark's smile. 'It's not so simple to kill a man, and it's a messy business with a knife. You might find you don't take to it.' He directed the suggestion at the freckled boy, who had developed a twitch in one eye. 'Now if you'd brought guns…'

They might lack experience, but they weren't to be diverted so easily. Carefully, they spread apart a little to come at him from four different angles. If there'd been two of them, maybe even three, he would have fancied his chances, but not four. He considered telling them he was on their side. That he was working for the Underground. But he doubted they'd believe him. Even if they did, sooner or later they'd end up screaming under the pliers and the hooks and the knives in a Gestapo basement, and when the name Jan Kalisz came out, it would be all over anyway. No, it might as well be now.

So close he could see the acne on their cheeks, he shuffled his feet to improve his stance and hunched his shoulders as if he was in the ring. His guts were churning at the thought of those gleaming points lancing into his body, but he showed no fear and that evidently confused them.

'Now,' he continued, to keep them off balance, 'I don't reckon I can kill you all, but I'm fairly certain I'll get at least two. You're new to this, but I've been here before with my back to the wall and the shiny steel in my face, and I'm still around.'

His eyes flicked from one to the other, and he saw the first true uncertainty there. Their breath came in rasping grunts, but despite their doubts, they were brave Polish boys and determined to see it through. Kalisz felt his heart plummet, but he had to keep trying.

'That will make it awkward for the ones who are left standing once you've cut me up,' he predicted. 'I don't see you carrying the bodies through the streets. The Nazis don't like that kind of thing. That means the unlucky ones will be identified, and if my detective's nose smells it right, you're old pals. Buddies from school, right? So the first people the Gestapo will come looking for will be you and you.' He nodded to the tall boy and Poldek and saw the consternation on the others' faces as they realised the significance of what he was saying. 'Of course, you could run away—' He was forced to sway back as the tall boy took a tentative swing and the knife point cut the air inches from his face. Still, the others held off and he knew he had their interest. 'But it won't end there. They'll come for your father and your mother and your sisters and brothers, your grandmother and grandfather. They'll round up your friends, and every last one will end up in the cellars at Szucha Avenue. You know what that means? And when they're finished, they'll put them up against a wall and shoot them. Not far from here, the Nazis killed a hundred men for shooting two dumb Wehrmacht pioneers. I reckon I'm worth at least that. The question is, am I worth it to you? The deaths of a hundred innocent people?'

Tall Boy would have gone through with it, but he'd felt the resolve fading from his companions and he knew there was no guarantee he could take Kalisz alone. His mouth worked with rage, but he lowered the knife and backed slowly away. 'Your time will come, traitor,' he snarled. 'And when it does, I'll spit in your face as I watch you dying.'

Kalisz waved a weary hand in the direction of the river and they took the hint and moved off, watching him over their shoulders and shouting insults as they went. When they were at a safe distance, he closed his eyes and tried to stop his hands from shaking. *Mother of…* He flinched at the buzz saw rasp of a machine pistol and the hiss of bullets passing close enough to his head that he could feel the disturbed air of their passage. *Jesus, no!* When he opened his eyes, the four young Poles were writhing in a heap in the bloody snow, clawing at their bodies where the bullets had torn them. Behind him, he heard the sharp click of a magazine being changed, and his back tensed for the strike of the rounds that would kill him. Instead, he heard the sound of a match being struck. He turned to see a man in a long overcoat and a black fedora standing at the top of a brick pile, his face illuminated by the flare of the match he'd just used to light his cigarette.

'Blum?' Kalisz struggled to keep the hatred from his voice.

'That's right, Kalisz. Your saviour.' The SS man flicked the match away. 'But don't thank me too much. I nearly couldn't shoot for laughing. Worth a hundred hostages? I wouldn't give five Polacks and a rabbi for you.' He began picking his way down the rubble, but Kalisz noticed the gun's muzzle never strayed far from his body.

'You didn't need to kill them. They were leaving. They were just kids.'

'You heard them.' Blum snorted. 'They would have come for you eventually. This way, you don't have to watch your back.' He leered. 'At least not for them. Anyway, if they didn't kill you, the little bastards would have killed someone else.' A terrible agonised groan came from the little huddle of bodies. 'Here.' Blum reached inside his coat and pulled out the Nagant he cleaned so obsessively. 'You finish him.' Kalisz's fist closed on the familiar cross-hatched butt of the pistol and his finger poised over the trigger. Blum brought the muzzle of the machine gun up to Kalisz's chest. He was grinning, but the dark eyes were like ice chips. 'On you go.'

Kalisz turned and walked to the shattered bodies. Three of them were clearly dead, their eyes already dimming as they lay back in spreading pools of darkness. Poldek clutched convulsively at his stomach, trying to push a blue-grey coil back into the torn cavity where the bullets had nearly torn him in half. The boy's eyes were screwed tight shut and tears ran down his cheeks. Like putting an animal out of its misery, Kalisz persuaded himself. He said a silent prayer and held the pistol at arm's length, sighted on the freckled forehead and pulled the trigger.

As the echoes of the shot faded, he felt Blum come to his side to stare down at the bullet-ripped bodies and the boy with the shattered skull whose brains had spattered Kalisz's shoes. The

SS man reached out to take the pistol from Kalisz's unresisting hand.

'You're a cool one, Kalisz.' He grinned. 'To be honest, I didn't think you had it in you.' He flicked open the cylinder and showed it to the other man. It was empty. 'Just the one bullet. You never can tell.'

He clapped Kalisz on the shoulder like an old comrade, slipped the MP38 under his coat and walked away, whistling to himself.

'What about them?' Kalisz called.

'What about them?' Blum looked over his shoulder. 'Polish terrorists die in cowardly attack on representatives of the Reich. Don't worry, I'll do the paperwork.'

Kalisz stood over the bodies for a long time. His foolish reassurances of a few hours earlier about being true to himself seemed hollow now. Oh, he could rationalise his decision – all he'd done was save the boy a few minutes of pain – but there'd been a line he'd vowed he would never cross. Now that line was behind him. He had a terrible premonition of other lines, each requiring a filthier act than the one before, each corroding the thing that made Jan Kalisz Jan Kalisz. How could a man live without a soul?

At last, he turned away. Four more debts to pay. He felt a sudden chill as he realised that if he'd succumbed to the temptation to tell them he was working with the Resistance, he would be lying there beside them.

And why had Blum been following him in the first place?

CHAPTER 20

Through the following days, Kalisz noticed Ziegler becoming increasingly tense in their dealings together. It was so obvious, he wondered if the young SS officer had come to regret his impulsive decision to attend a Mass where he was unlikely to get any kind of welcome. For his part, Kalisz lived in the constant hope that Ziegler would call it off and save them both what was likely to be an embarrassing – if not excruciating – experience. But as the day approached, the young SS man found a new determination, and on the Friday he suggested to Kalisz they should rendezvous outside the church a few minutes before the Mass.

Ziegler lived in an apartment in the German-only zone around Piłsudski Square – now renamed Adolf Hitler Platz in honour of the Führer. Kalisz decided the address provided a potential opportunity. He told the SS man he had business to conduct in the area, and suggested an alternative rendezvous a little earlier than planned and close to Plac Teatralny, just outside the zone. The meeting would give him a ready excuse to follow up a hunch that had been niggling him since Feinbaum knocked on the door of his apartment on Christmas Eve.

On Sunday morning, Kalisz put on his best suit and spit-shined his shoes before he escorted Maria and Stefan to Mass. When they returned to the apartment, Maria was surprised he didn't change into a sweater and trousers, as he normally did before they sat down to lunch. He felt her staring at him as they ate their rough bread with a little lard bought on the black market.

'You're going out?' she said as he stood up.

'I thought I'd visit my father.' He shrugged on his overcoat and picked up his hat. 'I haven't seen him since Christmas.' He hadn't told her about Ziegler, because to do so would have invited an argument, one that would highlight seemingly fundamental differences that might do yet more harm to their marriage.

'To visit Stan, you need to look like you're going to a wedding?' Clearly she'd have liked to have been more direct, but not in front of Stefan. 'And your only decent pair of shoes?' He didn't answer, and she followed him to the door. 'Are you sure there isn't anything else you want to say to me, Jan?'

He moved to kiss her on the cheek but she flinched away. He shook his head. 'No, Maria.'

Her jaw tightened, but she accepted the lie.

Kalisz tried again and this time she didn't move. Her skin was cold, but so were his lips.

He deliberately took a circuitous route to his destination, inwardly regretting every scuff of leather sole that would probably never be replaced. New shoes were virtually unobtainable, except on the black market, and even with his Occupation marks he'd struggle to afford the six or seven hundred zlotys they'd cost. Along Świętokrzyska, up the diagonal of Bagno and through Plac Grzybowski. He hadn't been this way since the great raids of late September, and he was struck again by the lottery of war. Whole blocks entirely destroyed on the one hand, while the next street would be utterly untouched: not even a broken window. A left into Graniczna and a quick right into the shattered ruin of Rynkowa. Before the war, Iron-Gate

Square had been the site of two large Jewish markets. Now it only held one, and the burnt-out ruins of the second, Wielopole, where Hannah Goldberg had vanished.

Kalisz remembered Wielopole as an astonishing building that dominated the square: a lozenge-shaped masterpiece of soaring cast-iron pillars and canopies, where you could buy anything and buy it cheap. Now, as he walked into the square from Rynkowa, his heart fell at the sight of the shattered, rusting skeletons of once-thriving arcades and an enormous heap of twisted metal and stone. He'd planned to take a closer look at the derelict site where Hannah had vanished, but one glance was enough to tell him his Sunday suit would never survive the maze of ragged, razor-edged iron. This was the place Hannah Goldberg had thought of as a playground and a storehouse?

Another reason for a change of plan was the temporary Nazi checkpoint manned by a squad of watchful SD men and presided over by an armoured car with another of their number crouched behind a machine gun. There seemed no apparent reason for its presence, other than intimidation, but it was enough to make people stay on the left side of the street. Here, dozens of traders – some of them presumably the previous occupants of the Wielopole – had set up their stalls. This cloth city, and the building looming behind it, comprised the famous Bazaar Janasz. Kalisz slipped seamlessly among the crowds who bought and sold in little huddled groups, anonymous but for one thing: every man and woman around him wore the six-pointed blue star. A few stared at him, conscious of an interloper in their midst. He was among them, but not of them. A curiosity, because the Nazis 'encouraged' their isolation, and few Poles dared challenge that position – at least conspicuously. Many – and it was surprising how many – did so when they were certain they wouldn't be seen. There was no law yet segregating the races, but the educated among these Jews knew the recent history of their German brethren, and nobody doubted what was coming. Most, though, ignored the well-dressed Gentile, too intent on doing business, finding food or fuel, those essentials for survival, or bartering some treasured valuable for a lesser item that could more easily be traded for the necessities of life. A diamond ring or an Old Master was no good to anyone if the Nazis were about to take it away, but a fur coat or a thick blanket could save your life if you had no coal.

Kalisz moved among the stalls, refusing offers of tea from great steaming urns, and home-brewed potato vodka strong enough to blind you. He remembered this place from his childhood as a riot of colour, but the multicoloured gowns and men's shirts that had fluttered like medieval banners were gone, replaced by sullen greys and browns. In season, there'd been a rainbow spectrum of red apples, pink-fleshed watermelon, yellow raisins, golden apricots and green gooseberries, and even barrels of fish that glittered blue-silver in the sunshine.

It had been a place of thieves, gangsters and opportunists, poor people taking their revenge on those who had the audacity and the good fortune to be a little bit richer. The memory made him check his wallet and keep his overcoat buttoned tight. Kalisz had seen young men from the market leap on to the back of a passing truck, lift a box of goods and disappear among the crowds before anyone could react. The local cops applauded along with the rest. Men like Szymele Blacharz and Isaac Goldberg ruled here, and you crossed them at your peril. Throw a punch and the answer would be a knife in the ribs. Pull a blade, and they'd like as not shoot you.

He paused. Something caught his eye at the very periphery of his vision, and he turned to stare at a stall selling rabbit traps.

Simple tunnels of wire and wood, but a bonus if you knew a little piece of ground where the *kroliki* grazed. What was it that had made him stop, though? The stallholder's son completed his latest trap and threw it onto the heap on the table, where it made a distinctive rattling sound. Slowly it all came together. The long beard and the dark coat, his back festooned with cages and traps that rattled and jingled as he walked. Not so many around these days, but he remembered them from his childhood: the Jewish rat-catcher.

Kalisz studied his surroundings, trying to work out the layout of the area from his time on the streets. This was a district that had been frozen in time for a hundred years – give or take a few Luftwaffe bombs. What had been here a dozen years ago should still be here. He cast a wary glance towards the checkpoint in front of the Wielopole ruins. From his experience of the Germans, it was a bit too static, not quite threatening enough. It was there to draw attention, and that meant he had to move quickly. He pushed his way through the crowd and moved north. Across Mirowska, between the big palace to his right and the Tarnowa Halls, and still no warning shout. All right. Why not? He took a chance and sprinted into the cover of Zimna.

When he reached the shadows, he slowed to a walk and checked the shop signs until he came to the one he was looking for. A deceptive place, with a narrow frontage and an empty window, but he remembered what lay behind. It looked closed – and these days, who knew? – but it was all he had. He hammered on the door and waited. Nothing happened, so he knocked again. This time the door cracked open and a single eye appeared in the narrow gap. 'We've nothing to sell. I'm sick of telling people—'

'Mosicki, Department V.' Kalisz flashed his old warrant badge quickly enough that the man wouldn't see the name on it.

The eye closed and a great sigh emanated as the door swung open. '*Shteyner af zayne beyner*,' the shop owner muttered in Yiddish. 'What have I done to deserve this?'

'Nothing to worry about.' Kalisz pushed his way past the man, into the gloomy interior of a shop filled with the musty scent of decaying flour. It had once sold beans and pulses and grain by the sack, even exotics like rice, but now the shelves were empty. 'I'm just trying to trace someone.'

'Don't we have enough trouble already?' The shopkeeper followed him, muttering to himself. 'Trying to find someone? With the Nazis picking people off the streets every day?' A short, stocky figure in a white overall, he had the broad back of a man who'd shouldered sacks of grain all his life, but his face was a picture of defeat, lined and lugubrious. 'Who's this person you're looking for?'

'You still have the grain store through the back?'

A hesitation – *now why would you ask that?* 'Certainly.' He led the way through a pair of swing doors into a vast, cavernous warehouse that must take up half the block, partly lit by windows in the roof. 'Not much use for all this space now. Maybe I should start hosting dances, eh?' He pointed to a few sacks piled beside the door. 'This is my allocation these days. The Germans, they come in the morning and weigh them. Then they come at night and weigh them again, and old Mandelbaum must account for every gram. Who received what and when.' He shook his head and gave a deep sigh that was like the life bleeding from him. 'Now, it is difficult. Soon, it will be impossible. I know these things. I grew up in a *shtetl* near Zhovkva.' Kalisz knew of the town, up near Lwów on the

153

Ukrainian border. A hard place to make a life, and harder still to be a Jew. 'I saw the pogroms. First they humiliate you, then they grind you down, then they kill you.'

'I'm looking for the local rat-catcher. Long grey beard, dark coat?'

'Sure.' Mandelbaum's face brightened. 'Old Salomon. He used to come round once a week, but when the grain went the rats weren't so interested any more. I haven't seen him for maybe three weeks. A pity – I could make more money selling rats than I can wheat. You can get five zloty down the market for a good fat rat.'

'Do you know where Salomon lives?' Kalisz persisted. 'Any places he visits regularly?'

'No.' The shopkeeper frowned. 'He moved around a lot. He would appear, take his money and then disappear again. You never know when he'll turn up. The local kids throw stones at him. It's not in his interest to hang around.'

Kalisz thanked him and moved towards the door. 'Just one last thing. Do you know a girl called Hannah Goldberg? A bright kid, about thirteen?' Mandelbaum shook his head. 'Daughter of Isaac Goldberg.'

A shadow fell like a shutter over the haggard features. 'I know nothing of Isaac Goldberg.'

Out in the street, Kalisz made his way back to Iron-Gate Square. He was early for his rendezvous with Ziegler, but he'd have to make a detour around the edges of the *Nur für Deutsche* zone. He decided to have one last look at the Wielopole arcade and make some plans for a future visit. As soon as he entered the square, he knew he'd made a mistake. The Germans at the checkpoint stood in a line, holding their weapons in a way that told you they were ready to use them. The machine-gunner crouched a little lower behind his MG34, sighting along the barrel. The Jewish crowd in front of the bazaar had sensed it, too. They jostled restlessly, little flurries of panic visible as they swept through the mass of people like a breeze over a field of summer corn. A few of the more nervous were already scuttling for the surrounding streets. Stallholders hurriedly dismantled their tables and canopies. Kalisz reversed his direction in a single movement and joined a group hurrying back up Zimna. Too late.

He searched desperately for some place of refuge as the clatter of hob-nailed boots echoed from the walls of the narrow street. Nothing. Every door was closed. From ahead and behind, shouted orders and the sound of barking dogs.

'*Łapanka*,' an anguished voice cried out: Round-up.

Kalisz was swept up with the rest and herded back into the square by a line of Wehrmacht troopers, pleased to have the opportunity to use their rifle butts or long whips. Behind them, others battered in the doors of the tenements and hustled the occupants into the streets with roars of '*Raus*'. He tried to keep his head clear as he shuffled along with the crowd, caught like a piece of flotsam on the tide, but there were too many questions. The *łapanka* might be aimed at the market and the illegal activities of many of the Jewish traders. Then again, it could be that they were looking for someone specific, which might mean nothing more than a long wait. On the other hand, if you were the right age, with the wrong documents, there was an increasing chance you'd be pushed on to a train and carried off to do forced labour in a Silesian coal mine or on a Bavarian farm. Sometimes, though, they used these surprise swoops to provide a fresh crop of hostages: gallows fodder who'd be driven directly to Pawiak Prison and kept to provide an example in the event of a German soldier being attacked. The Poles were as powerless as sheep being rounded up for the slaughterhouse.

Kalisz looked at the face of the man next to him, and saw a mask of dismay and utter helplessness he knew must mirror his own.

–

'I'm sorry I'm late, sir,' Kalisz gasped. 'I was temporarily detained by the security police.'

A different Ziegler this, much younger out of uniform, trim and correct in a pinstripe suit, looking like a newly graduated student attending his first job interview. The German pursed his lips in irritation at Kalisz's dishevelled appearance, taking in the grey pallor and the dark hair plastered to his brow by sweat. It had taken twenty of the longest minutes in Kalisz's life to persuade a granite-faced Gestapo major that he worked for the Kripo and had an appointment with an SS lieutenant 'that must be kept, sir, for all love'. It had been touch and go for a few moments whether his reward would be a bellyful of rifle butt and being thrown into the back of the truck with the rest.

'Then we must hurry.' Ziegler glanced at his watch. 'Six, you said?'

'Yes, sir. If you will follow me.' Kalisz set off at a brisk pace in the direction of the city centre with the SS man at his side.

Ziegler turned to him as they crossed the street. 'Would it help if I ordered you to call me by my name, Kalisz?'

'No, Herr *Obersturmführer*.'

Ziegler shook his head. 'Then tell me about this church.'

'There's not much to say, sir. My church is the Church of St Joseph and the Visitationists. The building dates to the eighteenth century, but there has been a church on the site for almost three hundred years. It has a fine interior.' It also had many fine artworks from all over Europe, but that wasn't the sort of thing you mentioned to a Nazi, not even one like

Ziegler. 'But I suppose the most significant thing I can tell you about it is that Chopin was once our church organist.'

It was the type of fact Kalisz thought would interest Ziegler, but the German didn't react. Now that Kalisz had the time to notice, his companion looked unnaturally pale. Ziegler's pensive, distracted air reminded him of that dreadful morning in the bloodied snow out in Wawer.

'And your priest? You would describe him how? Compassionate? Understanding?'

Kalisz hesitated, unsure how to respond to this odd line of questioning. 'I would say so, sir. I've known Father Panasik for twenty years. He conducted my marriage ceremony and baptised my son.'

'And his politics?'

Kalisz almost missed a stride.

'I don't believe he has any, sir.'

'Good.'

It was a long Mass, but Ziegler didn't embarrass Kalisz. They sat together at the back of the near empty church. The German knelt when he should and made the Latin responses at the appropriate time. Only the cut of his suit distinguished him from any other worshipper. An intense man, Kalisz noted, who lost himself in the traditional rituals. A difficult man to hate.

After the blessing, the priest made an announcement. Kalisz stood up to leave, but Ziegler pulled at his jacket.

'What did he say?'

'He said he will take confession from anyone who wishes it, sir.'

Ziegler bowed his head and whispered a prayer, his hands clasped together.

'Sir.'

The SS officer looked up, and Kalisz was surprised by the intensity in his eyes.

'Your priest, Kalisz? He speaks German?'

Kalisz considered a lie, but instead he nodded. Ziegler rose and made his way to the confessional booth.

Fifteen minutes passed.

Kalisz stared at the curtain of the confessional booth, instinct telling him that no good would come of this. Ziegler confirmed his fears when he stumbled from the confessional and staggered blindly past him up the aisle with his hand over his eyes.

'Sir… Willi?'

He rose to follow the other man from the church.

'Mr Kalisz.' The shout was sharp and raw-edged. He turned to find Father Panasik staring at him, his face pink and inflamed. Kalisz looked from the priest to the doorway, uncertain how to respond. 'We must talk, Jan. Please.'

Panasik was a big man with a commanding presence, now made more so by the power of his emotions. In Kalisz's experience he was a genuinely good man. Certainly not a man to get angry. Yet here he was struggling to suppress some fierce passion. Kalisz felt an overwhelming dread that he was about to discover the reason for it. Panasik clearly wanted to convey a message about what had just happened, but was uncertain how to articulate it without breaking the confidence of the confessional.

'Sometimes, my son…' The priest spoke with great deliberation, and the muscles in his face worked as he searched for the proper form of words. 'I speak purely in general terms… A priest sometimes hears things that challenge his faith in God. It is one of the great tests of our calling. Another is that – fortunately, very rarely – he hears of acts so unspeakable they are almost beyond his powers of forgiveness.'

Kalisz listened with growing alarm and confusion. What was the priest telling him? And what did it have to do with Ziegler? Something terrible, certainly, to make him go even this far. He remembered the SS man's lack of reaction to the Wawer executions. It had seemed unnatural at the time, but was there a darker reason for his behaviour?

Panasik nodded solemnly. 'I see you understand.'

'No, Father, I don't.'

'I must ask you never to bring that man to this church again.'

'He's a German, I'm not sure I can stop him.'

'I am asking you as a valued member of my congregation, Jan. He would not come here without you.'

'I'll do what I can.' Kalisz turned towards the door.

'And… Jan?'

'Yes, Father?'

'I understand you are working for the Nazis.'

Kalisz went very still. 'I'm doing my job, Father. People still need to be shielded from crime, even in these times.'

He felt the other man's eyes boring into him. Someone else would have sneered with contempt at this transparent hypocrisy, but Panasik only allowed the long silence to prolong Kalisz's torment.

'You are a good man, Jan. A good father, a good husband and a good friend. These are indeed difficult times, times when the right path is sometimes obscured by confusion, a sense of misplaced duty – or fear. I implore you to look deep into your heart and ask yourself if the path you have taken is the right path. Seek God's guidance, and should you choose to walk another path, one which I believe is the true path, the Church will do everything it can to ease your way ahead. Do you understand me, Jan?'

Kalisz understood well enough, but he also knew there was no turning back now. 'I think I do, Father.' He drew a long breath. 'But the path I am on is the path I've chosen. Unlike you, I have a family to provide for.' He saw the other man flinch, but he felt no shame. The priest had begun this, and Jan Kalisz was running out of patience with people who tried to dictate how he lived these potentially final few days of his life. 'I will not abandon them. Not for you, or the Church or any false sense of duty. Do you understand?'

'Then may God forgive you.' The priest gave a curt nod. 'Because your country will not.'

CHAPTER 21

The Artist

Spring 1940

The Artist had cultivated her for three days, like a gardener coaxing a rose to bloom.

He had been right about the uniform. In one way or another, it gave him power over them. This one had been easy because it held attraction for her, rather than fear. The symbolism it projected was like a magnetic pull: a combination of authority and the very essence of the conqueror's strength. Was it normal to admire your country's enemy? In his short experience of Poland, he'd come to understand that some females were weak that way. Scores of Polish women walked arm in arm with German soldiers in the Ogród Saksi near his accommodation, in the hope that their favours would earn them a ration coupon or a meal. The way she stared at the silver trinkets that adorned his collar contained an eroticism – a love, verging on the sexual – for the uniform, and a curiosity about the man who wore it.

He hated her.

On the outside she was beautiful, with the silken waves of blonde hair, ripe peach complexion and glowing blue eyes he had first fallen in love with as a boy. But beneath the veneer, she was the same as all the rest. It had taken him years to understand that.

It had begun in his third year at secondary school. He had admired Christa since they were seven. A precocious and lively girl, she lived a few doors away and it was natural that they should walk together to school. Natural, too, that he should carry her satchel; his mother had brought him up to be a gentleman. To the boy, her eyes shone like glistening sapphires and her pale skin glowed gold in the summer sunshine, and when she smiled it made his stomach turn somersaults of pure joy. His mother had called him handsome, a perfect specimen of Aryan manhood, and he had believed her. One day, he would marry the girl of his dreams.

He had watched Christa change and grow. At first, it was a matter of poise and confidence, a certainty in her ability to control the boys in class by the force of her personality and some all but imperceptible transformation in the way she moved. Then came the physical: a gradual increase in the proportions of her lower half which began to draw the eyes of not just her class-mates, but her teachers, too: the swelling in her blouse seemed to bud and become full-grown over the length of a season. He was hypnotised by every millimetre of these changes, and the very fact of them wrought a breathlessness and a reaction beyond his control every time they were in proximity. Even the scent of her seemed to reach out to him and draw him to her. Eventually, he realised he loved her.

He decided to tell her on her fifteenth birthday.

The Artist suppressed a groan of anguish at the memory. The boys in the class were a rough crowd, and he had never made friends with them. When they wanted to go for long marches in the countryside, all he wanted to do was study. When they wrestled with each other he stayed a step back, declining to become involved. Swimming in a river repelled him because he was clever enough to know what he was sharing the water with. But in the *Hitlerjugend* he had no choice but to get involved. Every boy must be able to climb a tree. Every boy must endure an early morning swim in a freezing lake. He discovered that his mother was wrong. He was *not* the perfect specimen of Aryan manhood. But he still had Christa.

When he told her, she glowed with pleasure and he reflected that glow when she kissed him on the cheek. Naturally, Christa took command. Tomorrow, she said, they would go for a walk and talk about the future. She had seen him looking at her, and she implied with a lift of her breasts that she was not averse to letting him see more. The touch of her lips burned like a brand all through the long night.

The next day, they had set out with the sun on their backs to the special place she had found. They took a picnic, and Christa had danced and laughed and held his hand. Her eyes had been full of fun and promise. The special place was a dell, a little depression in the woods far away from any path. She led him there with an assurance that puzzled him, as if she'd been here many times before.

She sat down among the beech leaves and patted the ground beside her. He thought she had never looked more beautiful, something expectant and wonderful in the way she held herself. His heart pounded with a mixture of exhilaration and fear as he took his place beside her.

'Do you truly love me?' she'd asked.

'Of course,' he'd told her.

'Then you must show me.'

He'd reached for her, ready to take her in his arms and put his mouth on hers and almost exploding with the wonders that would follow.

'No.' She pushed him away, and her voice contained an unexpected edge of irritation. 'That's not what I meant. You must show me —' she pointed a finger at the groin of his shorts — 'and I —' her hands reached to her breasts and cupped them in the blouse, almost making him groan with pleasure — 'will show you.'

'But...'

Her lips formed a pout.

He was confused. This wasn't how it was meant to be. She'd been supposed to melt into his arms, the way the girls did in the books and magazines his mother didn't know about. Then things would take their course and...

'You don't love me.' She made to get up.

'No, Christa. I—'

'You will?' The smile was back. 'I promise... I will make it worth your while.'

'All right.' His throat felt as if it was filled with sand, and something seemed to be happening in the pit of his stomach. Was it excitement? Or fear? His hands reached for the buttons on the front of his shorts, fumbling on each one, but eventually he had undone them all.

'Take them off.'

'No, please...'

Her hands were back on her breasts. 'Take them off. For me.'

Reluctantly, he stood and shrugged his shorts to his ankles. Her hands went to her mouth and he felt a guilty pleasure at her shock at seeing a man for the first time. It took him a few moments to realise she was laughing behind her fingers.

'What is it?' he demanded.

She took her hands away, pink with the effort of keeping her sniggers caged. 'I've... I've seen bigger *Rostbratwurst*.'

He froze. *No. No, it wasn't meant to be…* He snatched for his shorts, but she stretched out her hand to keep them where they were.

'Make it grow,' she ordered. 'It can't be that small always. I want to see you make it grow. Touch it. You do touch it, don't you, at night? I touch mine.' Now her hands went under her skirts to stroke her thighs.

Desperately, his hands reached for the wilted thing beneath his legs. He pulled at it, massaged it. Nothing happened. His movements became quicker, more urgent, but still nothing happened. That was when he realised she was giggling and looking around at the surrounding trees. He looked up to see twenty pairs of eyes on them. His *Hitlerjugend* platoon, grins on their faces, trying and failing to stifle their laughter. It started slowly, but grew to a rhythmic, jubilant chant.

'*Rostbrat. Rostbrat. Rostbrat. Rostbrat.*'

He'd torn his shorts from Christa's grasp and run away, not caring which direction he went or how far.

The knowing grins and the nickname stayed with him for five interminable years.

That was when he'd learned how to hate.

Over the years he'd come to understand that they were all the same. No matter how radiant their outer beauty, inside was a foul ugliness. Every one was filled with bile and spite. They were as loathsome to him as any reptile. He'd tried to cleanse himself of that day and the humiliations that followed – even going so far as visiting a Jewish quack in Vienna – but nothing removed the pain of the memory. Then had come the grand revelation in Munich. He would take what was foul and ugly and transform it into something beautiful. A work of art that men would look upon and wonder at.

The girl had seen him and waved. He waved back, smiling warmly.

Warsaw was perfect. He enjoyed being a German in a conquered land.

–

He left the black Mercedes with its engine running, checked the street was empty, and then opened the warehouse doors and drove the car inside. Before closing the doors again, he lit the kerosene lamp that was the room's only source of light. A pair of stained workman's overalls hung behind the door, and he pulled them on over his uniform.

When he opened the trunk she was still unconscious, which pleased him. He hadn't been certain how long the effects would last, and this way it was easier. The new mixture had worked perfectly and she'd succumbed in seconds. He reached inside and heaved her up and onto the steel workbench, the warehouse's only furnishing. Her wrists and ankles were tied, and he'd gagged her for fear the drug might wear off too quickly.

He tugged at her legs and body until she lay straight, then opened a drawer in the bench and pulled out a scalpel, testing it against the hairs of his arm for sharpness. *Perfect.* First he cut off the calf-length skirt and white blouse. The scalpel made a ripping noise as it sliced through the thin cloth, and he took little care not to nick her flesh. When he'd finished, he pulled the torn scraps of linen clear and threw them aside before doing the same with the flimsy brassiere and pants she wore, flinching in disgust at the yellow stains in the crotch area.

This must be how the gods of old felt, he thought, as he stood over the thin, milk-white body – *this surge of power and invincibility.* Naked, she was nowhere near as beautiful as she had been clothed – an impostor, her deceit exposed for all to see. Her body had been wasted by hunger, so he could see every bone. Small, barely discernible breasts and a tiny tuft of hair at the conjunction of her thighs.

He laid his hand on her stomach, feeling the warmth and the pulsing in her veins.

Her eyes snapped open.

He smiled at the pure terror he saw there as she began to struggle against her bonds, writhing and shaking her head.

He leaned over her and whispered 'shush' in her ear, at the same time stroking her forehead. It was curious how it always calmed them, even with the scalpel poised in front of their eyes. He brought it down and swept it across her throat.

The eyes widened and her body shook. A wave of bright, arterial blood gushed from the gaping wound and spread across the bench to drip from the edges onto the dirt floor. He took a practised step back to ensure his shoes weren't contaminated, and waited until the spurting declined and the body had stopped twitching. She was more beautiful to him dead than alive, her flesh the mottled creamy white of old marble.

He felt… nothing.

Avoiding the pooling blood, he bent over the corpse, placed the point of the scalpel into the little hollow above her pubis and drew it upwards to her breastbone in a single flowing movement.

There would be no hurry this time. It had become clear to him that the next part of the process was by far the most important. If he achieved perfection at this stage, when he created the components of the artwork, then it was more likely that the end result would be just as perfect.

Later, he drove to the cleared bomb site where he'd decided the work would be displayed. Tonight was a full moon. He had ample light to position the pieces, and the curfew provided peace of mind that no one would disturb him. His breath quickened as he realised that, finally, he had created a masterpiece worthy of his talents.

At last, the city and the whole world would see an artist at the peak of his powers.

Yet, three days later there were no cries of horror and wonder at what he'd done. One of Warsaw's German-language newspapers contained a single paragraph announcing that a prostitute had been found murdered. He might have felt sorry for her – she had been no whore – but for the rage that bubbled inside him. If they'd found the girl, they must have found his creation, yet there was not a word of it.

What do I have to do to get their attention?

Was it because she was only a Pole? Or the nature of the location where he'd left her that had allowed them to disregard his endeavours?

In that moment, he vowed that his next creation would be so spectacular it would be impossible to ignore.

CHAPTER 22

Kalisz made his roundabout way via Senatorska to his father's apartment on a beautiful evening, with the sun trying to chase the war away for a while. But a little warmth on his back and the emerald glow of the lime trees couldn't make up for the hunger gnawing at his belly, or the knowledge that a thousand miles to the west, Hitler was teaching the French and British a lesson in how to wage war. The Nazi newspapers crowed about every German success, and loudspeaker vans on street corners relayed each stage of the campaign with messianic fervour. It turned out that the Maginot Line had been nothing but a French fig leaf, which the Wehrmacht laughed at on the way past as they attacked through Belgium and Holland. A hundred and thirty-six divisions, with flocks of bombers and thousands of paratroops paving the way, had smashed the defensive forts at Rotterdam, The Hague and the Albert Canal, on their way to the River Meuse and French soil. If the Nazi propaganda was to be believed, the British and the French – and the brave Poles who fought alongside them – were being pushed back on all fronts.

There'd been jubilation and backslapping at Nowy Sjazd 1, and Kalisz was forced to smile even as the bile came into his throat. Just for a moment, he was left wondering if his sacrifice had any point. If France and Britain sued for peace, what future did Poland have?

Still, he would continue to fight his lonely war, though how long it would last he didn't care to speculate. He'd been taking more and more risks to satisfy the ravenous hunger for intelligence displayed by Kazimierz's chiefs: advance notice of raids; names of men and women marked for arrest; any tiny nugget of information that would give an indication of the Nazi strategy for fighting the *Związek Walki Zbrojnej*, the Union of Armed Struggle. Kazimierz, for his part, pleaded with him to be more careful. Yes, the product was important, but, 'The very fact of your existence at the heart of the Kripo is a victory for us,' he assured Kalisz. 'Just by staying alive and in place, you give us options we would not otherwise have.'

Now *that* had brought a wry smile to Kalisz's lips. The truth was that for every supporter in whatever department Kazimierz reported to, there'd be another who'd question the point of continuing to court the source known as 'Bullet' or 'Butterfly', or whatever silly code name they'd given Kalisz.

But Kalisz's loyalty was to Kazimierz, not the men in the shadows behind him.

Then there was the enigma of *Obersturmführer* Willi Ziegler. That morning, the SS man had approached Kalisz about his odd behaviour at the Church of St Joseph.

'I should like to apologise for rushing away without saying goodbye,' Ziegler said. 'The truth is that I was quite over-whelmed by the occasion.'

'There's no need for that, sir,' Kalisz assured him, but Ziegler wasn't finished.

'I also have to inform you that I will be going on extended leave, which means you may be reassigned. *Hauptsturmführer* Hoth would like to see you in his office at your earliest convenience.'

Hoth had been quite apologetic about it, but with Ziegler gone, he'd had no choice. Kalisz was temporarily back checking lists in the basement.

The latest had contained the names and addresses of thousands of Jewish families due to be relocated from their current homes to the workers' district in the city centre. *Ryngman, Hershel, family of four, Żelasna 33, to Leszno 67 (5). Garfinkel, Isaac, family of three, Chmielna 47, to Leszno 67 (5). Lederberg, Yekhiel, family of three, Bagno 156, to Leszno 67 (5). Feinbaum, Julius, family of four, from Kopernika 35, to Leszno 67 (5).* Kalisz had queried with the official overseeing the lists why so many families were being placed in the same apartment. He'd been told the apartments were 'spacious', and that each family had been allocated a single room. Should he inform Feinbaum of the impending disaster about to befall his family? After some agonised deliberation, he'd decided not to. Better, in Kalisz's mind at least, to be allowed another few weeks' relative peace of mind before the blow struck. In any case, Feinbaum would have made his preparations for something like this. They all would have.

Not too far now.

The scream of tyres and the sound of a racing engine froze his blood. Only the Nazis drove cars, and a Nazi in a hurry meant trouble. Kalisz could see fear in the faces of the people coming towards him, and he steeled himself for the inevitable: rough hands taking him by the shoulder and forcing him into the rear of the vehicle; the instant barrage of punches just to let him know what was coming; the hood and the shackles. Who had betrayed him?

A small black saloon car slammed to a halt in the street at his side. 'Get in the passenger side.'

'Sir?'

'You're not fucking deaf, Kalisz,' Kripo Investigator Günther Gruhl snarled through the open window. 'I said, get in the passenger side, and make it quick before I get annoyed.'

Kalisz's mind reeled with relief and bewilderment. He slipped into the leather passenger seat, glancing into the rear just to make sure Müller wasn't hiding there with a garotte. Gruhl didn't seem to notice.

'That fat turd Zurowski called in sick –' he moved the car, an unassuming little Polski Fiat 508, into gear – 'just when I need someone who knows his way around the rat runs of this city for a hush-hush job. I saw you coming this way, so you get the vote.'

Zurowski was the Polish interpreter Gruhl normally worked with, and Kalisz allowed himself to relax. 'I'd be happy to help you, sir, but I thought—'

'You thought I hated your Polish guts, and you were correct. But Blum says you're all right, and I trust his judgement. He can sniff out a traitor at a hundred paces, that one. Blum told me you put the lights out on one of those little Polish bastards who ambushed you. That sends you up in my estimation, Kalisz. It takes guts to put a gun against a man's head and pull the trigger. Believe me, I know. It's not for the nervous. You have to be as hard as Krupp steel. So I reckon Hoth may be right, and there's some good German blood in you.'

Gruhl drove out of Senatorska into Plac Bankowy. Kalisz's father's house lay a couple of hundred paces to the north. 'My father is—'

'Your old man will have to wait.' Gruhl veered left into Elektoralna, continuing westwards. 'And you'd best stop whining before my good opinion of you changes.' They drove past a family of Orthodox Jews and the Nazi's lip curled. 'Fucking Yids parading around in fancy dress. The Führer's got the right idea for them, and it won't be long now. The daughter's not bad, though.' He turned to grin at Kalisz. 'You'd be surprised how many good German boys go wild for a piece of Jewish snatch. I thought your pal Ziegler was a fruit, but I've seen him sniffing around the Yid skirt on Leszno Street when he didn't think anyone was looking. You know Wola?'

Kalisz had switched off Gruhl's rant, and the sudden change of subject took him by surprise. 'I was stationed there when I was in uniform.'

'Good. There's a warehouse, somewhere close to the motor-cycle factory – this is the address.' He passed over a sheet of paper, one hand on the steering wheel. 'Some people will be meeting there tonight, and we'll make sure they all arrive before I call in the cavalry on this.' He patted a short-wave radio transmitter attached to the dashboard. 'Erich Marten and his snatch squad will be waiting for word.'

Kalisz felt a thrill of alarm. What had he been dragged into? In Warsaw's pantheon of fear, Marten was a name that stood out for cruelty and viciousness. Even the Gestapo oper-ated within some semblance of legal framework, but Marten's *Rollkommando* were notorious for their murderous unpredict-ability. They would scour the streets, seeking out potential targets for torture and execution without any form of judicial sanction. Their victims would simply disappear, never to be seen again, unless some animal unearthed a shallow grave or a bloated corpse surfaced in the Vistula. It looked as if some unfortunate group had been betrayed by one of its members. *Should I risk my position to try and stop it happening?* As soon as he posed the question, he knew what Kazimierz's answer would be: *Whoever they were, they must be left to their fate.* The debit side of the currency of resistance. It sickened Kalisz to his stomach, but that was the way it had to be.

'May one ask who these people are?'

'No, one may not, Kalisz. All you need to know is that they are enemies of the state, and that when they're in the bag, Günther Gruhl's career will be on the rise. Nobody knows apart from me and my source, and nobody gets to share the glory, understand?'

'Of course, sir.'

'Don't worry.' Gruhl took his eyes off the road to flash Kalisz a leer. 'I'll make sure you're seen all right. Here's something on account.' He reached into his pocket and threw the Pole a packet of German cigarettes. 'Hoth's not the only one with contacts.'

'Thank you, sir.' Kalisz managed an answering grimace.

'Right, tell me what you know about this place.'

Wola was home to some of the giants of Poland's heavy industry: the Gerlach engineering works; the state-owned National Arms Factory; the Joint Stock Locomotive works; Philips, who made light bulbs and radio parts. Some of the costliest battles in the defence of Warsaw had been fought in and around Wola. Before it had been destroyed in an air raid, the Dobrolin chemical plant on Wolska had provided the Polish defenders with hundreds of barrels of turpentine they'd used to incinerate the crews of several dozen Wehrmacht tanks, but Gruhl probably wouldn't want to hear that.

'Many of the factories and homes in this area were destroyed in raids or during the fighting. It might not be so easy to find this street.'

Gruhl turned to glare at him. 'We have plenty of time, the meeting's not due to start until after eight. I'm depending on you to get me close, Kalisz, and you'd best not fuck this up, because that'll make me angry, and you really don't want to see me angry. We need to get there with just enough light so I can identify who goes in. That's all I need. Five minutes in the right place.'

'I'll do my best, sir.'

'Fucking right you will.'

Gruhl drove slowly around the shattered streets, past giant piles of twisted metal and rubble that had once been thriving factories. In the end they settled on a secluded, partially cleared bomb site. As they waited, Gruhl began to pare his fingernails with what looked like a razor-edged pocket knife. Kalisz endured the scraping sound until he could stand it no longer.

'Best we should be in place soon,' he suggested. 'We must be about ten minutes away.'

Gruhl nodded. He pulled out a Walther P38 automatic and nervously checked the magazine. Little beads of sweat had formed on his forehead. 'If anybody gets in our way, you talk us through, all right?'

'Yes, sir.'

'If they turn into a problem, I'll get behind them and take them out.' He saw Kalisz's look of alarm. 'No firing – not unless it turns into a complete fuck-up, which it won't. A little tap behind the ear, and into the cuffs with a gag in their chops. But it won't come to that.'

Fortunately, there weren't many people on the street so close to curfew. They managed to find a burnt-out building not too far from the warehouse, where a smoke-stained bedroom on the first floor gave a view of the approach. Gruhl checked his watch. 'Not long now.' He swallowed. He reached inside his voluminous overcoat and took out a small flask, taking a long pull, then hesitating before offering it to Kalisz with a lift of his chin.

'Thank you, sir.' Kalisz accepted and put the flask briefly to his lips before returning it. As dusk fell, Gruhl moved into position so he could see down the street, but was still hidden in the room's shadows. He produced a small pair of binoculars and studied the view from the window, and Kalisz moved in behind him so he had a similar aspect.

Minutes passed, and the *Volksdeutsche* detective's agitation increased as the street remained stubbornly empty.

'That little shit,' he grumbled. 'I'll hang him with his own guts and fuck his mother and sister if he's making a fool of me.' A few minutes later, Kalisz saw him stiffen. 'Yes.' The Pole's heart fell at Gruhl's whisper of elation. A man strode up the far pavement and disappeared from view. 'You'll be code name "Falcon".' One by one, Falcon was followed by four more men and one woman, and Gruhl listed them as they passed: Teofil, Danuta, André, Flash, Girder. Each name a death sentence. 'That's it,' Gruhl hissed to Kalisz. 'They're all in the bag. Back to the car and we'll call it in.' He was almost chuckling to himself as they made their tricky way down the charred stairway and out into the back garden. Ten minutes later, they were approaching the car.

'Cigarette, sir?' Kalisz pulled the packet from his pocket and offered it to the other man.

'Christ, yes.' Gruhl let out a long sigh as he accepted. 'I'd almost forgotten how much I was needing one. Another minute won't make any difference. They're to be in there for two hours.'

Kalisz struck a match with his left hand and Gruhl bent his head to meet it.

The punch was a jawbreaker. It started below Kalisz's waist and came up with the power of a steam piston. His closed fist connected at the point where the mandible was weakest and the lower and upper jaws connected. Gruhl's mouth was partially open to draw in smoke, and the force of the blow snapped one of the arms of the condyle, forcing the bone up into the cartilage behind. Gruhl dropped with a grunt to sit on the dusty ground, holding his jaw in both hands.

Kalisz bent to go through the pockets of the stunned Nazi's overcoat, but he ignored the Walther. He'd been formulating some kind of plan since the moment he'd recognised 'Girder' as Kazimierz. The man's face had been invisible, but the clothes and the way he carried himself had instantly identified him. Kalisz took a pair of black leather gloves from a side pocket, then rummaged a little deeper, rejecting the pocket knife before he found what he was looking for. He'd heard Gruhl boasting about his little friend, the Equaliser: a set of brass knuckles, with protruding nodules of steel to ensure maximum damage to the victim.

Kalisz pulled on the gloves, slipped the knuckles over the fingers of his right hand and stood over the groaning detective. He took a deep breath. Kazimierz had signed one of their death warrants the moment he stepped into view. Gruhl looked up at him with stunned disbelief in his eyes, and Kalisz had a moment of doubt. But the German wouldn't hesitate if their roles were reversed. This was when Jan Kalisz went to war. He put all his strength into a vicious right hook that brought the steel fist plum against Gruhl's temple. The detective toppled on to his side with a low groan. Kalisz knelt over the defenceless man, punching repeatedly in short arm jabs until the side of Gruhl's skull was a bloody mess that was soft to the touch. Still, the Nazi wouldn't die. Ragged, grating breaths, like a pig grunting as it searched for food, emerged from his nostrils along with spurts of blood. Undeterred, Kalisz gripped the bulbous nose in the fingers of one hand, pinching off the airways, and clamped the other gloved hand over the open mouth. There was no resistance, but it felt like a very long time before Gruhl's chest stopped rising and falling and his corpse emitted a loud, drawn-out fart. When he was certain, Kalisz deftly searched the body, coming up with a little 'throwdown' pistol in a holster strapped to Gruhl's hairy white ankle, a model Kalisz didn't recognise. He pocketed the weapon and the car key, then unstrapped the holster and thought about it for a few moments before adding it to his haul.

He wasted no time; better to be doing something – anything – than thinking about the murder he'd just committed. Using the keys to open the boot, he somehow managed to drag the body across and heave it in to fill the confined space. Inside the Polski Fiat he discovered a battered attaché case with leather straps, containing documents connected with something called Aktion AB. He replaced the papers and got out and leaned against the car, aware of the inevitable reaction beginning to set in after the cold-blooded murder. His whole body started to shake. A sharp heat was born deep in the base of his stomach, and expanded to fill his chest before erupting from his mouth like a column of bitter fire. When he'd finished vomiting, he wiped his eyes and considered his position.

If the Germans discovered the car with the murdered Gruhl in the trunk, they'd never stop until they found his killer. Under questioning, someone somewhere would remember the Polski Fiat drawing up beside the slim, dark-haired man in Senatorska. One thing would inevitably lead to another, and Kalisz would end up in front of the firing squad that played such a big part in his life these days. Only one man could help him.

He made his way back to the warehouse, this time choosing an alleyway where he could watch the six ZWZ chiefs leaving the building, but without being seen. If he guessed right, they'd come out in the same order they went in, which suited his purposes. An hour or so later they began to emerge: Falcon, Teofil, Danuta, Andre, Flash. Then, after a suitable pause,

Girder. Kalisz waited until the familiar figure was directly opposite before he stepped out and came up behind him, the little throwdown gun in his hand. Moving silently, he simultaneously screwed the barrel into Kazimierz's neck and put his other arm round his throat to drag the struggling figure into the deeper darkness.

'Hello, Girder.'

Kazimierz froze. 'I don't know anyone by that name.'

'No?' Kalisz turned him around, keeping the pistol barrel firmly against his flesh.

'What the fuck…?' Kazimierz was infuriated and bewildered.

'Falcon. Teofil. Danuta. Andre. Flash.'

'I repeat my question.' The other man recovered some of his composure.

'Betrayed,' Kalisz said. 'Don't ask me how. It's up to you to find out, but they knew where and when, and they had your code names.'

'Shit.' Kalisz saw all the questions going through Kazimierz's mind. *Who knew? Who had they told? And why?* He was completely absorbed in the disaster facing his organisation until realisation gradually dawned. 'How did you come to be here?'

Kalisz told him the short version. 'Gruhl said he'd kept all the information to himself,' he finished, 'but I need help. It has to look like an accident.'

If anything, Kazimierz was even more astonished, but not for long. 'The car keys?' Kalisz handed them over. 'We'll deal with it.' He gave Kalisz an address close by. 'You'll be able to explain all this to your wife?'

Kalisz shrugged. Who knew? He'd come up with something.

'Someone will pick you up when the curfew's past and take you into town. Just go in to work as if nothing has happened.'

'Sure.'

'And, Jan, we appreciate this. I know how—'

'Forget it.' The last thing Kalisz wanted was thanks. 'Oh, and Gruhl mentioned a mother and sister.'

He saw a flash of disbelief in Kazimierz's eyes before they hardened.

CHAPTER 23

The Polski Fiat sat with its chassis crumpled but still upright, chrome bumper wrapped around the scarred trunk of a lime tree on Aleja Ujazdowskie, with the body of the late Kripo investigator Günther Gruhl draped across the bonnet. Oddly, Gruhl's battered felt hat remained in place on his head, only six inches closer to his neck than anyone could previously remember. He lay among shards of jagged glass from the windscreen, through which he'd been propelled head first into the tree by the impact of the crash. Gruhl's grieving colleague, Investigator Müller, took the foul-smelling meerschaum pipe from between his teeth and stuck his head through a shattered side window, his nostrils twitching at the pungent scent of vodka from a smashed bottle in the footwell.

'He wouldn't have stood a chance.' Kalisz injected a note of sympathy into his voice. He'd been ordered to the crash scene as soon as he'd arrived for work, and there was something unreal about standing beside the man he'd killed not twelve hours earlier. 'Catastrophic head injury.'

'Tell me something I don't know,' Müller said sourly.

'No tyre marks,' Kalisz pointed out. 'He didn't try to brake, or he didn't have the chance.'

Müller brought his face threateningly close to the Pole's. 'Are you trying to insinuate my good friend Günther might have done this deliberately?'

Kalisz ignored the thick sarcasm that threw as much doubt on Müller's friendship with Gruhl as it did on Kalisz's theory. 'I didn't know him that well.'

'All Günther Gruhl cared about was propping up a bar while pouring beer down his throat, followed by a warm bed and a warmer woman. He didn't have the brains to be depressed. Lucky the car didn't burn.'

'Yes, sir?'

'Yes.' Müller grinned. 'Because then we'd have had to shoot a couple of hundred Poles on the off chance he might have been murdered.'

Kalisz wandered to the front of the car and studied the body. 'You think it's a possibility, sir?'

'I wonder what happened to the little throwdown pistol he was so fond of.'

'Maybe he felt he didn't need it in Warsaw,' Kalisz suggested. 'Who was going to accuse him of anything just for shooting a few Poles?'

Kalisz winced as Müller spun him round and slammed him against the bodywork, drawing looks of surprise from the German guards and the Polish police who'd cordoned off the crash site. 'Don't think you can get clever with me, you little Polish shit.' Müller's bristling moustache seemed to have taken on a life of its own. His grip relaxed a little and his eyes turned knowing. 'If I frighten you, Kalisz, you hide it well.'

'I don't understand, sir.' Kalisz feigned puzzlement.

'The question I ask myself is, what else are you good at hiding? You see, I don't buy the dumb, submissive Polack routine.'

'Begging your pardon, but I only try to do my duty.'

'Gruhl hinted just yesterday that he was on to something big,' Müller continued as if Kalisz hadn't spoken. 'He reckoned the Gestapo would be giving him a call this morning to offer him a job.' He released Kalisz and gave the corpse a pat on the shoulder. 'How are the mighty fallen, eh? That means whatever he was on to was due to happen last night. He'd even told my old pal Erich Marten to expect a call. So what's Günther Gruhl, who can barely string two words together in that barbarian gabble of yours, doing swanning about Warsaw alone in the middle of the night? And getting himself killed into the bargain. Now that's careless. Me, I'm not so careless. So I checked with Gruhl's usual interpreter, Zurowski, who tells me he had a touch of the squirts last night and couldn't go out with his boss. Gruhl told him it didn't matter, because he knew where he could find a replacement. Now, who would that be?'

'I don't know, sir.'

'By the way, where did you spend last night, Kalisz?'

Something in the way he asked the question made Kalisz's blood freeze, but he dared not allow his expression to falter.

'I was where I normally am, sir. With my family.'

Müller studied him for a long time, his dark, beady eyes glittering like a snake's as it sizes up a mouse for the strike. Eventually, he brought his hand up to Kalisz's cheek and the Pole winced as he pinched the flesh between two fingers.

'Just as well for you that's what your wife told me when I called on her after I spoke to Zurowski.' The words were accompanied by a wintry smile. 'But there'll be something else, Kalisz. You'll slip up eventually, and when you do, I'll be there to pull the trigger on you. I'll enjoy that. Now, let's get this cleared up.' He raised his voice so it could be heard by everyone at the scene. 'I want to know if anyone finds any inconsistency. Anything at all that may not point to an accident. Every one of you should assume Investigator Gruhl may have been deliberately killed.'

A murmur went through the ranks of the soldiers and policemen, but it was interrupted by the growl of a powerful engine and the arrival of a large Mercedes staff car. *Hauptsturmführer* Hoth emerged, accompanied by one of his aides, and they walked briskly towards Müller. Kalisz stepped to one side and watched as the two men went to the car and Hoth inspected Gruhl's body. Hoth pursed his lips and shook his head. It was impossible to hear what was said, but clearly Müller wasn't happy. Eventually, Hoth gave his languid Hitler salute and Müller responded with a rigid straight arm that brought a wry half-smile from his superior.

'Kalisz, get your arse over here,' Müller shouted.

'Yes, sir?'

'The case is closed.'

'Closed, sir?'

'That's right – it's fucking closed. Captain Hoth has decided, against my better judgement, that Gruhl died as a result of an unfortunate traffic accident. I'm assigned to a new case and, God knows why, but you're with me. Do you know the Krasiński Gardens?'

'Of course, sir.'

'Then let's go. There's a villa overlooking the gardens, home to a big-time industrialist, name of Kleist, who's taken over the railway-engine plant out at Wola.' Müller let out a long breath. 'He's also an old party man, close to the Führer, and the brother of General Ewald von Kleist, whose Panzers are chasing the Frogs and the Tommies into the English Channel.'

'May I ask why he's of interest, sir?'

'His fucking daughter's just gone and got herself killed, that's why.'

CHAPTER 24

The villa was a handsome building of cream stucco and red tile, tucked away in its own secluded garden and surrounded by trees. *Hauptsturmführer* Hoth's Mercedes was already parked on the gravel outside. The head of Department V's presence would have been a surprise, but for the full company of watchful SS guards who'd cordoned off the area, and the number of senior Gestapo officers visible. They waved Müller and Kalisz through. Hoth had announced he would take personal charge of the investigation, with Müller and a team of detectives doing the day-to-day legwork.

'They say Hans Frank himself is coming personally to offer his condolences.' Müller grunted. 'You stay here, while I go and talk to the father and get my instructions.'

Kalisz studied his surroundings. Away to his left, the line of trees ended just in front of a complex of bombed-out buildings where the SS presence seemed to be strongest. He walked towards the skeletal remains of the buildings until two soldiers raised their rifles and demanded his identity papers.

'I'm with *Hauptsturmführer* Hoth, Warsaw Kripo.' Kalisz flashed his old badge. 'Where's the body?'

'Through there, Herr…?' The guard frowned, taking in the crumpled suit and careworn features.

'Kalisz. Investigator Kalisz.'

'We were just told to guard the place and not let anyone near until the investigation team arrived.'

'Well, then?' Kalisz stared at them. 'The investigation team is here. Let's get on with it.'

The two men glanced at each other, shrugged, and stood aside. Kalisz picked his way through the rubble towards a bomb crater where a camouflage tent had been erected. He felt a surge of irritation when he saw the tent. The body and its immediate surroundings should have been left undisturbed. Any footprints or other potential evidence would have been trampled by the men who'd erected it.

But that was Müller's problem.

In his years as an investigator, Kalisz had seen many corpses, but for some reason the breath caught in his throat as he approached the canvas entrance flap. He hesitated, trying to put aside his personal prejudices and rediscover the objectivity that had made him a good detective. Daughter of a Nazi or not, these weren't just the remains of a German; the victim was a human being: a young girl. The corpse would be a reference point on a map, the centrepiece of a process that had its beginnings even before she was dead. Who did she know? Who did she trust? Who knew her, but whose existence she didn't even acknowledge? Who were her friends? Who were her enemies? What was her relationship with her parents? The servants? All questions that would have to be answered even before the investigation truly began. She was a German in Warsaw – an enemy. Some Poles didn't need a reason to hate her... or to kill her.

He untied the tent flaps and ducked under the canopy and immediately understood why someone had felt the need to have the body covered. Traudl Kleist. Age thirteen. Kalisz tried to focus on something else as the acid rose in his throat in response to the sight that met him. According to Müller, her parents had last seen her the previous day when she'd gone to play in the nearby park. Well, Traudl would never go out to play again. A dead body was a dead body, but some bodies seemed deader than others, and Traudl Kleist was very dead indeed. The last time Kalisz had seen anything like this was in a mortuary, partway through a post mortem.

She lay on her back, naked, with her arms by her side and her legs together. Her throat had been cut, leaving a ragged, pink-lipped gash in flesh the colour of aged marble, though whether that was what had killed her only a proper examination would tell. She was just past puberty, and the twin swells of her teenage breasts were tipped by tiny brown nipples. Kalisz knew that if he touched those breasts they'd feel solid, because Traudl Kleist was now in the grip of rigor mortis. You could use rigor mortis to ascertain an approximate time of the victim's demise. It started between two and six hours after death, and began with the muscles of the eyelids, neck and jaw. Over the following four to six hours it spread to the other muscles. Using this evidence, Kalisz would have said Traudl had been killed some time between yesterday afternoon and the early hours of this morning. At just about the same time, come to think of it, he'd been bludgeoning the life out of Inspector Günther Gruhl.

What made Traudl Kleist different, and what told Kalisz she'd been murdered during the daylight hours of yesterday afternoon or evening, was what had been done to her lower body. From her breastbone to her pelvis, Traudl had been sliced open and eviscerated, so he could see into the bloody abdominal cavity and make out the line of her spine. But this was no haphazard frenzy of bloodletting. The cut was very precise, and the skin had been drawn back as if the murderer wanted those who followed to have a glimpse into the very essence of his victim. If he guessed right, her killer had also removed her sex organs.

'Excuse me.'

Kalisz flinched as the tent flaps opened and another man pushed into the tent. He'd stayed longer than he intended, and he'd be in deep trouble with Müller. The newcomer wore an SS uniform, and he half-turned to stare at the other occupant of the tent with steady brown eyes.

'Kalisz, Herr *Obersturmführer*.' Kalisz introduced himself hurriedly. 'I'm with *Hauptsturmführer* Hoth of the Warsaw Kripo.'

The newcomer took off his peaked officer's cap and ran a hand through thick dark hair. 'Mengele,' he introduced himself as he crouched over the corpse. 'They've appointed me to oversee the forensics of the case. I'm sure a Pole could have done it perfectly well, but...' He shrugged. 'Politics. I was on assignment in Warsaw. So here I am.' While he talked, his eyes roamed across Traudl Kleist's body and he nodded to himself. 'Dead for sixteen to eighteen hours, would you say?'

'Last seen in Krasiński Gardens at around four, sir.'

'"Doctor" will do for now, Kalisz.'

'Yes, Herr Doctor.'

'She must have been a lovely young thing, don't you think?' Mengele studied the dead girl's face, and the staring blue eyes. 'Still is. Odd, that expression of complete serenity, given the horrors that have been perpetrated on her.'

'I was wondering if there might be a reason for that, sir.'

'Yes.' Mengele gave a slow nod of agreement. 'I suspect we'll find some sort of incapacitating drug in her system. It might give you fellows a clue to who her killer was. That, and the way it was administered.'

'An injection puncture would certainly raise some inter-esting theories, sir.'

Mengele picked up Traudl's right arm and examined it for marks. The lower part of the arm was bruised black where what little remained of her blood had gathered. The SS doctor did the same with the other arm. Kalisz noted that he appeared familiar, indeed entirely at ease, with a dead body. 'Help me turn her on her side.' Kalisz moved so he could take Traudl's shoulder, and heaved her up so her back and buttocks were visible. Again there was extensive bruising on the parts of her torso where she'd been lying. 'Nothing to be seen here, but I'll know better when I have her on a slab in some decent light.'

'Strange that he should do this to her, but go to so much effort to make sure she felt no pain?'

'Excuse me, young lady.' Mengele bent low so he could see between Traudl's legs. 'No sign of bruising. That doesn't categorically rule out rape. Of course, it would help if we could find her bits and pieces.'

'Her clothing, too – it's nowhere to be seen,' Kalisz offered. 'I wondered whether the guards who put up the tent also searched the surrounding area.'

'No, they haven't.' Mengele frowned. 'I asked when I arrived. All they'd been told was to cover the body and cordon off the house.'

Kalisz saw an opportunity to get out of the tent before Müller or Hoth arrived. 'Then perhaps I should take a look, Herr Doctor?'

'That sounds sensible.' Kalisz felt the intense gaze of the deep brown eyes. 'I'll accompany you. Poor little Traudl isn't going anywhere.'

They wandered through the ruins, on closer inspection a former school. Mengele picked up the charred remains of a child's book and shook his head. 'Who would have thought it would come to this? So many fine buildings damaged. Just think, Kalisz, even now this could be happening to Paris. What do you say to that?'

'It would be a pity, sir,' Kalisz said with conviction. 'It was certainly a pity for Warsaw.'

'I—' They froze at the sound of a cough that turned into a low growl. Mengele turned to Kalisz. 'A dog?'

The implications of the sound for their evidence hit them both in the same moment. 'Then we'd better be quick, Herr Doctor.'

They danced across the rubble heaps until they reached a corner of the school where three walls had survived. 'What…?' Mengele stopped dead and Kalisz followed his gaze.

'Mary, mother of Jesus. What is it?'

Framed on a cleared patch of ground in the corner of the walls was something beyond horror.

'Well, it appears we've found her large intestine,' Mengele said. 'It would seem to constitute some kind of inner framing.'

What they could see was a picture made up of organs and body parts: a picture of a vase of blooming flowers, outlined in a square of greyish powder.

'Roses, I think.' Mengele answered Kalisz's unspoken question. He seemed fascinated by the image and its constituents. 'This fellow of ours is an artist in more ways than one. Three blooms,' he said, almost to himself. 'I suppose that could be significant.'

'Are you saying Traudl Kleist may not be his… Let's call him "The Artist". She may not be his first victim, sir?'

'You're the policeman, Kalisz, but it's a theory, isn't it?' He turned back to the artwork. 'The main stem of the flowers appears to be made from the aorta. I believe those rather odd-looking leaves are slices of kidney, and see how he's used an ovary as the centre and patches of skin for the petals. It even has stamens, though God only knows what they are. A rather crude representation, though, when you think about it. As if the killer was in a hurry. I'm not sure that Spanish fellow would be proud of it.'

'Picasso, sir. Blood Roses.'

'I beg your pardon.'

'The killer has created Blood Roses.'

'Oh, yes, I see what you mean.' The Nazi frowned. 'Now why would the dogs ignore it.' He reached down and put his finger in the white powder. 'Pepper?'

He was about to touch it to his lips when Kalisz grabbed his arm.

'Pepper with more of a kick than you'd be comfortable with.'

For a moment, something beyond anger appeared in Mengele's eyes. Later those eyes would appear in Kalisz's dreams, but the look subsided when Mengele realised what the Pole had heard: a soft moaning sound from beyond the furthest wall.

They moved slowly towards the noise till they could hear it was accompanied by frantic heavy breathing. Behind the wall, some sort of large mongrel dog lay on its side, panting fiercely, saliva dripping from its jaws and a pool of vomit near its head. Even as they watched, it stiffened and the breathing stopped.

'Poison.' Mengele studied the white powder on his fingers with a sickly look on his face. 'I suppose you think I should thank you for saving my life?'

'That won't be necessary, Herr Doctor.'

'Well, I believe it is, Kalisz. Thank you. I'd shake your hand, but in the circumstances...' They grinned at each other. 'I'd better have this analysed. Be a good fellow and see if you can find some sort of container.'

Before Kalisz could move, he heard shouting from the direction of the tent. 'Kalisz, where the fuck have you been?' Müller demanded. 'If you've fucked up this crime scene, I'll—'

'Investigator Kalisz has been assisting me,' Mengele informed him curtly.

'My apologies, sir, I wasn't aware… I thought—'

'Perhaps you could be of some use, and arrange for a photographer to come and record this oddity that seems to have been created by the perpetrator.' Müller's jaw dropped as he noticed the gruesome collage for the first time. 'Once it is done, I'll have an assistant separate out the individual pieces for tests and eventual return to the body. I'd also be grateful if you can have someone who understands a crime scene to carefully collect this grey powder you see here. I say carefully, because it appears to be a deadly poison. Can you do that?'

'Of course, sir.' Müller directed Kalisz towards the Kleist house with a sideways tilt of the head. 'You're to report to Pawiak Prison.'

'Sir?' Kalisz's voice reflected his dismay. Pawiak, the great concrete slab of a building between Pawia and Dzielna streets, was where the thousands rounded up in *łapanka* swoops were held before they were either executed or sent to one of the Nazis' feared new detention camps. The prison didn't have Szucha Avenue's reputation for torture, but many of the guards were reputed to be little more than beasts.

'We're rounding up every Pole and Jew within a five-hundred-metre radius of the Kleist villa for questioning. The father reckons you Polacks don't much like the fact that he's taken over the railway engine plant. He's had threats and dirty looks.'

'But, sir, there's no evidence—'

Kalisz saw the punch coming and could easily have blocked it. Instead, he took the blow on the cheek and rode it backwards, providing Müller with the satisfaction of contact, but sustaining no real damage. He found himself on his back, looking up at Müller's mask of fury, and a mildly puzzled Mengele. Müller hauled him to his feet by the front of his jacket.

'You don't question my orders – you hear that, Kalisz? We're going to solve this case quickly to Governor Frank's satisfaction, or heads will roll, and I'm damned sure mine won't be one of them. So unless you'd welcome a trip to Szucha Avenue, you'll keep your mouth shut and get on with the job. Meet me back at the car.'

'Yes, Herr Investigator.'

Mengele bent down to pick up Kalisz's hat, which had fallen to one side, and dusted it off on his uniform trousers. 'An unfortunate incident,' he said mildly. 'For a moment, Mr Kalisz,' the SS man lowered his voice, 'you allowed another man to reveal himself. Take my advice and learn to keep him out of sight, or you will not survive all this.'

Kalisz accepted the hat. 'Thank you, sir.' He bowed his head. 'My temper...' He shrugged, but Mengele's expression told him it wasn't temper he'd seen, but something more interesting.

–

Kalisz had had worse nights, but not many. Hour after hour in the tiny, soulless interview room in Pawiak, with the dreadful spirit of the place a constant menacing presence. Guards hustled dozens of ashen-faced Poles and Jews into the room one by one. No wall of silence here, quite the opposite. Some of them would have talked all night, many gabbled, and a few asked him what he wanted them to say. Not silence, but consternation.

They knew nothing of murder. They knew nothing of Traudl Kleist. They kept to themselves. In other rooms and cells, the team of interviewers would be hearing various versions of the same theme.

One girl Kalisz spoke to, of a similar age to Traudl, admitted talking to her in the park about the latest fashions and boys. Kalisz had a feeling she was keeping something back, but he didn't note that down. Instead, he took her address and filed it in his inside pocket. At the end, nothing. Dawn was breaking somewhere over the Vistula when the decision was made. The women and children would be released, but the men held as hostages. As he trudged home, Kalisz struggled to keep his eyes open and one foot in front of the other. The only consolation was that he was so tired, his stomach preferred to forget he hadn't eaten for more than twenty-four hours.

When he reached Kopernika, he didn't go directly to the apartment. Instead, he turned left down Obóźna, past the Warsaw University botany department, and continued until he reached a small fountain set into a substantial masonry wall. He stopped for a moment, picked up a metal cup on a chain and filled it from the spout, taking the opportunity to check his surroundings as he drank. When he was sure he was alone, he pulled from his pocket the packet of coloured chalks that Kazimierz had supplied him. Selecting three different colours, he bent and chalked three separate stripes on the wall beside the fountain. It was a dry morning, with little chance of rain. If the protocol worked as it always had done in the past, one of Kazimierz's agents would visit the fountain in an hour or two and the colours of the three stripes would tell Kalisz's contact the date, place and time of their next meeting. Kazimierz had to know about the Traudl Kleist killing. Kalisz had a feeling that the consequences of her death might threaten to engulf them all.

When he finally reached home, he didn't know what to expect when he burrowed into bed beside Maria. The reality – '*Two nights away from home? Have I become such a shrew that you must seek consolation elsewhere?*' – was probably better than he deserved. He told her about the ants' nest Traudl Kleist's murder had stirred up, and his fears for the men still held at Pawiak. 'Why did you tell the German I was at home with you when you knew I wasn't, Maria?'

The question was followed by a long hesitation, and she kept her back to him. Eventually, she murmured, 'I thought that if they were asking where you were, the best place you could be was with me.' Another long pause. 'Are you sure there isn't something you want to tell me, Jan?'

'No, Maria.' The words tore his throat like a jagged fishbone. 'Sometimes with the Germans, the left hand doesn't want the right one to know what it is doing.'

He wanted to hold her then, but he didn't dare for fear of her reaction.

Later, he dreamed of the snowy day in the ruins of the vodka distillery, and the young Polish boys who'd been cut down by Blum's machine gun. It was an odd dream, because it duplicated the events precisely as they happened… right up to the moment he pointed the gun at the dying kid's head, and the face staring up at him was Stefan.

'Nooooooo.'

The word rasped from his throat, but in the dream no sound emerged. He began running and he would have run forever, but for the touch of Maria's lips on his forehead. He opened his eyes.

'You were having a nightmare, Jan. You must have been terrified because you screamed out Stefan's name. What was it about?'

'Just the war, Maria,' he lied. 'Sometimes I think it will never let us go.'

CHAPTER 25

Jan Kalisz walked into his worst nightmare. All around, glamorous uniforms and colourful gowns made him feel like a little grey mouse in his tired suit and scuffed shoes. What other civilians there were – Polish collaborators, middlemen and contractors who were making a fortune from the occupation – had the same well-fed look and cheerful demeanour as the soldiers who mingled and chatted beneath the glittering chandeliers. Like Kalisz, their host had negotiated dispensation for them, for one night only, from the venue's *Nur für Deutsche* rule.

It was impossible for a Pole to refuse an invitation to help celebrate the award of the Knight's Cross to *Obersturmführer* Willi Ziegler in the private room at the exclusive Café Club. Free-flowing champagne – everyone knew there'd soon be plenty more where that came from – and fillet steak canapés, with a five-piece orchestra, so the SS officers and their beautiful escorts could glide effortlessly across the polished wooden dance floor.

The single consolation was that it gave Kalisz the chance to pick up a few morsels of information Kazimierz might appreciate. Drink made the most inhibited of men garrulous, and these confident Black Knights of the Third Reich were far from diffident. Not that they'd talk directly to a lowly Pole, but as Kalisz circulated with a glass of Moët and Chandon clutched in his fist, he was able to tune in to snatches of conversation.

If he'd picked it up correctly, the Germans were planning a mass confiscation of fur coats and other winter clothing. A small thing that would condemn thousands of Poles to a freezing winter, but perhaps of wider significance to the people Kazimierz worked with. He'd also heard two SS officers talking about 'penning in the Jews', but he wasn't certain what it meant.

He was making his way towards another group when Ziegler noticed him; the German was more than slightly drunk.

'So you came, Kalisz? I wasn't sure you would. I hope you are enjoying my party?'

'It was kind of you to invite me, sir.' Kalisz managed a smile. 'It's a long time since I tasted champagne, and I intend to fill my pockets with the contents of the buffet. May I congratulate you on your award.' He indicated the black metal cross hanging from a ribbon at Ziegler's neck.

Ziegler's hand went up to touch the medal and he gave a self-conscious laugh. 'A little throat ache will do my career no harm. I'm not sure I deserved it, but Governor General Frank was very complimentary.'

'May one ask what you did, sir?'

'Did?' Ziegler frowned and swayed slightly on his feet. 'I can barely remember. A village in some godforsaken Polish forest. They had a few well dug-in machine guns. I thought my men were with me, but it turned out I was on my own.' He grinned. 'Not quite as heroic as you thought, eh, Kalisz?'

'I'm sure the Herr *Obersturmführer* is being too modest.'

'A pity about poor Gruhl.' Kalisz blinked at this dangerous change of subject. 'A rather coarse fellow, but he didn't deserve that. They tell me you're working with Müller now? That girl who was murdered.' He shook his head. 'A terrible end.'

'Yes, sir,' Kalisz said, though as far as he was aware, none of the details of the Kleist killing had been released. 'Will you be rejoining us soon, sir?'

Ziegler's face went blank. 'When my leave is finished, it's possible I may return to my unit.'

'I'm sorry to hear that, sir.'

'One can't escape one's duty, Kalisz. Now, if you'll excuse me.' Ziegler drifted off into the crowd, to be instantly replaced by another familiar face.

Mengele.

'So you know Willi Ziegler, Kalisz?'

'Yes, Herr Doctor. And you?'

'We're old acquaintances from university in Munich. An unlikely hero, I would have thought. I always found him rather sensitive.'

'Sometimes, on the battlefield, it's the least likely people who surprise you.'

Mengele stared at him. 'You speak from personal experience?'

'No, sir.' Kalisz cursed himself for his stupidity. 'It was something my father said.' Mengele nodded thoughtfully, but Kalisz had a feeling he wasn't convinced.

'Would you be interested to know that I've been chatting with *Hauptsturmführer* Hoth about you?'

Kalisz didn't like that at all, but he could hardly say so. 'I'm flattered by your interest in my career, though I admit I find it surprising.'

'I like to know the calibre of the men I'm dealing with, Kalisz.' Mengele pulled a silver cigarette case from his pocket and lit one without offering it to Kalisz. 'It's important we understand each other.' He blew a plume of smoke towards the ceiling. 'The pressures from on high mean we must solve this terrible crime swiftly. Himmler himself is taking a personal interest in the case. I doubt someone like Müller is capable of doing so – all he seems interested in is finding a scapegoat. So, I ask myself who is?'

'And *Hauptsturmführer* Hoth suggested me?'

'He is an admirer.' Mengele shrugged. 'Even though you are a Pole.'

'It's the one quarter German he admires,' Kalisz pointed out.

Without warning, Mengele moved his face close to Kalisz's, and the Pole felt as if the brown eyes were measuring him. 'Does the word "physiognomy" mean anything to you, Kalisz?'

The sudden change of tack caught Kalisz off balance. 'I believe it's something to do with the face, sir.'

'Precisely.' The SS doctor's hands came up in what was clearly a practised movement. Mengele created the bottom half of a window, thumbs together and fingers vertical. He peered directly at Kalisz through the frame from a distance of a dozen centimetres. 'Did you know you have a very German face? Fine-boned, regular features, eyes neither too wide nor too narrow, nose and mouth in proportion and a strong jawline.'

'The Herr *Obersturmführer* is too kind.'

'And dark.' Mengele ignored the sarcasm in Kalisz's tone. The orchestral music faded and the first bars of a strident tune rang out from a piano, to drunken cheers from the revellers. Kalisz looked to where Willi Ziegler was seated at the keys of a baby grand, surrounded by a band of roaring SS men and watched by a tall man in a civilian suit whom Kalisz thought he vaguely recognised. Mengele dropped his hands and studied the scene. 'How very patriotic. But don't believe anyone who tells you these blond, blue-eyed giants are of perfect German stock, Kalisz. You only have to look at their eyes to know they were created for peering through the fog from the prow of a

Viking longship. No, it's men like you and me who have true German characteristics. Why, we could be brothers.'

'If you say so, Herr Doctor. But isn't your theory verging on heresy?' Kalisz realised the champagne was making him brave. He'd read about SS chief Heinrich Himmler's obsession with the origins of the German people. Blond, blue-eyed giants were the personification of the owlish *Reichsführer*'s 'master race'.

'It may be.' Mengele was momentarily distracted by a very young female version of the tribe he'd just mocked. 'But it has always been the responsibility of scientists to stand up against beliefs which are inherently false, even if it means they go to the fire. Wasn't Copernicus, an ethnic German with a Polish soul, condemned after his death as a heretic?'

'I believe so, sir.' Kalisz searched for the nearest exit. He was beginning to find Mengele's interest in him overpowering.

'Think on that, Kalisz. A German with a Polish soul. The most dangerous of combinations. Now, where did she go?' He took two steps before he halted again. 'How could I have forgotten?' he said. 'Our poison – I have had the preliminary results. It's a form of cyanide, but with some interesting characteristics. It could be significant, I believe. Ah, Raoul…' Kalisz looked round to see a swarthy, tanned man in an expensive suit approaching. 'Kalisz, this is a friend of mine visiting us from South America. He's a former police chief so you should have something in common. Now, if you don't mind, I have some research to do.'

When he was gone, Kalisz engaged in desultory conversation with the South American – a beef farmer from Buenos Aires in Argentina – but it quickly became clear the man had little interest in him, and he soon managed to slip away. He had to get out of here or he'd go mad. But the place seemed to be even more crowded, and the true aristocracy of Nazi Warsaw were only now making their entrance. He saw Hoth talking to *Standartenführer* Josef Meisinger, head of the SS and the security police in Warsaw. *Who is more productive?* he asked himself. *Kalisz, the not very good spy, or the Kalisz who mentally walked from the kitchens with an MP38 and sprayed the room with bullets?* He thought he knew the answer, but he didn't have a machine pistol. Instead, he waited for a gap in the wall of increasingly boisterous Germans.

A shift in the crowd, and he saw his chance. He laid his glass on a nearby table, slipped through an opening between two groups, and made for the door with his eyes to the ground. Kalisz, the invisible man.

Not, it turned out, invisible enough.

'How refreshing to meet someone else who's not in uniform.' Kalisz recognised his interceptor as Ziegler's friend from the Hotel de Saxe. He struggled for a name, but the other man saved him the trouble. 'Wolff, engineer.' The German fitted Mengele's description of tall, blond and blue-eyed to perfection. He wore an immaculate pinstripe suit with a Nazi party badge prominent on the lapel, and the pin on his silk tie was set with a diamond. Kalisz reluctantly took the outstretched hand and was surprised at the delicacy of the grip.

'Kalisz. I work with *Obersturmführer* Ziegler at Department V.'

A waiter passed with a tray of champagne and Wolff liberated two glasses, giving Kalisz no choice but to accept the one he was handed. 'You speak excellent German, but am I correct that you are a Pole? It must be irksome to be excluded from places like this because of your origins.' Someone knocked his elbow on the way past and Wolff only just missed spilling champagne on his suit. He flicked a few drops from his hand in irritation. 'Or perhaps not. May I be frank, Herr Kalisz?' The smile became just a little too intense, and Kalisz noticed that the ice-blue eyes were entirely devoid of humour. He was beginning to wish he'd walked straight past the man. 'I find it surprising that a person like you – in fact, any Pole – would willingly work with his country's invaders. Certainly, if it were me, I'd be out there in the forest with a rifle, fighting back. I look at you and I ask myself, is this man a coward or an opportunist? My problem is that I see neither. Of course, I could be wrong, but I don't think so. One day, when you think the time is right, you *will* be out there in the forest, or on the street with a rifle, and then –' he snapped his fingers with a sharp click – 'it will be all over for you, because my country knows how to deal with its enemies.'

Kalisz listened with growing anger, and he had to fight to conceal his true feelings. 'Thank you for your advice, Herr Wolff.' He accompanied the words with a bow of his head. 'Now, I have to be going. We Poles must keep to the curfew.'

He made for the door, but the other man stood his ground. 'I will make it my business to discover more about you, Herr Kalisz. I believe we'll meet again.'

After a moment, Wolff allowed Kalisz to pass. When he emerged into the open air, the Pole released a long breath and willed himself to be calm. The sun hung low in the western sky, and the soft Warsaw evening made the contrast with the humiliation he'd just endured all the more unsettling.

On the other side of the road, the gates of the Pałac Branickich, which had been the home of the British ambassador to Poland, were chained and padlocked. Kalisz crossed and walked east along Aleja Jerozolimskie, his conflicting responsibilities weighing on his shoulders like a giant yoke. Kazimierz would be waiting on the corner of Czerwonego Krzyża and Solec, the meeting a supposed chance encounter that would allow them to make the short walk to Kopernika together.

He was so lost in thought, he barely registered the small crowd up ahead at the entrance to Warsaw's main hospital. Two grey-green lorries were parked nearby and squads of troops were spreading out into the surrounding buildings to herd their occupants into the street. He made to turn back, but a group of *Ordnungspolizei* trotted out from a side street to form a cordon across the road. *Łapanka?* It didn't feel like it. Maybe they were looking for someone specific. He allowed himself to be pushed towards the hospital gates.

There were five men, and their captors had placed them against a grass bank beside the hospital entrance.

They were about to die.

An officer read out the proclamation in German and Polish. These men were terrorists and enemies of the state. They were to be executed in retaliation for an attack on a German dispatch rider injured in Mokotów. Orpo troopers stalked through the crowd, snarling that anyone who turned away or looked down would join the men in front of the firing squad.

'You will watch,' they told the Poles, 'and you will learn the price of resistance.'

Kalisz buried his true self somewhere deep inside and willed his mind to go numb. He would not watch. He would witness. Five of them. The boy on the right wept and pleaded for his life, his hands clawing at his shirt and his body shaking, which amused the twenty or so off-duty Wehrmacht soldiers who'd come to enjoy the spectacle. Beside him stood a man in a suit, who looked as if he'd just left the office and appeared more perplexed than frightened. On the far side stood two workmen in blue overalls, one of them with half his face swollen like a football and the other with his eyes skywards.

Kalisz's heart seemed to stop as his eyes settled on a tall, imposing figure in a dark clerical suit and a priest's collar. Father

Panasik stood in the centre of the line with his hands clasped behind his back, staring calmly at his executioners. A woman mumbled a prayer that ended in a yelp as one of the German guards slapped her. Kalisz kept his eyes on the doomed priest. *I will not watch. I will witness.* The boy's cries became ever more frenzied, then, curiously, faded. Father Panasik made the sign of the cross. A single word of command was followed by the whiplash crack of twelve Mausers. Kalisz watched the priest crumple without a sound, saw the firing squad commander march forward with a pistol and put an unnecessary bullet into each head. *Remember. Record. Another debt to pay.*

Stay numb. The shattered bodies mean nothing. The spreading pools of blood mean nothing. Soldiers dispersed the crowd with the encouragement of their rifle butts, and Kalisz walked on. What they didn't understand was that their pitiless brutality would eventually work against them. If anything, the butchery would strengthen the resolve of those forced to witness it. Better, surely, to be shot for doing something than for doing nothing? Somewhere along the line, the Nazis would pay for the sacrifice of Father Panasik and the men who had died beside him.

Kalisz turned a corner and almost walked into two boys. They looked at him like startled rabbits, then ran off in the opposite direction. They left behind a tin and a brush stained with red paint. On the wall near where they'd been, a curious symbol stood out against the grey brick: A sixty-centimetre-high *P* which descended to form a *W*. Kalisz knew the emblem stood for *Pomścimy Wawer* – We will avenge Wawer. The boys were around Stefan's age, and he had a feeling he recognised one of them from his son's scout troop.

If they'd been caught, they'd have been arrested and taken to Pawiak, or more likely shot on the spot. Though he had no direct evidence, Kalisz was certain his son was involved in similar acts of rebellion. The knowledge inspired a curious mix of fear and pride. But pride was no consolation if your son was dead.

He reached the rendezvous with Kazimierz almost without being aware of it, and he was startled when the other man took step with him: two acquaintances exchanging news as they walked together. Kalisz reported the execution and Father Panasik's courage in the face of certain death. Kazimierz only nodded. The confirmation that it had been carried out by Orpo Battalion 101 animated him more: here was information that could be acted on. Some sort of revenge might be arranged. Kalisz mentioned Ziegler's award and the incident at the church.

'Yes, we've confirmed he was with one of their murder squads. Your friend has been involved in some horrors.'

'I know it's wrong,' Kalisz said, 'but I feel a little sorry for him.'

'He's as happy pulling the trigger as he is giving the order.' No sympathy from Kazimierz. 'We'll deal with the likes of him when this is over.'

'You still think we'll win the war?'

'What choice do we have?' the other man answered. 'Look, Jan.' His voice took on a new enthusiasm. 'You don't know it, and there's very little evidence on the surface, but big things are happening. While you're doing your bit, an entire secret state is growing up around you despite the kind of thing that happened today. We are everywhere. Of every political dimension. In every aspect of life. Everything that has gone before, exists again. Government. Order. Justice. Retribution. Look out upon Warsaw and though it's invisible, it is there, Jan. You are part of something enormous. Something that will endure whatever the Nazis do.'

Kalisz would never understand how he allowed it to happen, but it was like a dam breaking. He dragged the other man into a shop doorway. 'It's all right for you, Kazimierz.' The hissed words erupted in a torrent of frustration. 'You're a part of this "secret state" you talk of. If anything happens to you, there's a chance people will get you out or hide you somewhere safe. The best I can hope for is a swift death like Father Panasik, and even that's unlikely. The burden I carry is mine alone. Every day of my life I place my family in danger, yet I can't reveal my true self because the knowledge would endanger them even more. Maria hates that I work with the Nazis. How long before she hates *me*? Stefan doesn't understand why his father collaborates with the Germans, while other fathers fight them. His father shames him, therefore he must outdo his friends in his personal resistance. He takes risks, Kazimierz, I know it. I don't try to stop him because I don't know how. Eventually, he'll get himself killed and I'll be to blame. Every day I sit among murderers and sadists. I listen to tales of how they beat the truth out of so-and-so, or watched the Gestapo pull some poor girl's nails out. I smile at their jokes when all I want to do is put my hands round their necks and throttle the life out of them. The more time I spend with them, the more I fear I am becoming one of them.'

'No, Jan—'

'I didn't kill Gruhl to save you. I killed him to save myself. And the worst thing about it is that I *enjoyed* killing him. How do you think that makes me feel?'

Kalisz realised he'd been gripping the front of Kazimierz's coat, and he dropped his hands. Kazimierz took a step back and gazed at him with eyes filled with compassion. 'Oh, my poor friend.' He laid a hand on Kalisz's shoulder. 'What can I do to help you?'

The answer, of course, was nothing. The outburst was a safety valve, a release of the unremitting pressure and tension that had come close to exploding in the insanity of the Café Club and the shooting. He'd *had* to tell somebody, and logically Kazimierz was the only person he could talk to. The answer was nothing, and nothing had changed. *The burden I carry is mine alone.*

'Just tell me it's worthwhile.'

'It's worthwhile, Jan.' Kazimierz sounded passionate in his certainty. 'It may not feel like it, but you're making a difference.'

'Then it goes on.' Kalisz studied the street in both directions before they walked out of the doorway.

'Our security people found the informer, by the way. He was one of our best people - clever, trustworthy – we thought – and as brave as a lion. But when they took his mother and sister, he couldn't stand the thought of them being tortured. He knew Gruhl was with the Kripo and offered himself as a substitute. Of course, Gruhl used him, in that disgusting way these people do. He convinced the boy the only way to save them was to work for him. When our people questioned him he didn't even deny it, he just asked for a pistol and walked into the woods. No one had the heart to tell him the Gestapo had shot the women the day they were arrested.'

They talked about France, where things were going badly. Wehrmacht and SS Panzer divisions had driven a wedge through the Allied forces. The French and most of the Poles were withdrawing in the direction of Paris, while the British Expeditionary Force was in danger of being annihilated somewhere near the Channel coast.

'I'm sorry about your wife's brother.'

'Tadeusz?' Kalisz stopped abruptly. 'What's happened to him?'

Kazimierz looked horrified. 'You don't know. They haven't told you?'

'We've heard nothing since a letter his father passed on in February.'

'I'm sorry, Jan. Tadeusz was killed during take-off on the first day of the German offensive. He didn't even get off the ground.'

CHAPTER 26

Dread clawed at Kalisz's heart as he climbed the stairs.

How was he going to tell Maria?

Poor Tad, always with his head in the clouds one way or the other, so full of life and laughter. It was impossible to think of him dead, but there could be no doubt. This horrible fucking war.

Kalisz opened the front door and stood in the hall for a long moment, trying to get the words right in his head. If he didn't act now his courage would fail him completely.

Maria sat at the table, her shoulders hunched and her face hidden by the silken curtain of her dark hair. Her hands lay clutched almost violently together on the wooden surface, as if the only thing anchoring her to this world was the grip of her own flesh. Kalisz felt a guilty surge of relief. She already knew. August must have been informed and visited the house to tell her. But why would he leave her alone?

'Maria?'

She looked up, face almost as pale as Traudl Kleist's and black circles round her eyes. At first he thought she didn't recognise him, but she blinked and her hand came up to her mouth in a convulsive movement. 'My father has disappeared, Jan.'

–

Kalisz was waiting in the office when Hoth arrived the next morning. Maria had eventually recovered her composure enough to tell how she'd gone to her father's house on Marsza-łkowska, only to learn from his housekeeper that August hadn't been seen since the previous afternoon. He'd gone out on an errand and hadn't returned. Maria knew her father had contacts in the Underground, but she had no idea how active he was. She was terrified he'd been arrested, or worse. Kalisz had assured her he'd find out what had happened to the old man, even if he had to beg his superiors. He'd also decided this wasn't the time to give her the news of Tad's death.

'May I beg a few moments of your time, sir?'

Hoth looked up from the paperwork on his desk, puzzlement and irritation on his blunt features. 'All right, Kalisz. You have five minutes. It had better be important. *Standartenführer* Meisinger took me aside at Ziegler's party yesterday and told me Governor Frank is looking for immediate answers in the Traudl Klein case – and I don't have any. It doesn't help that Müller wasted everybody's time extracting a confession from one of the Polish neighbours, only for a little further investigation to prove the man couldn't have been involved. It all leaves a sour taste in the mouth.'

Kalisz explained about his father-in-law's disappearance. Hoth's expression darkened with every passing moment. Kalisz could see what he was thinking: *A missing Pole?* He shook his head. 'I'm not sure what I can do, Kalisz.'

'A phone call,' Kalisz pleaded. 'Anything that would help, sir. My wife…'

His voice trailed away at Hoth's grunt of irritation, but the SS officer picked up his pen. 'All right, all right. The name, please.'

'August Klimecki.'

An hour later, Hoth called him back to the office. Something in the *Hauptsturmführer*'s expression told him not to be hopeful. Hoth confirmed his suspicion with his first words.

'I'm afraid the news isn't good.' He waved towards a chair and Kalisz took a seat. 'On Tuesday, *Brigadeführer* Streckenbach, head of the SD, ordered the arrest of two hundred suspected terrorists and Polish political and community leaders in retaliation for the killing of Traudl Kleist. August Klimecki was one of the people taken into custody, but I'm not aware of which category he falls into.'

'Do you know where he's being held, sir? Perhaps a visit could be arranged?'

'Those arrested are currently in Pawiak Prison.'

'Thank you, sir.' Kalisz got up to go.

'There is one more thing, Kalisz.'

'Yes, sir?'

'I'm afraid *Brigadeführer* Streckenbach ordered that ten of the hostages should be shot every day until the Pole or the Jew who killed Traudl Kleist either gives himself up or is handed over.'

'But, sir,' Kalisz protested, 'there's no evidence the killer was either.' He saw Hoth's face harden at the implication of his words and hurried on. 'You saw the body, sir,' he said desperately. 'At the post mortem, Doctor Mengele himself commented that our killer was someone who enjoyed their work and who has probably killed before. And there's the missing clothes. A certain kind of multiple killer will keep trophies from his victims. We're looking for a psychopath, sir, and no psychopath is going to give himself up to save two hundred people he doesn't know. It's more likely someone will settle an old score by informing on one of their neighbours.' He had a moment of inspiration. 'How would Department V look if we had the wrong man in custody and the killer struck again?'

Hoth sucked at his pencil. 'It's true that we can't afford any more instances of overenthusiasm like Müller's.' The hard eyes fixed on Kalisz. 'All the more reason for us to solve the case quickly, then, wouldn't you say? Have you – as a former investigator – any suggestions?'

Kalisz considered the question for a moment. He had to do something for August. He had his own idea where the next line of inquiry should be, but Hannah Goldberg was a Jew and might not exist as far as the likes of Hoth were concerned. But another faint possibility provided some room for manoeuvre.

'I took the liberty yesterday morning of asking Investigator Gersten to go through the files, to see if there were any reports of missing girls around the time of Traudl Kleist's death. It turns out the Blues had a report from Wola of a family whose daughter had disappeared about three weeks earlier. We did some further checks and discovered that she'd later been found dead.'

'Surely we would know about it?' Hoth frowned. 'The Blues would have called it in immediately.'

'It appears they did, sir, but they were told we were too busy and they should look into it themselves.' Hoth was clearly unhappy about this breakdown of the system, and Kalisz hurried on. 'I believe you were on leave, and it's true we were short-staffed at the time. In the light of what's happened since, sir, it might be an idea to go out there and talk to her parents.'

'All right.' Hoth tapped the pencil on the desk. 'In the circumstances it may be worth a try. But we can't have you running about the city on your own playing detective.' He smiled at Kalisz's visible disappointment. 'Müller will accompany you.'

'Yes, sir.' Kalisz hesitated at the door. 'Do you know when the... executions... will begin?'

'I'm afraid the first batch were due to be carried out this morning.'

–

Müller drove with the window of the Mercedes wound down, but Kalisz still choked on the fierce cloud of tobacco smoke from the smelly meerschaum clamped between the Kripo man's teeth. Hoth had promised to call the SD and request that August Klimecki be placed at the bottom of the execution list. If Streckenbach kept his word, ten Polish prisoners would still die every day, but Kalisz had nineteen days to save Maria's father.

He had an odd feeling of déjà vu as they drove along Chłodna. Müller was following the exact route Günther Gruhl had taken on the night he'd died. Kalisz studied the German from the corner of his eye, felt hat low on his head and the narrow eyes peering through the thick lenses of his spectacles. He'd heard about the 'confession' the investigator had beaten out of a chemist who'd admitted to having Traudl Kleist in his shop. The man had only truly broken when Müller stripped his wife naked in front of him and threatened to sodomise her with the butt of the whip he was using on her husband. The detective sensed him staring and glanced across.

'If this is a waste of time...' Müller muttered.

'We won't know until we get there.'

'We should be concentrating on the neighbours,' the Nazi grumbled. 'My detective's nose tells me there's a stinking Pole at the bottom of this particular sewage pit.'

'I hear your detective's nose didn't do so well a couple of days ago.' Kalisz didn't bother to conceal his scorn. 'Hoth wasn't too impressed.'

Müller shot him a look of hatred. 'Don't push your luck, Polack. Your time is coming, Kalisz. We'll deal with the Jew boys first, then it will be the turn of you Poles. Your shithole of a city will be wiped off the map and replaced by a new Warsaw – a German Warsaw, populated by good German stock.' A sneer wreathed his pasty features. 'Believe me, I've seen the plans, and the only Poles they include are slave workers to clean the latrines. So it's a bullet for you, and I'll be at the head of the queue to put you away.'

Kalisz kept his eyes on the road ahead, annoyed at himself for reacting to Müller. He wondered if the Nazi's boasts about the German plans for Warsaw were true, or just another provocation. Either way, another morsel for Kazimierz.

Wola had been a farming community before distilleries, breweries and wind-driven flour mills flourished on the produce from the fertile black earth. When the suburb became a stop on the Warsaw–Vienna railway line, the old industries were followed by steelworks, tanning yards and textile mills. Heavy industries required big workforces and workers needed housing. The answer had been tenements, cheap and quick to build, where families lived packed together in tiny rooms, separated by paper-thin walls. Close proximity and hard, stubborn men – more often than not fuelled by vodka – bred social problems. For as long as Kalisz could remember, Wola had been a thorn in the flesh of the state police.

The tenement where two uniformed Polish policemen waited for Kalisz and Müller was typical of the area. Five storeys high and built of soot-stained brick, peeling paint and cracked and broken windows gave it an air of decay and decline. One of the cops handed Müller a file, but the Nazi thrust it at Kalisz without looking at it.

'This is *your* waste of time.'

Kalisz glanced at the contents. He would read it properly later, but he flicked through to the post mortem report and felt a buzz of anticipation. The injuries suffered by fourteen-year-old Krystyna Lenski were remarkably similar to those sustained by Traudl Kleist. There was no mention of any unusual use of the missing organs, but otherwise the similarities were too obvious to be ignored.

'Where was the body found?' He addressed the question to the senior of the two men, who'd introduced himself as Sergeant Piskorski.

'On a half-cleared bomb site not far from here.' He gestured with his thumb. 'Over that way.'

'We'll take a look at it later,' Kalisz told him. 'But first I'll speak to the parents.' He saw the look that passed between the two men. 'Should we expect trouble?'

'Probably best if you find out for yourself, sir.' Piskorski's tone put a dent in Kalisz's optimism.

The sergeant led the way up a narrow, ill-lit stairway to the third floor and along a corridor until he reached a door with a faded number painted on the scarred wood.

Beaten, was the word Kalisz would use to describe the man who answered Piskorski's knock. Tall and thin, with a drooping moustache, he might have been forty but had the washed-out, rheumy eyes of a man twenty years older. He wore a stained vest that displayed pale shoulders and skinny liver-spotted arms, and his trousers were held up by a piece of rope. His eyes darted from Piskorski to the two men at his back, and Kalisz saw them dilate with fear when he recognised Müller for what he was. 'These gentlemen are here to talk to you about your daughter, Lenski,' the sergeant said. 'It would be polite to let them in.'

Lenski's prominent Adam's apple jerked as he swallowed nervously. 'I've got nothing to say about that, sir. What's done is done.'

Müller shifted impatiently and Piskorski put a hand on Lenski's chest and pushed him inside. 'Like I say, it would be polite.' He stepped aside and ushered Kalisz and the German forward. 'I'll stay out here, sirs, if you don't mind. You'll see why.'

'Why' was immediately apparent when they were inside the room, which was probably about three metres by five. It was already occupied by Lenski's patently terrified wife, two boys and a girl aged between four and ten, a baby in a pram, and an aged relative of indefinite sex who lay snoring beneath the blankets of a bed at the far end of the room. The smell of cooking vegetables competed with the combined scents of unwashed humanity, fear and – unless Kalisz's nose lied – a nappy that needed changing. Religious icons covered the walls: pictures of long-dead saints and popes and Bible scenes. Kalisz's eye was drawn to a wooden chest, where a photograph of a young girl with large solemn eyes and a pert upturned nose, her features framed by blonde curls, was draped in black crêpe paper.

'Please do not be frightened.' Kalisz addressed his words to the woman. 'All we ask is a few moments of your time to talk about Krystyna. My colleague is here only to observe. He speaks no Polish. Do you understand what I'm saying?' Mrs Lenski glanced at Müller and back to Kalisz. She nodded.

'Good. Anything you tell me will be helpful in finding her killer.'

Kalisz heard the scratch of a match, and the reek of Müller's meerschaum joined the unsavoury olfactory blend. Kalisz turned to glare at the German, but Müller was unrepentant. 'My Pöschl is easier on the nose than your Polish stink.'

The three older children stared at the exotic pipe with rapt fascination until Mrs Lenski shooed them through a door on the opposite side of the room and closed it behind them. She went to stand by the pram with her husband, and indicated that Kalisz and Müller should take the chairs.

Müller snorted.

'We will stand, if you don't mind,' Kalisz said. 'May I ask what age your daughter was?'

It was a simple question, designed to ease the tension, and Kalisz already knew the answer, but Mrs Lenski looked up at her husband with fear in her eyes. Lenski just stared at Kalisz, his hands clutched together to stop them shaking.

Kalisz tried again. 'What kind of girl was she? Did she have many friends?'

Now they both stared at him, like rabbits quivering under the gaze of a stoat.

'Are they fucking dumb?' Müller growled.

'Please, you must help me. Did she go out with friends on the day she died, or was she alone?'

'We don't know.' It was the woman who spoke, but her husband's hand shot out to grab her wrist and she bit her lip.

More questions, and more answers that weren't answers. Kalisz struggled to conceal his frustration from Müller.

'Please, sir,' the woman whispered. 'You are not one of them. You seem a good man. You must understand that we have been told… ordered… not to co-operate with the authorities. Things would be very difficult for us.'

'What did she say?' Müller demanded.

'They don't know anything that would help us.'

'Then let's get out of this cesspit.'

218

The murder scene had been a metal works until the night the Heinkels came, and the Wehrmacht had finished the job when they'd tried to blast their way through Wola in the early days of October. Now it was just a patchwork of scarred concrete and flattened earth with orderly rubble piles dotted around. Kalisz felt a chill run through him when he saw it. Krystyna Lenski had come here – or had been brought here – and she'd died here. Sergeant Piskorski showed Kalisz where Krystyna's body had lain.

'One thing you should know, sir,' he said quietly to Kalisz, 'is that Krystyna hadn't made herself too popular lately. She spoke a bit of German and would hang around the temporary barracks up by the hospital, practising it on the soldiers. One of her friends heard her saying she admired the bas— Them.'

Kalisz quietly thanked him and opened the file to study the photographs of the body in situ and on the slab in the mortuary. He paid particular attention to the wounds in the girl's throat and torso.

'I just about threw up when I saw it,' the policeman admitted. 'Poor kid. Nobody deserves that.'

'No sign of blood anywhere near the body?'

'No,' Piskorski said. 'We reckon she was killed elsewhere and then brought here and laid out as you see her in the photos.'

'Her clothes?'

'Nowhere to be found.'

'What about her… organs?'

'You saw the pictures.' Piskorski turned a little paler at the memory. 'He'd taken everything.'

'No, I mean did you find any of them.'

The sergeant shrugged. 'By the time we got here, the dogs—'

'Hey, Kalisz, let me have a look at that file.'

Kalisz strode over to where Müller had crouched over a patch of dusty earth and handed over the folder.

'What is it, sir?'

The Nazi detective pulled a sheet from the file. 'Tyre tracks and what might be bloodstains, but the murder scene diagram doesn't show either.'

Kalisz called Piskorski across. 'We checked every inch of this place,' the sergeant insisted. 'They weren't here when we found Krystyna's body. Something must have happened since.'

'He says they must have missed it,' Kalisz lied. 'He apologises for their negligence.'

'Useless fucking Poles.' Müller glared at the sergeant. 'The tracks might have given us something to follow up, but they're too disturbed now.'

'That's too bad.' Kalisz tried to slow his racing heart. Too bad they'd never be matched to the little Polski Fiat signed out by the late and unlamented Investigator Günther Gruhl on the night he died. Kalisz pretended to study the pattern of blood spots from when he'd shattered Gruhl's head with the knuckleduster. 'What do you think?'

Müller straightened and rubbed his back. 'I think there's enough evidence to link the case to Traudl Kleist,' he said reluctantly. 'But I'm not sure it helps us. And you?'

'I think if he's killed twice, he'll kill again.'

CHAPTER 27

The following Saturday, Kalisz took the tram from Nowy Świat to Zielna. The Nazis had restored the service a few weeks earlier, although the newest cars were kept for the German-only routes. None of the passengers wore the distinctive blue stars because Jews were forbidden from setting foot on any Warsaw tram. He disembarked when they reached Świętokrzyska and took the familiar route up Bagno, through Plac Grzybowski and along Rynkowa. When he reached Iron-Gate Square he did a circuit, noting with relief that there was no visible German presence this time. As he passed the ruins of the destroyed shopping hall his eyes sought out possible entry points. It took him ten or fifteen minutes before he made his decision.

A surviving metal arch seemed to offer the best opportunity. Beyond it lay a sea of twisted metal and brick, but he'd dressed for the occasion in stout boots, old trousers of thick mole-skin and, despite the warm sunshine, a sturdy jacket that had once belonged to a Vistula bargeman. He crossed the road and crunched his way beneath the arch as if he had every right to be there, then stopped for a moment to study his surround-ings. This was the last place Hannah Goldberg had been seen; logically, it was where he should start looking for her.

He picked his way through the rubble, avoiding severed wires and fractured gas pipes, and running his mind through what Feinbaum and Mrs Goldberg had told him. The remains of the shops would have been stripped by the scavengers who had frightened Hannah's friends, but that wouldn't stop people left destitute from searching for anything useful. If the body had been above ground, it would have been found. No point in searching here. He had to find his way into the cellars.

Kalisz tried to visualise the former layout of the hall. He guessed there'd be two or three main cellars in the foundations, but they'd also accommodate secure storage for each of the twenty or thirty individual shops in the arcade. Most, if not all, of those shops would have had their own entrance. In places the mass of rubble and girders must be nearly three metres deep, but Hannah had discovered a way in. If she could do it, so could he. He found a narrow path through the debris and followed it, his eyes searching the ground for the clues he sought. In places the floor creaked beneath his feet, and he trod warily. Blast and fire had weakened the entire structure. Put one foot wrong and the floor would give way and plunge him three or four metres into whatever lay below. A piece of corrugated iron drew his attention, perhaps torn from a roof. He lifted it, but the only thing below was scorched parquet flooring.

He was close to giving up when he glanced to his left and saw a piece of wooden board weighed down by large stones. A surge of anticipation ran through him, prompted by the suspiciously regular positioning of the pieces of rubble. He removed them one by one and carefully lifted the board: a sign for a jeweller's shop. Below it, set into the floor, was a wooden panel a metre and a half square with a recessed brass ring close to one edge. Kalisz reached into the deep pocket of the bargeman's jacket and withdrew a torch. He hooked the fingers of his other hand through the brass ring and raised the trapdoor to reveal a black void. A throat-clogging stench rose from the opening that made him recoil in disgust. A smell instantly recognisable from the battlefield. Something had died down there, but what – or who? He clicked the torch button and its beam illuminated a set of steep wooden stairs.

With a last sweep of the area to ensure he was alone, he slipped down the stairway and closed the hatch behind him. When he reached the bottom he stood for a few moments, scanning his surroundings with the light. His first glance confirmed that the search was going to be much more difficult than he'd imagined. He'd expected a big open space, or perhaps two or three large rooms. Instead, he seemed to be at the centre of a rabbit warren of corridors and rooms, walled with bare wooden planks or the reused sides of packing cases, that had developed and mutated over the hundred years since the building opened. Behind him, the cellar had been obliterated when the building collapsed, and a wall of rubble filled the room from one side to the other. He looked closer and noticed a small gap in the corner where a man might squeeze through. He knew he couldn't discount the area, no matter how dangerous it looked. Each room must have had a locked door, because the ones he could see had all been ripped from their hinges. Logic told him he had nothing to fear down here, except the dangerous environment, but sometimes logic wasn't enough to keep your demons at bay.

Three possible corridors to choose from. Right, left or centre? He chose left.

He searched systematically, checking every storeroom. Most had been stripped bare, but a few held objects that had been too heavy to steal, and he was forced to look inside toppled filing cabinets and metal workbenches, any of which might hide a small body. Dust filtered from the roof, creating little pinpricks of light in the beam of the torch. At one point he froze at the sound of muffled footsteps overhead, but they quickly faded. Room after room and always nothing.

Kalisz's fingers had just closed on the handle of a half-open door when some buried sense told him a dynamic in his underground world had altered. Not a noise as such, but the faint whisper of disturbed air on the back of his neck and a change in the pattern of the dust motes in the torchlight. He clicked off the beam and froze, listening intently in the stifling darkness.

He heard nothing at first, and as the minutes passed he wondered if he'd imagined it. Then he registered the faintest hint of a soft shuffling in the distance. His hand gripped the torch like a club and he backed along the wall until he could sidle into the room he'd been about to search. He closed his eyes and fought for calm. Someone had followed him, but who? Müller? Blum? Someone from the Underground? When he opened his eyes again, something had changed. He didn't realise what it was at first, but gradually he became aware of a minute alteration in the darkness. A softening that lasted a second, and came and went at intervals of about a minute. The shuffling increased in volume until it was transformed into wary, suspicious footsteps.

As they approached, Kalisz made his decision. He was trapped, but that didn't make him helpless. He'd allow whoever was hunting him to pass the door. If there was only one pursuer, he should be able to time it so he'd be able to brain him with the torch before he could react. He'd try not to do too much damage to man or torch, but knocking people out wasn't an exact science. Of course, that was the optimistic scenario. More likely, he'd stumble over something in the dark and the bastard would shoot him.

He waited.

Closer and closer still. A hesitation. A torch flicked on, then off again. He tensed, ready to step out into the corridor. *One, two...*

Without warning, light seared his eyeballs and filled his brain, blinding and stunning him in the same instant. He stepped forward, flailing wildly with the torch.

'Dada!'

'Stefan? How...?'

Suddenly his son let out a howl of terror.

'Stefan, what is it? Please, it's all right.'

Something soft hammered into his chest and the cry was muffled by the folds of his coat. Kalisz could only hang on blindly to the boy and pray that whatever had terrified him wasn't physical, because he was as helpless as a mole who'd emerged into a convention of foxes.

Gradually Stefan's wails subsided and Kalisz sensed his sight returning. The red flare that scored his eyeballs faded to black. Stefan had dropped his torch and they were still in total darkness. Kalisz murmured words of reassurance to his son and switched on his own light.

'What frightened you, Stefan.'

'There, Dada.' Stefan pointed a shaking finger at the corner of the room.

'Close your eyes, son.'

He shone the torch at the area Stefan had indicated and was met by a scene that reminded him of a painting of the Spanish Inquisition.

A tall man with a long beard and thick unkempt hair hung by the arms from a pipe running along the wall. His coat and shirt had been torn open to bare his chest. Even though the skin was darkened by the onset of decomposition, Kalisz could see that someone had gone to work on him with pliers and a soldering iron. But that wasn't what had killed him. When they'd tired of their work, his torturers had rammed a dead rat down his throat, so the rear end and worm-like tail protruded from his gaping mouth. Kalisz had to stifle the urge to vomit.

'Wait for me outside, Stefan.'

When he was alone, he approached the dead man, trying not to see the expression of wide-eyed horror. On closer inspection, he found extensive bruising to the man's face and someone had broken three of his fingers. Kalisz could picture the scene: Salomon knocked about by his captors; *a little gentle pressure, snap, snap, snap. See how we can hurt you? Make it easy on yourself and confess*. But of course Salomon couldn't confess, because Salomon hadn't killed Hannah Goldberg. So out had come the instruments of true pain, the way they always had over the centuries for unlucky people like Salomon. Did he give a false confession to save himself more agony? Or had Isaac Goldberg stuffed the flea-bitten corpse of the rat into Salomon's mouth in frustration at being denied?

But why here? Goldberg could have taken his revenge on Salomon in any of a dozen apartments or warehouses in Muranów. Instead, he'd chosen this awkward and potentially dangerous location. To Kalisz, that meant only one thing: Hannah *had* been killed here. He doubted very much whether her body still remained, but sometimes the scene could provide an investigator with as much information as the corpse. He must continue the search.

Should he send Stefan back? After the horror of seeing Salomon, the boy would be terrified to walk through the maze of corridors alone. No time to escort him to the entrance, so he'd have to come along. Fortunately, Stefan appeared to have recovered swiftly from his shock. He was more curious than frightened as they set off in the light provided by Kalisz's torch.

'Who was he, Dada?'

'Just a poor old man in the wrong place at the wrong time.'

'Will you catch the people who killed him?'

'How did you follow me here?' Kalisz steered the conversation in a safer direction.

'I rode the tit,' Stefan said proudly. Despite their predicament, Kalisz smiled. 'Riding the tit' – jumping on the back of a moving tram – was a rite of passage for Warsaw's youth. 'And at the scouts they teach us how to follow people without being seen.' The Germans had ordered the ZHP, the Polish scouting association, to disband soon after the invasion, but Stefan still attended weekly meetings under the guise of a prayer group. Kalisz wondered moodily what else they were teaching boys at the scouts these days. Maybe it was better not to know. 'I've been worried about you,' the boy continued. 'You've been acting strangely lately. Mama's worried, too, I can tell. I thought I'd follow you so I could tell her everything is all right.'

'You're a good boy.' Kalisz ruffled his son's hair. 'All you had to do was ask. But I meant, how did you follow me through this rabbit warren?'

Stefan switched on his torch, which he'd recovered while Kalisz inspected Salomon's corpse. 'See.' He half-turned and swept the ground behind them. Two pairs of fresh footprints, one large and one small, clearly visible in the dust. There were older ones, too, but they'd been blurred by the dust that fell like fine snow from the floorboards above and lacked the sharp-edged clarity of the more recent tracks. 'It was easy. All I had to do was switch on the torch every minute or so to make sure I was going the right way.'

'But it was dark.'

'I'm not afraid of the dark, Dada. I'm not afraid of anything.'

'Well, maybe you should be.'

They continued, searching each room in turn, until Kalisz guessed they were at the far northern end of the Wielopole complex. He was about ready to give up and resume the search another day.

'Dada?'

Kalisz went to where his son was shining his torch through the door of what looked like a self-contained cellar. 'Stay here.'

Hannah Goldberg had died hard. No drug-smoothed passing for the Jewish girl from Muranów. The blood spattered in great arcs across the walls told him she'd fought and struggled even as she knew she was dying. Someone had brought her here, coerced her in some way. Perhaps flattered her or made her an offer she'd found too good to refuse. Hannah had been brave and confident, her mother said; perhaps she believed she could accept the offer, but not give anything in return? But she'd been wrong. No amount of courage or cunning would help her escape once her killer had her trapped here. No amount of screaming would have brought help. The body was long gone, so there was no way of knowing what horrors had been perpetrated upon it before it had been moved. Though, as he swept the torch over the dirt floor, he saw they'd left at least one clue. About ten paces from the stained walls a patch of earth appeared subtly different from the rest. The evidence was in the scale, remarkably similar to the frame that had contained the 'picture' associated with Traudl Kleist's body. This area had been wiped clean, with only a fine covering of dust in contrast to the undisturbed parts of the floor, which were thick with it.

Kalisz imagined someone on their knees frantically scouring the ground until they'd collected every last scrap of flesh that had been removed from the body. Why not the blood-stained walls, too? Because what he'd found on that patch of floor had been an obscenity. A desecration that must be wiped out to the last trace if Hannah was ever to have peace.

He stood there for a long time, until Stefan said quietly, 'I think we should go, Dada.'

Kalisz nodded. 'I think so, too.'

But he knew this was not the end of this search. If Hannah was ever to have peace, her murderer must be brought to justice. The only way to do that was to find out exactly what had happened here. And that meant he must confront the merciless killer who'd tortured Salomon the rat-catcher to death.

CHAPTER 28

When Kalisz left home the next day for his meeting with Kazimierz he sensed the mood on the streets of Warsaw was becoming increasingly sullen and tense. By mid-June of 1940 it had dawned on people that this was as good as it got unless somebody did something about it. They didn't smile much, because nobody had anything to smile about. Any open acts of resistance were sporadic and small-scale, and always met with brutal retaliation.

We'll give one of your patrols a fright.

All right, *we'll* shoot ten hostages.

We'll empty an MP38 into a *Nur für Deutsche* cafe.

We'll hang twenty academics from the long balcony on Marszałkowska Street, see how you like that.

The real resistance existed inside people's heads, and the Nazis seemed to sense that because they didn't need an excuse to lash out with boot or fists.

'Sometimes I think we should get it over with and kill as many of the bastards as we can before they slaughter us,' Kalisz said. 'They're going to do it anyway.'

'We have to be patient and build our strength.' Lately, Kazimierz had gravitated erratically between manic enthusiasm and near exhaustion. Kalisz had never seen him look so tired. The flesh seemed to have fallen away from his bones, and the eyes behind the thick glasses had the leaden sheen of buried musket balls. 'The Nazis will overstretch themselves, and that is when we must be ready to strike.'

'By then we'll probably all be dead.'

To Kalisz's surprise, Kazimierz nodded. 'You must not think I will always be here, Jan.'

'Why do you say that?' Kalisz wished he hadn't raised the subject. It was early evening, and they were sitting on a bench by the murky Vistula, looking out to where the east wind created battalions of white-capped wavelets on the river.

Kazimierz shrugged. 'You get a feeling for these things, and you know better than I how the Nazis work. They're methodical and relentless.' He hesitated. 'We've lost a lot of people lately. Good people. A man appears at this checkpoint at this date, and that one at another. His appearance is cross-referenced to information that so-and-so was in the area at the time, or whispers of a meeting that reach the Gestapo from one of their informers. His name goes on a list, and the next time he's stopped they take him in for questioning… just in case.' Something in Kazimierz's manner told Kalisz his friend was talking from experience, and the experience had frightened him. 'Maybe his story stands up, maybe it doesn't. He won't know, because it's possible they'll play him on a long line, just in case. His every move is followed and reported by a team of Gestapo agents.' Kalisz glanced over his shoulder and Kazimierz produced a grunt of bitter laughter. 'I don't *think* it's happened yet, but I can feel them closing in. I sleep with a gun under my pillow and I never go anywhere without a cyanide capsule. I wish you'd reconsider, Jan.'

They watched a German patrol boat forge its way upriver with the choppy waters forming a white *V* beneath the bow. Bored sailors manned twin machine guns in the stern, and did whatever it is sailors do to pass the time on little boats. When it was gone, Kalisz returned to the point of the meeting.

'You haven't told me whether you'll try to get him out. I promised Maria I'd do everything in my power to keep August alive, and I meant it.'

'That's because I don't know,' Kazimierz said testily. 'It's been done, I can tell you that. We have people on the inside at Pawiak. The question that will be asked is whether August Klimecki is worth the risk, and even if that's the case, is there a greater benefit to be gained in freeing X or Y. There'll be no mass breakout – that's certain. The Nazis would tear Warsaw apart, and the organisation we've been patiently building with it. You can't take responsibility for everyone, Jan. All right, they're being shot to encourage the killer to give himself up, but we both know they'd probably be dying in any case. We managed to copy that Aktion AB document you took from Gruhl's car before he had his *accident*. Thirty thousand Polish intellectuals, politicians, aristocrats and cultural figures are to be eliminated. No trial, no hearing, no appeal. If you're on the list, you'll be arrested and shot. We're trying to save as many as we can, but hundreds of men and women are trucked out to Palmiry every day and executed.'

'Then why aren't we doing something about it?' Kalisz snapped.

'Because I don't make the decisions, and because we must have patience. What I'm saying is that ten lives a day doesn't compare with murder on the scale of Aktion AB. You're doing your job, trying to catch the killer. For the moment, be satisfied with that.' Another momentary hesitation. 'We hear that France will sue for peace in the next few days. Our troops and pilots are already being evacuated to England.'

'What?' Kalisz couldn't believe what he was hearing.

'I'm saying it's over for France, for now.'

'Mother of Christ,' Kalisz exploded. 'What's wrong with them? The Nazis have barely threatened Paris.'

'Their government is rotten to its festering core.' Kazimierz voiced the undeniable truth. Nothing new there, not for a long time. 'We thought the generals would fight, but the army has lost the will. You could say they never had it in the first place. They put their faith in the Maginot Line. When it was shown to be an illusion, the *poilus* decided everything else must be, too. Maybe they're not far wrong.'

Kalisz felt all the energy drain from him. 'So it's truly over.'

'The British will fight on, with Polish help. Churchill, at least, won't give in.'

'Hitler may not give him any choice.'

'Oh, we hope that's the case.' Kazimierz tried without success to inject some genuine confidence into his tone. 'Forty kilometres of English Channel may not seem much, but it will drown an awful lot of men and their ships. To make it work, Hitler must destroy the RAF. His bombers possess the range, but his Bf 109s have only ten minutes' endurance over British soil. We don't think they can do it.'

'We didn't think they could defeat Poland,' Kalisz pointed out bitterly.

'Then we must pray.' Kazimierz sighed. 'Have you heard from your brother?'

'The old man had a postcard from Henryk in March, saying he was in a camp near Kozelsk and he'd appreciate some warm clothing if we could put together a parcel. Since then, nothing.'

'It's the same for everyone.' Kazimierz's head dropped and Kalisz wondered if he, too, had a relative imprisoned by the Soviets. 'We're worried they've been taken east.'

'Siberia?' Kalisz winced. 'Poor Henryk.'

'Poor all of them.' From somewhere the other man seemed to find a fresh energy – a soldier returned to his duty. 'If there's anything we can do to help you find this killer, just let me know.'

Kalisz nodded distractedly. 'I think Hoth is genuinely convinced a Pole is responsible. He can't believe one of her own countrymen would do that to Traudl Kleist. I'm not so sure. The killings didn't start until the Nazis took over Warsaw. I have a feeling the girl out in Wawer was intended to be his first victim, but he made a mess of it. Part of a psychopath's persona is a tendency to act on impulse and a need for immediate gratification, which fits the description of the attack perfectly. I went out there to speak to her on Sunday, but Baruch, the boy we rescued from the execution, says she left the day after because she was certain they'd kill her. She said she was coming to Warsaw to join the Resistance. Her name is Janina Berman.'

'If she's with us, I will find her,' Kazimierz promised.

'And, if it's possible, to get a list of places in Wola with a link to the Nazis?'

'That might be a long list.'

'Barracks. Police posts. Supply bases. Factories in the process of being taken over. Krystyna Lenski was known to fraternise with German soldiers. I know it's a lot to ask, but it might help.'

'I'll do my best,' Kazimierz said. 'And while I remember, there's something that might help you with that SS corporal, Blum.'

–

When Kalisz reached home, two men in workers' overalls were loading furniture into a horse-drawn wagon, and as he climbed the stairs he met the Feinbaum twins edging down with brown paper parcels. They greeted him politely enough, but there was something about their look that told him they understood what was happening to them. At the top, Feinbaum struggled out of his doorway with a stack of dining room chairs teetering in his arms.

'Perhaps I can help you, Mr Feinbaum?'

Feinbaum craned his neck to look behind Kalisz, as if he expected to find the Gestapo accompanying him. 'No thank you, sir,' he said. 'My wife's brother—'

'Do I understand you're leaving? If that's the case, we'll be very sorry. You and Mrs Feinbaum have been good neighbours to us.'

Feinbaum avoided his eyes, but a twitch showed in the muscle of his cheek.

'Yes, sir,' he snapped in an unlikely show of temper. 'But now you will have good Polish neighbours, not we filthy Jews.'

'Mr Feinbaum, I can understand you are angry—'

'Angry, sir?' The other man's voice shook and he laid down the chairs. 'Yes, I am angry. The Germans have taken everything from us. I am not allowed to run my business. I am not allowed to have money. I must wear a brand that proclaims me a non-citizen of my country and makes me feel like an animal marked for slaughter. They say my family carries Jewish diseases, so to save the Poles we must move to a new Jewish district. Four people living in a single room. Jewish district, sir? Let us call it what it is – a ghetto.'

Kalisz remembered the words of Mandelbaum, the grain merchant: *First they humiliate you, then they grind you down, then they kill you.* 'I can only say how sorry I am, sir, and repeat my offer – any help we can provide.'

Feinbaum couldn't help glancing at the door of Kalisz's apartment. The Pole read something significant in the look, but this wasn't the time to discuss it. 'I am sorry,' the Jew said, regathering his chairs. 'None of this is your fault, but Marta – my wife – is taking it very badly. I must hurry.'

'Please wait a second, Mr Feinbaum. I need your help. On Christmas Eve you wanted me to accompany you to Mrs Goldberg's home on Elektoralna. Can you tell me the number of the house?'

'Six months?' Feinbaum gaped. 'Six months after that poor girl was killed you finally take an interest.'

'Please, sir.' Kalisz felt his face redden. 'I will beg if I must. It could save the life of another girl like Hannah Goldberg.'

The disbelief faded from Feinbaum's half-starved features, to be replaced by an almost quizzical look. 'You don't know, do you?'

'Know what, sir?'

'If you don't know, I cannot be the one to tell you. We are about to become Isaac Goldberg's neighbours. If he knew I had co-operated with you it would go badly for us.'

'Goldberg will never know. I give you my word.'

Feinbaum sighed, a man resigned to another inevitable defeat in a life of nothing else. 'Very well, Mr Kalisz, I'll give you the address. You people –' the way he said it made Kalisz feel like the lowest form of vermin – 'would find out one way or the other. The Goldbergs' home is Elektoralna 10, third floor, apartment six.'

Feinbaum picked up his chairs and struggled down the stairs without looking back. His brother-in-law appeared with an empty packing case. On the way past he shot Kalisz a look of naked hatred.

Kalisz opened the door to find Maria waiting for him in the hall. He'd half-expected it.

'Were you with Stefan yesterday?' She saw the flash of anger in his eyes and raced on before he could interrupt. 'He didn't

236

want to tell me, but I insisted. He said he was helping you. I've never seen him so quiet and reserved.'

'He followed me. By the time I found out, it was too late. We searched some cellars. It was to do with the Traudl Kleist case, Maria.'

'Does Stefan know about my father?' Kalisz could almost feel her heart pounding at the prospect.

'Not unless you've told him.'

'So what happened?'

'Nothing.'

'Nothing? You expect me to believe that?'

'I was hoping you'd *accept* it, Maria.'

'Is this what we've become? Two people without the mutual respect to be honest with each other? For God's sake, Jan, what kind of marriage is that? Is it not enough that you collaborate with the Germans. That you leave me in a cold bed wondering if you're dead or alive. What else are you deceiving me about?'

Kalisz grabbed his wife by the wrists. 'Keep your voice down,' he hissed, 'or Stefan will hear.'

'Stefan is with his friends.' She shrugged her arms free and dashed a hand across her face.

'You mean at a scout meeting?'

'Yes, that's what I mean. You're not blind, you've known all along.'

'We should stop him.' Kalisz remembered the boys with the paint. 'If he gets into trouble, the Germans will—'

'And keep him in his room like a prisoner? The scouts and his lessons are all he has. His only link with what was once normal.'

'It's dangerous, Maria.'

'I know, Jan.' Without warning, she slumped forward into his arms and he had to bear her weight. It came as a surprise. She was almost feather-light. He hadn't realised how much weight she'd lost. 'Stefan, Tad, my father and you. I fear for you all. Every time you or Stefan go out of the door I think you might not come back. Every day I fear I'll see my father's name on one of the posters.' Her head shook against his chest. 'So many people. So many families in mourning. And Tad, too brave for his own good, fighting the Germans in France.'

Hearing Tadeusz's name from her lips felt like a knife in Kalisz's chest. He struggled to keep his voice steady. 'If I solve this case they'll free August, Maria. I have a new lead. Stefan helped. I'll follow it up tomorrow.'

'And Tad will be safe?'

'Yes.' He was glad she couldn't see his face. 'Tad will be safe.'

CHAPTER 29

Ten more Kleist hostages had been butchered that morning in the Palmiry Forest. That made forty so far. Kalisz felt crushed by the weight of expectation he'd placed on himself. Who was he to think he could play God and save these doomed men and women? It was just the war.

But he knew it wasn't really just the war. This was his *personal* war. The one he'd signed up to that night a lifetime ago, with Kazimierz in the hospital room on Czerwonego Krzyża. He tried to push the images of the firing squad to the back of his mind, and concentrated on the dilemma he'd struggled with since the previous night.

'Your papers.'

Mother of Christ, he'd almost sleepwalked through a checkpoint. Of all the ways to get himself killed, that would be the stupidest. He handed over his identity card and the *Arbeitskarte* identifying him as a Kripo employee. Normally, this would be enough to see him passed through by the guard, but this one's nose twitched as if Kalisz had placed something rotten beneath it. A square jaw and suspicious eyes. Still a teenager, probably, but they were often the worst – easily bored, and the true products of Hitler's system thanks to years in the *Hitlerjugend*. Kalisz avoided eye contact and braced himself for whatever humiliation was about to come.

'Raise your arms.'

Kalisz did as he was ordered, and the young man ran big worker's hands roughly over his body and checked the contents of his pockets. The usual sweat, wondering whether he was carrying anything illicit. Of course he was; everything was illicit these days. It was just a question of whether his tormentor wanted to make an issue of it. Kalisz had a feeling this one might.

'Kalisz.'

'Excuse me, sir.' Kalisz indicated with his head to where Doctor Mengele was tapping impatiently on the sill of his car window. 'The lieutenant...'

Pursed lips and an expression of suppressed fury. Clearly this one had had something in mind for Kalisz. But the rank insignia on Mengele's black collar patch convinced him it wasn't worth the trouble. He nodded for Kalisz to lower his arms, gave him a look that promised they'd be seeing each other again, and handed back his papers.

As Kalisz walked shakily across the street to the car he could feel every eye on his back. People who knew what he did for a living wouldn't quite spit at him in the street – they wouldn't dare. They just let him know that retribution was coming and that they hoped it was sooner rather than later. Maybe some people got used to that kind of thing, but not Kalisz. He put up with it, but it still hurt.

'Get in,' Mengele ordered. The doctor occupied one of the rear seats while an SS trooper drove and a sergeant sat in the front passenger seat with a machine pistol on his lap. 'I have some information for you.'

Kalisz levered himself into the back beside the SS officer.

'Drive, but take your time,' Mengele instructed the trooper. He pulled a sheaf of paper from his briefcase and turned to Kalisz. 'I can't let you view this document for security reasons, but I can give you an overview of the contents. If you have any questions, keep them till I'm finished. Yes?'

Kalisz nodded.

'The powder the killer employed to deter dogs from feasting on his unusual montage is a chemical called Zyklon B. It is used as a pesticide – principally a delousing agent – on ships, trains and the like, and one of its main components is hydrogen cyanide in a stabilised form. As I understand it, when the powder reaches a certain temperature it releases a gas that kills the lice and other pests, and then quickly disperses. Zyklon B is not widely available in Poland.' He saw Kalisz's interest and smiled. 'It is manufactured by a German firm, Degesch, under licence from IG Farben. Questions?'

Kalisz considered for a moment. The use of such a powerful and deadly poison had been puzzling him since Mengele mentioned it at Ziegler's party. He had no real idea of this Zyklon B's significance to the investigation, but it might be important. 'Do we have a list of Polish distributors?'

'No, but I'm sure it can be arranged.'

Kalisz hesitated. 'I may also have some new information for you, Doctor.'

He told Mengele about the Krystyna Lenski murder, and Mengele pursed his lips in annoyance.

'Idiots. Why wasn't I informed?'

'There is something else, Herr Doctor, but I'm not sure how to approach it.'

Mengele stared at him with those unreadable brown eyes. 'It is traditional to start at the beginning, Kalisz. What is it?'

'I believe there is a possible third victim.' Mengele listened without comment as Kalisz related the Christmas Eve visit from Hannah Goldberg's mother.

'No one is going to blame you for not following up on the disappearance of a Jewess, Kalisz,' Mengele assured him. 'But I'm intrigued. What makes you think this may be linked to the other killings?'

'I visited the place she was last seen, a bombed-out Jewish market in Iron-Gate Square. Below the ruins is a maze of cellars.' Salomon the rat-catcher's murder only complicated matters, so he gave Mengele the short version for now. 'In one of the cellars, I found suggestions that serious violence had been done. Blood patterns on the wall and evidence, admittedly circumstantial evidence only, that something had been created on the floor nearby.'

Mengele raised an eyebrow. 'So, in short, you subverted the main investigation for what might well have been the wrong reasons.'

Kalisz nodded warily.

'You also failed to report this to your superiors. Investigator Müller will undoubtedly be aggrieved. Not to mention *Hauptsturmführer* Hoth.' The Pole felt a flare of alarm. Had he misjudged his man? 'And your conclusion is…?' A little half-smile told Kalisz that Mengele had been toying with him.

Bastard.

'That Hannah Goldberg was killed in the cellar by persons unknown. That her father searched the building and found her body. And that he probably later buried her, and whatever was found with her, in the Jewish cemetery.'

'And why are you telling me this now?'

Because if I question Isaac Goldberg alone, I'll probably end up in the same condition as Salomon, but with something else rammed down my throat. Kalisz had been formulating the idea since Mengele hailed him. If he was going to confront a man like Goldberg, it would be wise to have some insurance. Müller was out of the question, but, for a Nazi, Mengele might just be open-minded enough to take a chance on.

'Because I believe it's vital to the Traudl Kleist case that we question Isaac Goldberg. Your presence –' he glanced at the two guards – 'would add weight and authority to the occasion.'

To Kalisz's ears it sounded pompous, but Mengele laughed. 'If only the Poles had used your diplomatic skills last summer, we might have been spared this war. Where are we going?' Kalisz gave him the address and he passed it on to the driver.

'You're an odd one, Kalisz.' The Pole once more found himself in the unsettling focus of those shrewd eyes. 'A mind quick enough to discover patterns in this case that Müller would never have seen in a hundred years. Brave to the point of foolishness – wasting time on the Jewish girl might have got you killed. And yet…' Mengele took a cigarette from his silver case and tapped both ends on the casing before lighting it. He wound down the window to allow the smoke to escape. 'Your submissiveness at the checkpoint today, for instance.' He pulled a shred of tobacco from his lip with the tips of two fingers and flicked it away. 'I found it interesting in the light of what I've come to know of you. I'm talking purely in a scientific sense, of course.'

'Of course, Herr Doctor.' Kalisz tried to make his face an unreadable mask. 'You have to understand that history has educated we Poles in how to react to changing circumstances. When a soldier with a gun suggests you put your hands up, it would take a foolish man not to comply. Thank you, by the way, for intervening. I think he took a dislike to my face and had a mind to rearrange it with his rifle butt.'

'You think our soldiers brutal, Kalisz?' Kalisz could see the SS driver grinning at his discomfort in the rear-view mirror.

'You may be honest, we are all friends here. Is that not so, Dietrich?'

The grinning face immediately disappeared.

'I think all soldiers have a capacity for brutality, Herr Doctor,' Kalisz said.

'Precisely. It is a soldier's duty to be stern and unyielding. To follow orders from his superiors without question. And to be loyal to his comrades. It is my belief that this good German soldier saw the same thing in you as I have done. Some mixture of pride, courage and will that, though it does not pose an immediate threat, may be a long-term danger. When he broke your jaw, it would not have been an act of brutality. On the contrary, it would have been an act of kindness that might have saved your life in the future. Am I making sense?'

'I'll certainly bear the sentiment in mind, sir. May I say, though, that I don't believe your picture of me is accurate.'

'That is of no matter. What does matter is that you understand what is happening in Poland is for the benefit of all.' He sighed. 'I see you still don't believe me.'

'No, sir, I—'

But Mengele wasn't finished. 'Then let me put it this way. A man may seem uncaring, even callous, but if that man is your doctor, such qualities are an asset. Believe me, Kalisz, you don't want your doctor to murmur sympathetically in your ear while he makes a misdiagnosis. You don't want him to burst into tears the moment he sees your injuries. The best doctors don't see a patient as an individual. They see a body made up of many thousands of living parts, each of which depends on the function of the others for life. Your pain won't concern him, unless it has the effect of incapacitating you further. If saving your life requires the amputation of a limb, he will not hesitate. I can see that, from the point of view of a Pole, the Führer might seem callous, but that would be an entirely erroneous conclusion. Poland forced Germany into the war, and Polish intransigence prolonged it. He is committed to excising the poison from what was once Poland and creating a new, healthy entity. It may be painful in the short term, but believe me, it will be worth the suffering.'

'Yes, sir, just like my rifle butt.'

They'd been forced to take a circuitous route because the authorities had embarked on a project to block certain streets in order to contain what was officially known as the Epidemic Quarantine District. Naturally, the Jews, through the *Judenrat*, the Jewish Council, were obliged to pay for the four-metre-high walls, and Jewish labourers were carrying out the work. Kalisz saw the sign for Elektoralna with relief. 'I think we're here, sir.'

'Good.' A dry smile flickered on the SS doctor's lips. 'But I'm glad we had time for our little chat.'

The car drew in to the kerb and the driver leapt out and ran round to open the rear passenger door for Mengele. Kalisz sat for a moment, wondering just how big a mistake he'd made not facing down Isaac Goldberg alone.

Mengele stuck his head through the door. 'Come along, Kalisz, we haven't all day. By the way, Willi Ziegler kindly allowed me the use of his apartment for a few days while mine was having a burst pipe repaired. If you get the opportunity, I encourage you to have a look at his paintings.'

CHAPTER 30

'Stay with the car, Sergeant,' Mengele ordered. 'Dietrich will accompany us.'

Dietrich ran to the rear of the Mercedes and opened it to retrieve an MP38, checked the magazine, and slung it across his neck by the leather sling. He snapped his boots together. 'At your orders, sir.'

The sergeant looked up doubtfully at the building, which rose five storeys above a row of shops on the ground floor, all marked with a white star on the window. Apartments occupied the upper floors. 'Are you sure about this, sir?'

'Oh, I think we'll be safe enough.' Mengele surveyed the nearly empty street that thirty seconds earlier had been busy with shoppers and loafers. 'Kalisz, this is your territory. You take the lead.' Between two of the shops, Kalisz noticed a blue painted door with a number 10 and started towards it. 'By the way, Kalisz, I should warn you that Dietrich has a certain amount of Polish, don't you, Dietrich?'

'Enough to buy a beer or chat up a woman.' The soldier grinned.

'That's very kind of you, sir.'

'Yes, it is.' Mengele smiled. 'You see, Kalisz, we Germans do have your best interests at heart.'

Moments later they entered the kind of gloomy, ill-painted stairway that Kalisz had spent his career climbing with a mixture of apprehension, exhilaration and occasionally outright fear. They reached the third floor without encountering another soul. Kalisz heard the click as Mengele unclasped the flap of his holster, and they emerged onto a landing illuminated by a small window that looked out over the street.

'Apartment six, sir.' Dietrich pointed to a surprisingly fine oak-panelled door on the left.

'Carry on, Investigator.'

Kalisz ignored Mengele's sarcasm and rapped on the door with his knuckles. Dietrich stood to one side, but he had his finger on the trigger and Mengele's hand was inside the flap of his holster. All very calm and professional and ready to react when all hell was let loose.

They heard the sound of frantic movement from behind the door, and it must have been a minute before the handle turned and it opened. At first Kalisz couldn't see anyone behind it, but his eyes drifted downwards to where an elfin, wide-eyed face stared back up at him from waist height. 'Please tell your father we wish to speak to him,' he told the child. Without a word, the door closed. Kalisz straightened and turned to find Mengele studying him with a look of amusement.

'My friend here would have taken a different approach.' He nodded towards Dietrich. 'But it's interesting to see you at work, Kalisz.'

More muffled sounds from the apartment before the door opened again. This time it was a woman, and Kalisz recognised her from the December night when Feinbaum had knocked on his door. Her hand went to her mouth when she saw the SS uniforms and Dietrich's machine pistol. 'You have nothing to fear, Mrs Goldberg,' Kalisz reassured her quickly. 'We're here to speak to your husband about Hannah.'

Mrs Goldberg's expression didn't change, but she stepped back and let them enter a large room with a high ceiling, bay windows and five or six doors leading off it. This had clearly been a spacious apartment for a middle-class family. Every internal door was open, and from each of them four or five pairs of eyes followed the newcomers as they edged their way into the room. To Kalisz's surprise, the owner of one pair was familiar, but he gave no sign of recognition for fear of alerting Mengele.

Despite the open windows, the air was heavy with the scent of unwashed humanity, a blocked toilet and an unmistakable hint of fear. What must have been furniture from all over the house crammed much of the floor: three beds lay side by side against the far wall; a dining table with the chairs stacked on top; a sofa and two chairs almost invisible beneath heaps of washing; packing cases piled on top of one another until they threatened to topple over. Kalisz's shirt, clammy with sweat, clung to him in the stifling atmosphere.

Mrs Goldberg sidled past the Germans through the jumble of furniture to stand in the centre of the room beside her husband and three surviving children. In Kalisz's experience, gangland enforcers tended to be big men, all muscle and threat and barely suppressed savagery. Isaac Goldberg was the type of person you could lose on any Warsaw street, wiry in build and of medium height, with a long, thin nose and a few thin strands of hair scraped across his peeling, sun-reddened scalp. Nothing about him said *Jewish*, as far as Kalisz could tell, apart from the white armband with its blue star which everyone in sight wore, apart from the very youngest children.

'Mr Goldberg.' They'd met once, in Kalisz's recollection, but Goldberg showed no sign of recognition.

'What do you want?' A soft voice. Abrupt and to the point and entirely without fear. It was the eyes, Kalisz decided, that made him so formidable: hard, unforgiving and pitiless. That, and the impression of suppressed power beneath the striped shirt.

Kalisz took his time, studying the room. 'I'm curious. How many people live here?'

Goldberg shrugged. 'Thirty-five.'

'Thirty-seven,' a voice corrected him from inside one of the side rooms. 'You always forget the Greenspan boys.'

'Shut up, Sym.'

'Is there anywhere more private we can talk?'

'What do you think?' Goldberg laughed, but there was no humour in it.

'Maybe we could go out into the hall?'

The Jew looked towards the two SS men. 'You dumped these people on us. There's nothing I could say out there I can't say in front of them.'

Kalisz gave him a warning look. 'You should know the private speaks some Polish.'

'So?' Goldberg looked Dietrich up and down as if he was sizing him up for a coffin. The SS man shifted on his feet and Kalisz had a feeling he'd be gripping the machine pistol a little more tightly. 'Today. Tomorrow. Next week or next year. What difference does it make?'

'Any time you want it, Jew,' Dietrich grunted in Polish. 'Just say the word.'

'What did Dietrich say?' Mengele demanded.

'He just threatened our witness.'

'Get the fuck out of here, Dietrich,' the SS man snapped. 'I'll deal with you later.' Kalisz heard the scuffle of feet and the door opening and closing. 'Tell him I apologise.'

'The Herr *Obersturmführer* says he is sorry.'

'Does he think I care?' A genuine laugh from Goldberg. 'Some day there will be a reckoning between his kind and our kind. The Germans think they know all about blood, but there are a few things we can teach them.'

'Kalisz?'

'He thanks you, Herr Doctor.'

'Can we get on with it?' Mengele sniffed. 'I haven't got all day.'

'Yes, sir.' So far Goldberg had had it all his own way, but Kalisz decided to turn up the heat a few degrees. 'I know about Salomon the rat-catcher,' he said quietly. 'But for the moment I'm prepared to leave that to you and your conscience. All I'm interested in is finding the man who really killed Hannah.'

'Salomon?' A curtain dropped over Goldberg's eyes. 'I don't know of any Salomon.'

Mrs Goldberg had been weeping quietly since the first mention of Hannah's name. Goldberg put his arm round his wife's shoulders and whispered something to her. She nodded and ushered the children – twin boys of about six and the elfin girl – towards the door. Kalisz stepped aside to let them pass, but to his surprise Mengele dropped to a crouch and smiled at the boys, fumbling in the pocket of his tunic. 'Tell them not to be afraid, Kalisz.' The SS doctor brought out a paper bag and plucked something from it, holding it between two fingers so they could see. 'Boiled sweets.' The children gaped at the delicacy and licked their lips. 'May I?'

Mrs Goldberg understood the sentiment, if not the words. She looked to her husband, who shrugged, then nodded. Mengele handed one to each of the twins and, almost as an afterthought, to the little girl, patting each of them on the cheek. It was an odd little interlude, but Kalisz didn't have time to dwell on it. He resumed his questioning of Goldberg.

'But you did find her body?'

'You think I don't know what has brought you here, Mr Polish investigator who now works with the Nazis?' Clearly Kalisz wasn't the only one who knew how to turn up the heat. 'All you're interested in is the German girl we read about in the newspaper. You wish to know what happened to Hannah? She died. She went to try to find some food, because she was a good girl who liked to help her mama. A good girl, but maybe a bit too adventurous for her own good because she went into the cellars. And there she died.'

'We need to know how she died.'

'You know how she died.' Goldberg's eyes flared, and his mouth worked with sheer fury. 'I can see it in your face. But I will not say how she died. Only that I, her own father, gathered her up and carried her to her grave. The words were said over her. Finish. Now get out.'

He turned away, but for the sake of August Klimecki, Kalisz couldn't let it drop. 'We could always dig up the body to find out. It might provide the evidence we need.'

Goldberg slowly swivelled, and Kalisz had never been the focus of a stare so bleak or so dangerous. 'Yes, you could do that, but first you would have to find the grave. Only I know where it is, and you could do to me what they did to Hannah and still I wouldn't tell you. And when you'd killed me, what then?'

Kalisz felt the atmosphere in the room subtly alter. The men and women in the side rooms had been listening to the tense dialogue with rapt attention. Now their eyes homed in on Kalisz, and they weren't friendly. An unmistakable message.

If anything happened to Isaac Goldberg, the best Kalisz could hope for was a knife in the back.

'Nobody's going to kill you, Goldberg,' he said. 'But if we're going to find Hannah's murderer we need your help.'

'Finish.'

The word was aimed at Kalisz, but Goldberg's eyes were on the man behind him.

Mengele sensed the conversation had ended. 'Do we have what we came for?'

'I think so, sir,' Kalisz said hesitantly.

'Think so?'

'May we discuss it outside?'

'Gladly.' Mengele's eyes surveyed the room. 'God, these people live like pigs, and the stink…'

The SS man turned towards the door and Kalisz stared after him, wondering how such an intelligent man could be blind to the fact that the conditions *these people* were living in had been forced upon them by him and his like.

'Thank you for your time,' he said to Goldberg. 'My condolences to you and your family. I'm sorry you don't want to help, but I promise I will do my best to find Hannah's killer.'

By way of an answer, Goldberg went to the window and spat into the street. Kalisz ignored the insult. He was more interested in the familiar pair of eyes and the message they were trying to convey.

Mengele was waiting for him in the corridor with Dietrich. Kalisz approached him and said quietly, 'I think Goldberg suspected you spoke some Polish. There are certain things he is keeping from us. Things he wouldn't say in front of a German officer.'

'Then perhaps we should return with a suitable escort and ask him more forcefully.' A flash of venom in the SS officer's

252

eyes reminded Kalisz that, for all Mengele's polished manners, he was still a Nazi.

'If the Herr Doctor would permit it, I'd like to go back in alone.'

Mengele studied him. 'I hope you are not playing games with me, Kalisz. That would not be wise.'

'If you don't trust me...'

'No.' Mengele looked at his watch. 'How long will it take?'

'Five minutes, ten at most. If you could wait in the car.'

'All right, but be quick. I'll want a report on exactly what he says.'

'Of course, sir.'

'Five minutes, then.'

When Mengele had gone, Kalisz didn't return to Goldberg's apartment. Instead, he stood at the top of the stairs and waited. A door opened close by.

'To say I was surprised to see you would be an understatement.'

Doctor Novak, the surgeon who'd treated him in hospital after he'd been wounded, and who had paved the way for his first meeting with Kazimierz, answered with a shrug. 'Forty years a lapsed Catholic, and the Nazis come along.' The familiar voice carried a hint of strain, but the wry humour survived. Novak adopted a mock German accent. 'Sir, you do not know how fortunate you are. Look here, your great-grandmother is called Ruth. You are a Jew. You no longer need to work every day. You may live a life of leisure. And by the way, we need this beautiful house you have occupied all your married life.' His voice took on its normal tone. 'My wife was reluctantly packed off to her parents. No children, God be thanked. I don't think I could have endured that.' A great sigh. 'I am no longer allowed to practise medicine. I now live with thieves and gangsters, a farmer from Modlin who stinks like his cows, and worse, a so-called novelist who wants to bore me to death before the Germans kill me.'

'It's good to see you, Doctor,' Kalisz said.

'I wish I could say the same, Lieutenant Kalisz.'

Novak put out his hand to be shaken, and Kalisz took it with a formal bow of his head. He studied Novak for a moment. The plump, cheerful doctor was gone, replaced by a pale wraith whose clothes hung loose on him and who had the haunted look of a man on the run. Of course, one couldn't acknowledge that; circumstances dictated that they must pretend nothing had changed.

'I owe you a great deal, sir.'

Novak smiled sadly. 'If I remember rightly, perhaps yes, and perhaps no. But we won't discuss that.'

Kalisz didn't respond directly. 'If there is anything I can do to help you? Perhaps—'

The doctor held up a hand. 'You must not do anything that would endanger your position, whatever that position is. There is nothing anyone can do for us here. Herr Hitler has made it quite plain what will happen to us eventually. Have you read *Mein Kampf*?'

'Yes,' Kalisz admitted. 'I had to do a presentation on it to a promotion board. Not the easiest book to read.'

'Then you know what he said about the Jew: *And so he advances on his fatal road*. I don't think Hitler meant any ambiguity in that word "fatal". I believe he intended it as a portent. And here we are, Lieutenant Kalisz, at the mercy of Hitler's demonic guard. Men like the SS officer you brought with you today.'

'His name's Mengele – a doctor. He's in charge of forensics in the Traudl Kleist case. I felt I couldn't come alone.'

A bitter smile from Novak. 'Yes, that would not have been wise. From Goldberg, precisely nothing?'

'You heard him. He found the body, he gathered up the body, he buried the body. Finish.'

'But what if there was more?'

'What I didn't tell Goldberg was that every day we fail to catch this killer, ten hostages are being executed. My wife's father is one of those being held.'

Novak nodded. 'I had to be sure. You understand that? When you didn't respond to Mrs Goldberg after I sent her to you with the help of Mr Feinbaum, I asked myself – Is this the same man? Has something changed him? It does happen. Especially in war.' He shrugged despondently. 'Perhaps you had your reasons.'

'I had my reasons.' *An empty space where my heart should be; at least that's what it feels like.* 'But that doesn't make it right.'

Novak's voice took on a new urgency. 'We haven't got much time. I was with Isaac when he found Hannah's body…' They heard a door opening below and Novak went pale. 'There is more. Much more,' he hissed. 'We must meet again.' He shot a frightened glance at the staircase and scuttled back towards the apartment.

Kalisz walked quickly to the stairs just as Dietrich appeared below. 'Where the fuck have you been?'

CHAPTER 31

He'd been so close. *There is more. Much more.* What did Novak have to tell him? It was clearly vital to set up another meeting, but Kalisz wasn't sure how. He couldn't just walk into the apartment building and knock on Isaac Goldberg's door. Yet the only other option was to hang around Elektoralna after work in the hope of contacting the Jewish doctor. Kazimierz would think of a way, but he couldn't go running to Kazimierz every time he had a problem or he'd compromise them both. The simple fact was that he wasn't very good at this.

Hoth was still in his office, but otherwise Kalisz had the place to himself for the moment. He could hear the *Hauptsturmführer* murmuring into the phone. Polish staff were forbidden to make calls unless under supervision by a German. Could he take a chance? He slipped across to where he had an oblique view of the SS man. Hoth seemed completely engrossed in conversation and Kalisz had a feeling he was talking to his wife. *Now or never.*

He walked quickly to an isolated desk normally occupied by Gersten, one of the friendlier investigators on the squad, and gently picked up the Bakelite telephone. It was the one used by the night cover detective, and had a direct connection. He'd memorised the numbers, so he picked out the first of them on the dial and waited.

'*Kriminalpolizei München*,' a clipped female voice replied.

'May I speak to Chief Commissar Lange, please?' Kalisz kept his voice low. 'Investigator Kalisz, Warsaw Kripo.'

'Please hold on.'

Kalisz glanced towards Hoth's office, but there was still no sign of the SS man. He could hear voices from the bottom of the stairs. If someone appeared, should he hang up or brazen it out? The seconds passed; Kalisz became more nervous.

'Kalisz?' a voice boomed at the other end of the line, so loudly Kalisz winced. Hans Lange had been Kalisz's German liaison officer during two weeks he'd spent in Munich on exchange, and they'd kept in touch before the war. 'You're about the last person I'd have expected to hear from. Shouldn't you be in a PoW camp, or in England?'

'It turns out I'm more German than I thought I was, Hansi.' Kalisz put a smile in his voice to show he wasn't offended. 'Germans eat better, for a start. I'm back in the old job.'

'Hey, I can barely hear you.' Lange laughed. 'You'll have to speak up.'

'It must be a bad line.' Kalisz raised his voice as high as he dared. 'Look, I have a favour to ask. An official favour. We have a murderer on the loose in Warsaw. One of the bad ones – know what I mean?'

'Another Kürten?' Peter Kürten had been an infamous serial killer, murdering more than a dozen men and women in Düsseldorf in the Twenties. Before his execution he'd boasted that the sight of blood gave him sexual pleasure.

'That's right, Hansi, but this one has a different style.' Kalisz explained about the victims being of a certain age and appearance, the removal of the organs, and, finally, the strange artwork. 'We call him "The Artist".'

'Jesus Christ.' Lange whistled. 'I thought I'd heard it all. But what has this to do with me, Jan?'

'We've checked out any possible Polish suspects, Hansi. I'm just covering all the angles. We think this isn't his first time.

He may have started somewhere else. One of the victims is the niece of General Kleist. There's pressure coming from so high it has wings. Nobody here is kidding themselves. There are about fifty thousand German tourists in Warsaw right now, and until we catch the killer all of them are suspects. Can you check your records for any unsolved killings with a similar style?'

He could almost feel the shrug at the other end of the line. 'That shouldn't take long. In fact, if we'd had anything like that, I'm fairly certain I'd have known about it. Give me your number and I'll get back to you.'

'Soon, Hansi?' Kalisz read out the number on Gersten's phone.

'Of course.'

He'd hoped to put through another call to a contact in Berlin, but footsteps echoed in the stairwell and Kalisz quickly hung up. He hurried across to his own desk as two or three detectives, including Gersten, walked into the office. When he looked up, Hoth was standing over him with a pensive look on his face.

'Yes, sir?'

'Detective Müller isn't around, so I suppose you should have these for now.' He handed Kalisz the case files for the Kleist and Lenski killings. 'Oh, and Dr Mengele just called to say that he will be at the laboratory or out in Wola for the rest of the day.'

'Thank you, sir.'

When Hoth was gone, Kalisz placed the two files side by side on the desk. There should have been a third, but Mengele had decreed they didn't have enough information yet to link Hannah Goldberg's disappearance to the other killings. Kalisz opened the folders and removed the photographs of the murder scenes, staring at the flat monochrome pictures for a long time, trying to find some message he hadn't picked up previously.

The similarities were obvious: two young girls on the brink of womanhood, taken from public places to be killed for a psychopath's pleasure. Their throats had been cut and they'd been eviscerated, laid out carefully in the form of a cross, and then – it turned out enough evidence had been gathered at the Lenski scene to be certain – pieces of their organs had been used to form some sort of montage. In the case of Traudl Kleist, that montage had been a still life scene of flowers – Blood Roses, as Kalisz had christened them. The Lenski girl's organs had been too scattered to be sure of the subject matter.

But there were also puzzling disparities.

He picked up a picture from the Kleist file and compared it to a similar one of Krystyna Lenski. The pool of blood beneath her head proved Traudl had been murdered in the bomb site where she lay, but Krystyna had been killed elsewhere. Two portraits, taken to show close-up detail of the wounds in the girls' throats, also brought their facial expressions into tight focus. As Mengele had remarked, Traudl Kleist might have been sleeping, such was her seeming serenity, but Kalisz looked into Krystyna Lenski's face and saw a girl who knew she was dying. The lips were drawn back and her mouth was open as if she was crying out. Perhaps he was imagining it, but he thought he could see the terror of her passing in the dull eyes. He spent the next hour reading and rereading the post mortem reports and witness interviews. The interviews told him nothing new. Nobody in the vicinity of the bomb site in Wola would admit to seeing Krystyna around the time she was murdered, or even to knowing her. The post mortems threw up more questions than answers. Was the difference in methodology between the two killings a result of a change in the killer's mental state, a product of circumstances, or was some other factor involved? It was impossible to be certain. Kalisz had a suspicion the answer lay with Hannah Goldberg. Novak had certainly given the impression the information he held was important.

'Investigator Gersten,' he called across the office. 'Do you have a map of the city I could take a look at, please?'

'What's wrong, Kalisz, can't find your way home?' Gersten grinned. He rummaged in a drawer until he found what he was looking for. 'Here you are.'

Kalisz took the map and thanked him. He replaced the pictures in their files and spread the sheet on the desk. Three killings that they knew of and, if Kalisz was right, a botched kidnap attempt. Hannah Goldberg had been the first, a young girl in the wrong place at the wrong time, lured into the depths of the Wielopole ruins and murdered. The way Kalisz saw it, an opportunity had arisen and – despite the risk – the man he now thought of as The Artist had acted upon it. The attempted kidnap of Janina Berman, with its dreadful consequences, had been next. Again, this was the behaviour of a man acting on impulse. Then a gap to Krystyna Lenski, a killing that had the hallmarks of a much more pre-planned and clinical attack – as, apart from the slight inconsistencies, had Traudl Kleist's murder.

He traced the locations with his finger: Wawer in the east, beyond the river; Wola in the west; then the two killings in the city centre, within a few blocks of each other. A man able to move at will, with the means and the authority to travel through a city with a checkpoint on every second corner. Kalisz was becoming increasingly certain the perpetrator was a member of the occupying forces. But was that the logic of a detective or the result of his own prejudice? Before he could answer, he became aware of a malignant presence behind him.

'What the fuck is going on here?' Fury twisted Müller's face into a contorted mask. 'Are you playing detective, Kalisz, or making a list of juicy places for your terrorist friends to attack?'

'I can assure you—'

'You'll assure me nothing, you Polish turd.' Müller brought his face close and his voice dropped so only Kalisz could hear what he said. 'I heard what you've been up to with that shiny-arsed SS doctor at the Jew house on Elektoralna. Not everybody keeps secrets around here. So we have another murder, do we? But old Müller doesn't get to hear about it, even though he's the senior investigator on this case —' he poked a steely finger in Kalisz's chest — 'which you seem to have forgotten.'

'I apologise, sir—'

'And not just that.' Müller allowed his voice to rise, and he looked triumphantly around the room at the other detectives. 'She's a fucking Jew who was probably butchered by her Yid relatives. Ritual slaughter - isn't that what they call it? And haven't the baby killers been doing it for fucking centuries? So if there are any similarities to the Traudl Kleist murder – not that Senior Investigator Müller would know, of course — who's to say the Yids aren't *her* killers, too?' He paused, and his glittering dark eyes fixed on Kalisz. 'Luckily, Senior Investigator Müller, with all his experience, has a bit more savvy than your SS doctor. So he did what should have been done the moment the case was reported, and had every male over the age of fourteen in the building arrested by the Gestapo. Szucha Avenue will soon get the truth out of them...'

Müller's voice faded, and in Kalisz's head his twisted features transformed into Novak's placid features. He'd killed him. Killed them all by his stupidity. He clenched his hands together to resist the urge to take the Nazi by the throat.

'Are you fucking listening to me, Kalisz?'

'Yes, sir.'

'I said, maybe when they start singing, your name will be one of the ones they spill. I'd like that, Kalisz. I'd like to see you strapped to a chair in Szucha Avenue. My good friend Alfie Spilker lets me sit in on some of their fun, sometimes even invites me to join in. You know what happens down in the basement, Kalisz? Some of the things I could tell you –' his face twisted into a grin – 'but we'll let it come as a surprise. Yids and terrorists, that's your sort, Kalisz. But until that happy day, you remember you work for me, and crawling after the SS man will just make it all the worse for you. Understand?'

Kalisz swallowed the ball of rage that filled his throat. 'I understand, Herr Investigator.'

'Good. Then we'll get along just fine for now.' He turned away, then swung back abruptly. 'Oh, and that wife and kid of yours?' Kalisz froze, and Müller's grin grew broader when he saw the impact of his words. 'I'll be taking a look at their files, too, the next time I'm down at Szucha Avenue.'

Kalisz watched the detective's retreating back as Müller marched off in the direction of the stairs.

'Don't you worry about old Müller.' A hand clapped him on the shoulder: Gersten, a sympathetic smile on his face. 'His piles must be acting up and he's a prime shit in the first place.'

Hauptsturmführer Hoth appeared at his office door. 'Where's Müller?' he demanded.

'I think he went out, sir,' Kalisz said.

'Well, get him back. They've found another body.'

PART FOUR: REVELATION

CHAPTER 32

The weather had more in common with autumn than summer as they waited by the cemetery gates beneath clouds the colour of old ashes A thick, all-enveloping drizzle soaked everything it touched, and they had to hunch their shoulders to keep the rain from running down their necks. Müller sucked morosely at his pipe. With the water dripping from his moustache, he looked increasingly like a bedraggled dog otter. His acid mood wasn't helped by the need to listen for the car that would announce the overdue arrival of Doctor Mengele.

Kalisz knew the *Volksdeutsche* detective was fretting about his impulsive and unsanctioned arrest of the adult male residents of the Goldberg house on Elektoralna. The pressure continued to grow from Berlin for a swift resolution to the Traudl Kleist case, and the last thing *Hauptsturmführer* Hoth needed was any suggestion that he was wasting his resources on a wild goose chase. Their location seemed to make that increasingly likely, because this was a Christian cemetery and, unusually in Poland, a Protestant one. The scions of Warsaw's Lutheran community had been jostling for the most prestigious slots in the Evangelical-Augsburg Cemetery for more than two hundred years. Adjacent, to the north, lay the Jewish cemetery where Kalisz was certain Isaac Goldberg had laid his daughter to rest, and beyond it the much larger Catholic cemetery. Warsaw had always been tidy that way.

'At last,' Müller muttered. A black Mercedes turned into the driveway and drove sedately over the gravel towards them. The SS doctor's big car parked beside the Polski Fiat Müller had signed out from the Department V motor pool, and the big police van that had brought the uniformed Blues who'd secured the scene. Mengele emerged from the Mercedes accompanied by the trusty Dietrich, inseparable, as ever, from his MP38.

'Thank you for waiting for me, gentlemen,' Mengele said. '*Hauptsturmführer* Hoth is anxious this investigation is conducted in an exemplary fashion. Do we know the identity of the victim?'

'Not yet, sir,' Müller said. 'But the Blues are certain she's not German.'

'And that will not influence our thinking in any way.' Mengele pulled on a pair of surgical gloves. 'We should all be conscious that a failure to give proper consideration to the deaths of Krystyna Lenski, and, to a lesser extent, Kalisz's Jewess, may have been a factor in the murder of Traudl Kleist. That is certainly how Governor Frank will see it.'

One of the Blues who'd been guarding the gate led them through the heavily wooded cemetery, past simple gravestones almost buried in the weeds and long since eroded to anonymity by the elements, and more recent interments which proclaimed the identities of their occupants in marble and gold leaf. They passed a couple of Blues on the path, and Kalisz spotted more among the trees to left and right. The fact none of them would meet his eyes didn't bode well for what he was about to see.

They emerged from the trees into a clearing with a large mausoleum at its centre.

'Jesus Christ,' Dietrich hissed.

A stone wall topped by a fence of spiked metal stakes surrounded the main vault of the mausoleum. From the top of the fence, the naked body of a young girl hung suspended by her arms, which were each impaled by a pair of spikes. The whole effect, which Kalisz felt certain was as the killer intended, resembled a crude parody of the crucifixion. Her head was slumped forward on her chest and her face was invisible behind a curtain of sodden, jet-black hair. The slender form was so pale as to be almost translucent, and even from this distance Kalisz could see the dark line of the long incision through which her killer had eviscerated the body.

'Well, our fellow certainly knows how to put on a show,' Mengele said as he made his way towards the macabre tableau with Müller.

'You sound as if you almost admire him, Doctor,' Kalisz said, but if Mengele heard his words, he ignored them. Kalisz looked for the senior uniformed policeman and called him across to shelter beneath the broad canopy of an ancient oak. He recognised the man, and searched his memory for a name. *Piskorski – that's it.* Sergeant Piskorski, who'd shown him round the Krystyna Lenski murder scene. It hadn't occurred to Kalisz how close the cemetery was to Wola. 'Who found the body?' he asked.

'An old woman.' The sergeant checked his notebook. 'A Mrs Petzel. She passed by the mausoleum most mornings, bringing fresh flowers to her husband's grave. The caretaker heard her screams and ran to help her. When he saw the victim he decided his first priority should be to call us and close the park – he's an ex-cop. Retired.'

'Good man,' Kalisz acknowledged.

'I was first Blue on the scene. As soon as I recognised the injuries to the girl I radioed for Department V. You can't imagine the shit that's been flying around over the Lenski investigation.' He glared in the direction of Müller. 'Someone's putting the word about that the Blues fucked up by not sending for Kripo.'

'I heard you did send for us.'

'That's right. My lieutenant spoke to one of your investigators. He said *Hauptsturmführer* Hoth wasn't available and that he was in charge. When he heard the details, he claimed the department was too short-staffed to worry about dead Polish whores, and the Blues should handle it themselves.'

For some reason, it was an image of Ziegler that appeared in Kalisz's mind. But why wouldn't the SS officer have mentioned a murder? 'Do you know the investigator's name?'

The sergeant shook his head. 'I only heard it once, in a sentence that was mostly curses. Sounds unlikely, but could it have been Ghoul, or something like that?'

Günther Gruhl.

'Kalisz, come and take a look at this,' Mengele called.

'We'll need to talk to Mrs Petzel and the caretaker.' He threw the words over his shoulder as he jogged to where the SS doctor and Müller stood beside the gated entrance to the mausoleum enclosure.

'We have found another of his artworks.' Mengele pointed through the gate. 'Look upon it and wonder.'

'What do you mean?' Kalisz grimaced at the mosaic of sliced body parts that formed the familiar image of a vase filled with roses. He noted there were six blooms now, but he understood that wasn't the only thing different about The Artist's latest creation.

'Oh, come, Kalisz. I'd expect this of Müller here, he hasn't got an artistic bone in his body, but I thought better of you. Surely you recognise a masterpiece when you see one?'

'I don't see a masterpiece, I see an obscenity.' Kalisz tried to keep his tone even, but Mengele's enthusiasm for the killer's work was beginning to anger him.

'You have to look beyond the material of the individual components, which I'll grant you is unusual,' Mengele continued. 'But the composition, the way each individual item has been shaped to fit precisely with its neighbour, the delicacy of their positioning, are all perfect. It's a pity we were never able to see his earlier attempts, but our Artist has come a long way in a short time from the crudity of his Traudl Kleist creation. I look upon this and I can't help thinking we bask in the presence of genius.'

Kalisz stared at him, but before he could say anything, Müller interrupted.

'Does this mean he's had more practice than we know about?' he asked Mengele. 'That there are more bodies out there, waiting to be discovered?'

Mengele didn't answer, but he looked to Kalisz, who shook his head.

'I don't think so,' he said. 'The Artist isn't a man who just wants his creations to be seen. He *needs* them to be seen.' He recalled Mengele's words of just a few moments earlier. 'In fact, the kind of praise you've just provided gives him the validation for everything he does. The women whose bodies he desecrates are nothing to him. His only reason for keeping them and displaying them like this is to provide a context for his creations, which would be lost without the origins of the components. No, if there were other victims he would have left them where we couldn't miss them, just like this.'

'So the bastard would like nothing better than for everybody to be talking about him?'

'That's right, Investigator Müller, which is why I think we should keep any mention of this *thing* out of any newspaper reports about the killings. It will frustrate him and, with luck, make him take more risks. Your psychopath is a chameleon with a lust to see his name in lights. It wouldn't surprise me if he was watching us now, just to see our reaction to what we've found.'

Mengele asked Müller to question the witnesses, and he gestured to Kalisz to come and take a look at the corpse.

'You really believe the killer could be close by, Kalisz?' Mengele asked.

'Yes, sir. What we have here —' he nodded towards the girl hanging from the fence — 'is a kind of performance art. A performer is nothing without his audience, and so far we are the only audience he's got. Does she have anything to tell us?'

Mengele considered the victim for a moment before he replied. 'From the extent of her rigor mortis I'd say the timings are very similar to that of the Kleist murder. As you can see, the methodology appears identical. You noticed there was no sign of any white powder?'

'He didn't need any cyanide to keep the dogs away. The walls and gate did that for him, and provided him with the privacy to create what you call his masterpiece undisturbed.'

'There is just one thing.' Mengele stepped forward. He was just tall enough to gently lift the dead girl's head. Kalisz winced at the mask of horror on a face that was probably normally quite pretty. 'Unlike Traudl Kleist, this one doesn't appear to have been drugged, but I can't be certain until I've done the proper tests.'

'There's one thing that *is* certain, Doctor Mengele,' Kalisz said. 'And that's if we don't stop him, he'll kill again, sooner rather than later.'

CHAPTER 33

Kalisz felt as if he was wearing lead boots as he walked along Dobra to his meeting with Kazimierz. He wasn't sure how much longer he could go on with it. He could cope physically – just – but something at the very heart of him seemed to be fading, like a fire deprived of oxygen. An uncle who had fought in the war – the one they called the Great War – had once assured him courage was not an inexhaustible resource. Soldiers who were as brave as lions at the start of a campaign would refuse to leave their trenches at the end of it, even when threatened at gunpoint. Perhaps it was the same for a man living in the shadows? Perhaps there were only so many times you could lie to a loved one, or stand face to face with a man you wanted to kill, without showing your true feelings. When every door you walked through could lead to a firing squad, maybe the next was the one your hand would refuse to open?

The dead girl had eventually been identified as a Jew, fourteen-year-old Tosia Lipman, whose home address was given as an apartment on Grzybowska. The address was a puzzle, because it was on the opposite side of the city from where she'd been found. Her identity had allowed Müller to retain his fantasy that some kind of bloodthirsty sect among the captive Jewish population was responsible for the killings. That part of Grzybowska was inside the recently walled area of the Epidemic Quarantine District. No one knew how she'd got out, but if she'd stayed inside the walls she would almost certainly still be alive.

Kalisz had allowed himself his own short-lived fantasy that Günther Gruhl might be responsible for the early killings, with the active participation of Müller. It was based solely on Gruhl's seeming determination to keep Department V out of the Lenski investigation, and the razor-like pocket knife in his possession, but in truth his theory was laughable. Both men would kill without the slightest compunction, but Mengele was right: Müller didn't have an artistic bone in his body, and Gruhl had been cast from the same mould.

Kalisz had chosen Dobra because the street was wide and he knew it would be almost empty. He crossed to the west side of the road and glanced casually back. A surge of electricity replaced the lethargy when he caught a glimpse of someone ducking into a doorway. He mustn't break stride or give any sign he knew he was being followed. *No need to panic.* Losing his tail wouldn't be a problem. It was a complication, nothing more. The only question was whether he should keep his appointment with Kazimierz.

Another twenty paces, and that became a secondary consideration. Kalisz felt an equal measure of exhilaration and alarm as he recognised the man who stumbled from an alleyway a few dozen paces ahead of him. Either Novak had also been following him and somehow dashed up a parallel street to cut him off, or he'd gambled Kalisz would take this route home. How had he avoided arrest at the house in Elektoralna? That was for later. Now his face shone as he approached the man he hoped would be his salvation. Kalisz couldn't allow that.

His hand went to his pocket, and he hardened his features and his heart. A look of consternation appeared on Novak's face when he saw Kalisz's glare, and he wavered uncertainly in the street. Kalisz pushed him in the chest.

'I've told you before about asking me for money in the street, you filthy old man.' A passing couple gave Kalisz a startled glance, but quickly turned away, unwilling to become involved. He took the Jewish doctor by the front of his jacket and pulled him close, at the same time slipping the contents of his left hand into the jacket pocket. 'Kopernika,' he whispered. 'The basement.'

Novak opened his mouth, but Kalisz pushed him away, so he staggered. 'Never again, do you hear, or I'll give you a beating like you've never had before. Understand me?'

'Yes, sir. I'm sorry, sir.' Novak slipped away with the air of a man who'd already been beaten. Kalisz gave him a last stare as the doctor retreated up the alley from which he'd emerged. He walked on, willing his heart to slow. It had been a crude, spur of the moment ruse. If he was being followed by the Gestapo, the chances were they'd pick up Novak in case it had been a prearranged contact. There would be six or eight of them at least, behind and in front, alternating their positions, with a back-up of security police nearby. In that case, the game, as the English would say, was up. Doctor Novak was a fugitive from justice and his name would be on one of their lists. It would all come out: the *arrangement* at the hospital and the mysterious stranger in the night. The only conclusion? Conspiracy, and aimed at the very heart of the state. Department V had taken a viper to its bosom. Consternation and outrage from Hoth. At Aleja Szucha, rubber truncheons would be the least of it. For a moment, Kazimierz's little white capsule began to look attractive.

But what choice did he have but to play the game to its final conclusion?

A cafe at the next intersection gave him the opportunity he needed. A bell rang as he pushed the door, and he went down two steps into a tiny room with a bar at the rear. The couple who'd walked past as he abused Novak looked up from their discussion and glared when they recognised him. Kalisz ignored them. A fearsome-looking woman appeared from behind a curtain and took her place behind the counter, daring him to make an order.

'Coffee, please.'

He took a seat at a table in the corner with his back to the wall, where he'd be difficult to see from the door. This was the moment when his tail would have a choice to make. Kalisz had followed enough people to know what would be going through his mind. He could find somewhere to watch the door and wait, but Kalisz had deliberately chosen the cafe for its position in the heart of a residential area, with no handy shops to mark time studying the non-existent merchandise. Naturally, his tail would be concerned that the cafe could be the location for Kalisz's meeting with Kazimierz – or whoever – and he'd certainly be tempted to make a fleeting visit just to check. But the cafe was so small he'd immediately be compromised. In fact, that option suited Kalisz best, but he doubted his shadow would take it. He'd sensed an uncertainty in the fleeting glimpses that made it unlikely. Finally, there'd be that heart-stopping moment when the tail feared Kalisz was simply using the cafe to shake him off, and had walked straight through the door at the back of the counter to only God knew where.

The woman brought his coffee and laid down the tiny cup and saucer with a rattle on the table in front of him. A thimble's worth of black liquid nestled in the bottom of the cup. He picked it up and took a sip, the bitter tang making him purse his lips. *Mother of Christ, will I ever get used to the taste of roasted acorn dust and coal tar.* Still, it was hot. He took another sip. And somehow stimulating. He reached across to pick up a newspaper that had been left on a nearby table. At first glance, it might have been the once popular *Kurier*, but that was only until you noticed the tiny 'New' in the top left corner. The Nazis had closed down the *Kurier* the day after they'd entered Warsaw. This was the *Nowy Kurjer Warszawski*, a German propaganda sheet. Its stories and editorials sought to convince Poles that everything happening to them was what they deserved, and to blacken the names of their former rulers. Varsovians had taken to calling it the *Kurwa* – The Whore.

Normally, Kalisz would ignore the overblown reports of Wehrmacht victories, but today's front page had the ring of truth. Apparently 'armistice' was the new euphemism for surrender. France had concluded an armistice with the Nazis that gave up her army, her navy and two thirds of her territory to Germany. With typical malice, Hitler had compounded the French humiliation by making their representatives sign the peace terms in the same railway carriage used for the German surrender at the end of the last war. So, France had joined Poland, Norway, Denmark, Holland and Belgium under the German yoke. It had been coming for so long, the details had little impact on Kalisz. Though the story didn't say so, Britain's war leader Winston Churchill had pledged to continue the war 'on land, sea and air'. Whatever happened, Poland would fight on.

He looked up as a shadow passed the small window on to the street. Made eye contact. Allowed himself an inner smile. What would happen now? He went back to the newspaper and waited.

The bell above the door tinkled.

'Kalisz, fancy meeting you here.'

In other circumstances, Kalisz would have laughed.

'*Unterscharführer* Blum? I wouldn't have thought this was your kind of place.' They spoke in German, and there was a rustle as the couple at the other table gathered up their belongings and hurriedly left the cafe. Blum was in civilian clothing – a suit and tie and a felt hat – but the bulge under his left armpit told its own story. 'I'd buy you a coffee,' Kalisz said, 'but I'm just finishing up and I have to get home to my family.'

'Why don't I keep you company?'

Kalisz shrugged. 'Why not?' He threw a handful of coins on the table and they left under the accusing eyes of the proprietress.

They walked side by side for a few minutes as Kalisz observed his companion's increasing agitation. That evening in the ruins of the distillery had subtly altered the balance of their relationship, and not in a way either of them would have expected. Blum had been *genuinely* impressed that Kalisz had pulled the trigger on poor little Poldek. As a result, he treated the Pole, perhaps not as a comrade, exactly, but with a level of respect that gave Kalisz a certain… leeway.

'You're not really cut out for this, are you, Blum?'

'What do you mean?' A touch of outraged dignity in the SS corporal's tone.

Kalisz smiled, including the other man in the conspiracy. 'Come on, we both know you weren't just passing by that cafe. *Hauptsturmführer* Hoth told you to keep an eye on me. No.' He wagged a finger in Blum's face. 'Not Hoth. Müller. Müller said something like, *I don't quite trust that fellow Kalisz. Why don't you follow him and tell me who he meets?* Only I spotted you. Creeping about in civvies, for God's sake.'

Blum reddened. 'Maybe he thought you needed a nursemaid after what happened?'

Kalisz gave a 'pfaw' of laughter. 'Müller hates me, Blum, and you know why? Firstly because I'm a Pole, but mostly because he thinks I plan to find this Artist killer for myself. And he's right. If the killer is a Pole, who do you think is going to catch him? A German who doesn't speak the language, or a Pole, eh?' They reached the big red-brick Falanga film studio on the corner of Dobra and Leszczyńska, and Kalisz stopped and turned to the German. 'The question is, what do we about it?'

'What do you mean?' Beetle-browed puzzlement looked odd on Blum's habitually mean features.

'Well, you can't keep following me now that I know you're following me. That doesn't make sense. I'd have to tell Müller, and that would make you look like a fool. Worse, I'd have to complain to Hoth. He already thinks you're a Gestapo snitch—'

'What?'

'I hear the Führer is looking for volunteers to invade England. Hoth has a soft spot for me. He thinks I'm a German, but I just haven't realised it yet. He might just volunteer *Unter-scharführer* Blum for a spot up front in one of the first barges to hit the beach.' Kalisz shook his head at his companion's potential fate. 'Don't let anyone tell you the English fight fair, Blum. They'll give you a warm welcome. They'll set the sea on fire and fill the air with lead. Good luck with that.'

'But what can I do, Kalisz?' Blum protested. 'Müller outranks me. I can't just tell him I won't follow you any more.'

Kalisz pretended to consider for a moment. 'I have an idea. You tell Müller you're still following me, but instead, you use the time to go for a beer. You can either make something up to tell him, or if you like, I'll drop by your desk and give you a list of places I've been.' He saw Blum's frown of growing scepticism. 'Look, you think I don't know what a nice little number I have in Department V? I've an incentive to keep my nose clean.' He pushed his face close to the German's. 'And when I catch The Artist, not only will I shove Müller's nose right in the shit, but I'll make *Hauptsturmführer* Hoth a very happy man. Maybe even happy enough to put me on the People's List.'

'When you put it like that…'

'Of course, I'll be looking for a little incentive to keep my mouth shut.'

Blum's face twisted into a cynical smile. Now this was something he understood. 'And what would that be, Kalisz? You're not on the People's List yet.'

'No, but I intend to be. Do you and Losner still have that deal going with the boys down at the shunting yard? You know the one - eight cases for the quartermaster, one case for us, and the other for the railwaymen for keeping both eyes shut while it's happening.'

'Christ, how the fuck…?' Blum's face took on a look of horror, but Kalisz only winked. 'It's that bastard Gersten who's been flapping his gums, isn't it.'

'It doesn't matter how I know, Blum, only that I do. I'm not after a cut of the action - don't think that. All I'm asking is that you remember me from time to time. Maybe a bottle of brandy here – you must be drowning in the stuff after what's happened this week – and a carton of smokes there. Things I can trade for a decent pair of shoes –' he turned his foot so Blum could see the hole in his sole – 'and a few luxuries.'

'Christ, Kalisz.' There was something close to admiration in Blum's tone. 'You're a deep one. All right, I'll think about it. But it stops there, all right.'

Kalisz raised his hands. 'I've seen you at work, Blum, I'm not stupid enough to cross you.'

Blum nodded, pleased to have regained control. 'Good.' He turned in to Leszczyńska, but Kalisz called him back.

'No need for you to come all the way, is there? Why don't you go for a beer and think about what you're going to tell Müller?'

'You're right.' The SS corporal grinned. 'Why not?'

They separated and Kalisz walked in the direction of Kopernika. Not a bad hour's work. Müller's animosity was beginning to get in the way. Kalisz had needed to find a way to keep him at arm's length. Poor Blum. For all his bluster, he really wasn't cut out for this kind of thing. Kazimierz had given Kalisz the information about Losner and the smuggling as a lever in case of an event just like this. Kalisz had a feeling Blum would soon be too busy to bother with him. The Resistance had their own contacts in the black market, and before long the Nazi wouldn't know who he was working with, or for.

Now, what the hell am I going to do about Doctor Novak?

CHAPTER 34

'Are you sure we're safe here?' The hoarse whisper came from the rear of the pitch-dark cellar of number 35, where the terrified Novak had been hiding since Kalisz passed him the key.

'No one will come, I've locked the door.' Kalisz struck a match and lit the oil lamp that was the cellar's main illumination. Novak sat against the far wall with his arms around his knees, looking utterly defeated. He raised his head, squinting into the light.

'When I saw your face I thought you were going to turn me away. I was returning to the apartment when the Gestapo appeared with their whips and dogs. Three truck loads. I saw them take almost everyone except Isaac – I think he may have escaped, too. I didn't know what to do.'

'You did the right thing,' Kalisz assured him. 'I was being followed. We couldn't have met in the street.'

'Followed?'

'I've dealt with it.'

'Yes?' Meaning '*You're certain?*'

'You said you were with Goldberg when he found Hannah?'

Novak emitted a soft groan that might have meant yes or no. 'What about me? What will become of me?'

'We will talk about that later. I need to know. Now.'

'You did not seem so hard in the hospital,' the doctor said mournfully. 'Not like this. A heart made of granite.'

'Those were different times, Doctor Novak. Now, please.'

'Yes. I...' He put his head in his hands for a moment, holding his skull as if it was about to explode. When he raised it again, his eyes had the haunted look of a man on his way to his execution. 'I think it's best if I start at the beginning, yes?'

Kalisz nodded. *Let him tell it his own way and in his own time.*

'When Hannah didn't come home,' Novak began, 'Mrs Goldberg feared she might be lying hurt somewhere, and she asked me to accompany Isaac. We spoke to the girls who were with her. They told us she'd gone into the Wielopole ruins, but they'd seen the rat-catcher there and were too frightened to follow. It seems he'd chased after them on a previous occasion when they'd thrown stones at him...'

'Did they mention a car?'

'Yes.' Novak's eyes glittered in the lamplight. 'There was a car. You know what that means, of course?'

'Yes, I know.'

'It was close to curfew, but Goldberg wouldn't turn back until a German patrol appeared. We tried again the next day, but by then they'd set up a checkpoint so we were prevented from getting close. That was when I suggested to Mrs Goldberg she contact Feinbaum and arrange a meeting with you. It wasn't until the third evening we were able to search the ruins properly. Isaac found the entrance to the cellars—'

Novak froze at the sound of someone outside the cellar door. They sat for more than a minute, not daring to breathe. If it was the Gestapo, they were finished and they both knew it. Kalisz had a moment of raw fear at the thought of Maria and Stefan sleeping, innocent and unknowing, upstairs. He saw the doctor take something in his pocket and hold it in shaking hands in front of his lips, so it would only take a single movement to place it in his mouth.

'It's all right.' Kalisz placed a reassuring hand on his arm. 'I left the key in the lock. You went down there?'

'Yes. You have no idea what it's like…' Novak read something in Kalisz's eyes. 'But you do. You've been there. So you were investigating Hannah's death? You know?'

'Some of it, but I need to know it all. Tell it exactly as you experienced it.'

Novak hesitated, collecting his thoughts, or perhaps steeling himself for what was to come.

'Goldberg had the torch, and he led as we worked our way through that maze of rooms. I could feel his anger as his fear and frustration increased with every failure. It was like watching a man grow in front of your eyes. We both knew what we might find, and Isaac was no innocent. He would have prepared himself for it…' He shook his head and whimpered at the memory.

'Please, Doctor Novak.'

'Even… Even so, when we opened the door to that final room and his torch fell upon her, I watched a man die inside. He fell to his knees and—'

'The scene.' Kalisz urged him in the direction he wanted. 'Tell me about the scene.'

'Blood everywhere.' Novak's eyes were wide now. 'On the walls and on the floor, and at its centre, Hannah, arms extended and feet together in the shape of a cross, naked and pale as a marble statue except… Except for…'

'Except for what?'

'Her throat had been cut.' He took a deep breath and recovered his surgeon's composure and detachment. 'And her killer had opened her from pubis to sternum…'

'Pubis to sternum. You're certain?'

'Certain, yes. He then removed the major organs and associated viscera and laid them aside. This was used for…' He stared at Kalisz. 'I'm sorry, I'm not sure I know how to explain it.'

'Please try, it's important.'

'The viscera had been carefully sorted into its various components and – the only way I can describe it is "fashioned" – yes, parts had been fashioned into certain shapes designed to fit into a carefully planned and executed representation, or mural, of a… I know this is difficult to believe, but I saw it with my own eyes… A floral display.'

He waited for Kalisz's exclamation of wonder, but the investigator didn't react.

'You knew?'

'I guessed. Continue. How would you describe its presentation?'

'It was evident to me that each piece had been placed in position with almost loving care. Roses – red, of course. Can something so truly terrible be described as beautiful? If the discovery of his daughter's body had destroyed the man who had been Isaac Goldberg, the sight of this obscene montage created from her flesh drove him mad. He vowed all sorts of terrible revenge. Whoever was responsible would suffer as he'd suffered. It took all my persuasion to stop him taking the body and carrying it through the streets.' Novak closed his eyes, and the silence was so prolonged Kalisz wondered if he was asleep. Then, 'I pleaded with him to have the mural recorded in some way. "It is unique," I said. "The evidence that will undoubtedly snare Hannah's killer." "I will find Hannah's killer," he told me, "and when I do…" And he would wipe away this obscenity, so no other would see what had been done to her. So we stayed all night in that awful place and picked up each piece of her flesh and returned it to her body. In the morning, he sent me for a blanket and surgical needle and thread, so that when she was buried it would be with a certain dignity. I left him praying over her body while two of his men scrubbed the area of the mural clean.'

'Tell me about her wounds. Did she have any defensive injuries?'

'One of her fingers was broken,' Novak confirmed. 'And she had flesh beneath her nails where she had clawed at her killer. She was Isaac Goldberg's daughter, Lieutenant Kalisz. She fought. As to the cuts, they were very clean – the work of an extremely sharp instrument, something in the nature of a surgeon's scalpel. There was one other thing that may help you. A distinctive smell, sweet, almost a perfume. I should certainly recognise it again.'

Kalisz took time to think about what he'd been told. It all made sense: fitted. A picture was forming. But at the back of his mind, a warning bell rang. What was he missing?

'What do you know about Salomon the rat-catcher?'

'Only that in his initial grief and madness, Goldberg convinced himself Salomon must be the murderer, or at the very least an accomplice. He vowed to hunt him down. From what you said at the apartment, I gather he succeeded.'

Kalisz told him what he'd found in the cellars and Novak groaned. 'It's not enough that the Nazis kill us, now we must kill each other.' He sighed. 'I believe he may have learned something of significance from Salomon. He came home drunk from work one night, raging and growling. "I know," he repeated over and over. "I know." Then he started cursing that black devil and saying he'd teach him.'

'That black devil?'

'It was the name he used for the SS. Isaac was in Dresden a few years before the war, collecting a debt owed to his bosses.

His visit coincided with a big Nazi rally and some SS men cornered him in a bar and beat him up pretty badly. They wore black in those days, so whenever he sees those lightning flashes he remembers the black devils, no matter the colour of uniform they wear now. Black devils.'

A shiver ran through Kalisz at the implications of what he was hearing, but it was enough for now. He turned towards the door, then something struck him. 'You said he came home from work. I thought he worked for one of the Jewish crime syndicates?'

'No. He was trying to give all that up. He had a part-time job.' Novak named a well-known Warsaw factory.

Kalisz filed it away, just in case. 'But you think he escaped the round-up?' Novak nodded. 'Then I have to find him.'

The doctor shook his head. 'Then I wish you luck, my friend, because in his current state of mind, Isaac Goldberg is capable of anything. There is one other thing. Since Hannah's death there have been rumours of other girls in the Jewish district being followed. Watched.'

'By whom?'

Novak shook his head. 'If they know, they are too frightened to say.'

Kalisz thought of the girl's pale body crucified on the spiked railings.

Not frightened enough.

CHAPTER 35

Kalisz set up another meeting with Kazimierz using the emergency protocol. Two days later they sat, sharing a wizened pear brought by the Resistance agent, on the sunlight-dappled grass beneath a tree in the once-beautiful gardens of the bombed-out music conservatoire two streets from Kalisz's home. *Conspiracy doesn't always have to be uncomfortable, does it?* Kazimierz looked as worn as Kalisz had ever seen him, an almost spectral shadow of the man he'd first met. He could tell by the look in his eyes that the other man was seeing something similar.

Kalisz told him the news about Blum and Müller, and Kazimierz gave him a certain look. 'If you think this Müller is becoming a real problem, we can have him dealt with in a way that will leave you safe.'

'I'll think about it.' Kalisz considered the implications of the offer. 'But for the moment I can handle him. There is one other thing. Something that could be a danger to you as well as me. It's beginning to look as if Traudl Kleist's killer is a German, possibly an SS officer.'

'Shit.' Kazimierz grimaced. 'Are you sure you should be going ahead with this, Jan?'

'If I'm going to stop them killing August, I don't have any choice.' Kalisz told him about Novak. 'He can't stay in the basement for more than another day. I need to find him a new set of papers. Can you help? He was prepared to run, so he has his own photographs.'

Kazimierz thought for a moment. 'Remember Rozenblum, the forger whose file you brought me?' A thin smile flickered across the haggard features. Kalisz had released Rozenblum from custody as the Germans approached Warsaw, and had almost certainly saved his life. 'Well, he turned out to be as useful as you suggested. So far we've managed to keep him a step ahead of the Gestapo, but with the work he does and the way things are, we have to change his location every two or three weeks. We can find a place for Novak to hole up, too. In our world it never does any harm to have a surgeon you can call on. When the time comes, your Doctor Novak may well be worth his weight in gold. Do you want me to arrange it?'

'No, I'll deal with it.'

'Rozenblum is living in one of the outbuildings at the Warszawianka football ground.' Kazimierz gave him the directions. 'Don't take too long. An SS transport unit has just set up home in the old Department of Forests building next door, so we need to move him soon.'

'It shouldn't be a problem.' Kalisz nibbled the last flesh from the pear core and tossed it aside. 'It's odd. Hoth seems to have told Müller I'm semi-officially on the case. Müller thinks Blum is tailing me, so he doesn't worry where I am. Sometimes I wonder if they're giving me just enough rope to hang myself.'

'Don't take too many risks, my friend.' Almost as an afterthought, Kazimierz said, 'You wanted a list of places in Wola?' He reached into his inside pocket and handed it over. 'It's much as we expected. The SS barracks in the old school on Karolkowa, the supply depot at Sawki and the security police headquarters. They have a garrison at the railway station and the tram depot on Młynarska. Then there's the factories the Nazis have taken over and brought their own people to run. The most important will have an SS unit to provide security.'

Kalisz looked down the list and found the names he would have expected: the Philips light-bulb factory, the power plant, the Henneberg plating works, and the Bormann Swede metal works. One name caught his eye. *Could it be a coincidence?*

'I have one more favour to ask. Can we try to find out if any of these factories use a compound called Zyklon B. I'm told it's a delousing agent?'

Kazimierz gave him a wry look, but otherwise made no reply. Then he said, 'We've found Janina Berman.'

CHAPTER 36

Kalisz reckoned that Klub Sportowy Warszawianka had been one of the few beneficiaries of the German invasion of Poland. At the outbreak of the war they'd been ninth out of ten teams in the Polish football league, and if the season hadn't been abandoned they'd have been relegated. As a supporter of their arch-rivals Polonia, who'd been on the receiving end of a few such humiliations, he wouldn't have been too sad to see it happen.

The Warszawianka ground was in the south of the city, a few streets past the main water works. He was able to take a tram down Marszałkowska as far as Plac Zwabiciela. A strong security presence down here, not so far from Aleja Szucha, so watchful eyes and a sandbagged machine-gun post on every corner. He moved quickly in the opposite direction to the Gestapo headquarters, keeping to the smaller side streets, modifying his pace and doubling back on himself in a pattern that was now second nature. When he was as certain as he could be that he was alone, he walked unhurriedly down a narrow lane to Wawelska.

By some astonishing quirk of good fortune, he emerged next to a baker whose windows held a display of real bread. Such luck could not be ignored, especially when it was accompanied by the sweet, mouth-watering scent of loaves fresh from the oven. He paused and bought a round loaf which the baker wrapped in the pages of yesterday's *Kurier*. When he left the shop, Kalisz discovered a ZWZ news sheet slipped between them. It made him smile. Resistance didn't have to be all about guns and bombs – and at least someone thought he looked like a patriotic Pole.

In a way, Novak was a side issue he could have done without: to pass the fugitive doctor on to Kazimierz would create a direct link which might endanger them all. He'd been right when he'd told Novak these were different times. Back then, even with the bombs dropping, they'd treated it almost as a game, and Novak had little idea what he'd become involved in. Now, a single mistake would kill you. Better to allow the doctor to be absorbed into the Resistance by another route. Maybe it didn't matter. If Novak was caught and he talked, any Pole who'd helped him would be shot for aiding a Jew. But being careful had kept Kalisz alive so far, and he wasn't about to change.

He was certain now that Isaac Goldberg held the key to discovering the identity of Traudl Kleist's killer and saving August Klimecki from a firing squad. Somehow Salomon the rat-catcher had provided a clue that identified Hannah Goldberg's murderer as a member of the SS: the Jewish enforcer's black devil. Perhaps he'd seen the killer follow Hannah through the ruins, or remembered the number of the car he'd used? More significantly, Isaac Goldberg had referred to *that* black devil and *him*. Did that mean he'd been able to single out an individual? The only way to find out was to get to Goldberg before Müller or the Gestapo did. *And how in the name of Mary, mother of Christ, am I going to do that?*

Kazimierz's directions took him past the velodrome and athletics track to the soccer pitch. On the far side, hidden by trees, stood a group of buildings around a central courtyard; he walked towards it. This was where the ground staff kept their equipment, but, as the length of the grass testified, there'd been no need for ground staff since the previous October, when the Nazis added league football to the list of everything else they'd banned.

He stopped in front of a double door with peeling mud-green paint, knocked gently, and stepped quickly to one side. Kazimierz had explained that Rozenblum would normally be guarded, but the mother of the boy given the job was sick and he'd gone off to be with her. It meant Kalisz was less likely to be met by a bullet and a bellyful of splinters. Still...

No answer. So he knocked again. After a few moments the door opened to reveal the pale, anxious face of a man who was, nevertheless, resigned to his fate. All it needed to complete the picture was a pair of narrow wrists extended ready for the shackles.

'Mr Rozenblum. You remember me?'

Hershel Rozenblum nodded wordlessly, his misery, if anything, compounded. He had always looked underfed, but now his opaque skin and pink eyes gave him the look of an emaciated cave dweller.

'May I come in?'

The door swung back and Kalisz stepped past the little Jew into a gloomy interior lit only by a small roof light. The scents of printer's ink and mouldering grass made an odd, but not unpleasant, combination. Stacked by the walls, the tools of the groundsmen's trade – mowers, rollers, rakes and garden forks – left space for an antiquated, hand-cranked printing press in the centre of the concrete floor. On the other side of the room stood a pair of benches equipped with countless small drawers, many of which jutted open. Despite the poor light, Kalisz could see they were filled with metal and wooden blocks each cut with a single letter, and in many different fonts and sizes. On top of the benches sat flat metal frames, one or two filled with the blocks of type.

Kalisz laid the loaf on top of one of the benches and unwrapped it. Rozenblum wiped his inky hands on his stained apron and eyed the bread hungrily, the hope rapidly fading as Kalisz held up the news sheet. 'One of yours?'

The printer hung his head. 'Yes, sir.'

Kalisz tore a piece from the loaf and offered it. Rozenblum's eyes turned suspicious, but he accepted it and put the bread to his nose, breathing in the scent and emitting a little moan of pleasure. He took a bite and chewed as if he feared it was going to be taken from him.

'Mr Rozenblum.' Kalisz allowed his tone to harden a little. 'I am not interested in what you do here, or who you are. I am interested in your... creative talents. I have a friend who has mislaid his papers and requires a new set. Naturally, I'm prepared to pay.'

He had expected opposition, or at least prevarication, but Rozenblum looked up, still chewing.

'Does his name matter?'

Kalisz shrugged. 'No, I suppose it doesn't.'

'His age?'

'Around fifty-five, I would say, but he could be a few years younger, a few years older.'

Rozenblum pondered for a moment, his eyes flicking to the closer of the two benches and his lips murmuring something to himself. 'Naturally, you will need them yesterday?'

'Naturally.' Kalisz smiled.

'Then all I will need is his photograph.'

Kalisz handed over a small envelope. Rozenblum accepted it and squinted at the two pictures it contained. 'Good. Yes. Poor quality, but not too poor.' He peered at Kalisz. 'You can come back in the morning?'

'I'd prefer to stay until the job's done.'

Rozenblum stared at him as if he were mad, then shrugged. 'All right. I'll work through the night. There's a mattress behind the lawnmower.'

–

A rough hand shook Kalisz awake from a dream where he'd been chased across open fields by a relentless Bf 109 fighter, towards a line of men waiting with knives and bunches of roses. He stretched and groaned, gradually remembering where he was. An itch in his groin seemed to confirm his initial fear the mattress might be infested with fleas.

'I thought *I* didn't sleep too well, but you've been at it all night.' Rozenblum thrust the remains of the loaf into Kalisz's hand. 'Groaning and whimpering.'

Bright sunlight streamed in through the roof light. Kalisz ran a hand over his chin and decided he must look like hell and smell worse.

'There's a bucket if you want to wash.' Rozenblum pointed to a corner. 'And I have coffee – not the real sort, of course…'

After 'breakfast' Rozenblum handed Kalisz a set of cardboard rectangles. '*Kenncarte, Arbeitsbuche* – I hope your friend knows something about metalworking, that's all I had for someone his age – and a set of ration cards.'

'He can learn.' Kalisz opened the identity card and compared it with his own. Novak's grim face stared back at him from a blizzard of official stamps and signatures. He'd known Rozenblum was good, but not this good. 'They're perfect.'

'They should be.' Rozenblum glared at him. 'They're the real thing. The cards came from the administrative offices of the General Government. So did the typewriter I used to fill in the details. All of the stamps are official. Only the ink isn't real, but after you've roughed them up a little to age them that doesn't matter so much. Your friend will have to work on his signature. I couldn't afford to leave it blank. The one thing I can't replicate is his fingerprints, so he should apply them as soon as he can. Tell him not to take too much care, they're usually badly smudged. Is there anything else?'

Kalisz held his gaze for a moment: this wizened little gnome of a man, condemned by his own blood and forced to live the life of a fugitive, but still with an inner fire that made him twice the person he appeared. 'Only to say thank you.' He reached for his jacket pocket.

'Keep your money, Investigator. As you've noticed, I don't get out much these days. Maybe buy me a beer when this is over, huh?'

'Of course,' Kalisz said, and they grinned at each other, knowing how unlikely it was either of them would live to make the appointment. 'I thought you might be more reluctant to help, Mr Rozenblum. I appreciate your co-operation.'

Rozenblum dismissed him with a wave of the hand. 'If you hadn't sprung me loose when you did, I'd be in one of those new concentration camps, or more likely propping up two metres of earth. You told me someone would come knocking and I'd know what to do. Besides…' He laughed. 'For a cop, you were always a *mensh*.'

—

Kalisz found Doctor Novak crouched against the rear wall in the basement of the apartment block, shaking with fear and cold. If anything, he seemed even more diminished than before.

His entire demeanour changed when Kalisz handed over the identity papers, and he flicked through them. 'But these are—'

'Yes, they're real.' He told Novak about the fingerprints that were required. 'You'll need to memorise your new name and look the part of a workman. I have a pair of overalls in the cupboard that should fit you.'

'How can I thank you, Lieutenant?' Novak was on the brink of tears.

'By not staying a moment longer than you need to. Do you have somewhere else to go for a short while?'

Novak considered for a moment. 'The hospital. There is a bed in the basement where the boiler man sometimes sleeps over.'

'That might be best. Can you trust this man?'

'Once, but now…' *Who can trust anybody?* is what he meant.

Kalisz felt in his pockets and pulled out a handful of Occupation marks and zloty. 'Here.' He placed the crumpled notes in Novak's hand. 'Go to the hospital and stay there. Have him buy you food on the black market. A friend will be in touch.'

'A friend?'

'A friend from the old days.'

'And then?'

'That will be entirely up to you, Doctor Novak. Now, I am going to leave. Give me ten minutes and follow me. You should have ample time to reach the hospital before curfew. Should you be stopped by a patrol…'

'You need not worry, Lieutenant Kalisz.' Novak patted his pocket. 'They will not take me. A hospital contains many things that help ease the path. Some act more swiftly than others.'

'Then good luck, Doctor.' Kalisz doused the lamp he'd lit when he entered. 'Just one last thing.' The soft voice came from the darkness. 'You mentioned an odd smell in the cellar when

295

you found Hannah. Sweet, almost perfumed. Could it possibly have been cigarette smoke?'

Novak struggled to remember the scent that had tickled his nostrils. 'It's possible, but I can't be certain.' He blinked as the cellar door opened and a figure appeared, silhouetted for a single heartbeat against the light, and then was gone.

CHAPTER 37

The Artist

He'd spotted her quite by chance. Just another potential subject walking in the street and worth a glance as he drove by. It took moments before he realised it was *her*. He remembered the feel of the pliant flesh and hard muscle. During the struggle he'd managed to get his hand on her stomach, where he could feel the living elements of his masterpiece squirming beneath his fingers. The glorious anticipation of what was to come.

Being forced to abandon her by the men of the village had plunged him into a black pit of depression that made him question his very existence. When he looked in the mirror he saw a different man: flawed and twisted – a monster? At one point he'd found himself drawn to his pistol. That was when he knew he had to find another subject, or it was over.

Yet, despite the desperate urge to resume his work, he knew he had to be careful. Just as he'd planned, the police had found the Jewish girl and the wonderful creation she had inspired. She'd been so easy he'd feared it might be a trap. He'd seen her crossing at an unfinished part of the ghetto wall and followed her. When he approached her, the uniform and the power it represented froze her in place, and she'd done everything he said without the slightest protest. The hunt had almost been disappointing, but, paradoxically, she was responsible for his greatest work. By now, Department V knew precisely what was happening, and they would be carefully putting together all the pieces of evidence they had. Not that there was much – he'd made certain of that. All of his targets, apart from the Polish farm girl, had died alone and in terror, and no one had witnessed the disposal of their bodies. He'd created a smokescreen to hide him from detection, using pool cars and planting seeds of doubt and deception along the way.

They'd call him a depraved madman, because they still didn't appreciate the true genius of what he was doing. Or, at least, not all of them. From his observations, the little Pole, Kalisz, was the most perceptive of them – clever, with a trained police mind – while the others were largely mere brutes in uniform. But the very fact that Kalisz was a Pole meant he had little to fear. Kalisz might believe he was trusted, and even valued, but they would never allow him to be more than a dogsbody, fetching and carrying for his German betters. Then there was the carefully concealed side of his personality – the secret pride that Kalisz tried so hard not to show – that would eventually see the end of him. Men like Hoth would never listen to someone like Kalisz, and that meant the little Polish farm girl was once more at his mercy.

She wouldn't escape this time.

He'd watched her on three separate evenings until he'd been sure of her route and the murky business she conducted in the hour before curfew. Whatever her destination, she always passed the alley where he stood, looked back to check she wasn't followed and then crossed the road. He'd parked the car opposite the entrance, close to the pavement with the door open. The moment she looked back he'd step out, put the pad over her mouth and drag her into the car. At this hour the streets were virtually empty, and in any case no one would question the actions of an SS officer.

His heart stuttered as he saw her emerge from the clothes shop. A moment of doubt as she hesitated before starting in his direction. Another two minutes and he would have her.

He studied her from the shadows, taking in the way she walked, seeking out any hidden threat she might carry. His attention was so focused on his target that he barely registered the moment the man in the dark suit appeared behind her. He pulled his head back, and a thrill of fear rushed through him as he experienced a moment of recognition.

Kalisz.

For a few terrified heartbeats he checked his surroundings for the inevitable arrest squad who'd accompanied the Polish interpreter. No sound of thundering boots. No rattle of hand-cuffs or impact of spring-loaded cosh. He released a long breath as he realised he was safe.

Kalisz had seen the car, and some instinct made him steer the girl towards the far side of the street.

What could she tell him? He was certain she hadn't been able to get a good look at his face. Yet everything she said would add to the interpreter's knowledge. He forced himself to relax. There would be plenty of time for the Wawer girl. Her fate was not in doubt.

Maybe he'd been wrong, and the Pole was more of a threat than he'd thought. Perhaps it was time to rid himself of a nuisance.

After all, what was another dead Pole in a city where hundreds were butchered every day?

CHAPTER 38

Janina Berman's first thought as the man appeared beside her was for the cyanide capsule sewn into the lapel of her blouse.

'You have nothing to fear from me, Janina.' Kalisz kept his voice low, hoping she would hear calm and confidence in his tone, though he knew that would mean little to a girl who'd experienced what Janina had. Nazis knew all about the iron fist disguised by the velvet glove. 'I only want to ask you a few questions. No one will ever know we've spoken.'

Pretty as a porcelain doll, Kazimierz had described her, but with the heart of a lion. Be gentle with her, he'd said. Janina was fifteen years old, and since fleeing to the city she'd worked as a courier for a ZWZ Resistance cell, carrying messages between different addresses and delivering clandestine newspapers. As underground jobs went, it couldn't have been more dangerous. Her predecessor had lasted two months before she was caught, but Janina Berman's luminous beauty gave her an advantage. They'd be too busy looking at her to wonder what she was carrying in the leather shoulder bag. The only flaw was a mark on her cheek beneath her eye that might have been an old bruise, but which she'd subtly camouflaged with make-up.

'I have nothing to say to you.'

'How will you know until you hear my question?'

She continued walking without looking at him.

'I'm trying to find the man who attacked you. The man who was responsible for what happened afterwards.'

She stopped abruptly and looked up at him with eyes so deep and blue you could dive into them.

'Don't you understand?' She had a child's voice, but spoke with an adult's authority. 'I'm responsible for the deaths of all those men. The death of my own father. If I'd only gone with him, none of this would have happened.'

She turned to walk away, but Kalisz pulled her back.

'Don't be a fool, Janina. If you'd gone with him he'd have killed you, just as he may have killed at least three other girls since. Do you think your cousin would have done anything different if he'd taken you? I need to know what the man looked like. What he was wearing. Anything you can tell me about him.'

She'd gone very pale. 'Three other girls?'

'Yes, I'm sorry.'

'What did he do to them?'

Kalisz hesitated. He'd hoped it wouldn't come to this. 'He cut their throats.' At least he could spare her the details. She shook her head, and something in her eyes told him her legs were about to go. He supported her to a pavement cafe nearby. 'Two coffees, please,' he called to the man behind the counter. Janina sat with her face in her hands.

'I'm sorry,' she mumbled.

'Don't worry. It's not unusual to have a reaction when you hear something like that.'

'It could have been me.'

'Yes, it could. But you're here, and it's your duty to tell me what you know.'

She looked up. 'You're with us?' Her voice dropped to a whisper.

'I'm a policeman.'

She hesitated and he could tell what she was thinking. *Something isn't right here. If he isn't ZWZ, how has he found me? The police work with the Germans. Can I trust him?* Kalisz said nothing. Janina would have to come up with the answer for herself. The cafe owner appeared and laid two tiny cups on the table. When he'd gone, Janina started to talk in a low voice, so Kalisz had to lean forward to hear the words.

'I can't tell you what he looked like.' She saw the disappointment on his face. 'I'm sorry, but I can't tell you what I don't know.'

'Then tell me what you do know.'

'He was SS,' she said. 'I wouldn't have known it then, but I've seen enough of *them* since coming to Warsaw to be able to tell the difference.'

'An ordinary soldier or an officer?'

'Officer.' Her reply was confident. 'An *Obersturmführer.* He grabbed me from behind and I never saw his face, but before he hit me I was able to raise my head enough to see the three diamonds on his collar patch.'

'You're sure?'

She took a sip of her coffee and grimaced. 'They make us learn these things.'

He didn't need to ask who *they* were. 'Was he a big man? How tall?'

The blue eyes studied him. 'Taller than you.'

Kalisz laughed. 'Most people are taller than me.'

'Tall.' Janina smiled for the first time. 'A little under two metres. A slim build, I would say, but strong. I can feel his hands on me yet. It was as if they were testing a piece of meat.'

Kalisz had a vision of Traudl Kleist, and had to take a mouthful of his coffee to clear his throat. To think of Janina Berman lying there…

'Are you all right?'

He nodded, not trusting himself to speak just yet. Her voice told him he'd missed something.

She continued. 'I was saying that before it happened, a car had just drawn up on the road nearby and I heard someone whistling a tune, something quite cheerful, as if the whistler was in good spirits. It was odd, and I sometimes ask myself if I'd truly heard it. Why would a man who was going to do what he was going to do warn me by whistling?'

'Did you know this tune?'

'No.' She was sorry to disappoint him again. 'I'd never heard it before.' Her voice brightened. 'But I could sing it for you.'

He smiled. 'Why not? It's worth a try.'

She closed her eyes for a moment, nodding her head to an unheard rhythm. 'Da-da-da, de-dum, de-dum, dum, dum, dum, de-dum, dum dum dum, de-dum…'

It sounded vaguely Teutonic, and Kalisz thought he'd heard it somewhere before. He looked up to find the cafe owner in the doorway, his face a mask of disapproval.

'I'm sorry, sir, we didn't mean to offend you. My friend heard this tune somewhere and wondered if I knew it. You have heard it before?'

'I've heard it,' the man confirmed grimly. 'I lived in Berlin for two years back in the Thirties. Those Brownshirt bastards would strut around the streets roaring that, and their other favourite song, the "*Horst Wessel Lied*".'

Kalisz exchanged a glance with Janina. 'Does it have a title?' he asked the proprietor.

'They call it "*Die Wacht am Rhein*" – "The Watch on the Rhine".'

Kalisz stood up and laid a note on the table, about twice the value of the coffees. 'Thank you,' he said.

As he and Janina walked away, he asked her, 'Is there anything else you can tell me about him? Anything at all?'

She carried on for a few paces, chewing her lip in concentration. 'Yes.' She frowned. 'He smelled funny.'

'Smelled funny?' Kalisz felt a thrill of expectation run through him.

'Sweet. Like perfume, but more earthy.' She saw the look that crossed his face 'Have I been of help to you? Are you going to find him?'

'I'm going to try.'

'Then I'll be responsible for your death, too,' she said, with an assurance that belied her age. 'They'll kill you. That's what they do to people they believe are a threat to them.'

The matter-of-fact way she spoke sent a shiver through Kalisz. She wasn't only predicting his future; she was also foretelling her own.

CHAPTER 39

It was beginning to fall into place. Kalisz bent over the table and, by the flickering light of the oil lamp, wrote down the main elements of the case with the stub of a pencil on an old police notepad.

The sweet smell in the cellar linked the attack on Hannah Goldberg to the one on Janina Berman. The man who attempted to kidnap Janina was an officer in the SS. The terrible – near identical – injuries suffered by Hannah, Krystyna Lenski, Traudl Kleist and Tosia Lipman indicated that they were all killed by the same man. When you added up all the evidence, the killer was a German soldier, an SS officer, who carried a sweet smell around with him. Kalisz would bet that one of the things Isaac Goldberg's men had cleaned up in the cellar was a cigarette butt.

There were probably hundreds of *SS-Obersturmführers* in Warsaw, and from this moment, each of them was a suspect. But did that really matter? All the evidence was so circumstantial, Hoth would either laugh in his face or, more likely, have him hustled off to Pawiak to share the fate of the next batch destined for the wall. Goldberg's testimony might hold the key, but Goldberg was on the run and was hardly going to make himself easy to find. There had to be another way.

'Another night away, Jan. Perhaps you should just move in with her permanently.'

Jan looked up from his notebook. Maria was standing in the doorway in her dressing gown, studying him. Not angry, which he could have coped with, but detached, as if it didn't really matter to her any more.

'It's the Germans,' he said. 'They work us hard. You never know what's coming next.'

'Is it work?' She came to stand beside him at the table. 'Or something else? Something I'm not supposed to know about? More secrets.'

Kalisz's first instinct was to cover up the papers, but he had a feeling that if he did the cracks in his marriage would become fractures that could never be repaired. He willed his hand to stay still and allowed her to look over his shoulder.

'It's new information that could be linked to the Kleist case, but I'm not certain what to do with it.' He hesitated. 'It could be dangerous.'

'Walking in the street can be dangerous.' She drew up a seat beside him. 'Could it help my father?'

'It's possible.'

'Then tell me about it. Maybe I can be of use to you for a change.'

'All right.' He made his decision, for better or worse. 'Whoever murdered Traudl Kleist has probably killed three other girls.' He saw the shock register on her face. 'The bodies of two Jewish girls, Hannah Goldberg and Tosia Lipman, and Krystyna Lenski, a Pole, suffered similar injuries to Traudl.' As a nurse, Maria had seen more than her share of dead and shattered bodies, but Kalisz spared her the details.

'This man has killed four children?'

'Yes, but for the moment the department is only interested in one – Traudl Kleist.'

'That's ridiculous. Surely they understand that the deaths of the others may provide the evidence to identify her killer?'

Kalisz shook his head. 'As far as the Nazis are concerned, Hannah, Tosia and Krystyna might as well not exist. I think Hannah gives us the best chance of finding the killer.' He told her what Novak had said about Isaac Goldberg.

Maria stared at him. 'Why would you keep important information like this a secret?'

'You know why. Releasing it might get my informant killed.'

'But my father—'

'And because his information appears to indicate that our killer is an SS officer.' He told her about his conversation with Janina Berman. He expected expressions of horror and outrage, but she surprised him.

'Don't you see, Jan?' she cried. 'This can save my father! They can't keep shooting hostages to try to force a Pole to give himself up when the killer is one of them. You have to give this information to Hoth and ask him to stop the shootings.'

The expression of hope was so genuine and so improbable, Kalisz couldn't quite believe what he was hearing. Could she really be so naive? The last thing he wanted was to hurt her, but she had to be made to understand, or the hurt might end up being fatal.

'It's only one witness, Maria.' He took her hands and held them tight to emphasise the importance of what he was telling her. 'A fifteen-year-old girl who would be committing suicide if she stood up in court and accused a member of the SS. What do you think Hoth is going to say if I go into his office with a single piece of evidence and accuse a fellow SS officer of being a multiple murderer? The only way to make him listen is to find more evidence and try to identify the killer. Hoth won't act until he has no other choice, and even then there's no telling what he'll do. The SS is a brotherhood. Himmler modelled them on the Jesuits. They protect their own.'

'So my father will die – is that what you're saying?' She was angry now, but that was better than the alternative.

'Not if we can provide proof.'

'You're not frightened of them, Jan?'

'Yes, I am, Maria.' Kalisz didn't attempt to hide it. 'I know them too well not to be.' He showed her his notes. 'See, we have the sites of the four killings and the attack on Janina Berman. Traudl Kleist here, just south of Krasiński Gardens.' He marked the positions with the pencil. 'Hannah Goldberg found dead in Iron-Gate Square. Everything points to the Berman attack being a chance encounter when he was passing through Wawer. Which means this is the odd one out.' His brow furrowed in a frown of concentration. 'Krystyna Lenski, here in Wola.' He saw her look of doubt. 'I know. I thought Tosia's death might be another link to Wola, but look – her home address is here in Grzybowska, not far from the Ogród Saksi. The likelihood is that her killer snatched her close to her home, and used the cemetery site where she was found to make a point. That means three abductions within a radius of, say, a kilometre of Piłsudski Square, and there are suggestions other girls have been followed nearby. Yet Krystyna is kidnapped and later dumped three or four kilometres away on a bomb site between the Philips electrical plant and the Wola tram depot. Why?'

'Opportunity?' she suggested.

'Exactly,' he agreed. 'His hunting ground is the government area around Piłsudski Square and the Saxon Garden. There must be dozens of SS officers billeted in apartments in the *Nur für Deutsche* sector. But the man we're looking for has a reason or reasons to visit Wola, and that could be significant. The girls all disappeared in the late afternoon or early evening, which gives us an indication of his work patterns. Also, for reasons I can't disclose at the moment, the suspect is, or considers himself to be, some kind of artist…' His voice trailed off.

'Is something wrong, Jan?'

'I was just remembering something someone said recently.'

'Is it important?'

'It may be.'

Maria reached out and her hand covered his. 'Do you truly think you can find this man and save August, Jan?'

'I think so, Maria.' In his heart of hearts, Kalisz didn't believe his own words, but he needed to give her something. 'He's out there somewhere, but I'm going to need some specialist help to track him down.'

'What kind of specialist?'

'Someone in the SS.'

Yet it occurred to him that the someone he had in mind would fit all but one of the categories he'd just spelled out to Maria.

Doctor Josef Mengele had shown a decided lack of interest in art when they'd stumbled upon the montage The Artist had created from the organs of Traudl Kleist. No one who considered themselves an art lover would describe Pablo Picasso as 'that Spanish fellow'. But could that have been an attempt by Mengele to divert attention from himself? And, those words that had just come back to him. Hadn't Mengele drawn Kalisz's attention to Ziegler's paintings? Another part of the smokescreen? And if not, what had he meant by it? On the other hand, he'd also displayed an almost theatrical enthusiasm for the way The Artist had displayed Tosia Lipman's internal organs. The cigarettes he used could be said to have a sweet scent. Then there was Ziegler – another who fitted the killer's profile. The apartment he'd lived in was exactly where Kalisz had in mind when he'd pointed to the *Nur für Deutsche* sector on the map. Ziegler had been in Warsaw during the period the killings were carried out, and his reaction to the Wawer executions had shown a marked indifference to death. Yet did Ziegler's personality exhibit the kind of cold calculation and raw nerve Traudl Kleist's murderer had shown? If it did, he kept it buried deep, but then that's what made psychopaths so difficult to catch. In their normal lives they were actors playing a part, wearing a smile and buying you a drink as they chose you as their next victim.

Approaching Mengele entailed a calculated risk, but he had to do something. Kalisz would protect Novak by claiming he'd received the information from an anonymous Jew who'd been with Goldberg when he'd found Hannah's body. Of course, if Mengele *was* the killer, he'd simply shoot Kalisz, claim he'd been attacked, and that would be the end of it. In the eyes of the General Government, every Pole was a potential terrorist and no one would question the word of an SS officer. And if by some chance he – they – did succeed in tracking the murderer down and he was a member of the SS, what then? Hoth might well find it preferable to protect the service's reputation and dispose of the killer without going through the courts. In that case, Kalisz would become a loose end that required tidying up.

He saw from Maria's expression that she'd finally realised what she was asking of him and what it might cost them. 'Jan…' She shook her head, torn by the competing loyalties that threatened to destroy her. 'My father would never ask you to risk your life to save his. I was upset when I made you promise to save him.'

'It's not that, Maria. I—'

She put a finger on his lips to silence him. 'I spoke to him about what he was doing… with the Resistance. He knew exactly what could happen. Perhaps it was coincidence he was picked up over Traudl Kleist, perhaps not, but he knew they might come for him one day.'

'No, Maria.' Kalisz kissed her finger and moved it aside. 'You don't understand. It's not about August any more. It's not even about the others who still face death with him every day Traudl's killer isn't caught. It's about me – Jan Kalisz. I took a decision to work with the Germans.' It was his turn to raise a hand to ask for silence. 'There's no need to go into the reasons now, but I still believe I was right. As a family we've paid a price for that decision. I hope one day you and Stefan will understand that price was worth paying. Finding Traudl Kleist's killer and saving the lives of those people in Pawiak is my chance to be a Pole again, if only for one day. My act of resistance. If there is a risk to me, what about the risks all those other men and women are taking every day by resisting and refusing to co-operate? This is something I have to do. I pray it saves your father's life, but it is as much about restoring my own pride.'

Maria reached out, a hand moving behind his head and drawing him to her. They kissed, lightly at first, then with more passion. His heart, which had been in limbo for six long months, found new life and took wing. They had survived.

Maria drew away, her eyes shining.

'Tadeusz was right. I should have trusted you.'

CHAPTER 40

Kazimierz had suggested the restaurant and provided the money so Kalisz could afford to eat there. They sat at a corner table, well out of the hearing of the other diners.

'I'm impressed, Kalisz,' said Doctor Josef Mengele as he studied the leather-covered menu, 'though I'd been given to believe you Poles were going hungry. Isn't there supposed to be rationing?'

Mengele wore a smart civilian suit this lunchtime, as did the men at most of the cloth-covered tables, none of whom, at first glance, looked as if they were going hungry. Waiters dashed between the tables bearing trays piled high with steaming dishes that made Kalisz's stomach groan in anticipation. *Another surreal moment in a world gone mad. The vanquished Polish invest-igator and his SS conqueror contemplate a gourmet lunch in a city starving to death.* Kalisz had to remind himself that the food was a secondary consideration. On the other side of the room, Department V's former guest, Petrov, 'The Bulgarian', raised an ironic glass in welcome before turning his attention back to the beautiful woman who shared his table. In the opposite corner, a pianist was playing something from a Beethoven concerto.

'This place is run by the black market,' Kalisz said by way of explanation. 'A special refrigerated wagon in one of your weekly supply trains brings the chef the finest food and drink Paris can provide. Since I can't go to a German-only restaurant, and you don't seem the type to appreciate turnip soup, it was an obvious choice.'

Mengele raised a single cultivated eyebrow. 'And why would you believe a conscientious German officer would not report this blatant criminality?'

'Apart from the obvious attraction of the menu –' Kalisz smiled to let Mengele know he knew he was joking – 'it would be a very rash German officer who decided to jeopardise an enterprise in which *Standartenführer* Meisinger has such a substantial stake. They tell me he and a very senior Wehrmacht general, who has his headquarters not far from here, are regular customers.'

'That shines a slightly different light on the situation.' The German's lips twitched. 'I was intrigued at your suggestion we should meet away from the office and I wonder why... I'm considering the Chateaubriand, by the way. Are you sure you can afford this?'

'If I can't, I suppose I could always offer to wash the dishes.'

'Then I insist on paying for the wine. A Chambertin, I think, would go well, and 1929 was an excellent vintage. As I say, I'm intrigued.'

'You suggested I might be interested in *Obersturmführer* Ziegler's paintings. Was there a particular reason for that?'

'Ah...' Mengele smiled. 'Ziegler. Now I see. Yes, I found his paintings fascinating. A rather surprising insight into the inner Ziegler. They weren't on display...' A waiter approached and Mengele paused as Kalisz ordered for them both. 'He had them stacked facing the wall in a little room that he used as a studio, just to the left of the front door. It was almost as if he was ashamed of them.'

'Can you tell me about them?'

'Oh, no, Kalisz. That would spoil the surprise. I think you'd have to see for yourself. Perhaps you can ask him for a viewing?'

'I may do that. What do you think of the music?'

The abrupt change of subject clearly puzzled Mengele. 'Personally, I prefer Haydn or Bach.' He shrugged. 'Beethoven is very popular, of course, because of the Führer's interest, and there's something quite martial about his work.'

'What about other martial songs? I understand the SS are very fond of them.'

Something in the other man's eyes told Kalisz he'd overstepped a mark, but he was saved by the arrival of the sommelier, who went through the ritual of opening the wine, which Mengele pronounced 'very adequate'.

'What shall we drink to?' Mengele wondered idly. 'We have so little in common, you and I, Kalisz.'

'How about the future?' Kalisz suggested.

'The future.' Mengele raised his glass. 'May it be a prolonged one in your case.' Kalisz noted the suggestion that the opposite might be true should the conversation proceed the wrong way. 'Now,' the German continued, 'I really must insist you tell me what is going on.'

'I was specifically wondering if you enjoyed a song entitled "*Die Wacht am Rhein*"?'

Mengele studied him for a long moment. 'You know, of course, that "*Die Wacht am Rhein*" was the first tune Ziegler played on the piano at that ridiculous party?'

'What if I was to tell you that all the evidence points to the The Artist being an SS officer?'

Mengele leaned back in his chair. 'I was led to believe there was no evidence to suggest the killer's identity.' He took a sip of wine. 'Unless, of course, you've been doing a little investigating of your own? I'm sure Müller will be delighted to hear about it. Have you considered Hoth's reaction when you announce this?'

'He must listen.' Kalisz reached for his pocket. 'I've spoken to witnesses. When you see what—'

The German cut him short. 'I'm sure your evidence is perfectly adequate, but I don't wish to know about it.'

'But you've seen what this man's done,' Kalisz protested. 'Someone has butchered four innocent young girls. If it is Ziegler, he has to be brought to justice before he kills again.'

'Perhaps,' Mengele conceded. 'But not by me. Can you imagine the uproar if I accused a brother SS officer of murder? Guilty or not, my career would be finished. No, Kalisz, you're on your own. And consider this. It is quite possible that Hoth's first consideration will be the good of the service. He won't want any scandal, and he won't thank the interfering Pole who presented him with one. Even if you succeed in incriminating Ziegler, you might be signing your own death warrant. The SS looks after its own.'

Kalisz held the other man's gaze. 'I don't have any choice. Every day The Artist goes free, another ten of my countrymen are dying.'

'I admire your tenacity, but I seem to have lost my appetite...' Mengele took out his wallet. He paused as a thought struck him. 'When you came here, you couldn't be certain Ziegler was The Artist. All you suspected was that the killer was an SS *Obersturmführer.*' His hand went to his collar, where the three diamonds of his rank would normally be displayed. 'And of course...' He shook his head with a little half-smile of disbelief. 'What would you have done if I'd said I sang "*Die Wacht am Rhein*" before breakfast every morning?'

Kalisz struggled to hide his growing anger. 'I'd have thought of something, Herr *Obersturmführer.*'

Mengele studied him for a long moment, then reached into the inside pocket of his suit and pulled out what looked like a flat leather pouch. 'I see you require another lesson, Investigator.' He unstrapped the pouch's binding and opened it on the table. 'This is an emergency surgical kit,' he explained. 'I carry it everywhere with me. As you can see, it contains scissors, tweezers, probes, safety pins, and this —' he held up a scalpel so the recently honed edge glinted in the light of the restaurant's lamps — 'which, as we both know, is probably identical to the one The Artist uses. Are we agreed.'

'I think so, sir. Perhaps—'

'No.' Mengele's voice hardened. 'Let me continue. In the event that your unlikely theory was correct, and I *am* The Artist, I could reach out like this —' he extended his arm across the table so Kalisz could feel the cold steel of the scalpel blade against the side of his neck — 'and slice the edge across your throat, severing carotid artery and windpipe and silencing your foolish accusations forever. And the only inconvenience would be to a few people who had their lunch spoiled, and possibly my laundry maid. Why, I could cut off your head and carry it away as a souvenir, and all they'd do is clean up the table for the next guest. Do you know why, Kalisz?' Mengele withdrew the scalpel and placed it back in the wallet.

Kalisz swallowed and touched his neck where the blade had been. 'Because you're a German and an SS officer?'

'No – because you are a Pole, an impudent Pole with ideas above his station, and the life of a Pole in Warsaw has a value of precisely nothing. You're a fool, Kalisz,' Mengele sneered. 'A brave fool, but still a fool. Take my advice and give it up.' He placed a handful of notes on the table. 'That should cover the bill. Enjoy your Chateaubriand.'

He walked out of the restaurant and Kalisz found himself the focus of a puzzled waiter carrying two plates filled with enormous slabs of meat. He considered for a moment before picking up his napkin. *Why not? The condemned man should eat a hearty meal.* 'I don't think I can manage two. Perhaps you might find some kind of bag for the other one,' he suggested.

It was only when he reached for his wine he noticed the key partly hidden by Mengele's pile of Occupation marks.

CHAPTER 41

Kalisz was translating a document from Polish to German when the phone on Gersten's desk rang. The German investigator answered it and spoke for a few moments before gesturing to Kalisz with a puzzled frown.

'It's for you.'

'Thank you, sir.'

He picked up the handset.

'Kalisz?'

'Yes.'

'Lange here. I'm sorry, Jani, but we drew a blank. No eviscerated girls or mosaics made from their bits and pieces.'

Kalisz tried to hide his disappointment. 'It was a long shot, Hans, but I appreciate the time you put in. I'll buy you a beer if I'm ever back in Munich.' There was a momentary hesitation at the end of the line. 'Hansi?'

'Look, Jan, this is probably nothing and I don't see how it helps you, but I did come across something odd in the files. It happened in '38 when I was on secondment to the Gestapo in Frankfurt, so I didn't hear about it at the time. We had a whole list of complaints involving young girls being touched up or assaulted. One or two of them ended up in a pretty bad way. The reason I mention it is that they'd all been lured into posing for a pervert who called himself an artist.'

Kalisz felt the excitement rising inside him. He picked up a pencil from Gersten's desk. 'Do you have an identity?'

'That's what's so odd about the case, Jan. The case files are all there, and Munich Kripo were in a position to make an arrest at the end of last year, but we had orders from on high not to proceed, and the skirt-lifter's personal file vanished.'

'From on high?'

'Like you said, Jani. So high that whoever was giving those orders must have had wings. The note came from a pen-pusher at the Reich Main Security Office, but it had been initialled by someone important. The initials were R.H. You understand?' Yes, Kalisz understood. Hans Lange would never say the name over the telephone, but Himmler's deputy, Reinhardt Heydrich, had taken a personal interest in the case.

'Like I say, I'm not sure how it helps. I'm curious, Jani. What do you plan to do about it?'

'To be honest, I'm not sure, Hans.'

Lange was chuckling when he hung up.

Willi Ziegler was from Munich.

'Not going home tonight, Kalisz?' Hoth asked.

'I have to finish translating this witness statement for Investigator Gersten, sir. He's coming back in half an hour to collect it.'

When Hoth had left, Kalisz waited, barely daring to breathe and his ears straining to catch the sounds from below, where the SS clerk would be manning the front desk. The almost imperceptible flick of a page being turned. A soft thud as a file was closed, and a second as it was returned to its pile. The scratch of a match and a long exhalation, accompanied by the scent of a newly lit cigarette.

He walked quickly to Müller's desk by the window. As Senior Investigator, Müller handed out the various forms that authorised entry for his junior detectives to the likes of Pawiak Prison and the Gestapo Headquarters at Aleja Szucha. He also kept a book of passes that allowed the department's Polish interpreters to accompany them into areas designated *Nur für Deutsche*. Ziegler had signed one for Kalisz to get him into the Café Club on the night of his party.

Each detective had to lock his desk up at night or face disciplinary action, but the desk Müller used had once belonged to Kalisz. The Pole had handed over the original key and the spare on the day the Nazis took over, but, given Kazimierz's mission, it had seemed like a good idea to have a second spare cut before he did so. Now he slipped it into the lock and turned it gently, grimacing as it clicked to give him access to all four drawers.

The forms were in the third drawer he tried, and he quickly found the *Nur für Deutsche* passes. They had to be filled out in duplicate with one left in the book. Kalisz had already thought about that. He took a razor blade from his pocket and carefully cut *both* sheets from the book, as close to the spine as he could manage. When he'd completed the task he returned the book and locked the desk. The whole operation had taken a matter of seconds, but as he crossed the four paces to his own desk he could already hear the footsteps he'd been expecting on the stairs.

The SS clerk's head appeared in the opening. 'The *Hauptstur-mführer* told me to come up and stay with you until Investigator Gersten arrives.'

'It's all right,' Kalisz assured him. 'I'm just leaving. Kurt's note was hidden beneath the papers on my desk.' He showed the young SS man a piece of paper with a scrawled message that read 'It can wait till tomorrow. G'.

'Fair enough.' The soldier shrugged. 'Just make sure you lock the file away overnight.'

'Yes, sir. Thank you, sir.'

Next morning, Kalisz handed his temporary pass to the guard at the Ogród Saksi entrance to the *Nur für Deutsche* sector, hoping the spiky Germanic script and a fair representation of Müller's signature would be enough to get him through.

He was walking into the lion's den: the only question was whether the lion was waiting there, ready to gobble him up. Why would Mengele warn him off continuing the investigation, then leave him the key to Ziegler's apartment? It could be that he wanted the killer caught, but was protecting himself and his career. *We can't have people going around killing other people for no good reason. It would be anarchy.* That was the way the German mind worked, even in a city where they waited round every corner, ready to dispense death for the slightest of reasons. But Mengele, too, had his links with Munich. Hadn't he said he and Ziegler had been at university there together? His little performance in the restaurant was yet more evidence of his love of theatrics. What he'd said was entirely true: Kalisz's life was worth nothing in German eyes. Yet killing Kalisz in public wouldn't have been the act of someone who planned to murder again. Why cause a fuss, when it would be so much easier to simply make him disappear like so many thousands of other Poles?

The guard frowned beneath the rim of his steel helmet. 'It says here you should be accompanied by an investigator?'

'He told me to meet him by the fountain, sir.'

The Nazi tapped the piece of paper against his palm, his narrow eyes sizing up Kalisz. He could keep him here all day, but was it worth it? If the investigator was on an important case and that case was delayed, the shit would eventually filter down and dribble all over the man who caused it. Of course, it was probably just some thieving Polish cleaner stealing a general's socks, and the guard was bored enough to consider kicking this particularly uppity Polack twice round the park for a bit of fun. But…

'On your way.' He handed back the pass. 'But tell him from me, he should follow the rules next time.'

'I will, sir.' Kalisz bowed his head and walked past with his eyes on the ground. Of course, there might be another reason for Mengele's encouraging him to work on his own. What if *Hauptsturmführer* Hoth wasn't the only one with the good of the service at heart? How convenient if the troublesome Pole turned out to be a terrorist who tricked his way into Ziegler's apartment, planning to kill him? There were any number of convenient ways that scenario might work out, and none of them was good for Kalisz's health.

Kazimierz would have told him to turn back – the hostages weren't his responsibility. But as Kalisz had told Maria, it wasn't about the hostages any more. He was sick of the double life he was forced to lead. Sick of working alongside monsters like Müller and Gruhl, and suave thugs like Hoth. Sick of being manipulated. Today he was Jan Kalisz, former deputy head of Department V, and he would see it through to the end. Just like the old days.

The thought brought a grim smile. He hadn't been in the Ogród Saksi since before the war and the open space made his head spin: hectares of lovingly manicured grass, criss-crossed by gravel walkways and clumps of lime trees. German officers and their wives or Polish mistresses walked languidly beneath the emerald canopy enjoying the sunshine, while off-duty soldiers sat in groups on the grass chatting, smoking and dozing, as if the war was none of their business. Kalisz tried to look as if he belonged. He walked with his head high and met any puzzled look with a brief nod, but he knew his worn suit and scuffed shoes marked him as a Pole, just as obviously as a white armband marked the Jews. He didn't look around, but he was aware of the burnt-out ruin of the summer theatre to his left, a victim of the big raids of the previous September. To his right, the swimming pool where he'd swum as a boy was now occupied by tanned Wehrmacht *Landsers* sunbathing on the boards or cavorting in the blue waters. When he was past the pool, he cut across the grass. Ziegler had his apartment on Królewska – now, of course, renamed Königstraße – in a block that had survived the bombing while many others nearby were piles of rubble.

As he approached the apartment building, Kalisz was relieved to see it wasn't important enough to merit a guard. A year ago this street had been lined with rowan trees, but they'd been chopped down to provide a clear field of fire for the Nazi security forces in this sensitive zone.

He felt an unnatural calm. No turning back now. He would play the cards as they fell. If Ziegler was home, he'd confront him about the killings and hope his reaction wasn't fatal. If he was out, it would give Kalisz the opportunity to search for evidence that might be presented to Hoth and force his hand.

The building had an arched doorway, and Kalisz pushed his way inside to discover that the block might not warrant an armed guard, but it had the next best thing. A scrawny, bald man in a dark suit two sizes too large sat at the window of a booth to one side of the stairs. One of a *type*: feral eyes and a Hitler moustache. Kalisz knew that, no matter the outcome of his confrontation with Ziegler, a report of his visit would be with the Gestapo by nightfall.

'Your business here?' The voice matched his looks, a mixture of vinegar and belladonna.

'Investigator Kalisz.' Kalisz gave his German a throaty Silesian growl as he flashed his warrant disc and continued towards the stairs. 'Kripo, to see SS *Obersturmführer* Ziegler. Second floor, apartment five, is that right?'

'Wait. You can't go up. He's out.'

Think like a Nazi. Act like a Nazi. You don't frighten me, little man. 'That'll be why he gave me the key, then.'

'But it's against the rules.'

Kalisz stopped with his hand on the rail and his foot on the bottom step. 'Some people would call that obstructing a state official in the pursuance of his duty.'

'I'm just doing my job,' the man blustered.

'Then stay in your hutch. And let me do mine.'

Kalisz could still hear muttering as he strode up the stairs, but he was inside. He'd worry about the future later. He felt a bolt of elation. Ziegler was out. He'd be able to search the place. The kind of man who'd killed Hannah and Traudl and Krystyna was a collector. If Ziegler was his man, somewhere in those rooms Kalisz would find the evidence that would convict him.

He reached the second floor and counted the doors: three, four, five. As he went to put the key in the lock, he heard voices from above and footsteps on the stairs. He ducked into a passageway. The fewer people who saw him, the better. Two voices, talking in matter-of-fact tones.

'...the general was in no doubt about it. Himmler was quite serious.'

'But that many? The numbers are huge, and the country is bloody enormous.'

'Nevertheless, the Soviet Union will be Jew-free from Minsk to Chelyabinsk.'

'Well, I'm glad I won't have to...'

It took a few moments before the enormity of what he'd heard dawned on Kalisz. The Soviet Union? His initial reaction was to abandon Ziegler and run to Kazimierz, but a second's thought made him pause. What *had* he just heard? Of course, it made sense. Hitler had never made any secret of his ambitions in the East. Poland was just the appetiser before the main course. But what *hadn't* he heard? The men could have been talking about a contingency plan. Every army made them. *What if…?* And perhaps he'd missed '…*after we settle with England…*' It might be a while before that happened. Kalisz thought about the logistics. The Russian winter had swallowed up Napoleon's Grand Army. It was too late in the season for it to be this year. That meant next spring at the earliest, and a huge build-up of troops in advance, from the Baltic to the Black Sea: millions of soldiers, thousands of tanks, airfields and hospitals. No, he'd report it to Kazimierz, but there was no reason for haste. He slipped silently from the corridor, inserted the key, and opened the door to Ziegler's apartment.

The first thing that struck him was the smell: the rank scent of unwashed clothing, mixed with the heavy, bittersweet odour of last night's alcohol, old vomit and stale cigarette smoke. The stink was matched by what he could see in the sunlight streaming through the big double window.

Underwear and shirts strewn everywhere, overflowing ashtrays, and an astonishing number of empty cognac bottles. It was so totally unexpected that he didn't know what to think, or where to start. If the other rooms were in a similar condition, he could search for days and never know if he'd found anything significant. This chaos didn't fit with either of the Zieglers he knew. When they'd first met, Ziegler had worn an air of haunted tragedy that Kalisz thought he now understood, but the reasons for which he could never condone. Yet he'd held himself together enough to do his duty, and his uniform had always been immaculate. But this room? It was a window into a soul that had given up on life.

Still, there'd been no rush of feet and truncheon-wielding Gestapo. No pistol muzzle on the back of the neck when he came through the door. Kalisz had to make the most of the opportunity while it lasted.

Mengele had mentioned a room to the left of the door, and once again Kalisz was reminded of the way the SS doctor had dangled Ziegler's paintings in front of him like a baited hook. Something still didn't feel right about that, but he'd never know unless he looked. He opened the door. The room – little more than a cupboard, really – had no windows, and he switched on the light.

Torn and shattered canvases lay scattered across the floor, kicked, punched and – judging by the scars in the plaster – deliberately smashed to pieces against the walls. Some remained intact enough that Kalisz could identify the subject matter, and it was this that made him feel as if the point of a dagger had been run down his spine. Blood. Blood in fountains, splashed across walls and flowing in torrents. Blood hazing the air and oozing from the ground. Blood on grass, and on the golden straw of a corn field. And mixed with the blood, crudely portrayed, but recognisable, ripped flesh and splintered bone. Only one picture remained intact, and in its way it was the most haunting of all. In the midst of a field of earth that oozed blood, a single, delicate, almost certainly female hand rose from the ground, the fingers hooked like claws.

No cold muzzle on the back of my neck? How wrong could I have been?

'Give me one reason why I shouldn't pull the trigger.'

CHAPTER 42

Kalisz carefully raised his arms.

'I'm here to help you, Willi.'

'Turn around – slowly.'

Kalisz did as he was ordered and looked into the face of a day-old corpse. Willi Ziegler wore a crumpled SS uniform jacket and trousers and a white shirt open at the neck, stained with flecks of vomit. He'd clearly just woken, and his face was the unhealthy, washed-out dirty yellow of ancient ivory. His red-rimmed eyes were sunk so deep, it was like looking into the pistol barrel Ziegler now pointed at Kalisz's forehead.

'The concierge said you were out.' Kalisz allowed himself a glance downwards. 'You're wearing socks. That's why I didn't hear you coming.'

'How did you get in?'

'Doctor Mengele very kindly lent me your key so I could visit you. We've been worried about you, Willi.'

'You're a lying Polish shit, Kalisz.' Ziegler's words emerged as a throaty growl, and a nerve in his left cheek twitched alarmingly. 'The very fact you're here gives me all the reason I need to put a bullet in your brain and no questions asked. I'm very good at putting bullets in people's brains. I was averaging about twenty a day for a while. Of course, I only needed to do it when those incompetent animals in my unit were too drunk to shoot straight, and blew bits off all the Jews and Poles instead of killing them. Do you know what it's like to shoot a baby, Kalisz? A very tiny one?' Kalisz shook his head, and wished he was anywhere else in the world than listening to Willi Ziegler's version of Hell.

'I didn't do it because I enjoyed it, of course, but Corporal Jäger and his friends had taken to swinging them by the legs and smashing their heads against trees. So shooting was a blessing, really. Of course the mothers didn't think that, but we worked out it was best to kill them first.' He spoke in the matter-of-fact tone of a lawyer explaining some obscure clause in a document, but without warning his breath quickened. The barrel of the Walther shook as his finger tightened on the trigger. 'Now, I will ask you one more time. Why… are… you… here?'

Kalisz knew that to hesitate invited a bullet, and what did it matter anyway? All he had was the truth. 'Doctor Mengele suggested I might like to look at your art collection.'

A puzzled frown flitted across Ziegler's damaged features. 'Why would he do that?'

'Since you went on leave, we've been having some trouble with a killer we call The Artist.' Kalisz nodded towards the paintings and Ziegler's frown deepened. 'All the evidence points to an SS officer, and you fit certain elements of his description and what we might call "windows of opportunity".'

'Why do you call him The Artist?'

'Because he likes to make pictures,' Kalisz said softly. 'Pictures not too different from these. He cuts open his victims and removes their organs to create a montage with them.'

Ziegler's brow creased in a frown and the gun dropped away slightly. 'What kind of montage?'

'He likes flowers.' Kalisz recalled a detail he'd noticed on his first survey of the other room. 'A bit like the ones in the vase on your windowsill. We call them "Blood Roses". So far, we know his Warsaw tally stands at four, but it could be more. He doesn't care who he kills as long as they're young and female – Poles, Jews, Germans, it makes no difference to him.'

'I don't believe you.' Ziegler's eyes flared and the Walther came up into Kalisz's face again. 'They've sent you here to drive me mad. That shit Fischer won't be satisfied until I'm in an asylum. I asked for a transfer and he called me a weakling. Said that if I ever tried to walk away he'd shoot me as a deserter. When he saw I was about to crack, he sent me to Warsaw for "a rest", knowing full well that going back would be worse than if I'd stayed. And now he's sent you.'

'No, sir,' Kalisz said quietly.

Ziegler stared at him. 'You mean you truly believe I am this maniac? This Artist?'

'Are you?'

For a moment, the other man seemed to look inside himself and his face reflected the horror of what he found there. 'I don't know.'

Kalisz had expected denial, or justification, or confession… anything but this.

'You don't know?'

The pistol dropped away and Willi Ziegler stumbled into the living room to slump into a chair. His hands hung over the side and he dropped the pistol to the floor. Kalisz picked it up and studied it before returning it to a holster draped from a door handle. If Ziegler was going to shoot him, he'd have done it by now.

'I… I have gaps.' Ziegler sounded as if his throat was coated with sandpaper. 'What the doctors call a blackout. It happened even before I started drinking. I would be walking along a street in a city and a moment later I would be in another district entirely, wondering where I was and how I'd got there.

Sometimes my feet would be wet, as if I'd crossed a stream, or I'd have mud on my shoes. Once –' he looked up despairingly into Kalisz's eyes – 'I had scratches on my face.'

'What kind of scratches? From thorns? Falling against something?'

'Don't, Kalisz.' It was almost a sob. 'You know what kind of scratches.'

'Defensive scratches? From a woman's nails.'

'I think so.'

'So you could be The Artist?'

'Yes.' A violent shake of the head. 'No. I cannot be. You say these women – these girls – were eviscerated. I could never do such a thing. There would be other signs. The blood... It would be everywhere. You may search my clothing.'

'You could have washed it.'

Ziegler gave a harsh laugh. 'Does it look as if I wash my clothes? Look.' The final word emerged almost as a scream, the kind a man makes as he realises he's falling from a cliff edge. Ziegler slumped back into the chair, almost in the foetal position. Kalisz suspected the SS officer was on the verge of a total breakdown. He'd seen it in the war. Men under intense shelling would enter a catatonic state that might last hours, days or weeks, or they'd collapse into shaking fits so intense they'd break bones. He made a show of checking the rank underwear and filthy shirts.

'Hannah Goldberg was the first,' he said, to keep Ziegler's attention. 'She disappeared in Iron-Gate Square on 23 December and her body was found below the ruins of the Wielopole shopping hall. Does that mean anything to you?'

'No.' A kind of mental shrug. 'I don't know.'

'Think,' Kalisz snapped. 'Everyone knows what they were doing over Christmas. You appeared at my door two days later. You were in a mess then?'

'It happens like that. I spend two or three days drinking, then I wake up with a black hole where my memory should be and sickened with myself.'

'All right.' Kalisz moved on. 'Traudl Kleist. She was killed on 13 May near her home out by Krasiński Gardens. Traudl was thirteen years old, and a true German beauty – all blonde curls, peach complexion and blue eyes. You would remember Traudl.'

'I remember nothing.' Ziegler had discovered a brandy bottle that was only half-empty, and he poured most of the contents down his throat as if they were water. Kalisz could have done with a slug himself, if only to stop his hands shaking. 'Maybe there were parks. Girls. I don't know.'

'We didn't find any of the victims' clothing. That means you – The Artist – may well have kept some of it. Do you mind if I check through your wardrobe and drawers?'

'Do what you have to.'

Kalisz opened a drawer. Oddly, it was a complete contrast to the chaos in the room, every item freshly pressed and placed precisely with its fellows. He felt almost guilty disturbing them. Nothing but men's socks and underpants. 'It was the song that led us to you.' He opened another drawer.

'The song?'

'"*Die Wacht am Rhein*." You played it at your party. The killer was known to whistle it.'

Ziegler snorted through his nose and took another drink. 'Half the SS must go around whistling "*Die Wacht am Rhein*". You'll have to do better than that if you're going to send me to the axe.'

'It's the poison I still don't understand,' Kalisz continued. 'When were you ever in a position to lay your hands on something like Zyklon B? What's this?'

'Zyklon B?' Ziegler looked up sharply, the remaining colour drained from his face. 'What is that?'

Kalisz studied the square of silk in his hand. 'It's a scarf. A lady's scarf. Krystyna Lenski was wearing one just like it on the day she was killed.'

CHAPTER 43

'No!' Ziegler was out of his seat, shouting. 'What is Zyklon B?'

'Forget Zyklon B.' Kalisz held out the scarf like an accusation. 'This belonged to Krystyna Lenski's mother.'

'Tell me what Zyklon B is.' Kalisz was caught by surprise as the German flew across the room at him, but he managed to sway aside at the last minute. Ziegler smashed into the wardrobe and collapsed on the floor. When he looked up, tears were streaming down his face. 'Please, Kalisz, you must tell me.'

Kalisz stood with the scarf in his hand, utterly bewildered by Ziegler's reaction. 'It's a poison. Some kind of chemical for pest control. How did you get it?'

'Not me.' Ziegler shook his head.

'But the scarf?'

'I've never seen it before. Someone must have put it there. Someone who's trying to implicate me in these killings.'

Kalisz almost felt pity at the feebleness of Ziegler's defence. Surely a lawyer could come up with something better than that. But he had to ask, though he already knew the answer. 'Who would do that?'

'Wolff.'

'Who?' Kalisz had expected him to accuse Mengele. He trawled his memory for the name until a face came to him: the tall blond civilian who'd confronted him at Ziegler's party. 'But Mr Wolff is a civilian. The man we're looking for is in the SS.'

'Honorary rank.' Ziegler's voice shook. '*Obersturmführer.*'

'But he wasn't wearing uniform.'

'That doesn't mean he doesn't have one.'

'No.' Kalisz refused to believe it. 'He told me he was an engineer.'

'He is – a chemical engineer. And it was Hans Wolff who suggested I play "*Die Wacht am Rhein*" at the party.'

And Kalisz had seen Wolff handing Ziegler the Turkish cigarettes whose smell Novak and Janina Berman remembered. Who was to say he didn't smoke them himself?

'He was setting you up?' It all came together in Kalisz's head. 'Half of the Warsaw Kripo would have been at the Café Club. Wolff's not the kind of man to take chances. He must have known that tune was a weakness that might link him to the killings. It was a simple thing to arrange.'

'I thought he was my friend.'

'If it ever came out that an SS officer might have been involved in the killings and they started looking—'

'But a song? It's hardly something that would hang a man.'

'No.' Kalisz helped Ziegler to his feet. 'But we have this –' he put the scarf to his nose and detected a faint whiff of perfume – 'and you can bet there'll be other clues that will point the Kripo or the Gestapo in the direction of Willi Ziegler.'

'That bastard.' Ziegler's voice shook with outrage. 'A brother SS officer. He would have let me be executed.'

'The question is, what do we do about it?'

'Do?' Ziegler was a different man now: energised and focused. He buttoned up his tunic and strapped on the Walther in its holster. 'We confront him. Where are my boots?'

Kalisz pointed to a pair of jackboots half-hidden behind the door. 'Are you sure you want to do this, sir? Shouldn't we take what evidence we have to Hoth and let him deal with it?'

'Don't you, of all people, understand, Kalisz? All we have is a few coincidences. I've known Hans Wolff since I was a student in Munich. I want to hear him tell me why he betrayed me. Then we'll do what needs to be done.'

'What if he just laughs it off?' Kalisz said. 'He didn't seem like the kind of man to go around admitting anything.'

Ziegler was undeterred. 'Then we'll search his hotel room at the Europejski.' He patted the pistol on his hip. 'If he kept this girl Lenski's scarf, there will certainly be other trophies. Let's go.' A smile flitted across Ziegler's face that reminded Kalisz of the first day they'd met. He pulled on his uniform cap and straightened it in front of the mirror, nodding to himself. 'Surely you want to be in at the death?'

That's what I'm afraid of.

–

Ziegler led the way from the apartment, across the tram tracks of Königstraße and on to the enormous paved parade ground of Adolf Hitler Platz. The great square, originally dedicated to the Polish hero Marshal Piłsudski, was being prepared for the official renaming ceremony. Billowing swastika banners fully six metres long fluttered from tall flagpoles, and all but concealed the pillared frontage of the magnificent palace that dominated the square. Engineers worked on a reviewing stand in front of the Poniatowski Monument, and the scarlet, white and black backdrop portrayed a giant Nazi eagle. Ziegler's boots clattered on the flagstones as he maintained a diagonal course towards the Europejski Hotel on the far side of the square.

When they reached the front entrance, Kalisz was unsurprised to see Doctor Josef Mengele emerge from a car parked nearby and cross the street to meet them.

'Josef – so you're in on it, too?' Ziegler pumped Mengele's hand. 'I'm just going up to confront Wolff. It's so difficult to believe.'

'You look terrible, Willi,' Mengele said. 'Do you think you're up to this?'

'I thought he was my closest friend, but he set me up to take the blame for this… these atrocities. How could anyone do such a thing?' Ziegler drew himself up to his full height and marched towards the entrance. Kalisz and Mengele held back.

'You knew all along,' the Pole said quietly.

Mengele dropped his cigarette and stubbed it out with his foot. 'It wasn't so difficult after you told me you suspected an SS officer.'

'So it was the poison?'

'Very clever, Kalisz.' The smile of acknowledgement appeared quite genuine. 'Once I discovered Degesch had taken ownership of a factory in Warsaw to develop further uses for the product, I was able to find out which company. After that, it was simple enough to track down the names of the officers who dealt with it.'

'The Chemikalia Handlowe Company in Wola.' Kalisz repeated the name he'd been given by Kazimierz. 'Krystyna Lenski's father worked there.'

Mengele clapped his hands, even more impressed.

Kalisz was curious. 'What would you have done if we hadn't come here?'

'That doesn't matter now. What does is that I was just passing and *Obersturmführer* Ziegler asked me to assist him. I doubt any of my brother officers would blame me for that. We should be joining our friend.' He turned and walked into the hotel.

Ziegler met them in a state of wild-eyed confusion, the concierge watching him warily from behind the check-in desk. 'He's not here. They don't know where he is.'

'Then we have the perfect opportunity to take a look at his rooms.' Mengele marched across to the desk. 'May I have the spare key for room...?' He turned to Ziegler.

'Room 320.'

'Indeed – 320.'

The concierge fairly bristled at this outrage. An elderly East Prussian with a Great War medal on the lapel of his dark suit, he was perfectly capable of making a stand if he must. 'Sir, I am not sure if it is possible... The regulations.'

'And I, sir, say that you certainly must.' Mengele held out his hand. 'I am Herr Wolff's physician and a fellow officer of the SS. I am concerned for my patient's welfare, and I can assure you that if anything happens to him because you have delayed us, there will be serious consequences. Do you understand?'

The concierge might be a war hero, but he was no fool. 'In that case, Herr *Obersturmführer*...' He reached below the desk and they heard a rattle as he rummaged in some kind of box. 'The spare key for room 320, sir.'

'You will mention our visit to no one.'

'Naturally.'

Mengele led the way up the carpeted stairs to the third floor. With every step, Kalisz felt his stomach squirm as if it were inhabited by a ball of mating snakes. He had brought them to this moment, but now there truly was no turning back. What would they find in Wolff's room? And, more importantly, how would the two men with him react? He had a suspicion Ziegler and Mengele were set on different courses. Ziegler believed he'd been betrayed by a friend, sought an explanation, and wanted Wolff brought to justice. Mengele appeared mildly amused by the situation, yet he'd warned Kalisz off the case while at the same time giving him the means to pursue it. But for what purpose? They reached the third floor, where an enormous gold urn on a pedestal dominated the landing.

'Room 320.' Mengele turned to Kalisz. 'Now we'll see. Investigator? After you, if you don't mind.' He twisted the key and turned the door handle. 'You're the one with experience of this kind of thing.'

Kalisz pushed the door open to reveal a sumptuous room with lime-painted walls, pristine white cornices and tall windows hung with thick curtains of lined gold brocade. Through an open door he could see into another large room, with an enormous bed covered by a spread of the same material and flanked by bow-legged chairs and tables. Persian rugs scattered the polished wooden floor. The wall space between the windows of the main room was filled by a large wardrobe inlaid with different types of wood and equipped with six visible drawers.

The two Germans followed him inside and Mengele closed the door behind them.

CHAPTER 44

'Well, Kalisz, where do we start?' the SS doctor asked.

Kalisz studied his surroundings. This was very different from Ziegler's chaotic apartment, with none of the usual clutter you would expect in a hotel room occupied by a semi-permanent resident. No shoes beside the bed or books on the table. No pyjamas cast aside to be picked up by the maids and folded, just so, on the bed cover. He had a moment of panic that Wolff might have checked out, until a glance into the bathroom and the sight of a razor and shaving brush reassured him.

'If you –' he indicated Ziegler – 'would watch the door in case our man returns, while the doctor and I have a look around.'

The suggestion produced an almost imperceptible nod of approval from Mengele – Ziegler had the look of a man who was about to start turning over the furniture – but the SS doctor visibly flinched when Ziegler drew his Walther pistol. 'Do you really think you need that, Willi?' he asked.

'Wolff is a dangerous man, Josef. There is no telling what he might do.'

Mengele might have pushed the point, but Kalisz caught his eye and the German shrugged. 'Very well. Let's get on with it. I'll check the bedroom, you start in here.'

He walked from the room, leaving Kalisz with Ziegler. The lawyer's eyes had taken on a glazed, half-distant look. Kalisz wondered how much use he'd be if Wolff did return before they finished.

He started with the big wardrobe. Rows of suits and shirts and silk ties on a rail. A full SS officer's uniform, with the same rank insignia worn by Ziegler and Mengele. He took the uniform from the rail and laid it on the bed to check for bloodstains or other evidence. Nothing. He lifted it up to his face and sniffed. A distinctive chemical smell told him it was newly back from the laundry. Wolff's recently shined jackboots proved equally frustrating: even the soles had been wiped clean. To a detective, such obsessive cleanliness was almost an admission of guilt, but not one that would stand up in court. He checked the drawers one by one without result, before moving to a walnut-inlaid cabinet that proved to contain several brands of whisky. It was only when he'd completed his search that he noticed the ornate table with the room's Bakelite telephone that had been hidden behind the door. It also had two drawers and a small cupboard. He'd barely started on the first drawer when Mengele burst from the bedroom.

In one hand, the SS doctor held what looked like a piece of black cloth, in the other, a small knife similar to a surgeon's scalpel. His eyes glittered with triumph. 'These were in a case under his bed. This is a BDM beret that, according to the label, was owned by a girl from Munich called Ilse Kramer. There's more girls' clothing—'

'We have him.' Ziegler took a step towards Mengele. He'd barely moved when the door beside Kalisz swung open. Ziegler turned, bringing up his Walther in the same movement. The distinctive crack of a pistol reverberated round the room. Kalisz watched in horror as Ziegler crumpled with a sharp cry and a look of disbelief on his face.

Shielded by the open door, Kalisz eased himself to a crouch so he was able to reach his ankle with his right hand. He could see Mengele, face a ghastly white, desperately trying not to look in his direction.

'I think you should put the scalpel down, Doctor,' a familiar voice suggested. 'We don't want anyone else getting hurt, do we?' A hand reached round the door to pull it closed as the speaker stepped into the room. 'Now...' Hans Wolff froze in mid-sentence as he felt the muzzle of Kalisz's pistol against his temple.

The gun was the little throwdown the Pole had taken from Günther Gruhl: an almost toy-like British Webley .25. It fired a tiny bullet, but at point-blank range even a tiny bullet would make a hole in Wolff's skull. 'If you'll just drop your pistol, Mr Wolff.'

'I don't think I will for the moment.' Wolff sounded perfectly calm, almost as if he'd expected to be in this position. 'If you shoot me, it's very likely I'll involuntarily pull the trigger and put a bullet through Doctor Mengele's heart, which would leave you with some explaining to do. I'm sure we can work this out.'

'I don't make deals with murderers.'

'Please, Doctor Mengele.' Wolff sounded exasperated. Kalisz couldn't see his face, but he could tell the man was smiling. 'Explain the facts of life to this fool. Any evidence you have which appears to implicate me – and I deny being guilty of any crime – can only be circumstantial, and hardly likely to be enough to convict an officer of the SS.'

'The scalpel—'

'Is just a scalpel. You will find no trace of anything to suggest it has been used for illegal purposes. Perhaps,' Wolff's tone suggested he was being magnanimous, but his pistol never wavered from Mengele's chest, 'you will discover that I was in a certain place, at a certain time. But during your investigations you will also find that *Obersturmführer* Ziegler was also in several of those locations. Poor Ziegler, with his demons and his drink problem, is surely a much more likely candidate than I. And if that were not enough – Kalisz, isn't it? – I am currently involved in a secret project of vital importance to the Reich. So important that I report directly to *Brigadeführer* Reinhardt Heydrich, who is, as you know, deputy to the *Reichsführer* SS. Really, I am much too valuable to the Reich to be sacrificed in return for a few Jewish bitches.'

'Traudl Kleist wasn't a Jewish bitch,' Kalisz said.

'Traudl Kleist?' Wolff sounded incredulous. 'I don't know what you're talking about. You're more deluded than I thought. Even *if* anyone believed your fanciful tales – and I can see from Doctor Mengele's face that he already has his doubts – I will be quietly sent to a rather comfortable SS sanatorium outside Munich. Men in white coats will tut over me for a few months before they decide I am rehabilitated, and I will be able once again to resume my vital war work. So you see, Kalisz, there is no point in this. Better for all that you both walk away. Poor Ziegler's death can be easily explained. He appeared at my door in a distraught state, drew his gun, and I was forced to shoot him. An elegant solution that will bring no dishonour to the service.'

'Is this true?' Kalisz asked Mengele.

'I'm afraid it is, Investigator.'

Kalisz pulled the trigger.

The little pistol fired with more of a snap than a crack. Wolff instantly went into shock as the bullet entered his skull, and it took a heartbeat for his brain to understand it had been shot. He stood rigid for a long, agonising moment before dropping to the floor with a shriek. Blood spurted from the tiny hole in his temple as his feet scrabbled on the polished wood. Eventually the scrabbling movement faded, and he lay shuddering on his side for a few hoarse breaths before his body went still.

To Kalisz, it was as if the room had frozen in time. He stood holding the gun in the same position, his mind entirely calm, but aware he'd destroyed himself just as surely as the man already growing cold at his feet. A pity for Maria and Stefan, but others had died for Poland and many more would follow. Jan Kalisz would die for Poland and for justice. He only prayed that pride would be sufficient recompense for their loss, and the conflict that had marred their last few months together.

He felt no pity for Hans Wolff. In a just world, Wolff would have answered for his crimes before a court of law, but this wasn't a just world. Poland was ruled by Nazis, and the Nazis ruled by fear and savagery. They looked after their own. Likely, he would soon be the subject of that savagery. Naturally, he had regrets. Regret that he could no longer serve Kazimierz and his secret state. That he would never again hold Maria, or be able to help guide Stefan through this dangerous world. But he did not regret the death of a man like Hans Wolff, who had used the power given him by the Nazis to slaughter innocents. He could not let another family suffer what the Goldbergs, the Lenskis, the Lipmans – and, yes, the Kleists and the Kramers – had suffered.

But the room couldn't have gone still, because when Mengele eased the Webley from Kalisz's hand, he was holding his Walther and it was pointed at Kalisz's heart. The SS doctor took a step back and surveyed the scene, his brown eyes moving between the two corpses and Kalisz, the soon to be corpse.

'Yes.' He nodded, satisfied with what he saw. 'Very neat indeed. We were on our way to interview Wolff, but Ziegler beat us to it. Wolff shot him dead – he is dead, isn't he, would you mind checking? – and consumed by remorse, he killed himself. Of course, our report to *Hauptsturmführer* Hoth will be more detailed, providing certain evidence of Wolff's complicity in Traudl Kleist's death, and taking credit for uncovering it.'

'Our report?'

'Yes, Kalisz. Two dead bodies is tidy. Three would have tongues wagging, even if the third was a worthless Pole. The last thing Hoth wants is tongues wagging. You should be pleased. He certainly will be.'

'Then may I point out that although Wolff shot himself with a 9mm pistol, there's a very small hole in his head.'

'Of course,' Mengele said. 'The autopsy would probably find otherwise, since I'll be carrying it out, but let's make certain, shall we?' He bent and arranged Wolff's head so the bullet hole was accessible, placed the fallen Walther directly against the dead man's head, and pulled the trigger. Kalisz winced at the bang, but Mengele was more interested in the results. 'Messy,' he said cheerfully, 'but a mess can cover up an abundance of sins.'

'And the dead man was left-handed, but he has a hole – a rather large one now – in his right temple.'

'No wonder you're such a good detective, Kalisz, with observation like that, but let me worry about it. Have you never heard of someone being ambidextrous?'

Kalisz nodded distractedly. 'Why?'

Mengele knew what he was asking, but he affected not to. 'Because I despise weaklings like Wolff – men who allow their needs to overcome their discipline, and who prey on innocents like Traudl Kleist. And don't grieve for Ziegler, Kalisz. Wolff did him a favour, believe me.'

'No – I meant, why leave me alive?'

The SS man hesitated, an almost regretful smile flickering across the thin lips. 'Because, as I explained, it's neater this

344

way… and because, despite our differences, I rather like you, Kalisz. You have some admirable qualities in a world in which they're in short supply. If you're going to be beaten to death in a Gestapo cell, I'd rather it was for something more worthwhile than slaughtering an animal like Wolff. Shall we?' He opened the door and ushered Kalisz out with an elegant hand. 'I think we'll allow the concierge to report this little tragedy, but I believe I'll have a word with him first. You know…?' He took one last look at Wolff's body. 'He almost had me convinced he didn't kill Traudl Kleist.'

–

The following morning, Hoth sent an orderly to summon Kalisz to his office.

Kalisz complied on legs that felt as if they were made of concrete; he was physically and mentally spent after a long night lying listening to Maria breathing and trying to understand why he was still alive. But his senses were as well-honed as ever. The *Hauptsturmführer*'s bull-like frame betrayed an uncharacteristic nervousness. Was there, after all, to be a reckoning for Wolff's death?

Hoth's first words should have reassured him, but curiously they didn't. 'You have my thanks for a fine piece of detective work, Kalisz, and for ensuring the reputation of the service remains untarnished. A tragedy, of course, that *Obersturmführer* Ziegler had to become involved, but Doctor Mengele was most impressed by the way you handled things.'

'I'm very grateful to him, sir. I only did what I thought was my duty.'

'Of course.' Hoth cleared his throat noisily. 'As we all would.'

'May I inquire when my father-in— When August Klimecki and the surviving hostages will be released?'

Hoth rose from behind the desk and turned to the window, almost blocking out the light, and Kalisz knew his premonition was about to be confirmed. He felt a terrible coldness, and his hands sought the desktop to stay in contact with something tangible.

'I'm sorry, Kalisz. There was never any chance of their being released, you should have known that. They were terrorists and troublemakers, Klimecki among the worst.' He turned to meet Kalisz's eyes. 'I had to fight to keep his family out of it.'

Good manners dictated that Kalisz should thank his superior officer for his efforts, which might well have saved Maria's life, but he couldn't find the words. In any case, he was certain there was more to come.

'You won't have heard yet, but poor Müller was in a cafe last night when it was attacked by terrorists with grenades and pistols. Governor General Frank ordered the immediate execution of the remaining hostages in retaliation for his murder.'

Kalisz had an image of August's brave, kindly old face, and his world blurred. So much pointless pain and death. Gradually, he realised Hoth had continued talking. He heard something about transfers to France and the Gestapo.

'…so the governor has finally taken my advice and decided to ease our manpower situation in the General Government. Reliable Polish investigators are to be brought into the service of the Reich, and you are the first in Department V.'

Hoth placed a small brass disc on the desk between them. In a daze, Kalisz recognised the Nazi eagle, with its wings spread and a swastika in its talons. On the reverse, he knew there'd be the word '*Kriminalpolizei*' and a four-digit number. His number.

'Congratulations, Kalisz.' Hoth stretched out his hand. 'You're one of us.'

CHAPTER 45

Jan Kalisz kept to the shadows. It was well after curfew, but his new Kripo investigator's warrant disc and a little bluster would probably have dealt with any patrols. Still, he preferred not to be seen. Better that way for everybody.

The utter desolation he'd felt in Hoth's office had faded, to be replaced by an emptiness, a dearth of spirit, that made him wonder if he was any better than Willi Ziegler. Oh, he could justify the deaths of Wolff and Gruhl, but that didn't make it any easier, and there was a little worm in his brain that constantly reminded him of the fact. His greatest fear, in the sleepless hour before the dawn, was that the worm would never leave him.

Maria had taken the news of her father's murder with a cold, distant acceptance that concerned him more than if she'd collapsed screaming at his feet. He understood that she'd known, deep in her soul, that August's fate had been determined the moment he was arrested, but there was more than that. War had changed her. The inner strength he'd always admired had been replaced by hardness, and part of her was closed to him as surely as if it were encased in an armoured carapace. And it wasn't just her feelings she was concealing. Once or twice he'd walked into a room and she'd swept something off the table before he could see what it was. Sometimes he wondered if what he saw in her eyes wasn't close to hatred.

Kazimierz, in his mysterious way, had provided the address, and Doctor Novak had reluctantly set up the meeting. Why was he here? It had something to do with the values ingrained in him by the men who'd guided his early career as an investigator. There came a moment in every murder case where a detective was able to close the file, in the knowledge he would never have to open it again. But before that point was reached, he had to be certain every piece of evidence was in place, exactly as it should be. It was important that any future investigator who opened the file should know the precise steps his predecessor had taken, and the logic that underpinned his conclusion.

This time, there would be no closing of the file, but Kalisz had one last piece to position.

The Germans might rule Warsaw, but they didn't have enough men to be everywhere at once. If you knew your way around the city, it was possible to avoid their patrols and check-points. He found the street he was looking for – little more than a narrow alley off Marszałkowska. A cobbler's workshop. The door was unlocked, as he'd been told it would be. He stopped just long enough to reach inside his jacket and unclip the flap of his shoulder holster, instinctively testing the Nagant's draw to ensure it wasn't going to be obstructed by an errant piece of stitching. No light, so he had to feel his way past the workbench and the cutting tables. His nostrils were filled with the pleasant scent of linseed oil and old leather, a ghostly reminder of the shop owner's former trade, because there was certainly none available now. Not for a Jew.

Straight out the back, and into a courtyard overlooked on all sides by windows, every unbroken pane reflecting the soft silver light of the dusk, the mirrored surfaces masking whatever life went on behind. He crossed to another door on the far side, conscious he was probably being watched all the way. Through the door. If they were going to take him, it would be now. But nothing. He made his way carefully up the darkened stairway and along a corridor, counting the doors as he went. There, he hesitated, tested the draw of the Nagant again, and turned the handle.

The man was sitting where Kalisz would have chosen to sit – in the corner, away from the window. The darkest part of the room, but with a good view of the door, where the new arrival would be just visible in the gloomy secondary light from the curtained window. Kalisz had a feeling he wasn't the only person in the room with a gun.

'Why are you here?' Isaac Goldberg's voice was so low it barely carried.

'No invitation to sit down, Isaac?'

'I asked you a question.'

'I'm here to tell you that Hannah's killer is dead.'

'You could have sent word without coming all this way. In any case, you owe me nothing.' A pause. 'You killed him?'

'Yes.'

'How?'

'I put a bullet in his head.'

'Not enough.' He sensed Goldberg shake his head.

'No,' Kalisz agreed. 'It never is.'

'But you didn't come here just to tell me that.'

Kalisz made him wait. 'I wanted you to know that I know.'

'I told you, I didn't kill Salomon.' Goldberg didn't hide his irritation.

'Not Salomon.' The room went very still, and Kalisz had a vision of fingers creeping towards a pistol butt. 'Before I shot Wolff he denied killing Traudl Kleist.'

'Of course he would.'

'But he said it in a way that made me think he was telling the truth.'

'The Germans are taught to lie at their mother's breast.' Goldberg's voice came from a slightly different angle, and Kalisz stepped away from the door.

'In fact, he sounded astonished by the suggestion,' Kalisz said. 'But then he would be. Because he didn't kill Traudl. You did.'

'I should kill you. Now.'

'But you won't, Isaac, because you're curious. You want to know how I know.' He slipped the Nagant from its holster. If it came to it, one shot was all he'd need. 'Maybe I'm not such a clever detective after all,' he continued. 'It's embarrassing to look back and see all the clues I missed that set the Kleist killing apart.'

Goldberg's breathing quickened, and Kalisz thought he had his position fixed in the darkness.

'Wolff was an artist. You're not. Novak described the thing he saw in the cellar of the Wielopole as an obscene work of beauty. Yours was crude and rushed. Wolff wanted to inflict pain. Whoever killed Traudl Kleist was a man who believed himself cursed by God, but at least he made sure she felt nothing when she died. I'm grateful for that, Isaac. Grateful you didn't entirely turn into the man who murdered your daughter.'

'Just talk,' Goldberg spat. 'All talk. You have proof of nothing.'

'The knife wound in Traudl's throat was a ragged slash, entirely different from the surgical cut that killed Krystyna Lenski. Traudl Kleist was cut from breast to pubis, but in the three other cases the blade had travelled in the opposite direction. Then there was the Zyklon B.'

'You know about Zyklon B?'

'I know you worked at the Chemikalia Handlowe company in Wola, which gave you access to whatever drug you used on Traudl Kleist, and the Zyklon B. The only place it was used was at the scene of Traudl's death.' Its absence had puzzled Kalisz until he'd been able to fit the information from Kazimierz about the chemical works with Novak's revelation that Isaac Goldberg had held a part-time position there. Hoth might be a Nazi, but he was a proper detective. He'd have worked it out eventually. If Wolff had continued to deny everything, Goldberg would have taken the blame for Traudl *and* the other killings, Wolff would have walked free, and all the hostages would have been shot anyway. So Wolff had always had to die.

'But you know about Zyklon B?' Goldberg persisted.

'I know it's used to kill lice.'

'That's not all it can be used to kill. We had a technician – a real Jew-hater called Ludwik. He worked closely with the Nazis when they came to take the place over. One day, he's on the line crowing about how Zyklon B was going to be Handlowe's best seller because the SS were planning to give every Yid a Zyklon B shower and kill off the vermin.'

'Maybe it was just talk?'

'He was taken away the same day and never came back. Pawiak, and then Palmiry, we heard. Which is what you have in mind for me.'

'What makes you think that?'

'If all that you say is true, why else would you be here?'

If Goldberg truly believed that, this could only end one way. Kalisz stood waiting for the muzzle flash and the bullet smashing into him from the darkness, but it never came. 'I'm putting my pistol back in its holster.'

'Your funeral.' Clearly, Goldberg thought he was a fool.

'If what you say about Zyklon B is true, things are going to go very badly for your people.'

'So?'

'What will you do?'

He heard Goldberg suck in a long breath. 'Resist. What else can we do?'

'Then you'll need help.' Kalisz had discussed it with Kazimierz. Soon – perhaps very soon – the Ghetto would be sealed off entirely, severing the ZWZ from contact with tens of thousands of potential combatants. They couldn't afford that when every finger on the trigger and every body behind a barricade was going to count.

'You?' Goldberg snorted. 'Since when has any Pole cared about what happened to the Jews? And you work for the Nazis.'

'No,' Kalisz said. 'I'm a Pole. A Polish soldier.' He was taking a risk of exposure, but it was a calculated risk. If there was one thing of which he could be certain, it was that Isaac Goldberg would never allow himself to be taken alive by the Nazis. 'At some point in the future we will have to fight the Germans. When that day comes, Isaac Goldberg will no longer be a Jew or Jan Kalisz a Gentile. They will be Poles. Poles fighting for survival. I have three things you do not have – freedom of movement, contacts, and access to resources. When the time comes, get in touch with Doctor Novak. We will do the rest.'

'What can you give us?'

'What do you need?'

Goldberg thought for a moment. 'Guns, ammunition and explosives. How will you get them to us?'

'We'll find a way.'

'Why me, Kalisz?' Goldberg said softly after a long silence. 'You said yourself I'm a murderer. A man cursed by God.'

The answer was simple.

'Because I know you're also a man who will fight the Nazis to his last breath. A man like me.'

AUTHOR'S NOTE

Adolf Hitler ordered the total destruction of Warsaw in the aftermath of the Uprising in 1944, and his orders were carried out with ruthless efficiency. The entire city centre was flattened by fire and high explosives, including some of the world's finest architectural treasures, and the population murdered or deported. One of the greatest challenges of writing *Blood Roses* was to reconstruct the streets Jan Kalisz walked and the sights he would have seen. For helping me achieve that, I have to thank the people behind www.warszawa1939.pl, a website that contains an interactive map of the city, complete with pictures of thousands of individual buildings, from ordinary houses and apartment blocks, hospitals and factories, to the great palaces which were such a feature of pre-war Warsaw, and the dates of their destruction. I'm also indebted to the authors of *The Eagle Unbowed* (Halik Kochanski), *For Your Freedom and Ours* (Lynne Olson and Stanley Cloud), and the early chapters of *Rising '44* (Norman Davies) for helping me paint a picture of everyday life in Warsaw during the first two years of the war. *Story of a Secret State* (Jan Karski) gave me an insight into the terrible strains imposed on those working for the Polish Underground and the lives they were forced to lead. I was also inspired by the story of Captain Witold Pilecki, an incredibly courageous Polish patriot whose feats, including having himself arrested and sent to Auschwitz and then escaping, are almost beyond belief. Heinz Höhne's *The Order of the Death's Head* provided chapter and verse on the SS. *Blood Roses* is the first of four books chronicling the double life of Jan Kalisz, and the ordeal of Warsaw and its citizens between 1939 and the end of 1944. It will be followed by *Blood Sacrifice*, *Blood Vengeance* and *Blood Enemy*, which will continue Kalisz's story through the creation and destruction of the Warsaw Ghetto, the murder of an aristocratic SOE agent, and the Warsaw Uprising of 1944. I'm indebted to my editor Craig Lye, my copy-editor Steve O'Gorman, and all at Canelo who have helped make this book what it is. As always, I'm grateful for the support of my agent, Mark Stanton, and my wonderful family.